CASTLE RACKRENT
and
THE ABSENTEE

CASTLE RACKRENT
and
THE ABSENTEE

Maria Edgeworth

WORDSWORTH CLASSICS

The paper in this book is produced from pure wood
pulp, without the use of chlorine or any other substance
harmful to the environment. The energy used in its
production consists almost entirely of hydroelectricity
and heat generated from waste material, thereby
conserving fossil fuels and contributing little to the
greenhouse effect.

This edition published 1994 by
Wordsworth Editions Limited
Cumberland House, Crib Street
Ware, Hertfordshire SG12 9ET

ISBN 1 85326 220 X

Printed and bound in Denmark by Nørhaven
Typeset in the UK by Antony Gray

INTRODUCTION

First published in 1800 and widely regarded as the first regional novel in English, *Castle Rackrent* describes the hopelessly dissolute life of the Rackrents, a family of eighteenth-century Irish landlords, who, watched by their good-humoured tenants, dissipate and debauch their fortune until they reach the very edge of ruin and destitution. The book's aged narrator is the Rackrents' long-serving steward, Thady Quirk. The novel begins even before Thady's time, with the wild and often drunken Sir Patrick, and continues through the ages of the mean and miserly Sir Murtagh and his brother, the dashing Sir Kit, who inherits and brings his Jewish English wife to live at the castle with explosive consequences. Meanwhile Thady's sharp lawyer son, Jason, is plotting how he can become the beneficiary of the Rackrent family's now almost inevitable downfall. The politician, Sir Condy, is the next to inherit. He marries Thady's grand-niece, Isabella, a choice made on the toss of a coin, and the final curtain for the family looms while Jason prepares himself for life as a landed gentleman. *Castle Rackrent* is a vital social commentary of not only literary but also of historical and political importance.

The Absentee (1812) was published in the second series of *Tales of Fashionable Life*. Set on a large property in Ireland and in London, the story contrasts the high life of London society, in which the socially ambitious Lady Clonbrony is determined to make her mark, with the poor state of the Irish peasantry and tenant farmers, and chronicles the continuous demands for more money made on the poor in Ireland to fund the extravagances of Lord and Lady Clonbrony's luxurious lifestyle in London. The Clonbrony's son, Lord Colambre, rejects the heiress whom his mother wishes him to marry and visits the family's Irish estates *incognito* to discover the truth of their financial circumstances and the condition of the people on them. He uncovers a terrible trail of indifference, injustice and embezzlement but, fortified by his love for his cousin Grace, he begins the arduous task of re-establishing probity, fair dealing and above all proper knowledge and presence in his family's ownership of their Irish holdings.

Maria Edgeworth was born at Black Bourton, near Witney, Oxfordshire in either 1767 or 1768. She was the second child of Richard Lovell Edgeworth, a wealthy Irish landowner, who exerted much influence on his daughter's interests and literary career. Maria first visited Ireland at the age of six, and in 1782, having attended schools in Derby and subsequently in London, she settled on her father's estate at Edgeworthstown in County Longford. During her life she was largely based in Ireland, but travelled from there to England, Scotland, Brussels, Paris and Switzerland. Sir Walter Scott was an admirer of her work, which influenced his Waverley novels, and she was his guest at Abbotsford for several weeks in 1823. Maria Edgeworth died in 1849.

FURTHER READING

M. Butler: *Maria Edgeworth: A Literary Biography* 1972
I. C. Clarke: *Maria Edgeworth: Her Family and Friends* 1950
C. Colvin (ed.): *Letters from England* 1971
C. Colvin (ed.): *Maria Edgeworth in France and Switzerland* 1979
E. Inglis-Jones: *The Great Maria* 1959
P. H. Newby: *Maria Edgeworth* 1950

CASTLE RACKRENT

Preface

THE PREVAILING TASTE of the public for anecdote has been censured and ridiculed by critics who aspire to the character of superior wisdom; but if we consider it in a proper point of view, this taste is an incontestable proof of the good sense and profoundly philosophic temper of the present times. Of the numbers who study, or at least who read history, how few derive any advantage from their labours! The heroes of history are so decked out by the fine fancy of the professed historian; they talk in such measured prose, and act from such sublime or such diabolical motives, that few have sufficient taste, wickedness, or heroism, to sympathise in their fate. Besides, there is much uncertainty even in the best authenticated ancient or modern histories; and that love of truth, which in some minds is innate and immutable, necessarily leads to a love of secret memoirs and private anecdotes. We cannot judge either of the feelings or of the characters of men with perfect accuracy, from their actions or their appearance in public; it is from their careless conversations, their half-finished sentences, that we may hope with the greatest probability of success to discover their real characters. The life of a great or of a little man written by himself, the familiar letters, the diary of any individual published by his friends or by his enemies, after his decease, are esteemed important literary curiosities. We are surely justified, in this eager desire, to collect the most minute facts relative to the domestic lives, not only of the great and good, but even of the worthless and insignificant, since it is only by a comparison of their actual happiness or misery in the privacy of domestic life that we can form a just estimate of the real reward of virtue, or the real punishment of vice. That the great are not as happy as they seem, that the external circumstances of fortune and rank do not constitute felicity, is asserted by every moralist: the historian can seldom, consistently with his dignity, pause to illustrate this truth; it is therefore to the biographer we must have recourse. After we have beheld splendid characters playing their parts on the great theatre of the world, with all the advantages of stage effect and decoration, we anxiously beg to be admitted behind the scenes, that we may take a nearer view of the actors and actresses.

Some may perhaps imagine that the value of biography depends upon the judgment and taste of the biographer; but on the contrary it may be maintained, that the merits of a biographer are inversely as the extent of his intellectual powers and of his literary talents. A plain unvarnished tale is preferable to the most highly ornamented narrative. Where we see that a man has the power, we may naturally suspect that he has the will to deceive us; and those who are used to literary manufacture know how much is often sacrificed to the rounding of a period, or the pointing of an antithesis.

That the ignorant may have their prejudices as well as the learned cannot be disputed; but we see and despise vulgar errors: we never bow to the authority of him who has no great name to sanction his absurdities. The partiality which blinds a biographer to the defects of his hero, in proportion as it is gross, ceases to be dangerous; but if it be concealed by the appearance of candour, which men of great abilities best know how to assume, it endangers our judgment sometimes, and sometimes our morals. If her Grace the Duchess of Newcastle, instead of penning her lord's elaborate eulogium, had undertaken to write the life of Savage, we should not have been in any danger of mistaking an idle, ungrateful libertine for a man of genius and virtue. The talents of a biographer are often fatal to his reader. For these reasons the public often judiciously countenance those who, without sagacity to discriminate character, without elegance of style to relieve the tediousness of narrative, without enlargement of mind to draw any conclusions from the facts they relate, simply pour forth anecdotes, and retail conversations, with all the minute prolixity of a gossip in a country town.

The author of the following Memoirs has upon these grounds fair claims to the public favour and attention; he was an illiterate old steward, whose partiality to *the family*, in which he was bred and born, must be obvious to the reader. He tells the history of the Rackrent family in his vernacular idiom, and in the full confidence that Sir Patrick, Sir Murtagh, Sir Kit, and Sir Condy Rackrent's affairs will be as interesting to all the world as they were to himself. Those who were acquainted with the manners of a certain class of the gentry of Ireland some years ago, will want no evidence of the truth of honest Thady's narrative; to those who are totally unacquainted with Ireland, the following Memoirs will perhaps be scarcely intelligible, or probably they may appear perfectly incredible. For the information of the *ignorant* English reader, a few notes have been subjoined by the editor, and he had it once in contemplation to translate the language of Thady into plain English; but Thady's idiom is incapable of translation, and, besides, the authenticity of his story would have been more exposed to doubt if it were not told in his own characteristic manner. Several years ago he related to the editor the history of the Rackrent family, and it was with some difficulty that he was persuaded to have it committed to writing; however, his feelings for '*the honour of the family*,' as he expressed himself, prevailed over his habitual laziness, and he at length completed the narrative which is now laid before the public.

The editor hopes his readers will observe that these are 'tales of other times;' that the manners depicted in the following pages are not those of the present age; the race of the Rackrents has long since been extinct in Ireland; and the drunken Sir Patrick, the litigious Sir Murtagh, the fighting Sir Kit, and the slovenly Sir Condy, are characters which could no more be met with at present in Ireland, than Squire Western or Parson Trulliber in England. There is a time when individuals can bear to be rallied for their past follies and absurdities, after they have acquired new habits and a new consciousness. Nations, as well as individuals, gradually lose attachment to their identity, and the present generation is amused, rather than offended, by the ridicule that is thrown upon its ancestors.

Probably we shall soon have it in our power, in a hundred instances, to verify the truth of these observations.

When Ireland loses her identity by an union with Great Britain, she will look back, with a smile of good-humoured complacency, on the Sir Kits and Sir Condys of her former existence.

1800

Castle Rackrent

HAVING, out of friendship for the family, upon whose estate, praised be Heaven! I and mine have lived rent-free time out of mind, voluntarily undertaken to publish the MEMOIRS OF THE RACKRENT FAMILY, I think it my duty to say a few words, in the first place, concerning myself. My real name is Thady Quirk, though in the family I have always been known by no other than 'Honest Thady,' afterward, in the time of Sir Murtagh, deceased, I remember to hear them calling me 'Old Thady,' and now I've come to 'Poor Thady'; for I wear a long greatcoat winter and summer, which is very handy, as I never put my arms into the sleeves; they are as good as new, though come Holantide next I've had it these seven years: it holds on by a single button round my neck, cloak fashion. To look at me, you would hardly think 'Poor Thady' was the father of Attorney Quirk; he is a high gentleman, and never minds what poor Thady says, and having better than fifteen hundred a year, landed estate, looks down upon honest Thady; but I wash my hands of his doings, and as I have lived so will I die, true and loyal to the family. The family of the Rackrents is, I am proud to say, one of the most ancient in the kingdom. Everybody knows this is not the old family name, which was O'Shaughlin, related to the kings of Ireland – but that was before my time. My grandfather was driver to the great Sir Patrick O'Shaughlin, and I heard him, when I was a boy, telling how the Castle Rackrent estate came to Sir Patrick; Sir Tallyhoo Rackrent was cousin-german to him, and had a fine estate of his own, only never a gate upon it, it being his maxim that a car was the best gate. Poor gentleman! he lost a fine hunter and his life, at last, by it, all in one day's hunt. But I ought to bless that day, for the estate came straight into *the* family, upon one condition, which Sir Patrick O'Shaughlin at the time took sadly to heart, they say, but thought better of it afterwards, seeing how large a stake depended upon it: that he should, by Act of Parliament, take and bear the surname and arms of Rackrent.

Now it was that the world was to see what was *in* Sir Patrick. On coming into the estate he gave the finest entertainment ever was heard of in the country; not a man could stand after supper but Sir Patrick himself, who could sit out the best man in Ireland, let alone the three kingdoms itself. He had his house, from one year's end to another, as full of company as ever it could hold, and fuller; for rather than be left out of the parties at Castle Rackrent, many gentlemen, and those men of the first consequence and landed estates in the country – such as the O'Neills of Ballynagrotty, and the Moneygawls of Mount Juliet's Town, and O'Shannons of New Town Tullyhog – made it their choice, often and often, when there was no room to be had for love nor money, in long winter nights, to sleep in the chicken-house, which Sir Patrick had fitted up for the purpose of accommodating his friends and the public in general, who honoured him with their company unex- pectedly at Castle Rackrent; and this went on I can't tell you how long. The whole country rang with his praises! – Long life to him! I'm sure I love to look upon his picture, now opposite to me; though I never saw him, he must have been a portly gentleman – his neck something short, and remarkable for the largest pimple on his nose, which, by his particular desire, is still extant in his picture, said to be a striking likeness, though taken when young. He is said also to be the inventor of raspberry whisky, which is very likely, as nobody has ever appeared to dispute it with him, and as there still exists a broken punch-bowl at Castle Rackrent, in the garret, with an inscription to that effect – a great curiosity. A few days before his death he was very merry; it being his honour's birthday, he called my grandfather in – God bless him! – to drink the company's health, and filled a bumper himself, but could not carry it to his head, on account of the great shake in his hand; on this he cast his joke, saying, 'What would my poor father say to me if he was to pop out of the grave, and see me now? I remember when I was a little boy, the first bumper of claret he gave me after dinner, how he praised me for carrying it so steady to my mouth. Here's my thanks to him – a bumper toast.' Then he fell to singing the favourite song he learned from his father – for the last time, poor gentleman – he sung it that night as loud and as hearty as ever, with a chorus:

> He that goes to bed, and goes to bed sober,
> Falls as the leaves do, falls as the leaves do, and dies in
> October;
> But he that goes to bed, and goes to bed mellow,
> Lives as he ought to do, lives as he ought to do, and dies
> honest fellow.

Sir Patrick died that night: just as the company rose to drink his health with three cheers, he fell down in a sort of fit, and was carried off; they sat it out, and were surprised, on inquiry in the morning, to find that it was all over with poor Sir Patrick. Never did any gentleman live and die more beloved in the country by rich and poor. His funeral was such a one as was never known before or since in the county! All the gentlemen in the three counties were at it; far and near, how they flocked! my great-grandfather said, that to see all the women, even in their red cloaks, you would have taken them for the army drawn out. Then such a fine whillaluh! you might have heard it to the farthest end of the county, and happy the man who could get but a sight of the hearse! But who'd have thought it? Just as all was going on right, through his own town they were passing, when the body was seized for debt – a rescue was apprehended from the mob; but the heir, who attended the funeral, was against that, for fear of consequences, seeing that those villains who came to serve acted under the disguise of the law: so, to be sure, the law must take its course, and little gain had the creditors for their pains. First and foremost, they had the curses of the country: and Sir Murtagh Rackrent, the new heir, in the next place, on account of this affront to the body, refused to pay a shilling of the debts, in which he was countenanced by all the best gentlemen of property, and others of his acquaintance; Sir Murtagh alleging in all companies that he all along meant to pay his father's debts of honour, but the moment the law was taken of him, there was an end of honour to be sure. It was whispered (but none but the enemies of the family believe it) that this was all a sham seizure to get quit of the debts which he had bound himself to pay in honour.

It's a long time ago, there's no saying how it was, but this for certain, the new man did not take at all after the old gentleman; the cellars were never filled after his death, and no open house, or anything as it used to be; the tenant even were sent away without their whisky. I was ashamed myself, and knew not what to say for the honour of the family; but I made the best of a bad case, and laid it all at my lady's door, for I did not like her anyhow, nor anybody else; she was of the family of the Skinflints, and a widow; it was a strange match for Sir Murtagh; the people in the country thought he demeaned himself greatly, but I said nothing: I knew how it was. Sir Murtagh was a great lawyer, and looked to the great Skinflint estate; there, however, he overshot himself; for though one of the co-heiresses, he was never the better for her, for she outlived him many's the long day – he could not see that to be sure when he married her. I must say for her, she made him the best of wives, being a very notable, stirring woman, and looking close to everything. But I always suspected she had Scotch blood in her veins; anything else I could have looked over in her, from a regard to the family. She was a strict observer, for self and servants, of Lent, and all fast-days, but not holidays. One of the maids having fainted three times the last day of Lent, to keep soul and body together, we put a morsel of roast beef into her mouth, which came from Sir Murtagh's dinner, who never fasted, not he; but somehow or other it unfortunately reached my lady's ears, and the priest of the parish had a complaint made of it the next day, and the poor girl was forced, as soon as she could walk, to do penance for it, before she could get any peace or absolution, in the house or out of it. However, my lady was very charitable in her own way. She had a charity school for poor children, where they were taught to read and write gratis, and where they were kept well to spinning gratis for my lady in return; for she had always heaps of duty yarn from the tenants, and got all her household linen out of the estate from first to last; for after the spinning, the weavers on the estate took it in hand for nothing, because of the looms my lady's interest could get from the Linen Board to distribute gratis. Then there was a bleach-yard near us, and the tenant dare refuse my lady nothing, for fear, of a lawsuit Sir Murtagh kept hanging over him about the watercourse. With these ways of managing, 'tis surprising how cheap my lady got things done, and how proud she was of it. Her table the same way, kept for next to nothing; duty follows, and duty turkeys, and duty geese, came as fast as we could eat 'em, for my lady kept a sharp look-out, and knew to a tub of butter everything the tenants had, all round. They knew her way, and what with fear of driving for rent and Sir Murtagh's lawsuits, they were kept in such good order, they never thought of coming near Castle Rackrent without a present of something or other – nothing too much or too little for my lady – eggs, honey, butter, meal, fish, game, grouse, and herrings, fresh or salt, all went for something. As for their young pigs, we had them, and the best bacon and hams they could make up, with all young chickens in spring; but they were a set of poor wretches, and we had nothing but misfortunes with them, always breaking and running away. This, Sir Murtagh and my lady said, was all their former landlord Sir Patrick's fault, who let 'em all get the half-year's rent into arrear; there was something in that to be sure. But Sir Murtagh was as much the contrary way; for let alone making English tenants of them, every soul, he was always driving and driving, and pounding and pounding, and canting and canting, and replevying and replevying, and he made a good living of trespassing cattle; there was always some tenant's pig, or horse, or cow, or calf, or goose, trespassing, which was so great a gain to Sir Murtagh, that he did not like to hear me talk of repairing fences. Then his heriots and duty-work brought him in something, his turf was cut, his potatoes set and dug, his hay brought home, and, in short, all the work about his house done for nothing; for in all our leases there were strict clauses heavy with penalties, which Sir Murtagh knew well how to enforce; so many days' duty-work of man and horse, from every tenant, he was to have, and had, every year; and when a man vexed him, why, the finest day he could pitch on, when the cratur was getting in his own harvest, or thatching his cabin, Sir Murtagh made it a principle to call upon him and his horse; so he taught 'em all, as he said, to know the law of landlord and tenant. As for law, I believe no man, dead or alive, ever loved it so well as Sir Murtagh. He had once sixteen suits pending at a time, and I never saw him so much himself: roads, lanes, bogs, wells, ponds, eel-wires, orchards, trees, tithes, vagrants, gravelpits, sandpits, dunghills, and nuisances, everything upon the face of the earth furnished him good matter for a suit. He used to boast that he had a lawsuit for every letter in the alphabet. How I used to wonder to see Sir Murtagh in the midst of the papers in his office! Why, he could hardly turn about for them. I made bold to shrug my shoulders once in his presence, and thanked my stars I was not born a gentleman to so much toil and trouble; but Sir Murtagh took me up short with his old proverb, 'Learning is better than house or land.' Out of forty-nine suits which he had, he never lost one but seventeen; the rest he gained with costs, double costs, treble costs sometimes; but even that did not pay. He was a very learned man in the law and had the character of it; but how it was I can't tell, these suits that he carried cost him a power of money: in the end he sold some hundreds a year of the family estate; but he was a very learned man in the law, and I know nothing of the matter, except having a great regard for the family; and I could not help grieving when he sent me to post up notices of the sale of the fee simple of the lands and appurtenances of Timoleague.

'I know, honest Thady,' says he, to comfort me, 'what I'm about better than you do; I'm only selling to get the ready money wanting to carry on my suit with spirit with the Nugents of Carrickashaughlin.'

He was very sanguine about that suit with the Nugents of Carrickashaughlin. He could have gained it, they say, for certain, had it pleased Heaven to have spared him to us, and it would have been at the least a plump two thousand a year in his way; but things were ordered otherwise – for the best to be sure. He dug up a fairy-mount against my advice, and had no luck afterwards. Though a learned man in the law, he was a little too incredulous in other matters. I warned him that I heard the very Banshee that my grandfather heard under Sir Patrick's window a few days before his death. But Sir Murtagh thought nothing of the Banshee, nor of his cough, with a spitting of blood, brought on, I understand, by catching cold in attending the courts, and overstraining his chest with making himself heard in one of his favourite causes. He was a great speaker with a powerful voice; but his last speech was not in the courts at all. He and my lady, though both of the same way of thinking in some things, and though she was as good a wife and great economist as you could see, and he the best of husbands, as to looking into his affairs, and making money for his family; yet I don't know how it was, they had a great deal of sparring and jarring between them. My lady had her privy purse; and she had her weed ashes, and her sealing money upon the signing of all the leases, with something to buy gloves besides; and, besides, again often took money from the tenants, if offered properly, to speak for them to Sir Murtagh about abatements and renewals. Now the weed ashes and the glove money he allowed her clear perquisites; though once when he saw her in a new gown saved out of the weed ashes, he told her to my face (for he could say a sharp thing) that she should not put on her weeds before her husband's death. But in a dispute about an abatement my lady would have the last word, and Sir Murtagh grew mad; I was within hearing of the door, and now I wish I had made bold to step in. He spoke so loud, the whole kitchen was out on the stairs. All on a sudden he stopped, and my lady too. Something has surely happened, thought I; and so it was, for Sir Murtagh in his passion broke a blood-vessel, and all the law in the land could do nothing in that case. My lady sent for five physicians, but Sir Murtagh died, and was buried. She had a fine jointure settled upon her, and took herself away, to the great joy of the tenantry. I never said any thing one way or the other whilst she was part of the family, but got up to see her go at three o'clock in the morning.

'It's a fine morning, honest Thady,' says she; 'good-bye to ye.' And into the carriage she stepped, without a word more, good or bad, or even half-a-crown; but I made my bow, and stood to see her safe out of sight for the sake of the family.

Then we were all bustle in the house, which made me keep out of the way, for I walk slow and hate a bustle; but the house was all hurry-skurry, preparing for my new master. Sir Murtagh, I forgot to notice, had no childer; so the Rackrent estate went to his younger brother, a young dashing officer, who came amongst us before I knew for the life of me whereabouts I was, in a gig or some of them things, with another spark along with him, and led horses, and servants, and dogs, and scarce a place to put any Christian of them into; for my late lady had sent all the feather-beds off before her, and blankets and household linen, down to the very knife-cloths, on the cars to Dublin, which were all her own, lawfully paid for out of her own money. So the house was quite bare, and my young master, the moment ever he set foot in it out of his gig, thought all those things must come of themselves, I believe, for he never looked after anything at all, but harum-scarum called for everything as if we were conjurors, or he in a public-house. For my part, I could not bestir myself anyhow; I had been so much used to my late master and mistress, all was upside down with me, and the new servants in the servants' hall were quite out of my way; I had nobody to talk to, and if it had not been for my pipe and tobacco, should, I verily believe, have broke my heart for poor Sir Murtagh.

But one morning my new master caught a glimpse of me as I was looking at his horse's heels, in hopes of a word from him. 'And is that old Thady?' says he, as he got into his gig: I loved him from that day to this, his voice was so like the family; and he threw me a guinea out of his waistcoat-pocket, as he drew up the reins with the other hand, his horse rearing too; I thought I never set my eyes on a finer figure of a man, quite another sort from Sir Murtagh, though withal, *to me*, a family likeness. A fine life we should have led, had he stayed amongst us, God bless him! He valued a guinea as little as any man: money to him was no more than dirt, and his gentleman and groom, and all belonging to him, the same; but the sporting season over, he grew tired of the place, and having got down a great architect for the house, and an improver for the grounds, and seen their plans and elevations, he fixed a day for settling with the tenants, but went off in a whirlwind to town, just as some of them came into the yard in the morning. A circular letter came next post from the new agent, with news that the master was sailed for England, and he must remit £500 to Bath for his use before a fortnight was at an end; bad news still for the poor tenants, no change still for the better with them. Sir Kit Rackrent, my young master, left all to the agent; and though he had the spirit of a prince, and lived away to the honour of his country abroad, which I was proud to hear of, what were we the better for that at home? The agent was one of your middlemen, who grind the face of the poor, and can never bear a man with a hat upon his head: he ferreted the tenants out of their lives; not a week without a call for money, drafts upon drafts from Sir Kit; but I laid it all to the fault of the agent; for, says I, what can Sir Kit do with so much cash, and he a single man? But still it went. Rents must be all paid up to the day, and afore; no allowance for improving tenants, no consideration for those who had built upon their farms: no sooner was a lease out, but the land was advertised to the highest bidder; all the old tenants turned out, when they spent their substance in the hope and trust of a renewal from the landlord. All was now let at the highest penny to a parcel of poor wretches, who meant to run away, and did so, after taking two crops out of the ground. Then fining down the year's rent came into fashion – anything for the ready penny; and with all this and presents to the agent and the driver, there was no such thing as standing it. I said nothing, for I had a regard for the family; but I walked about thinking if his honour Sir Kit knew all this, it would go hard with him but he'd see us righted; not that I had anything for my own share to complain of, for the agent was always very civil to me when he came down into the country, and took a great deal of notice of my son Jason. Jason Quirk, though he be my son, I must say was a good scholar from his birth, and a very 'cute lad: I thought to make him a priest, but he did better for himself; seeing how he was as good a clerk as any in the county, the agent gave him his rent accounts to copy, which he did first of all for the pleasure of obliging the gentleman, and would take nothing at all for his trouble, but was always proud to serve the family. By and by a good farm bounding us to the east fell into his honour's hands, and my son put in a proposal for it: why shouldn't he, as well as another? The proposals all went over to the master at the Bath, who knowing no more of the land than the child unborn, only having once been out a-grousing on it before he went to England; and the value of lands, as the agent informed him, falling every year in Ireland, his honour wrote over in all haste a bit of a letter, saying he left it all to the agent, and that he must let it as well as he could – to the best bidder, to be sure – and send him over £200 by return of post: with this the agent gave me a hint, and I spoke a good word for my son, and gave out in the country that nobody need bid against us. So his proposal was just the thing, and he a good tenant; and he got a promise of an abatement in the rent after the first year, for advancing the half-year's rent at signing the lease, which was wanting to complete the agent's £200 by the return of the post, with all which my master wrote back he was well satisfied. About this time we learnt from the agent, as a great secret, how the money went so fast, and the reason of the thick coming of the master's drafts: he was a little too fond of play; and Bath, they say, was no place for no young man of his fortune, where there were so many of his own countrymen, too, hunting him up and down, day and night, who had nothing to lose. At last, at Christmas, the agent wrote over to stop the drafts, for he could raise no more money on bond or mortgage, or from the tenants, or anyhow, nor had he any more to lend himself, and desired at the same time to decline the agency for the future, wishing Sir Kit his health and happiness, and the compliments of the season, for I saw the letter before ever it was sealed, when my son

copied it. When the answer came there was a new turn in affairs, and
the agent was turned out; and my son Jason, who had corresponded
privately with his honour occasionally on business, was forthwith
desired by his honour to take the accounts into his own hands, and look
them over, till further orders. It was a very spirited letter to be sure: Sir
Kit sent his service, and the compliments of the season, in return to the
agent, and he would fight him with pleasure tomorrow, or any day, for
sending him such a letter, if he was born a gentleman, which he was
sorry (for both their sakes) to find (too late) he was not. Then, in a
private postscript, he condescended to tell us that all would be speedily
settled to his satisfaction, and we should turn over a new leaf, for he was
going to be married in a fortnight to the grandest heiress in England,
and had only immediate occasion at present for £200, as he would not
choose to touch his lady's fortune for travelling expenses home to
Castle Rackrent, where he intended to be, wind and weather permit-
ting, early in the next month; and desired fires, and the house to be
painted, and the new building to go on as fast as possible, for the
reception of him and his lady before that time; with several words
besides in the letter, which we could not make out because, God bless
him! he wrote in such a flurry. My heart warmed to my new lady when
I read this: I was almost afraid it was too good news to be true; but the
girls fell to scouring, and it was well they did, for we soon saw his
marriage in the paper, to a lady with I don't know how many tens of
thousand pounds to her fortune: then I watched the post-office for his
landing; and the news came to my son of his and the bride being in
Dublin, and on the way home to Castle Rackrent. We had bonfires all
over the country, expecting him down the next day, and we had his
coming of age still to celebrate, which he had not time to do properly
before he left the country; therefore, a great ball was expected, and
great doings upon his coming, as it were, fresh to take possession of his
ancestors' estate. I never shall forget the day he came home; we had
waited and waited all day long till eleven o'clock at night, and I was
thinking of sending the boy to lock the gates, and giving them up for
that night, when there came the carriages thundering up to the great
hall door. I got the first sight of the bride; for when the carriage door
opened, just as she had her foot on the steps, I held the flam full in her
face to light her, at which she shut her eyes, but I had a full view of the
rest of her, and greatly shocked I was, for by that light she was little
better than a blackamoor, and seemed crippled; but that was only
sitting so long in the chariot.

'You're kindly welcome to Castle Rackrent, my lady,' says I (recollecting who she was). 'Did your honour hear of the bonfires?'

His honour spoke never a word, nor so much as handed her up the steps – he looked to me no more like himself than nothing at all; I know I took him for the skeleton of his honour. I was not sure what to say next to one or t'other, but seeing she was a stranger in a foreign country, I thought it but right to speak cheerful to her; so I went back again to the bonfires.

'My lady,' says I, as she crossed the hall, 'there would have been fifty times as many; but for fear of the horses, and frightening your ladyship, Jason and I forbid them, please your honour.'

With that she looked at me a little bewildered.

'Will I have a fire lighted in the state-room tonight?' was the next question I put to her, but never a word she answered; so I concluded she could not speak a word of English, and was from foreign parts. The short and the long of it was, I couldn't tell what to make of her; so I left her to herself, and went straight down to the servants' hall to learn something for certain about her. Sir Kit's own man was tired, but the groom set him a-talking at last, and we had it all out before ever I closed my eyes that night. The bride might well be a great fortune – she was a *Jewish* by all accounts, who are famous for their great riches. I had never seen any of that tribe or nation before, and could only gather that she spoke a strange kind of English of her own, that she could not abide pork or sausages, and went neither to church or mass. Mercy upon his honour's poor soul, thought I; what will become of him and his, and all of us, with his heretic blackamoor at the head of the Castle Rackrent estate? I never slept a wink all night for thinking of it; but before the servants I put my pipe in my mouth, and kept my mind to myself, for I had a great regard for the family; and after this, when strange gentlemen's servants came to the house, and would begin to talk about the bride, I took care to put the best foot foremost, and passed her for a nabob in the kitchen, which accounted for her dark complexion and everything.

The very morning after they came home, however, I saw plain enough how things were between Sir Kit and my lady, though they were walking together arm in arm after breakfast, looking at the new building and the improvements.

'Old Thady,' said my master, just as he used to do, 'how do you do?'

'Very well, I thank your honour's honour,' said I; but I saw he was not well pleased, and my heart was in my mouth as I walked along after him.

'Is the large room damp, Thady?' said his honour.

'Oh damp, your honour! how should it be but as dry as a bone,' says I, 'after all the fires we have kept in it day and night? It's the barrack-room your honour's talking on.'

'And what is a barrack-room, pray, my dear?' were the first words I ever heard out of my lady's lips.

'No matter, my dear,' said he, and went on talking to me, ashamed-like I should witness her ignorance. To be sure, to hear her talk one might have taken her for an innocent, for it was, 'What's this, Sir Kit? and what's that, Sir Kit?' all the way we went. To be sure, Sir Kit had enough to do to answer her.

'And what do you call that, Sir Kit?' said she; 'that – that looks like a pile of black bricks, pray, Sir Kit?'

'My turf-stack, my dear,' said my master, and bit his lip.

Where have you lived, my lady, all your life, not to know a turf-stack when you see it? thought I; but I said nothing. Then by and by she takes out her glass, and begins spying over the country.

'And what's all that black swamp out yonder, Sir Kit?' says she.

'My bog, my dear,' says he, and went on whistling.

'It's a very ugly prospect, my dear,' says she.

'You don't see it, my dear,' says he, 'for we've planted it out; when the trees grow up in summer-time – ' says he.

'Where are the trees,' said she, 'my dear?' still looking through her glass.

'You are blind, my dear,' says he; 'what are these under your eyes?'

'These shrubs?' said she.

'Trees,' said he.

'Maybe they are what you call trees in Ireland, my dear,' said she; 'but they are not a yard high, are they?'

'They were planted out but last year, my lady,' says I, to soften matters between them, for I saw she was going the way to make his honour mad with her: 'they are very well grown for their age, and you'll not see the bog of Allyballycarricko'shaughlin at-all-at-all through the skreen, when once the leaves come out. But, my lady, you must not quarrel with any part or parcel of Allyballycarricko'shaughlin, for you don't know how many hundred years that same bit of bog has been in the family; we would not part with the bog of Allyballycarricko'shaughlin upon no account at all; it cost the late Sir Murtagh two hundred good pounds to defend his title to it and boundaries against the O'Learys, who cut a road through it.'

Now one would have thought this would have been hint enough for my lady, but she fell to laughing like one out of their right mind, and made me say the name of the bog over, for her to get it by heart, a dozen times; then she must ask me how to spell it, and what was the meaning of it in English – Sir Kit standing by whistling all the while. I verily believed she laid the corner-stone of all her future misfortunes at that very instant; but I said no more, only looked at Sir Kit.

There were no balls, no dinners, no doings; the country was all disappointed – Sir Kit's gentleman said in a whisper to me, it was all my lady's own fault, because she was so obstinate about the cross.

'What cross?' says I; 'is it about her being a heretic?'

'Oh, no such matter,' says he; 'my master does not mind her heresies, but her diamond cross – it's worth I can't tell you how much, and she has thousands of English pounds concealed in diamonds about her, which she as good as promised to give up to my master before he married; but now she won't part with any of them, and she must take the consequences.'

Her honeymoon, at least her Irish honeymoon, was scarcely well over, when his honour one morning said to me, 'Thady, buy me a pig!' and then the sausages were ordered, and here was the first open breaking-out of my lady's troubles. My lady came down herself into the kitchen to speak to the cook about the sausages, and desired never to see them more at her table. Now my master had ordered them, and my lady knew that. The cook took my lady's part, because she never came down into the kitchen and was young and innocent in housekeeping, which raised her pity; besides, said she, at her own table, surely my lady should order and disorder what she pleases. But the cook soon changed her note, for my master made it a principle to have the sausages, and swore at her for a Jew herself, till he drove her fairly out of the kitchen; then, for fear of her place, and because he threatened that my lady should give her no discharge without the sausages, she gave up, and from that day forward always sausages, or bacon, or pig-meat in some shape or other, went up to table; upon which my lady shut herself up in her own room, and my master said she might stay there, with an oath: and to make sure of her, he turned the key in the door, and kept it ever after in his pocket. We none of us ever saw or heard her speak for seven years after that: he carried her dinner himself. Then his honour had a great deal of company to dine with him, and balls in the house, and was as gay and gallant, and as much himself as before he was married; and at dinner he always drank my Lady Rackrent's good health and so did the company, and he sent out always a servant with his compliments to my Lady Rackrent, and the company was drinking her ladyship's health, and begged to know if there was anything at table he might send her, and the man came back, after the sham errand, with my Lady Rackrent's compliments, and she was very much obliged to Sir Kit – she did not wish for anything, but drank the company's health. The country, to be sure, talked and wondered at my lady's being shut up, but nobody chose to interfere or ask any impertinent questions, for they knew my master was a man very apt to give a short answer himself, and likely to call a man out for it afterwards: he was a famous shot, had killed his man before he came of age, and nobody scarce dared look at him whilst at Bath. Sir Kit's character was so well known in the country that he lived in peace and quietness ever after, and was a great favourite with the ladies, especially when in process of time, in the fifth year of her confinement, my Lady Rackrent fell ill and took entirely to her bed, and he gave out that she was now skin and bone, and could not last through the winter. In this he had two physicians' opinions to back him (for now he called in two physicians for her), and tried all his arts to get the diamond cross from her on her death-bed, and to get her to make a will in his favour of her separate possessions; but there she was too tough for him. He used to swear at her behind her back after kneeling to her face, and call her in the presence of his gentleman his stiff-necked Israelite, though before he married her that same gentleman told me he used to call her (how he could bring it out, I don't know) 'my pretty Jessica!' To be sure it must have been hard for her to guess what sort of a husband he reckoned to make her. When she was lying, to all expectation, on her death-bed of a broken heart, I could not but pity her, though she was a Jewish, and considering too it was no fault of hers to be taken with my master, so young as she was at the Bath, and so fine a gentleman as Sir Kit was when he courted her; and considering too, after all they had heard and seen of him as a husband, there were now no less than three ladies in our county talked of for his second wife, all at daggers drawn with each other, as his gentleman swore, at the balls, for Sir Kit for their partner – I could not but think them bewitched, but they all reasoned with themselves that Sir Kit would make a good husband to any Christian but a Jewish, I suppose, and especially as he was now a reformed rake; and it was not known how my lady's fortune was settled in her will, nor how the Castle Rackrent estate was all mortgaged, and bonds out against him, for he was never cured of his gaming tricks; but that was the only fault he had, God bless him!

My lady had a sort of fit, and it was given out that she was dead, by mistake: this brought things to a sad crisis for my poor master. One of the three ladies showed his letters to her brother, and claimed his promises, whilst another did the same. I don't mention names. Sir Kit, in his defence, said he would meet any man who dared to question his conduct; and as to the ladies, they must settle it amongst them who was to be his second, and his third, and his fourth, whilst his first was still alive, to his mortification and theirs. Upon this, as upon all former occasions, he had the voice of the country with him, on account of the great spirit and propriety he acted with. He met and shot the first lady's brother: the next day he called out the second, who had a wooden leg, and their place of meeting by appointment being in a new-ploughed field, the wooden-leg man stuck fast in it. Sir Kit, seeing his situation, with great candour fired his pistol over his head; upon which the seconds interposed, and convinced the parties there had been a slight misunderstanding between them: thereupon they shook hands cordially, and went home to dinner together. This gentleman, to show the world how they stood together, and by the advice of the friends of both parties, to re-establish his sister's injured reputation, went out with Sir Kit as his second, and carried his message next day to the last of his adversaries: I never saw him in such fine spirits as that day he went out – sure enough he was within ames-ace of getting quit handsomely of all his enemies; but unluckily, after hitting the toothpick out of his adversary's finger and thumb, he received a ball in a vital part, and was brought home, in little better than an hour after the affair, speechless on a handbarrow to my lady. We got the key out of his pocket the first thing we did, and my son Jason ran to unlock the barrack-room, where my lady had been shut up for seven years, to acquaint her with the fatal accident. The surprise bereaved her of her senses at first, nor would she believe but we were putting some new trick upon her, to entrap her out of her jewels, for a great while, till Jason bethought himself of taking her to the window, and showed her the men bringing Sir Kit up the avenue upon the hand-barrow, which had immediately the desired effect; for directly she burst into tears, and pulling her cross from her bosom, she kissed it with as great devotion as ever I witnessed, and lifting up her eyes to heaven, uttered some ejaculation, which none present heard; but I take the sense of it to be, she returned thanks for this unexpected interposition in her favour when she had least reason to expect it. My master was greatly lamented: there was no life in him when we lifted him off the barrow, so he was laid out immediately, and 'waked' the same night. The country was all in an uproar about him, and not a soul but cried shame upon his murderer, who would have been hanged surely, if he could have been brought to his trial, whilst the gentlemen in the country were up about it; but he very prudently withdrew himself to the Continent before the affair was made public. As for the young lady who was the immediate cause of the fatal accident, however innocently, she could never show her head after at the balls in the county or any place; and by the advice of her friends and physicians, she was ordered soon after to Bath, where it was expected, if anywhere on this side of the grave, she would meet with the recovery of her health and lost peace of mind. As a proof of his great popularity, I

need only add that there was a song made upon my master's untimely
death in the newspapers, which was in everybody's mouth, singing up
and down through the country, even down to the mountains, only
three days after his unhappy exit. He was also greatly bemoaned at the
Curragh, where his cattle were well known; and all who had taken up
his bets were particularly inconsolable for his loss to society. His stud
sold at the cant at the greatest price ever known in the county; his
favourite horses were chiefly disposed of amongst his particular friends,
who would give any price for them for his sake; but no ready money
was required by the new heir, who wished not to displease any of the
gentlemen of the neighbourhood just upon his coming to settle
amongst them; so a long credit was given where requisite, and the cash
has never been gathered in from that day to this.

But to return to my lady. She got surprisingly well after my master's
decease. No sooner was it known for certain that he was dead, than all
the gentlemen within twenty miles of us came in a body, as it were, to
set my lady at liberty, and to protest against her confinement, which
they now for the first time understood was against her own consent.
The ladies too were as attentive as possible, striving who should be
foremost with their morning visits; and they that saw the diamonds
spoke very handsomely of them, but thought it a pity they were not
bestowed, if it had so pleased God, upon a lady who would have
become them better. All these civilities wrought little with my lady, for
she had taken an unaccountable prejudice against the country, and
everything belonging to it, and was so partial to her native land, that
after parting with the cook, which she did immediately upon my
master's decease, I never knew her easy one instant, night or day, but
when she was packing up to leave us. Had she meant to make any stay
in Ireland, I stood a great chance of being a great favourite with her; for
when she found I understood the weathercock, she was always finding
some pretence to be talking to me, and asking me which way the wind
blew, and was it likely, did I think, to continue fair for England. But
when I saw she had made up her mind to spend the rest of her days
upon her own income and jewels in England, I considered her quite as
a foreigner, and not at all any longer as part of the family. She gave no
vails to the servants at Castle Rackrent at parting, notwithstanding the
old proverb of 'as rich as a Jew,' which she, being a Jewish, they built
upon with reason. But from first to last she brought nothing but
misfortunes amongst us; and if it had not been all along with her, his
honour, Sir Kit, would have been now alive in all appearance. Her
diamond cross was, they say, at the bottom of it all; and it was a shame
for her, being his wife, not to show more duty, and to have given it up

when he condescended to ask so often for such a bit of a trifle in his distresses, especially when he all along made it no secret he married for money. But we will not bestow another thought upon her. This much I thought it lay upon my conscience to say, in justice to my poor master's memory.

'Tis an ill wind that blows nobody no good: the same wind that took the Jew Lady Rackrent over to England brought over the new heir to Castle Rackrent.

Here let me pause for breath in my story, for though I had a great regard for every member of the family, yet without compare Sir Conolly, commonly called, for short, amongst his friends, Sir Condy Rackrent, was ever my great favourite, and, indeed, the most universally beloved man I had ever seen or heard of, not excepting his great ancestor Sir Patrick, to whose memory he, amongst other instances of generosity, erected a handsome marble stone in the church of Castle Rackrent, setting forth in large letters his age, birth, parentage, and many other virtues, concluding with the compliment so justly due, that 'Sir Patrick Rackrent lived and died a monument of old Irish hospitality.'

Continuation of the Memoirs of the Rackrent Family – History of Sir Conolly Rackrent

SIR CONDY RACKRENT, by the grace of God heir-at-law to the Castle Rackrent estate, was a remote branch of the family. Born to little or no fortune of his own, he was bred to the bar, at which, having many friends to push him and no mean natural abilities of his own, he doubtless would in process of time, if he could have borne the drudgery of that study, have been rapidly made King's Counsel at the least; but things were disposed of otherwise, and he never went the circuit but twice, and then made no figure for want of a fee, and being unable to speak in public. He received his education chiefly in the college of Dublin, but before he came to years of discretion lived in the country, in a small but slated house within view of the end of the avenue. I remember him, bare footed and headed, running through the street of O'Shaughlin's Town, and playing at pitch-and-toss, ball, marbles, and what not, with the boys of the town, amongst whom my son Jason was a great favourite with him. As for me, he was ever my white-headed boy: often's the time, when I would call in at his father's, where I was always made welcome, he would slip down to me in the kitchen, and, love to sit on my knee whilst I told him stories of the family and the blood from which he was sprung, and how he might look forward, if the then present man should die without childer, to being at the head of the Castle Rackrent estate. This was then spoke quite and clear at random to please the child, but it pleased Heaven to accomplish my prophecy afterwards, which gave him a great opinion of my judgment in business. He went to a little grammar-school with many others, and my son amongst the rest, who was in his class, and not a little useful to him in his book-learning, which he acknowledged with gratitude ever after. These rudiments of his education thus completed, he got a-horseback, to which exercise he was ever addicted, and used to gallop over the country while yet but a slip of a boy, under the care of Sir Kit's huntsman, who was very fond of him, and often lent him his gun, and took him out a-shooting under his own eye. By these means he became well acquainted and popular amongst the poor in the neighbourhood early, for there was not a cabin at which he had not stopped some morning or other, along with the huntsman, to drink a glass of burnt whisky out of an eggshell, to do him good and warm his heart and drive the cold out of his stomach. The old people always told him he was a great likeness of Sir Patrick, which made him first have an ambition to take after him, as far as his fortune should allow. He left us when of an age to enter the college, and there completed his education and nineteenth year, for as he was not born to an estate, his friends thought it incumbent on them to give him the best education which could be had for love or money, and a great deal of money consequently was spent upon him at College and Temple. He was a very little altered for the worse by what he saw there of the great world, for when he came down into the country to pay us a visit, we thought him just the same man as ever – hand and glove with every one, and as far from high, though not without his own proper share of family pride, as any man ever you see. Latterly, seeing how Sir Kit and the Jewish lived together, and that there was no one between him and the Castle Rackrent estate, he neglected to apply to the law as much as was expected of him, and secretly many of the tenants and others advanced him cash upon his note of hand value received, promising bargains of leases and lawful interest, should he ever come into the estate. All this was kept a great secret for fear the present man, hearing of it, should take it into his head to take it ill of poor Condy, and so should cut him off for ever by levying a fine, and suffering a recovery to dock the entail. Sir Murtagh would have been the man for that; but Sir Kit was too much taken up philandering to consider the law in this case, or any other. These practices I have mentioned to account for the state of his affairs – I mean Sir Condy's upon his coming into the Castle Rackrent estate. He could not command a penny of his first year's income, which, and keeping no accounts, and the great sight of company he did, with many other causes too numerous to mention, was the origin of his distresses. My son Jason, who was now established agent, and knew everything, explained matters out of the face to Sir Conolly, and made him sensible of his embarrassed situation. With a great nominal rent-roll, it was almost all paid away in interest; which being for convenience suffered to run on, soon doubled the principal, and Sir Condy was obliged to pass new bonds for the interest, now grown principal, and so on. Whilst this was going on, my son requiring to be paid for his trouble and many years' service in the family gratis, and Sir Condy not willing to take his affairs into his own hands, or to look them even in the face, he gave my son a bargain of some acres which fell out of lease at a reasonable rent. Jason set the land, as soon as his lease was sealed, to under-tenants, to make the rent, and got two hundred a year profit rent; which was little enough considering his long agency. He bought the land at twelve years' purchase two years afterwards, when Sir Condy was pushed for money on an execution, and was at the same time allowed for his improvements thereon. There was a sort of hunting-lodge upon the estate, convenient to my son Jason's land, which he had his eye upon about this time; and he was a little jealous of Sir Condy, who talked of setting it to a stranger who was just come into the country – Captain Moneygawl was the man. He was son and heir to the Moneygawls of Mount Juliet's Town, who had a great estate in the next county to ours; and my master was loth to disoblige the young gentleman, whose heart was set upon the Lodge; so he wrote him back that the Lodge was at his service, and if he would honour him with his company at Castle Rackrent, they could ride over together some morning and look at it before signing the lease. Accordingly, the captain came over to us, and he and Sir Condy grew the greatest friends ever you see, and were for ever out a-shooting or hunting together, and were very merry in the evenings; and Sir Condy was invited of course to Mount Juliet's Town; and the family intimacy that had been in Sir Patrick's time was now recollected, and nothing would serve Sir Condy but he must be three times a week at the least with his new friends, which grieved me, who knew, by the captain's groom and gentleman, how they talked of him at Mount Juliet's Town, making him quite, as one may say, a laughing-stock and a butt for the whole company; but they were soon cured of that by an accident that surprised 'em not a little, as it did me. There was a bit of a scrawl found upon the waiting-maid of old Mr Moneygawl's youngest daughter, Miss Isabella, that laid open the whole; and her father, they say, was like one out of his right mind, and swore it was the last thing he ever should have thought of, when he invited my master to his house, that his daughter should think of such a match. But their talk signified not a straw, for as Miss Isabella's maid reported, her young mistress was fallen over head and ears in love with Sir Condy from the first time that ever her brother brought him into the house to dinner. The servant who waited that day behind my master's chair was the first who knew it, as he says; though it's hard to believe him, for he did not tell it till a great while afterwards; but, however, it's likely enough, as the thing turned out, that he was not far out of the way, for towards the middle of dinner, as he says, they were talking of stage-plays, having a playhouse, and being great play-actors at Mount Juliet's Town; and Miss Isabella turns short to my master, and says:

'Have you seen the play-bill, Sir Condy?'

'No, I have not,' said he.

'Then more shame for you,' said the captain her brother; 'not to know that my sister is to play Juliet tonight, who plays it better than any woman on or off the stage in all Ireland.'

'I am very happy to hear it,' said Sir Condy; and there the matter dropped for the present.

But Sir Condy all this time, and a great while afterwards, was at a terrible nonplus; for he had no liking, not he, to stage-plays, nor to Miss Isabella either – to his mind, as it came out over a bowl of whiskey-punch at home, his little Judy M'Quirk, who was daughter to a sister's son of mine, was worth twenty of Miss Isabella. He had seen her often when he stopped at her father's cabin to drink whiskey out of the eggshell, out hunting, before he came to the estate, and, as she gave out, was under something like a promise of marriage to her. Anyhow, I could not but pity my poor master, who was so bothered between them, and he an easy-hearted man, that could not disoblige nobody – God bless him! To be sure, it was not his place to behave ungenerous to Miss Isabella, who had disobliged all her relations for his sake, as he remarked; and then she was locked up in her chamber, and forbid to think of him any more, which raised his spirit, because his family was, as he observed, as good as theirs at any rate, and the Rackrents a suitable match for the Moneygawls any day in the year; all which was true enough. But it grieved me to see that, upon the strength of all this, Sir Condy was growing more in the mind to carry off Miss Isabella to Scotland, in spite of her relations, as she desired.

'It's all over with our poor Judy!' said I, with a heavy sigh, making bold to speak to him one night when he was a little cheerful, and standing in the servants' hall all alone with me, as was often his custom.

'Not at all,' said he; 'I never was fonder of Judy than at this present speaking; and to prove it to you,' said he – and he took from my hand a halfpenny change that I had just got along with my tobacco – 'and to prove it to you, Thady,' says he, 'it's a toss-up with me which I should marry this minute, her or Mr Moneygawl of Mount Juliet's Town's daughter – so it is.'

'Oh – boo! boo!' says I, making light of it, to see what he would go on to next; 'your honour's joking, to be sure; there's no compare between our poor Judy and Miss Isabella, who has a great fortune, they say.'

'I'm not a man to mind a fortune, nor never was,' said Sir Condy, proudly, 'whatever her friends may say; and to make short of it,' says he, 'I'm come to a determination upon the spot.' With that he swore such a terrible oath as made me cross myself. 'And by this book,' said he, snatching up my ballad-book, mistaking it for my prayer-book, which lay in the window, – 'and by this book,' says he, 'and by all the books that ever were shut and opened, it's come to a toss-up with me, and I'll stand or fall by the toss; and so Thady, hand me over that *pin* out of the ink-horn;' and he makes a cross on the smooth side of the halfpenny; 'Judy M'Quirk,' says he, 'her mark.'

God bless him! his hand was a little unsteadied by all the whiskey-punch he had taken, but it was plain to see his heart was for poor Judy. My heart was all as one as in my mouth when I saw the halfpenny up in the air, but I said nothing at all; and when it came down I was glad I had kept myself to myself, for to be sure now it was all over with poor Judy.

'Judy's out a luck,' said I, striving to laugh.

'I'm out a luck,' said he; and I never saw a man look so cast down: he took up the halfpenny off the flag, and walked away quite sober-like by the shock. Now, though as easy a man, you would think, as any in the wide world, there was no such thing as making him unsay one of these sort of vows, which he had learned to reverence when young, as I well remember teaching him to toss up for bog-berries on my knee. So I saw the affair was as good as settled between him and Miss Isabella, and I had no more to say but to wish her joy, which I did the week afterwards, upon her return from Scotland with my poor master.

My new lady was young, as might be supposed of a lady that had been carried off by her own consent to Scotland; but I could only see her at first through her veil, which, from bashfulness or fashion, she kept over her face.

'And am I to walk through all this crowd of people, my dearest love?' said she to Sir Condy, meaning us servants and tenants, who had gathered at the back gate.

'My dear,' said Sir Condy, 'there's nothing for it but to walk, or to let me carry you as far as the house, for you see the back road is too narrow for a carriage, and the great piers have tumbled down across the front approach; so there's no driving the right way, by reason of the ruins.'

'Plato, thou reasonest well!' said she, or words to that effect, which I could noways understand; and again, when her foot stumbled against a broken bit of a car-wheel, she cried out, 'Angels and ministers of grace defend us!' Well, thought I, to be sure, if she's no Jewish, like the last, she is a mad woman for certain, which is as bad: it would have been as well for my poor master to have taken up with poor Judy, who is in her right mind anyhow.

She was dressed like a mad woman, moreover, more than like any one I ever saw afore or since, and I could not take my eyes off her, but still followed behind her; and her feathers on the top of her hat were broke going in at the low back door, and she pulled out her little bottle out of her pocket to smell when she found herself in the kitchen, and said, 'I shall faint with the heat of this odious, odious place.'

'My dear, it's only three steps across the kitchen, and there's a fine air if your veil was up,' said Sir Condy; and with that threw back her veil, so that I had then a full sight of her face. She had not at all the colour of one going to faint, but a fine complexion of her own, as I then took it to be, though her maid told me after it was all put on; but even, complexion and all taken in, she was no way, in point of good looks, to compare to poor Judy, and withal she had a quality toss with her; but maybe it was my over-partiality to Judy, into whose place I may say she stepped, that made me notice all this.

To do her justice, however, she was, when we came to know her better, very liberal in her housekeeping – nothing at all of the skinflint in her; she left everything to the housekeeper, and her own maid, Mrs Jane, who went with her to Scotland, gave her the best of characters for generosity. She seldom or ever wore a thing twice the same way, Mrs Jane told us, and was always pulling her things to pieces and giving them away, never being used, in her father's house, to think of expense in anything; and she reckoned to be sure to go on the same way at Castle Rackrent; but when I came to inquire, I learned that her father was so mad with her for running off, after his locking her up and forbidding her to think any more of Sir Condy, that he would not give her a farthing; and it was lucky for her she had a few thousands of her own, which had been left to her by a good grandmother, and these were very convenient to begin with. My master and my lady set out in great style; they had the finest coach and chariot, and horses and liveries, and cut the greatest dash in the county, returning their wedding visits; and it was immediately reported that her father had undertaken to pay all my master's debts, and of course all his tradesmen gave him a new credit, and everything went on smack smooth, and I could not but admire my lady's spirit, and was proud to see Castle Rackrent again in all its glory. My lady had a fine taste for building, and furniture, and playhouses, and she turned everything topsy-turvy, and made the barrack-room into a theatre, as she called it, and she went on as if she had a mint of money at her elbow; and to be sure I thought she knew best, especially as Sir Condy said nothing to it one way or the other. All he asked – God bless him! – was to live in peace and quietness, and have his bottle or his whiskey-punch at night to himself. Now this was little enough, to be sure, for any gentleman; but my lady couldn't abide the smell of the whiskey-punch.

'My dear,' says he, 'you liked it well enough before we were married, and why not now?'

'My dear,' said she, 'I never smelt it, or I assure you I should never have prevailed upon myself to marry you.'

'My dear, I am sorry you did not smell it, but we can't help that now,' returned my master, without putting himself in a passion, or going out of his way, but just fair and easy helped himself to another glass, and drank it off to her good health.

All this the butler told me, who was going backwards and forwards unnoticed with the jug, and hot water, and sugar, and all he thought wanting. Upon my master's swallowing the last glass of whiskey-punch my lady burst into tears, calling him an ungrateful, base, barbarous wretch; and went off into a fit of hysterics, as I think Mrs Jane called it, and my poor master was greatly frightened, this being the first thing of the kind he had seen; and he fell straight on his knees before her, and, like a good-hearted cratur as he was, ordered the whiskey-punch out of the room, and bid 'em throw open all the windows, and cursed himself: and then my lady came to herself again, and when she saw him kneeling there, bid him get up, and not forswear himself any more, for that she was sure he did not love her, and never had. This we learned from Mrs Jane, who was the only person left present at all this.

'My dear,' returns my master, thinking, to be sure, of Judy, as well he might, 'whoever told you so is an incendiary, and I'll have 'em turned out of the house this minute, if you'll only let me know which of them it was.'

'Told me what?' said my lady, starting upright in her chair.

'Nothing at all, nothing at all,' said my master, seeing he had overshot himself, and that my lady spoke at random; 'but what you said just now, that I did not love you, Bella; who told you that?'

'My own sense,' she said, and she put her handkerchief to her face, and leant back upon Mrs Jane, and fell to sobbing as if her heart would break.

'Why now, Bella, this is very strange of you,' said my poor master; 'if nobody has told you nothing, what is it you are taking on for at this rate, and exposing yourself and me for this way?'

'Oh, say no more, say no more; every word you say kills me,' cried my lady; and she ran on like one, as Mrs Jane says, raving, 'Oh, Sir Condy, Sir Condy! I that had hoped to find in you – '

'Why now, faith, this is a little too much; do, Bella, try to recollect yourself, my dear; am not I your husband, and of your own choosing, and is not that enough?'

'Oh, too much! too much!' cried my lady, wringing her hands.

'Why, my dear, come to your right senses, for the love of heaven. See, is not the whiskey-punch, jug and bowl and all, gone out of the room long ago? What is it, in the wide world, you have to complain of?'

But still my lady sobbed and sobbed, and called herself the most wretched of women; and among other out-of-the-way provoking things, asked my master, was he fit company for her, and he drinking all night? This nettling him, which it was hard to do, he replied, that as to drinking all night, he was then as sober as she was herself, and that it was no matter how much a man drank, provided it did noways affect or stagger him: that as to being fit company for her, he thought himself of a family to be fit company for any lord or lady in the land; but that he never prevented her from seeing and keeping what company she pleased, and that he had done his best to make Castle Rackrent pleasing to her since her marriage, having always had the house full of visitors, and if her own relations were not amongst them, he said that was their own fault, and their pride's fault, of which he was sorry to find her ladyship had so unbecoming a share. So concluding, he took his candle and walked off to his room, and my lady was in her tantarums for three days after; and would have been so much longer, no doubt, but some of her friends, young ladies, and cousins, and second cousins, came to Castle Rackrent, by my poor master's express invitation, to see her, and she was in a hurry to get up, as Mrs Jane called it, a play for them, and so got well, and was as finely dressed, and as happy to look at, as ever; and all the young ladies, who used to be in her room dressing of her, said in Mrs Jane's hearing that my lady was the happiest bride ever they had seen, and that to be sure a love-match was the only thing for happiness, where the parties could any way afford it.

As to affording it, God knows it was little they knew of the matter; my lady's few thousands could not last for ever, especially the way she went on with them; and letters from tradesfolk came every post thick and threefold, with bills as long as my arm, of years' and years' standing. My son Jason had 'em all handed over to him, and the pressing letters were all unread by Sir Condy, who hated trouble, and could never be brought to hear talk of business, but still put it off and put it off, saying, 'Settle it anyhow,' or, 'Bid 'em call again tomorrow,' or, 'Speak to me about it some other time.' Now it was hard to find the right time to speak, for in the mornings he was a-bed, and in the evenings over his bottle, where no gentleman chooses to be disturbed. Things in a twelvemonth or so came to such a pass there was no making a shift to go on any longer, though we were all of us well enough used to live from hand to mouth at Castle Rackrent. One day, I remember, when there was a power of company, all sitting after dinner in the dusk, not to say dark, in the drawing-room, my lady having rung five times for candles, and none to go up, the housekeeper sent up the footman, who went to my mistress, and whispered behind her chair how it was.

'My lady,' says he, 'there are no candles in the house.'

'Bless me,' says she; 'then take a horse and gallop off as fast as you can to Carrick O'Fungus, and get some.'

'And in the meantime tell them to step into the playhouse, and try if there are not some bits left,' added Sir Condy, who happened to be within hearing. The man was sent up again to my lady, to let her know there was no horse to go, but one that wanted a shoe.

'Go to Sir Condy then; I know nothing at all about the horses,' said my lady; 'why do you plague me with these things?' How it was settled I really forget, but to the best of my remembrance, the boy was sent down to my son Jason's to borrow candles for the night. Another time, in the winter, and on a desperate cold day, there was no turf in for the parlour and above stairs, and scarce enough for the cook in the kitchen. The little *gossoon* was sent off to the neighbours, to see and beg or borrow some, but none could he bring back with him for love or money; so, as needs must, we were forced to trouble Sir Condy – 'Well, and if there's no turf to be had in the town or country, why, what signifies talking any more about it; can't ye go and cut down a tree?'

'Which tree, please your honour?' I made bold to say.

'Any tree at all that's good to burn,' said Sir Condy; 'send off smart and get one down, and the fires lighted, before my lady gets up to breakfast, or the house will be too hot to hold us.'

He was always very considerate in all things about my lady, and she wanted for nothing whilst he had it to give. Well, when things were tight with them about this time, my son Jason put in a word again about the Lodge, and made a genteel offer to lay down the purchase-money, to relieve Sir Condy's distresses. Now Sir Condy had it from the best authority that there were two writs come down to the sheriff against his person, and the sheriff, as ill-luck would have it, was no friend of his, and talked how he must do his duty, and how he would do it, if it was against the first man in the country, or even his own brother, let alone one who had voted against him at the last election, as Sir Condy had done. So Sir Condy was fain to take the purchase-money of the Lodge from my son Jason to settle matters; and sure enough it was a good bargain for both parties, for my son bought the fee-simple of a good house for him and his heirs for ever, for little or nothing, and by selling of it for that same my master saved himself from a gaol. Every way it turned out fortunate for Sir Condy, for before the money was all gone there came a general election, and he being so well beloved in the county, and one of the oldest families, no one had a better right to stand candidate for the vacancy; and he was called upon by all his friends, and the whole county I may say, to declare himself against the old member, who had little thought of a contest. My master did not relish the thoughts of a troublesome canvass, and all the ill-will he might bring upon himself by disturbing the peace of the county, besides the expense, which was no trifle; but all his friends called upon one another to subscribe, and they formed themselves into a committee, and wrote all his circular letters for him, and engaged all his agents, and did all the business unknown to him; and he was well pleased that it should be so at last, and my lady herself was very sanguine about the election; and there was open house! kept night and day at Castle Rackrent, and I thought I never saw my lady look so well in her life as she did at that time. There were grand dinners, and all the gentlemen drinking success to Sir Condy till they were carried off; and then dances and balls, and the ladies all finishing with a raking pot of tea in the morning. Indeed, it was well the company made it their choice to sit up all nights, for there were not half beds enough for the sights of people that were in it, though there were shake-downs in the drawing-room always made up before sunrise for those that liked it. For my part, when I saw the doings that were going on, and the loads of claret that went down the throats of them that had no right to be asking for it, and the sights of meat that went up to table and never came down, besides what was carried off to one or t'other below stair, I couldn't but pity my poor master, who was to pay for all; but I said nothing, for fear of gaining myself ill-will. The day of election will come some time or other, says I to myself, and all will be over; and so it did, and a glorious day it was as any I ever had the happiness to see.

'Huzza! huzza! Sir Condy Rackrent for ever!' was the first thing I hears in the morning, and the same and nothing else all day, and not a soul sober only just when polling, enough to give their votes as became 'em, and to stand the browbeating of the lawyers, who came tight enough upon us; and many of our freeholders were knocked off, having never a freehold that they could safely swear to, and Sir Condy was not willing to have any man perjure himself for his sake, as was done on the other side, God knows; but no matter for that. Some of our friends were dumbfounded by the lawyers asking them: Had they ever been upon the ground where their freeholds lay? Now, Sir Condy being tender of the consciences of them that had not been on the ground, and so could not swear to a freehold when cross-examined by them lawyers, sent out for a couple of cleavesful of the sods of his farm of Gulteeshinnagh; and as soon as the sods came into town, he set each man upon his sod, and so then, ever after, you know, they could fairly swear they had been upon the ground. We gained the day by this piece of honesty. I thought I should have died in the streets for joy when I seed my poor master chaired, and he bareheaded, and it raining as hard as it could pour; but all the crowds following him up and down, and he bowing and shaking hands with the whole town.

'Is that Sir Condy Rackrent in the chair?' says a stranger man in the crowd.

'The same,' says I. 'Who else should it be? God bless him!'

'And I take it, then, you belong to him?' says he.

'Not at all,' says I; 'but I live under him, and have done so these two hundred years and upwards, me and mine.'

'It's lucky for you, then,' rejoins he, 'that he is where he is; for was he anywhere else but in the chair, this minute he'd be in a worse place; for I was sent down on purpose to put him up, and here's my order for so doing in my pocket.'

It was a writ that villain the wine merchant had marked against my poor master for some hundreds of an old debt, which it was a shame to be talking of at such a time as this.

'Put it in your pocket again, and think no more of it anyways for seven years to come, my honest friend,' says I; 'he's a member of Parliament now, praised be God, and such as you can't touch him: and if you'll take a fool's advice, I'd have you keep out of the way this day, or you'll run a good chance of getting your deserts amongst my master's friends, unless you choose to drink his health like everybody else.'

'I've no objection to that in life,' said he. So we went into one of the public-houses kept open for my master; and we had a great deal of talk about this thing and that. 'And how is it,' says he, 'your master keeps on so well upon his legs? I heard say he was off Holantide twelvemonth past.'

'Never was better or heartier in his life,' said I.

'It's not that I'm after speaking of,' said he; 'but there was a great report of his being ruined.'

'No matter,' says I, 'the sheriffs two years running were his particular friends, and the sub-sheriffs were both of them gentlemen, and were properly spoken to; and so the writs lay snug with them, and they, as I understand by my son Jason the custom in them cases is, returned the writs as they came to them to those that sent 'em – much good may it do them! – with a word in Latin, that no such person as Sir Condy Rackrent, Bart., was to be found in those parts.'

'Oh, I understand all those ways better – no offence – than you,' says he, laughing, and at the same time filling his glass to my master's good health, which convinced me he was a warm friend in his heart after all, though appearances were a little suspicious or so at first. 'To be sure,' says he, still cutting his joke, 'when a man's over head and shoulders in debt, he may live the faster for it, and the better if he goes the right way about it; or else how is it so many live on so well, as we see every day, after they are ruined?'

'How is it,' says I, being a little merry at the time – 'how is it but just as you see the ducks in the chicken-yard, just after their heads are cut off by the cook, running round and round faster than when alive?'

At which conceit he fell a-laughing, and remarked he had never had the happiness yet to see the chicken-yard at Castle Rackrent.

'It won't be long so, I hope,' says I; 'you'll be kindly welcome there, as everybody is made by my master: there is not a freer-spoken gentleman, or a better beloved, high or low, in all Ireland.'

And of what passed after this I'm not sensible, for we drank Sir Condy's good health and the downfall of his enemies till we could stand no longer ourselves. And little did I think at the time, or till long after, how I was harbouring my poor master's greatest of enemies myself. This fellow had the impudence, after coming to see the chicken-yard, to get me to introduce him to my son Jason; little more than the man that never was born did I guess at his meaning by this visit: he gets him a correct list fairly drawn out from my son Jason of all my master's debts, and goes straight round to the creditors and buys them all up, which he did easy enough, seeing the half of them never expected to see their money out of Sir Condy's hands. Then, when this base-minded limb of the law, as I afterwards detected him in being, grew to be sole creditor over all, he takes him out a custodiam on all the denominations and sub-denominations, and even carton and half-carton upon the estate; and not content with that, must have an execution against the master's goods and down to the furniture, though little worth, of Castle Rackrent itself. But this is a part of my story I'm not come to yet, and it's bad to be forestalling: ill news flies fast enough all the world over.

To go back to the day of the election, which I never think of but with pleasure and tears of gratitude for those good times: after the election was quite and clean over, there comes shoals of people from all parts, claiming to have obliged my master with their votes, and putting him in mind of promises which he could never remember himself to have made: one was to have a freehold for each of his four sons; another was to have a renewal of a lease; another an abatement; one came to be paid ten guineas for a pair of silver buckles sold my master on the hustings, which turned out to be no better than copper gilt; another had a long bill for oats, the half of which never went into the granary to my certain knowledge, and the other half was not fit for the cattle to touch; but the bargain was made the week before the election, and the coach and saddle-horses were got into order for the day, besides a vote fairly got by them oats; so no more reasoning on that head. But then there was no end to them that were telling Sir Condy he had engaged to make their sons excisemen, or high constables, or the like; and as for them that had bills to give in for liquor, and beds, and straw, and ribands, and horses, and post-chaises for the gentlemen freeholders that came from all parts and other counties to vote for my master, and were not, to be sure, to be at any charges, there was no standing against all these; and, worse than all, the gentlemen of my master's committee, who managed all for him, and talked how they'd bring him in without costing him a penny, and subscribed by hundreds very genteelly, forgot to pay their subscriptions, and had laid out in agents' and lawyers' fees and secret service money to the Lord knows how much; and my master could never ask one of them for their subscription you are sensible, nor for the price of a fine horse he had sold one of them; so it all was left at his door. He could never, God bless him again! I say, bring himself to ask a gentleman for money, despising such sort of conversation himself; but others, who were not gentlemen born, behaved very uncivil in pressing him at this very time, and all he could do to content 'em all was to take himself out of the way as fast as possible to Dublin, where my lady had taken a house fitting for him as a member of Parliament, to attend his duty in there all the winter. I was very lonely when the whole family was gone, and all the things they had ordered to go, and forgot, sent after them by the car. There was then a great silence in Castle Rackrent, and I went moping from room to room, hearing the doors clap for want of right locks, and the wind through the broken windows, that the glazier never would come to mend, and the rain coming through the roof and best ceilings all over the house for want of the slater, whose bill was not paid, besides our having no slates or shingles for that part of the old building which was shingled and burnt when the chimney took fire, and had been open to the weather ever since. I took myself to the servants' hall in the evening to smoke my pipe as usual, but missed the bit of talk we used to have there sadly, and ever after was content to stay in the kitchen and boil my little potatoes, and put up my bed there, and every post-day I looked in the newspaper, but no news of my master in the House; he never spoke good or bad, but, as the butler wrote down word to my son Jason, was very ill-used by the Government about a place that was promised him and never given, after his supporting them against his conscience very honourably, and being greatly abused for it, which hurt him greatly, he having the name of a great patriot in the country before. The house and living in Dublin too were not to be had for nothing, and my son Jason said, 'Sir Condy must soon be looking out for a new agent, for I've done my part, and can do no more. If my lady had the bank of Ireland to spend, it would go all in one winter, and Sir Condy would never gainsay her, though he does not care the rind of a lemon for her all the while.'

Now I could not bear to hear Jason giving out after this manner against the family, and twenty people standing by in the street. Ever since he had lived at the Lodge of his own he looked down, howsomever, upon poor old Thady, and was grown quite a great gentleman, and had none of his relations near him; no wonder he was no kinder to poor Sir Condy than to his own kith or kin. In the spring it was the villain that got the list of the debts from him brought down the custodiam, Sir Condy still attending his duty in Parliament; and I could scarcely believe my own old eyes, or the spectacles with which I read it, when I was shown my son Jason's name joined in the custodiam; but he told me it was only for form's sake, and to make things easier than if all the land was under the power of a total stranger. Well, I did not know what to think; it was hard to be talking ill of my own, and I could not but grieve for my poor master's fine estate, all torn by these vultures of the law; so I said nothing, but just looked on to see how it would all end.

It was not till the month of June that he and my lady came down to the country. My master was pleased to take me aside with him to the brewhouse that same evening, to complain to me of my son and other matters, in which he said he was confident I had neither art nor part; he said a great deal more to me, to whom he had been fond to talk ever since he was my white-headed boy before he came to the estate; and all that he said about poor Judy I can never forget, but scorn to repeat. He did not say an unkind word of my lady, but wondered, as well he might, her relations would do nothing for him or her, and they in all this great distress. He did not take anything long to heart, let it be as it would, and had no more malice or thought of the like in him than a child that can't speak; this night it was all out of his head before he went to his bed. He took his jug of whiskey-punch – my lady was grown quite easy about the whiskey-punch by this time, and so I did suppose all was going on right betwixt them, till I learnt the truth through Mrs Jane, who talked over the affairs to the housekeeper, and I within hearing. The night my master came home, thinking of nothing at all but just making merry, he drank his bumper toast 'to the desserts of that old curmudgeon my father-in-law, and all enemies at Mount Juliet's Town.' Now my lady was no longer in the mind she formerly was, and did noways relish hearing her own friends abused in her presence, she said.

'Then why don't they show themselves your friends,' said my master, 'and oblige me with the loan of the money I condescended, by your advice, my dear, to ask? It's now three posts since I sent off my letter, desiring in the postscript a speedy answer by the return of the post, and no account at all from them yet.'

'I expect they'll write to *me* next post,' says my lady, and that was all that passed then; but it was easy from this to guess there was a coolness betwixt them, and with good cause.

The next morning, being post-day, I sent off the gossoon early to the post office, to see was there any letter likely to set matters to rights, and he brought back one with the proper post-mark upon it, sure enough, and I had no time to examine or make any conjecture more about it, for into the servants' hall pops Mrs Jane with a blue bandbox in her hand, quite entirely mad.

'Dear ma'am, and what's the matter?' says I.

'Matter enough,' says she; 'don't you see my bandbox is wet through, and my best bonnet here spoiled, besides my lady's, and all by the rain coming in through that gallery window that you might have got mended if you'd had any sense, Thady, all the time we were in town in the winter?'

'Sure, I could not get the glazier, ma'am,' says I.

'You might have stopped it up anyhow,' says she.

'So I did, ma'am, to the best of my ability; one of the panes with the old pillow-case, and the other with a piece of the old stage green curtain. Sure I was as careful as possible all the time you were away, and not a drop of rain came in at that window of all the windows in the house, all winter, ma'am, when under my care; and now the family's come home, and it's summer-time, I never thought no more about it, to be sure; but dear, it's a pity to think of your bonnet, ma'am. But here's what will please you, ma'am – a letter from Mount Juliet's Town for my lady.

With that she snatches it from me without a word more, and runs up the back stairs to my mistress; I follows with a slate to make up the window. This window was in the long passage, or gallery, as my lady gave out orders to have it called, in the gallery leading to my master's bedchamber and hers. And when I went up with the slate, the door having no lock, and the bolt spoilt, was ajar after Mrs Jane, and, as I was busy with the window, I heard all that was saying within.

'Well, what's in your letter, Bella, my dear?' says he: 'you're a long time spelling it over.'

'Won't you shave this morning, Sir Condy?' says she, and put the letter into her pocket.

'I shaved the day before yesterday,' said he, 'my dear, and that's not what I'm thinking of now; but anything to oblige you, and to have peace and quietness, my dear' – and presently I had a glimpse of him at the cracked glass over the chimney-piece, standing up shaving himself to please my lady. But she took no notice, but went on reading her book, and Mrs Jane doing her hair behind.

'What is it you're reading there, my dear? – phoo, I've cut myself with this razor; the man's a cheat that sold it me, but I have not paid him for it yet. What is it you're reading there? Did you hear me asking you, my dear?'

'*The Sorrows of Werter*,' replies my lady, as well as I could hear.

'I think more of the sorrows of Sir Condy,' says my master, joking like. 'What news from Mount Juliet's Town?'

'No news,' says she, 'but the old story over again; my friends all reproaching me still for what I can't help now.'

'Is it for marrying me?' said my master, still shaving. 'What signifies, as you say, talking of that, when it can't be help'd now?'

With that she heaved a great sigh that I heard plain enough in the passage.

'And did not you use me basely, Sir Condy,' says she, 'not to tell me you were ruined before I married you?'

'Tell you, my dear!' said he. 'Did you ever ask me one word about it. And had not your friends enough of your own, that were telling you nothing else from morning to night, if you'd have listened to them slanders?'

'No slanders, nor are my friends slanderers; and I can't bear to hear them treated with disrespect as I do,' says my lady, and took out her pocket-handkerchief; 'they are the best of friends, and if I had taken their advice – But my father was wrong to lock me up, I own. That was the only unkind thing I can charge him with; for if he had not locked me up, I should never have had a serious thought of running away as I did.'

'Well, my dear,' said my master, 'don't cry and make yourself uneasy about it now, when it's all over, and you have the man of your own choice, in spite of 'em all.'

'I was too young, I know, to make a choice at the time you ran away with me, I'm sure,' says my lady, and another sigh, which made my master, half-shaved as he was, turn round upon her in surprise.

'Why, Bell,' says he, 'you can't deny what you know as well as I do, that it was at your own particular desire, and that twice under your own hand and seal expressed, that I should carry you off as I did to Scotland, and marry you there.'

'Well, say no more about it, Sir Condy,' said my lady, pettish-like; 'I was a child then, you know.'

'And as far as I know, you're little better now, my dear Bella, to be talking in this manner to your husband's face; but I won't take it ill of you, for I know it's something in that letter you put into your pocket just now that has set you against me all on a sudden, and imposed upon your understanding.'

'It's not so very easy as you think it, Sir Condy, to impose upon my understanding,' said my lady.

'My dear,' says he, 'I have, and with reason, the best opinion of your understanding of any man now breathing; and you know I have never set my own in competition with it till now, my dear Bella,' says he, taking her hand from her book as kind as could be – 'till now, when I have the great advantage of being quite cool, and you not; so don't believe one word your friends say against your own Sir Condy, and lend me the letter out of your pocket, till I see what it is they can have to say.'

'Take it then,' says she; 'and as you are quite cool, I hope it is a proper time to request you'll allow me to comply with the wishes of all my own friends, and return to live with my father and family, during the remainder of my wretched existence, at Mount Juliet's Town.'

At this my poor master fell back a few paces, like one that had been shot.

'You're not serious, Bella,' says he; 'and could you find it in your heart to leave me this way in the very middle of my distresses, all alone?' But recollecting himself after his first surprise, and a moment's time for reflection, he said, with a great deal of consideration for my lady, 'Well, Bella, my dear, I believe you are right; for what could you do at Castle Rackrent, and an execution against the goods coming down, and the furniture to be canted, and an auction in the house all next week? So you have my full consent to go, since that is your desire; only you must not think of my accompanying you, which I could not in honour do upon the terms I always have been, since our marriage, with your friends. Besides, I have business to transact at home; so in the meantime, if we are to have any breakfast this morning, let us go down and have it for the last time in peace and comfort, Bella.'

Then as I heard my master coming to the passage door, I finished fastening up my slate against the broken pane; and when he came out I wiped down the window-seat with my wig, and bade him a 'good-morrow' as kindly as I could, seeing he was in trouble, though he strove and thought to hide it from me.

'This window is all racked and tattered,' says I, 'and it's what I'm striving to mend.'

'It *is* all racked and tattered, plain enough,' says he, 'and never mind mending it, honest old Thady,' says he; 'it will do well enough for you and I, and that's all the company we shall have left in the house by and by.'

'I'm sorry to see your honour so low this morning,' says I; 'but you'll
be better after taking your breakfast.'

'Step down to the servants' hall,' said he, 'and bring me up the pen
and ink into the parlour, and get a sheet of paper from Mrs Jane, for I
have business that can't brook to be delayed; and come into the parlour
with the pen and ink yourself, Thady, for I must have you to witness
my signing a paper I have to execute in a hurry.'

Well, while I was getting of the pen and ink-horn, and the sheet of
paper, I ransacked my brains to think what could be the papers my
poor master could have to execute in such a hurry, he that never
thought of such a thing as doing business afore breakfast in the whole
course of his life, for any man living; but this was for my lady, as I
afterwards found, and the more genteel of him after all her treatment.

I was just witnessing the paper that he had scrawled over, and was
shaking the ink out of my pen upon the carpet, when my lady came in
to breakfast, and she started as if it had been a ghost; as well she might,
when she saw Sir Condy writing at this unseasonable hour.

'That will do very well, Thady,' says he to me, and took the paper I
had signed to, without knowing what upon the earth it might be, out of
my hands, and walked, folding it up, to my lady.

'You are concerned in this, my Lady Rackrent,' said he, putting it
into her hands; 'and I beg you'll keep this memorandum safe, and show
it to your friends the first thing you do when you get home; but put it
in your pocket now, my dear, and let us eat our breakfast, in God's
name.'

'What is all this?' said my lady, opening the paper in great curiosity.

'It's only a bit of a memorandum of what I think becomes me to do
whenever I am able,' says my master; 'you know my situation, tied hand
and foot at the present time being, but that can't last always, and when
I'm dead and gone the land will be to the good, Thady, you know; and
take notice it's my intention your lady should have a clear five hundred
a year jointure off the estate afore any of my debts are paid.'

'Oh, please your honour,' says I, 'I can't expect to live to see that
time, being now upwards of fourscore years of age, and you a young
man, and likely to continue so, by the help of God.'

I was vexed to see my lady so insensible too, for all she said was, 'This
is very genteel of you, Sir Condy. You need not wait any longer,
Thady.' So I just picked up the pen and ink that had tumbled on the
floor, and heard my master finish with saying, 'You behaved very
genteel to me, my dear, when you threw all the little you had in your
power along with yourself into my hands; and as I don't deny but what
you may have had some things to complain of,' – to be sure he was

thinking then of Judy, or of the whiskey-punch, one or t'other, or both, – 'and as I don't deny but you may have had something to complain of, my dear, it is but fair you should have something in the form of compensation to look forward to agreeably in future; besides, it's an act of justice to myself, that none of your friends, my dear, may ever have it to say against me, I married for money, and not for love.'

'That is the last thing I should ever have thought of saying of you, Sir Condy,' said my lady, looking very gracious.

'Then, my dear,' said Sir Condy, 'we shall part as good friends as we met; so all's right.'

I was greatly rejoiced to hear this, and went out of the parlour to report it all to the kitchen. The next morning my lady and Mrs Jane set out for Mount Juliet's Town in the jaunting-car. Many wondered at my lady's choosing to go away, considering all things, upon the jaunting-car, as if it was only a party of pleasure; but they did not know till I told them that the coach was all broke in the journey down, and no other vehicle but the car to be had. Besides, my lady's friends were to send their coach to meet her at the cross-roads; so it was all done very proper.

My poor master was in great trouble after my lady left us. The execution came down, and everything at Castle Rackrent was seized by the gripers, and my son Jason, to his shame be it spoken, amongst them. I wondered, for the life of me, how he could harden himself to do it; but then he had been studying the law, and had made himself Attorney Quirk; so he brought down at once a heap of accounts upon my master's head. To cash lent, and to ditto, and to ditto, and to ditto and oats, and bills paid at the milliner's and linen-draper's, and many dresses for the fancy balls in Dublin for my lady, and all the bills to the workmen and tradesmen for the scenery of the theatre, and the chandler's and grocer's bills, and tailor's, besides butcher's and baker's, and, worse than all, the old one of that base wine merchant's, that wanted to arrest my poor master for the amount on the election day, for which amount Sir Condy afterwards passed his note of hand, bearing lawful interest from the date thereof; and the interest and compound interest was now mounted to a terrible deal on many other notes and bonds for money borrowed, and there was, besides, hush-money to the sub-sheriffs, and sheets upon sheets of old and new attorneys' bills, with heavy balances, 'as per former account furnished,' brought forward with interest thereon; then there was a powerful deal due to the Crown for sixteen years' arrear of quit-rent of the town-lands of Carrickshaughlin, with driver's fees, and a compliment to the receiver every year for letting the quit-rent run on to oblige Sir Condy, and Sir Kit afore him. Then there were bills for spirits and ribands at the election time, and the gentlemen of the committee's accounts unsettled, and their subscription never gathered; and there were cows to be paid for, with the smith and farrier's bills to be set against the rent of the demesne with calf and hay money; then there was all the servants' wages, since I don't know when, coming due to them, and sums advanced for them by my son Jason for clothes, and boots, and whips, and odd moneys for sundries expended by them in journeys to town and elsewhere, and pocket-money for the master continually, and messengers and postage before his being a Parliament man. I can't myself tell you what besides; but this I know, that when the evening came on the which Sir Condy had appointed to settle all with my son Jason, and when he comes into the parlour, and sees the sight of bills and load of papers all gathered on the great dining-table for him, he puts his hands before both his eyes, and cried out, 'Merciful Jasus! what is it I see before me?' Then I sets an armchair at the table for him, and with a deal of difficulty he sits him down, and my son Jason hands him over the pen and ink to sign to this man's bill and t'other man's bill, all which he did without making the least objections. Indeed, to give him his due, I never seen a man more fair and honest, and easy in all his dealings, from first to last, as Sir Condy, or more willing to pay every man his own as far as he was able, which is as much as any one can do.

'Well,' says he, joking like with Jason, 'I wish we could settle it all with a stroke of my grey goose quill. What signifies making me wade through all this ocean of papers here; can't you now, who understand drawing out an account, debtor and creditor, just sit down here at the corner of the table and get it done out for me, that I may have a clear view of the balance, which is all I need be talking about, you know?'

'Very true, Sir Condy; nobody understands business better than yourself,' says Jason.

'So I've a right to do, being born and bred to the bar,' says Sir Condy. 'Thady, do step out and see are they bringing in the things for the punch, for we've just done all we have to do for this evening.'

I goes out accordingly, and when I came back Jason was pointing to the balance, which was a terrible sight to my poor master.

'Pooh! pooh! pooh!' says he. 'Here's so many noughts they dazzle my eyes, so they do, and put me in mind of all I suffered larning of my numeration table, when I was a boy at the day-school along with you, Jason – units, tens, hundreds, tens of hundreds. Is the punch ready, Thady?' says he, seeing me.

'Immediately; the boy has the jug in his hand; it's coming upstairs, please your honour, as fast as possible,' says I, for I saw his honour was tired out of his life; but Jason, very short and cruel, cuts me off with – 'Don't be talking of punch yet awhile; it's no time for punch yet a bit – units, tens, hundreds,' goes he on, counting over the master's shoulder, units, tens, hundreds, thousands.

'A-a-ah! hold your hand,' cries my master. 'Where in this wide world am I to find hundreds, or units itself, let alone thousands?'

'The balance has been running on too long,' says Jason, sticking to him as I could not have done at the time, if you'd have given both the Indies and Cork to boot; 'the balance has been running on too long, and I'm distressed myself on your account, Sir Condy, for money, and the thing must be settled now on the spot, and the balance cleared off,' says Jason.

'I'll thank you if you'll only show me how,' says Sir Condy.

'There's but one way,' says Jason, 'and that's ready enough. When there's no cash, what can a gentleman do but go to the land?'

'How can you go to the land, and it under custodiam to yourself already?' says Sir Condy; 'and another custodiam hanging over it? And no one at all can touch it, you know, but the custodees.'

'Sure, can't you sell, though at a loss? Sure you can sell, and I've a purchaser ready for you,' says Jason.

'Have you so?' says Sir Condy. 'That's a great point gained. But there's a thing now beyond all, that perhaps you don't know yet, barring Thady has let you into the secret.'

'Sarrah bit of a secret, or anything at all of the kind, has he learned from me these fifteen weeks come St John's Eve,' says I, 'for we have scarce been upon speaking terms of late. But what is it your honour means of a secret?'

'Why, the secret of the little keepsake I gave my Lady Rackrent the morning she left us, that she might not go back empty-handed to her friends.'

'My Lady Rackrent, I'm sure, has baubles and keepsakes enough, as those bills on the table will show,' says Jason; 'but whatever it is,' says he, taking up his pen, 'we must add it to the balance, for to be sure it can't be paid for.'

'No, nor can't till after my decease,' says Sir Condy; 'that's one good thing.' Then colouring up a good deal, he tells Jason of the memorandum of the five hundred a-year jointure he had settled upon my lady; at which Jason was indeed mad, and said a great deal in very high words, that it was using a gentleman who had the management of his affairs, and was, moreover, his principal creditor, extremely ill to do such a thing without consulting him, and against his knowledge and consent. To all which Sir Condy had nothing to reply, but that, upon his conscience, it was in a hurry and without a moment's thought on his part, and he was very sorry for it, but if it was to do over again he would do the same; and he appealed to me, and I was ready to give my evidence, if that would do, to the truth of all he said.

So Jason with much ado was brought to agree to a compromise.

'The purchaser that I have ready,' says he, 'will be much displeased, to be sure, at the encumbrance on the land, but I must see and manage him. Here's a deed ready drawn up; we have nothing to do but to put in the consideration money and our names to it.'

'And how much am I going to sell? – the lands of O'Shaughlin's Town, and the lands of Gruneaghoolaghan, and the lands of Crookagnawaturgh,' says he, just reading to himself. 'And – oh, murder, Jason! sure you won't put this in – the castle, stable, and appurtenances of Castle Rackrent?'

'Oh, murder!' says I, clapping my hands; 'this is too bad, Jason.'

'Why so?' said Jason. 'When it's all, and a great deal more to the back of it, lawfully mine, was I to push for it.'

'Look at him,' says I, pointing to Sir Condy, who was just leaning back in his armchair, with his arms falling beside him like one stupefied; 'is it you, Jason, that can stand in his presence, and recollect all he has been to us, and all we have been to him, and yet use him so at the last?'

'Who will you find to use him better, I ask you?' said Jason; 'if he can get a better purchaser, I'm content; I only offer to purchase, to make things easy, and oblige him; though I don't see what compliment I am under, if you come to that.

I have never had, asked, or charged more than sixpence in the pound, receiver's fees, and where would he have got an agent for a penny less?'

'Oh, Jason! Jason! how will you stand to this in the face of the county, and all who know you?' says I; 'and what will people think and say when they see you living here in Castle Rackrent, and the lawful owner turned out of the seat of his ancestors, without a cabin to put his head into, or so much as a potato to eat?'

Jason, whilst I was saying this, and a great deal more, made me signs, and winks, and frowns; but I took no heed, for I was grieved and sick at heart for my poor master, and couldn't but speak.

'Here's the punch,' says Jason, for the door opened; 'here's the punch!'

Hearing that, my master starts up in his chair, and recollects himself, and Jason uncorks the whiskey.

'Set down the jug here,' says he, making room for it beside the papers opposite to Sir Condy, but still not stirring the deed that was to make over all.

Well, I was in great hopes he had some touch of mercy about him when I saw him making the punch, and my master took a glass; but Jason put it back as he was going to fill again, saying: 'No, Sir Condy, it shan't be said of me I got your signature to this deed when you were half-seas over: you know your name and handwriting in that condition would not, if brought before the courts, benefit me a straw; wherefore, let us settle all before we go deeper into the punch-bowl.'

'Settle all as you will,' said Sir Condy, clapping his hands to his ears; 'but let me hear no more. I'm bothered to death this night.'

'You've only to sign,' said Jason, putting the pen to him.

'Take all, and be content,' said my master. So he signed; and the man who brought in the punch witnessed it, for I was not able, but crying like a child; and besides, Jason said, which I was glad of, that I was no fit witness, being so old and doting. It was so bad with me, I could not taste a drop of the punch itself, though my master himself, God bless him! in the midst of his trouble, poured out a glass for me, and brought it up to my lips.

'Not a drop; I thank your honour's honour as much as if I took it, though.' And I just set down the glass as it was, and went out, and when I got to the street door the neighbours' childer, who were playing at marbles there, seeing me in great trouble, left their play, and gathered about me to know what ailed me; and I told them all, for it was a great relief to me to speak to these poor childer, that seemed to have some natural feeling left in them; and when they were made sensible that Sir Condy was going to leave Castle Rackrent for good and all, they set up a whillaluh that could be heard to the farthest end of the street; and one – fine boy he was – that my master had given an apple to that morning, cried the loudest; but they all were the same sorry, for Sir Condy was greatly beloved amongst the childer, for letting them go a-nutting in the demesne, without saying a word to them, though my lady objected to them. The people in the town, who were the most of them standing at their doors, hearing the childer cry, would know the reason of it; and when the report was made known, the people one and all gathered in great anger against my son Jason, and terror at the notion of his coming to be landlord over them, and they cried, 'No Jason! no Jason! Sir Condy! Sir Condy! Sir Condy Rackrent for ever!' And the mob grew so great and so loud, I was frightened, and made my way back to the house to warn my son to make his escape, or hide himself for fear of the consequences. Jason would not believe me till they came all round the house, and to the windows with great shouts. Then he grew quite pale, and asked Sir Condy what had he best do?

'I'll tell you what you had best do,' said Sir Condy, who was laughing to see his fright; 'finish your glass first, then let's go to the window and show ourselves, and I'll tell 'em – or you shall, if you please – that I'm going to the Lodge for change of air for my health, and by my own desire, for the rest of my days.'

'Do so,' said Jason, who never meant it should have been so, but could not refuse him the Lodge at this unseasonable time. Accordingly, Sir Condy threw up the sash and explained matters, and thanked all his friends, and bid them look in at the punch-bowl, and observe that Jason and he had been sitting over it very good friends; so the mob was content, and he sent them out some whiskey to drink his health, and that was the last time his honour's health was ever drunk at Castle Rackrent.

The very next day, being too proud, as he said to me, to stay an hour longer in a house that did not belong to him, he sets off to the Lodge, and I along with him not many hours after. And there was great bemoaning through all O'Shaughlin's Town, which I stayed to witness, and gave my poor master a full account of when I got to the Lodge. He was very low, and in his bed, when I got there, and complained of a great pain about his heart; but I guessed it was only trouble and all the business, let alone vexation, he had gone through of late; and knowing the nature of him from a boy, I took my pipe, and whilst smoking it by the chimney began telling him how he was beloved and regretted in the county, and it did him a deal of good to hear it.

'Your honour has a great many friends yet that you don't know of, rich and poor, in the county,' says I; 'for as I was coming along the road I met two gentlemen in their own carriages, who asked after you, knowing me, and wanted to know where you was and all about you, and even how old I was. Think of that.'

Then he wakened out of his doze, and began questioning me who the gentlemen were. And the next morning it came into my head to go, unknown to anybody, with my master's compliments, round to many of the gentlemen's houses, where he and my lady used to visit, and people that I knew were his great friends, and would go to Cork to serve him any day in the year, and I made bold to try to borrow a trifle of cash from them. They all treated me very civil for the most part, and asked a great many questions very kind about my lady and Sir Condy and all the family, and were greatly surprised to learn from me Castle Rackrent was sold, and my master at the Lodge for health; and they all pitied him greatly, and he had their good wishes, if that would do; but money was a thing they unfortunately had not any of them at this time to spare. I had my journey for my pains, and I, not used to walking, nor supple as formerly, was greatly tired, but had the satisfaction of telling my master, when I got to the Lodge, all the civil things said by high and low.

'Thady,' says he, 'all you've been telling me brings a strange thought into my head. I've a notion I shall not be long for this world anyhow, and I've a great fancy to see my own funeral afore I die.' I was greatly shocked, at the first speaking, to hear him speak so light about his funeral, and he to all appearance in good health; but recollecting myself, answered:

'To be sure it would be as fine a sight as one could see, I dared to say, and one I should be proud to witness, and I did not doubt his honour's would be as great a funeral as ever Sir Patrick O'Shaughlin's was, and such a one as that had never been known in the county afore or since.' But I never thought he was in earnest about seeing his own funeral himself till the next day he returns to it again.

'Thady,' says he, 'as far as the wake goes, sure I might without any great trouble have the satisfaction of seeing a bit of my own funeral.'

'Well, since your honour's honour's so bent upon it,' says I, not willing to cross him, and he in trouble, 'we must see what we can do.'

So he fell into a sort of sham disorder, which was easy done, as he kept his bed, and no one to see him; and I got my shister, who was an old woman very handy about the sick, and very skilful, to come up to the Lodge to nurse him; and we gave out, she knowing no better, that he was just at his latter end, and it answered beyond anything; and there was a great throng of people, men, women, and childer, and there being only two rooms at the Lodge, except what was locked up full of Jason's furniture and things, the house was soon as full and fuller than it could hold, and the heat, and smoke, and noise wonderful great; and standing amongst them that were near the bed, but not thinking at all of the dead, I was startled by the sound of my master's voice from under the greatcoats that had been thrown all at top, and I went close up, no one noticing.

'Thady,' says he, 'I've had enough of this; I'm smothering, and can't hear a word of all they're saying of the deceased.'

'God bless you, and lie still and quiet,' says I, 'a bit longer, for my shister's afraid of ghosts, and would die on the spot with fright was she to see you come to life all on a sudden this way without the least preparation.'

So he lays him still, though well nigh stifled, and I made all haste to tell the secret of the joke, whispering to one and t'other, and there was a great surprise, but not so great as we had laid out it would. 'And aren't we to have the pipes and tobacco, after coming so far tonight?' said some; but they were all well enough pleased when his honour got up to drink with them, and sent for more spirits from a shebeen-house, where they very civilly let him have it upon credit. So the night passed off very merrily, but to my mind Sir Condy was rather upon the sad order in the midst of it all, not finding there had been such a great talk about himself after his death as he had always expected to hear.

The next morning, when the house was cleared of them, and none but my shister and myself left in the kitchen with Sir Condy, one opens the door and walks in, and who should it be but Judy M'Quirk herself! I forgot to notice that she had been married long since, whilst young Captain Moneygawl lived at the Lodge, to the captain's huntsman, who after a whilst 'listed and left her, and was killed in the wars. Poor Judy fell off greatly in her good looks after her being married a year or two; and being smoke-dried in the cabin, and neglecting herself like, it was hard for Sir Condy himself to know her again till she spoke; but when she says, 'It's Judy M'Quirk, please your honour; don't you remember her?'

'Oh, Judy, is it you?' says his honour. 'Yes, sure, I remember you very well; but you're greatly altered, Judy.'

'Sure it's time for me,' says she. 'And I think your honour, since I seen you last – but that's a great while ago – is altered too.'

'And with reason, Judy,' says Sir Condy, fetching a sort of a sigh. 'But how's this, Judy?' he goes on. 'I take it a little amiss of you that you were not at my wake last night.'

'Ah, don't be being jealous of that,' says she; 'I didn't hear a sentence of your honour's wake till it was all over, or it would have gone hard with me but I would have been at it, sure; but I was forced to go ten miles up the country three days ago to a wedding of a relation of my own's, and didn't get home till after the wake was over. But,' says she, 'it won't be so, I hope, the next time, please your honour.'

'That we shall see, Judy,' says his honour, 'and maybe sooner than you think for, for I've been very unwell this while past, and don't reckon anyway I'm long for this world.'

At this Judy takes up the corner of her apron, and puts it first to one eye and then to t'other, being to all appearance in great trouble; and my shister put in her word, and bid his honour have a good heart, for she was sure it was only the gout that Sir Patrick used to have flying about him, and he ought to drink a glass or a bottle extraordinary to keep it out of his stomach; and he promised to take her advice, and sent out for more spirits immediately; and Judy made a sign to me, and I went over to the door to her, and she said, 'I wonder to see Sir Condy so low: has he heard the news?'

'What news?' says I.

'Didn't ye hear it, then?' says she; 'my Lady Rackrent that was is kilt and lying for dead, and I don't doubt but it's all over with her by this time.'

'Mercy on us all,' says I; 'how was it?'

'The jaunting-car it was that ran away with her,' says Judy. 'I was coming home that same time from Biddy M'Guggin's marriage, and a great crowd of people too upon the road, coming from the fair of Crookaghnawaturgh, and I sees a jaunting-car standing in the middle of the road, and with the two wheels off and all tattered. "What's this?" says I. "Didn't ye hear of it?" says they that were looking on; "it's my Lady Rackrent's car, that was running away from her husband, and the horse took fright at a carrion that lay across the road, and so ran away with the jaunting-car, and my Lady Rackrent and her maid screaming, and the horse ran with them against a car that was coming from the fair with the boy asleep on it, and the lady's petticoat hanging out of the jaunting-car caught, and she was dragged I can't tell you how far upon the road, and it all broken up with the stones just going to be pounded, and one of the road-makers, with his sledge-hammer in his hand, stops the horse at the last; but my Lady Rackrent was all kilt and smashed, and they lifted her into a cabin hard by, and the maid was found after where she had been thrown in the gripe of a ditch, her cap and bonnet all full of bog water, and they say my lady can't live anyway." Thady, pray now is it true what I'm told for sartain, that Sir Condy has made over all to your son Jason?'

'All,' says I.

'All entirely?' says she again.

'All entirely,' says I.

'Then,' says she, 'that's a great shame; but don't be telling Jason what I say.'

'And what is it you say?' cries Sir Condy, leaning over betwixt us, which made Judy start greatly. 'I know the time when Judy M'Quirk would never have stayed so long talking at the door and I in the house.'

'Oh!' says Judy, 'for shame, Sir Condy; times are altered since then, and it's my Lady Rackrent you ought to be thinking of.'

'And why should I be thinking of her, that's not thinking of me now?' says Sir Condy.

'No matter for that,' says Judy, very properly; 'it's time you should be thinking of her, if ever you mean to do it at all, for don't you know she's lying for death?'

'My Lady Rackrent!' says Sir Condy, in a surprise; 'why it's but two days since we parted, as you very well know, Thady, in her full health and spirits, and she, and her maid along with her, going to Mount Juliet's Town on her jaunting-car.'

'She'll never ride no more on her jaunting-car,' said Judy, 'for it has been the death of her, sure enough.'

'And is she dead then?' says his honour.

'As good as dead, I hear,' says Judy; 'but there's Thady here as just learnt the whole truth of the story as I had it, and it's fitter he or anybody else should be telling it you than I, Sir Condy: I must be going home to the childer.'

But he stops her, but rather from civility in him, as I could see very plainly, than anything else, for Judy was, as his honour remarked at her first coming in, greatly changed, and little likely, as far as I could see – though she did not seem to be clear of it herself – little likely to be my Lady Rackrent now, should there be a second toss-up to be made. But I told him the whole story out of the face, just as Judy had told it to me, and he sent off a messenger with his compliments to Mount Juliet's Town that evening, to learn the truth of the report, and Judy bid the boy that was going call in at Tim M'Enerney's shop in O'Shaughlin's Town and buy her a new shawl.

'Do so,' said Sir Condy, 'and tell Tim to take no money from you, for I must pay him for the shawl myself.' At this my shister throws me over a look, and I says nothing, but turned the tobacco in my mouth, whilst Judy began making a many words about it, and saying how she could not be beholden for shawls to any gentleman. I left her there to consult with my shister, did she think there was anything in it, and my shister thought I was blind to be asking her the question, and I thought my shister must see more into it than I did, and recollecting all past times and everything, I changed my mind, and came over to her way of thinking, and we settled it that Judy was very like to be my Lady Rackrent after all, if a vacancy should have happened.

The next day, before his honour was up, somebody comes with a double knock at the door, and I was greatly surprised to see it was my son Jason.

'Jason, is it you?' said I; 'what brings you to the Lodge?' says I. 'Is it my Lady Rackrent? We know that already since yesterday.'

'Maybe so,' says he; 'but I must see Sir Condy about it.'

'You can't see him yet,' says I; 'sure he is not awake.'

'What then,' says he, 'can't he be wakened, and I standing at the door?'

'I'll not be disturbing his honour for you, Jason,' says I; 'many's the hour you've waited in your time, and been proud to do it, till his honour was at leisure to speak to you. His honour,' says I, raising my voice, at which his honour wakens of his own accord, and calls to me from the room to know who it was I was speaking to. Jason made no more ceremony, but follows me into the room.

'How are you, Sir Condy?' says he; 'I'm happy to see you looking so well; I came up to know how you did today, and to see did you want for anything at the Lodge.'

'Nothing at all, Mr Jason, I thank you,' says he; for his honour had his own share of pride, and did not choose, after all that had passed, to be beholden, I suppose, to my son; 'but pray take a chair and be seated, Mr Jason.'

Jason sat him down upon the chest, for chair there was none, and after he had set there some time, and a silence on all sides,

'What news is there stirring in the country, Mr Jason M'Quirk?' says Sir Condy, very easy, yet high like.

'None that's news to you, Sir Condy, I hear,' says Jason. 'I am sorry to hear of my Lady Rackrent's accident.'

'I'm much obliged to you, and so is her ladyship, I'm sure,' answered Sir Condy, still stiff; and there was another sort of a silence, which seemed to lie the heaviest on my son Jason.

'Sir Condy,' says he at last, seeing Sir Condy disposing himself to go to sleep again, 'Sir Condy, I daresay you recollect mentioning to me the little memorandum you gave to Lady Rackrent about the £500 a year jointure.'

'Very true,' said Sir Condy; 'it is all in my recollection.'

'But if my Lady Rackrent dies, there's an end of all jointure,' says Jason.

'Of course,' says Sir Condy.

'But it's not a matter of certainty that my Lady Rackrent won't recover,' says Jason.

'Very true, sir,' says my master.

'It's a fair speculation, then, for you to consider what the chance of the jointure of those lands, when out of custodiam, will be to you.'

'Just five hundred a year, I take it, without any speculation at all,' said Sir Condy.

'That's supposing the life dropt, and the custodiam off, you know; begging your pardon, Sir Condy, who understands business, that is a wrong calculation.'

'Very likely so,' said Sir Condy; 'but, Mr Jason, if you have anything to say to me this morning about it, I'd be obliged to you to say it, for I had an indifferent night's rest last night, and wouldn't be sorry to sleep a little this morning.'

'I have only three words to say, and those more of consequence to you, Sir Condy, than me. You are a little cool, I observe; but I hope you will not be offended at what I have brought here in my pocket,' and he pulls out two long rolls, and showers down golden guineas upon the bed.

'What's this?' said Sir Condy; 'it's long since' – but his pride stops him.

'All these are your lawful property this minute, Sir Condy, if you please,' said Jason.

'Not for nothing, I'm sure,' said Sir Condy, and laughs a little. 'Nothing for nothing, or I'm under a mistake with you, Jason.'

'Oh, Sir Condy, we'll not be indulging ourselves in any unpleasant retrospects,' says Jason; 'it's my present intention to behave, as I'm sure you will, like a gentleman in this affair. Here's two hundred guineas, and a third I mean to add if you should think proper to make over to me all your right and title to those lands that you know of.'

'I'll consider of it,' said my master; and a great deal more, that I was tired listening to, was said by Jason, and all that, and the sight of the ready cash upon the bed, worked with his honour; and the short and the long of it was, Sir Condy gathered up the golden guineas, and tied them up in a handkerchief, and signed some paper Jason brought with him as usual, and there was an end of the business: Jason took himself away, and my master turned himself round and fell asleep again.

I soon found what had put Jason in such a hurry to conclude this business. The little gossoon we had sent off the day before with my master's compliments to Mount Juliet's Town, and to know how my lady did after her accident, was stopped early this morning, coming back with his answer through O'Shaughlin's Town, at Castle Rackrent, by my son Jason, and questioned of all he knew of my lady from the servant at Mount Juliet's Town; and the gossoon told him my Lady Rackrent was not expected to live over night; so Jason thought it high time to be moving to the Lodge, to make his bargain with my master about the jointure afore it should be too late, and afore the little gossoon should reach us with the news. My master was greatly vexed – that is, I may say, as much as ever I seen him – when he found how he had been taken in; but it was some comfort to have the ready cash for immediate consumption in the house, anyway.

And when Judy came up that evening, and brought the childer to see his honour, he unties the handkerchief, and – God bless him! whether it was little or much he had, 'twas all the same with him – he gives 'em all round guineas apiece.

'Hold up your head,' says my shister to Judy, as Sir Condy was busy filling out a glass of punch for her eldest boy – 'Hold up your head, Judy; for who knows but we may live to see you yet at the head of the Castle Rackrent estate?'

'Maybe so,' says she, 'but not the way you are thinking of.' I did not rightly understand which way Judy was looking when she made this speech till a while after.

'Why, Thady, you were telling me yesterday that Sir Condy had sold all entirely to Jason, and where then does all them guineas in the handkerchief come from?'

'They are the purchase-money of my lady's jointure,' says I.

Judy looks a little bit puzzled at this. 'A penny for your thoughts, Judy,' says my shister; 'hark, sure Sir Condy is drinking her health.'

He was at the table in the room, drinking with the exciseman and the gauger, who came up to see his honour, and we were standing over the fire in the kitchen.

'I don't much care is he drinking my health or not,' says Judy; 'and it is not Sir Condy I'm thinking of, with all your jokes, whatever he is of me.'

'Sure you wouldn't refuse to be my Lady Rackrent, Judy, if you had the offer?' says I.

'But if I could do better!' says she.

'How better?' says I and my shister both at once.

'How better?' says she. 'Why, what signifies it to be my Lady Rackrent and no castle? Sure what good is the car, and no horse to draw it?'

'And where will ye get the horse, Judy?' says I.

'Never mind that,' says she; 'maybe it is your own son Jason might find that.'

'Jason!' says I; 'don't be trusting to him, Judy. Sir Condy, as I have good reason to know, spoke well of you when Jason spoke very indifferently of you, Judy.'

'No matter,' says Judy; 'it's often men speak the contrary just to what they think of us.'

'And you the same way of them, no doubt,' answered I. 'Nay, don't be denying it, Judy, for I think the better of ye for it, and shouldn't be proud to call ye the daughter of a shister's son of mine, if I was to hear ye talk ungrateful, and anyway disrespectful of his honour.'

'What disrespect,' says she, 'to say I'd rather, if it was my luck, be the wife of another man?'

'You'll have no luck, mind my words, Judy,' says I; and all I remembered about my poor master's goodness in tossing up for her afore he married at all came across me, and I had a choking in my throat that hindered me to say more.

'Better luck, anyhow, Thady,' says she, 'than to be like some folk, following the fortunes of them that have none left.'

'Oh! King of Glory!' says I, 'hear the pride and ungratitude of her, and he giving his last guineas but a minute ago to her childer, and she with the fine shawl on her he made her a present of but yesterday!'

'Oh, troth, Judy, you're wrong now,' says my shister, looking at the shawl.

'And was not he wrong yesterday, then,' says she, 'to be telling me I was greatly altered, to affront me?'

'But, Judy,' says I, 'what is it brings you here then at all in the mind you are in; is it to make Jason think the better of you?'

'I'll tell you no more of my secrets, Thady,' says she, 'nor would have told you this much, had I taken you for such an unnatural fader as I find you are, not to wish your own son preferred to another.'

'Oh, troth, you are wrong now, Thady,' says my shister.

Well, I was never so put to it in my life: between these womens, and my son and my master, and all I felt and thought just now, I could not, upon my conscience, tell which was the wrong from the right. So I said not a word more, but was only glad his honour had not the luck to hear all Judy had been saying of him, for I reckoned it would have gone nigh to break his heart; not that I was of opinion he cared for her as much as she and my shister fancied, but the ungratitude of the whole from Judy might not plase him; and he could never stand the notion of not being well spoken of or beloved like behind his back. Fortunately for all parties concerned, he was so much elevated at this time, there was no danger of his understanding anything, even if it had reached his ears. There was a great horn at the Lodge, ever since my master and Captain Moneygawl was in together, that used to belong originally to the celebrated Sir Patrick, his ancestor; and his honour was fond often of telling the story that he learned from me when a child, how Sir Patrick drank the full of this horn without stopping, and this was what no other man afore or since could without drawing breath. Now Sir Condy challenged the gauger, who seemed to think little of the horn, to swallow the contents, and had it filled to the brim with punch; and the gauger said it was what he could not do for nothing, but he'd hold Sir Condy a hundred guineas he'd do it.

'Done,' says my master; 'I'll lay you a hundred golden guineas to a tester you don't.'

'Done,' says the gauger; and done and done's enough between two gentlemen. The gauger was cast, and my master won the bet, and thought he'd won a hundred guineas, but by the wording it was adjudged to be only a tester that was his due by the exciseman. It was all one to him; he was as well pleased, and I was glad to see him in such spirits again.

The gauger – bad luck to him! – was the man that next proposed to my master to try himself, could he take at a draught the contents of the great horn.

'Sir Patrick's horn!' said his honour; 'hand it to me: I'll hold you your own bet over again I'll swallow it.'

'Done,' says the gauger; 'I'll lay ye anything at all you do no such thing.'

'A hundred guineas to sixpence I do,' says he; 'bring me the handkerchief.' I was loth, knowing he meant the handkerchief with the gold in it, to bring it out in such company, and his honour not very able to reckon it. 'Bring me the handkerchief, then, Thady,' says he, and stamps with his foot; so with that I pulls it out of my greatcoat pocket, where I had put it for safety. Oh, how it grieved me to see the guineas counting upon the table, and they the last my master had! Says Sir Condy to me, 'Your hand is steadier than mine tonight, old Thady, and that's a wonder; fill you the horn for me.' And so, wishing his honour success, I did; but I filled it, little thinking of what would befall him. He swallows it down, and drops like one shot. We lifts him up, and he was speechless, and quite black in the face. We put him to bed, and in a short time he wakened, raving with a fever on his brain. He was shocking either to see or hear.

'Judy! Judy! have you no touch of feeling? Won't you stay to help us nurse him?' says I to her, and she putting on her shawl to go out of the house.

'I'm frightened to see him,' says she, 'and wouldn't nor couldn't stay in it; and what use? He can't last till the morning.' With that she ran off. There was none but my shister and myself left near him of all the many friends he had.

The fever came and went, and came and went, and lasted five days, and the sixth he was sensible for a few minutes, and said to me, knowing me very well, 'I'm in a burning pain all withinside of me, Thady.' I could not speak, but my shister asked him would he have this thing or t'other to do him good? 'No,' says he, 'nothing will do me good no more,' and he gave a terrible screech with the torture he was in; then again a minute's ease – 'brought to this by drink,' says he. 'Where are all the friends? – where's Judy? Gone, hey? Ay, Sir Condy has been a fool all his days,' said he; and there was the last word he spoke, and died. He had but a very poor funeral after all.

If you want to know any more, I'm not very well able to tell you; but my Lady Rackrent did not die, as was expected of her, but was only disfigured in the face ever after by the fall and bruises she got; and she and Jason, immediately after my poor master's death, set about going to law about that jointure; the memorandum not being on stamped paper, some say it is worth nothing, others again it may do; others say Jason won't have the lands at any rate; many wishes it so. For my part,

I'm tired wishing for anything in this world, after all I've seen in it; but I'll say nothing – it would be a folly to be getting myself ill-will in my old age. Jason did not marry, nor think of marrying Judy, as I prophesied, and I am not sorry for it: who is? As for all I have here set down from memory and hearsay of the family, there's nothing but truth in it from beginning to end. That you may depend upon, for where's the use of telling lies about the things which everybody knows as well as I do?

The Editor could have readily made the catastrophe of Sir Condy's history more dramatic and more pathetic, if he thought it allowable to varnish the plain round tale of faithful Thady. He lays it before the English reader as a specimen of manners and characters which are perhaps unknown in England. Indeed, the domestic habits of no nation in Europe were less known to the English than those of their sister country, till within these few years.

Mr Young's picture of Ireland, in his tour through that country, was the first faithful portrait of its inhabitants. All the features in the foregoing sketch were taken from the life, and they are characteristic of that mixture of quickness, simplicity, cunning, carelessness, dissipation, disinterestedness, shrewdness, and blunder, which, in different forms and with various success, has been brought upon the stage or delineated in novels.

It is a problem of difficult solution to determine whether a union will hasten or retard the amelioration of this country. The few gentlemen of education who now reside in this country will resort to England. They are few, but they are in nothing inferior to men of the same rank in Great Britain. The best that can happen will be the introduction of British manufacturers in their places.

Did the Warwickshire militia, who were chiefly artisans, teach the Irish to drink beer? or did they learn from the Irish to drink whiskey?

THE ABSENTEE

Chapter 1

'ARE YOU TO BE at Lady Clonbrony's gala next week?' said Lady Langdale to Mrs Dareville, whilst they were waiting for their carriages in the crush-room of the opera house.

'Oh yes! everybody's to be there, I hear,' replied Mrs Dareville. 'Your ladyship, of course?'

'Why, I don't know – if I possibly can. Lady Clonbrony makes it such a point with me, that I believe I must look in upon her for a few minutes. They are going to a prodigious expense on this occasion. Soho tells me the reception rooms are all to be new furnished, and in the most magnificent style.'

'At what a famous rate those Clonbronies are dashing on,' said Colonel Heathcock. 'Up to anything.'

'Who are they? – these Clonbronies, that one hears of so much of late?' said her Grace of Torcaster. 'Irish absentees, I know. But how do they support all this enormous expense?'

'The son *will* have a prodigiously fine estate when some Mr Quin dies,' said Mrs Dareville.

'Yes, everybody who comes from Ireland *will* have a fine estate when somebody dies,' said her grace. 'But what have they at present?'

'Twenty thousand a year, they say,' replied Mrs Dareville.

'Ten thousand, I believe,' cried Lady Langdale. 'Make it a rule, you know, to believe only half the world says.'

'Ten thousand, have they? – possibly,' said her grace. 'I know nothing about them – have no acquaintance among the Irish. Torcaster knows something of Lady Clonbrony; she has fastened herself, by some means, upon him: but I charge him not to *commit* me. Positively, I could not for anybody – and much less for that sort of person – extend the circle of my acquaintance.'

'Now that is so cruel of your grace,' said Mrs Dareville, laughing, 'when poor Lady Clonbrony works so hard, and pays so high, to get into certain circles.'

'If you knew all she endures, to look, speak, move, breathe like an Englishwoman, you would pity her,' said Lady Langdale.

'Yes, and you *cawnt* conceive the *peens* she *teekes* to talk of the *teebles* and *cheers*, and to thank *Q*, and, with so much *teeste*, to speak pure English,' said Mrs Dareville.

'Pure cockney, you mean,' said Lady Langdale.

'But why does Lady Clonbrony want to pass for English?' said the duchess.

'Oh! because she is not quite Irish *bred and born* – only bred, not born,' said Mrs Dareville. 'And she could not be five minutes in your grace's company before she would tell you, that she was *Henglish*, born in *Hoxfordshire*.'

'She must be a vastly amusing personage. I should like to meet her, if one could see and hear her incog.,' said the duchess. 'And Lord Clonbrony, what is he?'

'Nothing, nobody,' said Mrs Dareville;' 'one never even hears of him.'

'A tribe of daughters, too, I suppose?'

'No, no,' said Lady Langdale, 'daughters would be past all endurance.'

'There's a cousin, though, a Grace Nugent,' said Mrs Dareville, 'that Lady Clonbrony has with her.'

'Best part of her, too,' said Colonel Heathcock; 'd—d fine girl! – never saw her look better than at the opera tonight!'

'Fine *complexion*! as Lady Clonbrony says, when she means a high colour,' said Lady Langdale.

'Grace Nugent is not a lady's beauty,' said Mrs Dareville. 'Has she any fortune, colonel?'

' 'Pon honour, don't know,' said the colonel.

'There's a son, somewhere, is not there?' said Lady Langdale.

'Don't know, 'pon honour,' replied the colonel.

'Yes – at Cambridge – not of age yet,' said Mrs Dareville. 'Bless me! here is Lady Clonbrony come back. I thought she was gone half an hour ago!'

'Mamma,' whispered one of Lady Langdale's daughters, leaning between her mother and Mrs Dareville, 'who is that gentleman that passed us just now?'

'Which way?'

'Towards the door. There now, mamma, you can see him. He is speaking to Lady Clonbrony – to Miss Nugent. Now Lady Clonbrony is introducing him to Miss Broadhurst.'

'I see him now,' said Lady Langdale, examining him through her glass; 'a very gentlemanlike-looking young man, indeed.'

'Not an Irishman, I am sure, by his manner,' said her grace.

'Heathcock!' said Lady Langdale, 'who is Miss Broadhurst talking to?'

'Eh! now really – 'pon honour – don't know,' replied Heathcock.

'And yet he certainly looks like somebody one certainly should know,' pursued Lady Langdale, 'though I don't recollect seeing him anywhere before.'

'Really now!' was all the satisfaction she could gain from the insensible, immovable colonel. However, her ladyship, after sending a whisper along the line, gained the desired information, that the young gentleman was Lord Colambre, son, only son, of Lord and Lady Clonbrony – that he was just come from Cambridge – that he was not yet of age – that he would be of age within a year – that he would then, after the death of somebody, come into possession of a fine estate, by the mother's side – 'and therefore, Cat'rine, my dear,' said she, turning round to the daughter, who had first pointed him out, 'you understand, we should never talk about other people's affairs.'

'No, mamma, never. I hope to goodness, mamma, Lord Colambre did not hear what you and Mrs Dareville were saying!'

'How could he, child? He was quite at the other end of the world.'

'I beg your pardon, ma'am, he was at my elbow, close behind us; but I never thought about him till I heard somebody say, "My lord – " '

'Good heavens! I hope he didn't hear.'

'But, for my part, I said nothing,' cried Lady Langdale.

'And for my part, I said nothing but what everybody knows!' cried Mrs Dareville.

'And for my part, I am guilty only of hearing,' said the duchess. 'Do, pray, Colonel Heathcock, have the goodness to see what my people are about, and what chance we have of getting away tonight.'

'The Duchess of Torcaster's carriage stops the way!' – a joyful sound to Colonel Heathcock and to her grace, and not less agreeable, at this instant, to Lady Langdale, who, the moment she was disembarrassed of the duchess, pressed through the crowd to Lady Clonbrony, and, addressing her with smiles and complacency, was 'charmed to have a little moment to speak to her – could *not* sooner get through the crowd – would certainly do herself the honour to be at her ladyship's gala on Wednesday.' While Lady Langdale spoke, she never seemed to see or think of anybody but Lady Clonbrony, though, all the time, she was intent upon every motion of Lord Colambre, and, whilst she was obliged to listen with a face of sympathy to a long complaint of Lady Clonbrony's, about Mr Soho's want of taste in ottomans, she was vexed to perceive that his lordship showed no desire to be introduced to her, or to her daughters; but, on the contrary, was standing talking to Miss Nugent. His mother, at the end of her speech, looked round for Colambre – called him twice before he heard – introduced him to Lady Langdale, and to Lady Cat'rine, and Lady Anne — , and to Mrs Dareville; to all of whom he bowed with all air of proud coldness, which gave them reason to regret that their remarks upon his mother and his family had not been made *sotto voce*.

'Lady Langdale's carriage stops the way!' Lord Colambre made no offer of his services, notwithstanding a look from his mother. Incapable of the meanness of voluntarily listening to a conversation not intended for him to hear, he had, however, been compelled, by the pressure of the crowd, to remain a few minutes stationary, where he could not avoid hearing the remarks of the fashionable friends. Disdaining dissimulation, he made no attempt to conceal his displeasure. Perhaps his vexation was increased by his consciousness that there was some mixture of truth in their sarcasms. He was sensible that his mother, in some points – her manners, for instance – was obvious to ridicule and satire. In Lady Clonbrony's address there was a mixture of constraint, affectation, and indecision, unusual in a person of her birth, rank, and knowledge of the world. A natural and unnatural manner seemed struggling in all her gestures, and in every syllable that she articulated – a naturally free, familiar, good-natured, precipitate, Irish manner, had been schooled, and schooled late in life, into a sober, cold, still, stiff deportment, which she mistook for English. A strong, Hibernian accent, she had, with infinite difficulty, changed into an English tone. Mistaking reverse of wrong for right, she caricatured the English pronunciation; and the extraordinary precision of her London phraseology betrayed her not to be a Londoner, as the man, who strove to pass for an Athenian, was detected by his Attic dialect. Not aware of her real danger, Lady Clonbrony was, on the opposite side, in continual apprehension, every time she opened her lips, lest some treacherous *a* or *e*, some strong *r*, some puzzling aspirate, or non-aspirate, some unguarded note, interrogative or expostulatory, should betray her to be an Irishwoman. Mrs Dareville had, in her mimickry, perhaps a little exaggerated as to the *teebles* and *cheers*, but still the general likeness of the representation of Lady Clonbrony was strong enough to strike and vex her son. He had now, for the first time, an opportunity of judging of the estimation in which his mother and his family were held by certain leaders of the ton, of whom, in her letters, she had spoken so much, and into whose society, or rather into whose parties, she had been admitted. He saw that the renegado cowardice, with which she denied, abjured, and reviled her own country, gained nothing but ridicule and contempt. He loved his mother; and, whilst he endeavoured to conceal her faults and foibles as much as possible from his own heart, he could not endure those who dragged them to light and ridicule. The next morning the first thing that occurred to Lord Colambre's remembrance when he awoke was the sound of the contemptuous emphasis which had been laid on the words IRISH ABSENTEES! This led to recollections of his native country, to comparisons of past and present scenes, to future plans of life. Young and careless as he seemed, Lord Colambre was capable of serious reflection. Of naturally quick and strong capacity, ardent affections, impetuous temper, the early years of his childhood passed at his father's castle in Ireland, where, from the lowest servant to the well-dressed dependant of the family, everybody had conspired to wait upon, to fondle, to flatter, to worship, this darling of their lord. Yet he was not spoiled – not rendered selfish. For, in the midst of this flattery and servility, some strokes of genuine generous affection had gone home to his little heart; and, though unqualified submission had increased the natural impetuosity of his temper, and though visions of his future grandeur had touched his infant thought, yet, fortunately, before he acquired any fixed habits of insolence or tyranny, he was carried far away from all that were bound or willing to submit to his commands, far away from all signs of hereditary grandeur – plunged into one of our great public schools – into a new world. Forced to struggle, mind and body, with his equals, his rivals, the little lord became a spirited schoolboy, and, in time, a man. Fortunately for him, science and literature happened to be the fashion among a set of clever young men with whom he was at Cambridge. His ambition for intellectual superiority was raised, his views were enlarged, his tastes and his manners formed. The sobriety of English good sense mixed most advantageously with Irish vivacity; English prudence governed, but did not extinguish his Irish enthusiasm. But, in fact, English and Irish had not been invidiously contrasted in his mind: he had been so long resident in England, and so intimately connected with Englishmen, that he was not obvious to any of the commonplace ridicule thrown upon Hibernians; and he had lived with men who were too well informed and liberal to misjudge or depreciate a sister country. He had found, from experience, that, however reserved the English may be in manner, they are warm at heart; that, however averse they may be from forming new acquaintance, their esteem and confidence once gained, they make the most solid friends. He had formed friendships in England; he was fully sensible of the superior comforts, refinement, and information, of English society; but his own country was endeared to him by early association, and a sense of duty and patriotism attached him to Ireland. And shall I too be an absentee? was a question which resulted from these reflections – a question which he was not yet prepared to answer decidedly. In the meantime, the first business of the morning was to execute a commission for a Cambridge friend. Mr Berryl had bought from Mr Mordicai, a famous London coachmaker, a curricle, *warranted sound*, for which he had paid a sound price, upon express condition that Mr Mordicai, *barring accidents*, should be answerable for all repairs of the curricle for six months. In three, both the carriage and body were found to be good for nothing – the curricle had been returned to Mr Mordicai – nothing had since been heard of it, or from him – and Lord Colambre had undertaken to pay him and it a visit, and to make all proper inquiries. Accordingly, he went to the coachmaker's, and, obtaining no satisfaction from the underlings, desired to see the head of the house. He was answered, that Mr Mordicai was not at home. His lordship had never seen Mr Mordicai; but, just then, he saw, walking across the yard, a man, who looked something like a Bond Street coxcomb, but not the least like a gentleman, who called, in the tone of a master, for 'Mr Mordicai's barouche!' It appeared; and he was stepping into it when Lord Colambre took the liberty of stopping him; and, pointing to the wreck of Mr Berryl's curricle, now standing in the yard, began a statement of his friend's grievances, and an appeal to common justice and conscience, which he, unknowing the nature of the man with whom he had to deal, imagined must be irresistible. Mr Mordicai stood without moving a muscle of his dark wooden face. Indeed, in his face there appeared to be no muscles, or none which could move; so that, though he had what are generally called handsome features, there was, all together, something unnatural and shocking in his countenance. When, at last, his eyes turned, and his lips opened, this seemed to be done by machinery, and not by the will of a living creature, or from the impulse of a rational soul. Lord Colambre was so much struck with this strange physiognomy, that he actually forgot much he had to say of springs and wheels. But it was no matter. Whatever he had said, it would have come to the same thing; and Mordicai would have answered as he now did –

'Sir, it was my partner made that bargain, not myself; and I don't hold myself bound by it, for he is the sleeping partner only, and not empowered to act in the way of business. Had Mr Berryl bargained with me, I should have told him that he should have looked to these things before his carriage went out of our yard.'

The indignation of Lord Colambre kindled at these words – but in vain. To all that indignation could by word or look urge against Mordicai, he replied –

'Maybe so, sir; the law is open to your friend – the law is open to all men who can pay for it.'

Lord Colambre turned in despair from the callous coachmaker, and listened to one of his more compassionate-looking workmen, who was reviewing the disabled curricle; and, whilst he was waiting to know the sum of his friend's misfortune, a fat, jolly, Falstaff-looking personage came into the yard, accosted Mordicai with a degree of familiarity, which, from a gentleman, appeared to Lord Colambre to be almost impossible.

'How are you, Mordicai, my good fellow?' cried he, speaking with a strong Irish accent.

'Who is this?' whispered Lord Colambre to the foreman, who was examining the curricle.

'Sir Terence O'Fay, sir. There must be entire new wheels.'

'Now tell me, my tight fellow,' continued Sir Terence, holding Mordicai fast, 'when, in the name of all the saints, good or bad, in the calendar, do you reckon to let us sport the *suicide*?'

Mordicai forcibly drew his mouth into what he meant for a smile, and answered, 'As soon as possible, Sir Terence.'

Sir Terence, in a tone of jocose, wheedling expostulation, entreated him to have the carriage finished *out of hand*. 'Ah, now! Mordy, my precious! let us have it by the birthday, and come and dine with us o' Monday, at the Hibernian Hotel – there's a rare one – will you?'

'Mordicai accepted the invitation, and promised faithfully that the *suicide* should be finished by the birthday. Sir Terence shook hands upon this promise, and, after telling a good story, which made one of the workmen in the yard – an Irishman – grin with delight, walked off. Mordicai, first waiting till the knight was out of hearing, called aloud –

'You grinning rascal! mind, at your peril, and don't let that there carriage be touched, d'ye see, till further orders.'

One of Mr Mordicai's clerks, with a huge long-feathered pen behind his ear, observed that Mr Mordicai was right in that caution, for that, to the best of his comprehension, Sir Terence O'Fay and his principal, too, were over head and ears in debt.

Mordicai coolly answered that he was well aware of that; but that the estate could afford to dip further; that, for his part, he was under no apprehension; he knew how to look sharp, and to bite before he was bit. That he knew Sir Terence and his principal were leagued together to give the creditors *the go by*, but that, clever as they both were at that work, he trusted he was their match.

'Will you be so good, sir, to finish making out this estimate for me?' interrupted Lord Colambre.

'Immediately, sir. Sixty-nine pound four, and the perch. Let us see – Mr Mordicai, ask him, ask Paddy, about Sir Terence,' said the foreman, pointing back over his shoulder to the Irish workman, who was at this moment pretending to be wondrous hard at work. However, when Mr Mordicai defied him to tell him anything he did not know, Paddy, parting with an untasted bit of tobacco, began, and recounted some of Sir Terence O'Fay's exploits in evading duns, replevying cattle, fighting sheriffs, bribing *subs*, managing cants, tricking *custodees*, in language so strange, and with a countenance and gestures so full of enjoyment of the jest, that, whilst Mordicai stood for a moment aghast with astonishment, Lord Colambre could not help laughing, partly at, and partly with, his countryman. All the yard were in a roar of laughter, though they did not understand half of what they heard; but their risible muscles were acted upon mechanically, or maliciously, merely by the sound of the Irish brogue.

Mordicai, waiting till the laugh was over, dryly observed that 'the law is executed in another guess sort of way in England from what it is in Ireland'; therefore, for his part, he desired nothing better than to set his wits fairly against such *sharks*. That there was a pleasure in doing up a debtor which none but a creditor could know.

'In a moment, sir; if you'll have a moment's patience, sir, if you please,' said the slow foreman to Lord Colambre; 'I must go down the pounds once more, and then I'll let you have it.'

'I'll tell you what, Smithfield,' continued Mr Mordicai, coming close beside his foreman, and speaking very low, but with a voice trembling with anger, for he was piqued by his foreman's doubts of his capacity to cope with Sir Terence O'Fay; 'I'll tell you what, Smithfield, I'll be cursed, if I don't get every inch of them into my power. You know how?'

'You are the best judge, sir,' replied the foreman; 'but I would not undertake Sir Terence; and the question is, whether the estate will answer the *lot* of the debts, and whether you know them all for certain?'

'I do, sir, I tell you. There's Green – there's Blancham – there's Gray – there's Soho – naming several more – and, to my knowledge, Lord Clonbrony – '

'Stop, sir,' cried Lord Colambre in a voice which made Mordicai, and everybody present, start – 'I am his son – '

'The devil!' said Mordicai.

'God bless every bone in his body, then! – he's an Irishman,' cried Paddy; 'and there was the *ra*son my heart warmed to him from the first minute he come into the yard, though I did not know it till now.'

'What, sir! are you my Lord Colambre?' said Mr Mordicai, recovering, but not clearly recovering, his intellects. 'I beg pardon, but I did not know you *was* Lord Colambre. I thought you told me you was the friend of Mr Berryl.'

'I do not see the incompatibility of the assertion, sir,' replied Lord Colambre, taking from the bewildered foreman's unresisting hand the account, which he had been so long *furnishing*.

'Give me leave, my lord,' said Mordicai. 'I beg your pardon, my lord, perhaps we can compromise that business for your friend Mr Berryl; since he is your lordship's friend, perhaps we can contrive to *compromise* and *split the difference.*'

To compromise and split the difference, Mordicai thought were favourite phrases, and approved Hibernian modes of doing business, which would conciliate this young Irish nobleman, and dissipate the proud tempest which had gathered and now swelled in his breast.

'No, sir, no!' cried Lord Colambre, holding firm the paper. 'I want no favour from you. I will accept of none for my friend or for myself.'

'Favour! No, my lord, I should not presume to offer – But I should wish, if you'll allow me, to do your friend justice.'

Lord Colambre recollecting that he had no right, in his pride, to fling away his friend's money, let Mr Mordicai look at the account; and, his impetuous temper in a few moments recovered by good sense, he considered that, as his person was utterly unknown to Mr Mordicai, no offence could have been intended to him, and that, perhaps, in what had been said of his father's debts and distress, there might be more truth than he was aware of. Prudently, therefore, controlling his feelings, and commanding himself, he suffered Mr Mordicai to show him into a parlour, to *settle* his friend's business. In a few minutes the account was reduced to a reasonable form, and, in consideration of the partner's having made the bargain, by which Mr Mordicai felt himself influenced in honour, though not bound in law, he undertook to have the curricle made better than new again, for Mr Berryl, for twenty guineas. Then came awkward apologies to Lord Colambre, which he ill endured. 'Between ourselves, my lord,' continued Mordicai –

But the familiarity of the phrase, 'Between ourselves' – this implication of equality – Lord Colambre could not admit; he moved hastily towards the door and departed.

Chapter 2

FULL OF WHAT HE HAD HEARD, and impatient to obtain further information respecting the state of his father's affairs, Lord Colambre hastened home; but his father was out, and his mother was engaged with Mr Soho, directing, or rather being directed, how her apartments should be fitted up for her gala. As Lord Colambre entered the room, he saw his mother, Miss Nugent, and Mr Soho, standing at a large table, which was covered with rolls of paper, patterns, and drawings of furniture: Mr Soho was speaking in a conceited dictatorial tone, asserting that there was no 'colour in nature for that room equal to the *belly-o'-the fawn*;' which *belly-o'-the fawn* he so pronounced that Lady Clonbrony understood it to be *la belle uniforme*, and, under this mistake, repeated and assented to the assertion till it was set to rights, with condescending superiority, by the upholsterer. This first architectural upholsterer of the age, as he styled himself, and was universally admitted to be by all the world of fashion, then, with full powers given to him, spoke *en maître*. The whole face of things must be changed – there must be new hangings, new draperies, new cornices, new candelabras, new everything!

> The upholsterer's eye, in a fine frenzy rolling,
> Glances from ceiling to floor, from floor to ceiling;
> And, as imagination bodies forth
> The form of things unknown, th' upholsterer's pencil
> Turns to shape and gives to airy nothing
> A local habitation and a NAME.

Of the value of a NAME no one could be more sensible than Mr Soho.

'Your la'ship sees – this is merely a scratch of my pencil – your la'ship's sensible – just to give you an idea of the shape, the form of the thing. You fill up your angles here with *encoinières* – round your walls with the *Turkish tent drapery* – a fancy of my own – in apricot cloth, or crimson velvet, suppose, or *en flute*, in crimson satin draperies, fanned and riched with gold fringes, *en suite* – intermediate spaces, Apollo's heads with gold rays – and here, ma'am, you place four *chancelières*, with chimeras at the corners, covered with blue silk and silver fringe, elegantly fanciful – with my STATIRA CANOPY here – light blue silk draperies – aerial tint, with silver balls – and for seats here, the SERAGLIO OTTOMANS superfine scarlet – your paws – griffin – golden – and golden tripods, here, with antique cranes – and oriental alabaster tables here and there – quite appropriate, your la'ship feels.

'And – let me reflect. For the next apartment, it strikes me – as your la'ship don't value expense – *the Alhambra hangings* – my own thought entirely. Now, before I unroll them, Lady Clonbrony, I must beg you'll not mention I've shown them. I give you my sacred honour, not a soul has set eye upon the Alhambra hangings, except Mrs Dareville, who stole a peep; I refused, absolutely refused, the Duchess of Torcaster – but I can't refuse your la'ship. So see, ma'am – (unrolling them) – scagliola porphyry columns supporting the grand dome – entablature, silvered and decorated with imitative bronze ornaments; under the entablature, a *valance in pelmets*, of puffed scarlet silk, would have an unparalleled grand effect, seen through the arches – with the TREBISOND TRELLICE would make a *tout ensemble*, novel beyond example. On that Trebisond trellice paper, I confess, ladies, I do pique myself.

'Then, for the little room, I recommend turning it temporarily into a Chinese pagoda, with this *Chinese pagoda paper*, with the *porcelain border*, and josses, and jars, and beakers to match; and I can venture to promise one vase of pre-eminent size and beauty. Oh, indubitably! if your la'ship prefers it, you can have the *Egyptian hieroglyphic paper*, with the *ibis border* to match! The only objection is, one sees it everywhere – quite antediluvian – gone to the hotels even; but, to be sure, if your la'ship has a fancy – At all events, I humbly recommend, what her Grace of Torcaster longs to patronise, my MOON CURTAINS with candlelight draperies. A demisaison elegance this – I hit off yesterday – and – true, your la'ship's quite correct – out of the common, completely. And, of course, you'd have the *sphynx candelabras*, and the Phœnix argands. Oh! nothing else lights now, ma'am! Expense! Expense of the whole! Impossible to calculate here on the spot! – but nothing at all worth your ladyship's consideration!'

At another moment, Lord Colambre might have been amused with all this rhodomontade, and with the airs and voluble conceit of the orator; but, after what he had heard at Mr Mordicai's, this whole scene struck him more with melancholy than with mirth. He was alarmed by the prospect of new and unbounded expense; provoked, almost past enduring, by the jargon and impertinence of this upholsterer; mortified and vexed to the heart to see his mother the dupe, the sport of such a coxcomb.

'Prince of puppies! – Insufferable! – My own mother!' Lord Colambre repeated to himself, as he walked hastily up and down the room.

'Colambre, won't you let us have your judgment – your *teeste*?' said his mother.

'Excuse me, ma'am. I have no taste, no judgment, in these things.'

He sometimes paused, and looked at Mr Soho with a strong inclination to – But knowing that he should say too much, if he said anything, he was silent – never dared to approach the council table – but continued walking up and down the room, till he heard a voice, which at once arrested his attention, and soothed his ire. He approached the table instantly, and listened, whilst Grace Nugent said everything he wished to have said, and with all the propriety and delicacy with which he thought he could not have spoken. He leaned on the table, and fixed his eyes upon her – years ago, he had seen his cousin – last night, he had thought her handsome, pleasing, graceful – but now, he saw a new person, or he saw her in a new light. He marked the superior intelligence, the animation, the eloquence of her countenance, its variety, whilst alternately, with arch raillery or grave humour, she played off Mr Soho, and made him magnify the ridicule, till it was apparent even to Lady Clonbrony. He observed the anxiety, lest his mother should expose her own foibles – he was touched by the respectful, earnest kindness – the soft tones of persuasion, with which she addressed his mother – the care not to presume upon her own influence – the good sense, the taste she showed, yet not displaying her superiority – the address, temper, and patience, with which she at last accomplished her purpose, and prevented Lady Clonbrony from doing anything preposterously absurd, or exorbitantly extravagant.

Lord Colambre was actually sorry when the business was ended – when Mr Soho departed – for Grace Nugent was then silent; and it was necessary to remove his eyes from that countenance, on which he had gazed unobserved. Beautiful and graceful, yet so unconscious was she of her charms, that the eye of admiration could rest upon her without her perceiving it – she seemed so intent upon others as totally to forget herself. The whole train of Lord Colambre's thoughts was so completely deranged that, although he was sensible there was something of importance he had to say to his mother, yet, when Mr Soho's departure left him opportunity to speak, he stood silent, unable to recollect anything but – Grace Nugent.

When Grace Nugent left the room, after some minutes' silence, and some effort, Lord Colambre said to his mother, 'Pray, madam, do you know anything of Sir Terence O'Fay?'

'I!' said Lady Clonbrony, drawing up her head proudly; 'I know he is a person I cannot endure. He is no friend of mine, I can assure you – nor any such sort of person.'

'I thought it was impossible!' cried Colambre, with exultation.

'I only wish your father, Colambre, could say as much,' added Lady Clonbrony.

Lord Colambre's countenance fell again; and again he was silent for some time.

'Does my father dine at home, ma'am?'

'I suppose not; he seldom dines at home.'

'Perhaps, ma'am, my father may have some cause to be uneasy about – '

'About?' said Lady Clonbrony, in a tone, and with a look of curiosity which convinced her son that she knew nothing of his debts or distresses, if he had any. 'About what?' repeated her ladyship.

Here was no receding, and Lord Colambre never had recourse to artifice.

'About his affairs, I was going to say, madam. But, since you know nothing of any difficulties or embarrassments, I am persuaded that none exist.'

'Nay, I *cawnt* tell you that, Colambre. There are difficulties for ready money, I confess, when I ask for it, which surprise me often. I know nothing of affairs – ladies of a certain rank seldom do, you know. But, considering your father's estate, and the fortune I brought him,' added her ladyship, proudly, 'I *cawnt* conceive it at all. Grace Nugent, indeed, often talks to me of embarrassments and economy; but that, poor thing, is very natural for her, because her fortune is not particularly large, and she has left it all, or almost all, in her uncle and guardian's hands. I know she's often distressed for odd money to lend me, and that makes her anxious.'

'Is not Miss Nugent very much admired, ma'am, in London?'

'Of course – in the company she is in, you know, she has every advantage. And she has a natural family air of fashion – not but what she would have *got on* much better, if, when she first appeared in Lon'on, she had taken my advice, and wrote herself on her cards Miss de Nogent, which would have taken off the prejudice against the *Iricism* of Nugent, you know; and there is a Count de Nogent.'

'I did not know there was any such prejudice, ma'am. There may be among a certain set; but, I should think, not among well-informed, well-bred people.'

'I *big* your *pawdon*, Colambre; surely I, that was born in England, an Henglish-woman *bawn*! must be well *infawmed* on this *pint*, anyway.'

Lord Colambre was respectfully silent.

'Mother,' resumed he, 'I wonder that Miss Nugent is not married!'

'That is her own fau't, entirely; she has refused very good offers – establishments that, I own, I think, as Lady Langdale says, I was to blame to allow her to let pass; but young *ladies*, till they are twenty, always think they can do better. Mr Martingale, of Martingale, proposed for her, but she objected to him on account of he's being on the turf; and Mr St Albans' £7000 a year – because – I *reelly* forget what – I believe only because she did not like him – and something about principles. Now there is Colonel Heathcock, one of the most fashionable young men you see, always with the Duchess of Torcaster and that set – Heathcock takes a vast deal of notice of her, for him; and yet, I'm persuaded, she would not have him tomorrow, if he came to the *pint*, and for no reason, *reelly* now, that she can give me, but because she says he's a coxcomb. Grace has a tincture of Irish pride. But, for my part, I rejoice that she is so difficult, for I don't know what I should do without her.'

'Miss Nugent is indeed – very much attached to you, mother, I am convinced,' said Lord Colambre, beginning his sentence with great enthusiasm, and ending it with great sobriety.

'Indeed then, she's a sweet girl, and I am very partial to her, there's the truth,' cried Lady Clonbrony, in an undisguised Irish accent, and with her natural warm manner. But a moment afterwards her features and whole form resumed their constrained stillness and stiffness, and, in her English accent, she continued –

'Before you put my *idees* out of my head, Colambre, I had something to say to you – Oh! I know what it was – we were talking of embarrassments – and I wished to do your father the justice to mention to you that he has been *uncommon liberal* to me about this gala, and has *reelly* given me *carte blanche*; and I've a notion – indeed I know – that it is you, Colambre, I am to thank for this.'

'Me! – ma'am!'

'Yes! Did not your father give you any hint?'

'No, ma'am; I have seen my father but for half an hour since I came to town, and in that time he said nothing to me – of his affairs.'

'But what I allude to is more your affair.'

'He did not speak to me of any affairs, ma'am – he spoke only of my horses.'

'Then I suppose my lord leaves it to me to open the matter to you. I have the pleasure to tell you, that we have in view for you – and I think I may say with more than the approbation of all her family – an alliance – '

'Oh! my dear mother! you cannot be serious,' cried Lord Colambre; 'you know I am not of years of discretion yet – I shall not think of marrying these ten years, at least.'

'Why not? Nay, my dear Colambre, don't go, I beg – I am serious, I assure you – and, to convince you of it, I shall tell you candidly, at once, all your father told me: that now you've done with Cambridge, and are come to Lon'on, he agrees with me in wishing that you should make the figure you ought to make, Colambre, as sole heir-apparent to the Clonbrony estate, and all that sort of thing. But, on the other hand, living in Lon'on, and making you the handsome allowance you ought to have, are, both together, more than your father can afford, without inconvenience, he tells me.'

'I assure you, mother, I shall be content – '

'No, no; you must not be content, child, and you must hear me. You must live in a becoming style, and make a proper appearance. I could not present you to my friends here, nor be happy, if you did not, Colambre. Now the way is clear before you: you have birth and title, here is fortune ready made; you will have a noble estate of your own when old Quin dies, and you will not be any encumbrance or inconvenience to your father or anybody. Marrying an heiress accomplishes all this at once; and the young lady is everything we could wish, besides – you will meet again at the gala. Indeed, between ourselves, she is the grand object of the gala; all her friends will come *en masse*, and one should wish that they should see things in proper style. You have seen the young lady in question, Colambre – Miss Broadhurst. Don't you recollect the young lady I introduced you to last night after the opera?'

'The little, plain girl, covered with diamonds, who was standing beside Miss Nugent?'

'In di'monds, yes. But you won't think her plain when you see more of her – that wears off; I thought her plain, at first – I hope – '

'I hope,' said Lord Colambre, 'that you will not take it unkindly of me, my dear mother, if I tell you, at once, that I have no thoughts of marrying at present – and that I never will marry for money. Marrying an heiress is not even a new way of paying old debts – at all events, it is one to which no distress could persuade me to have recourse; and as I must, if I outlive old Mr Quin, have an independent fortune, *there is no* occasion to purchase one by marriage.'

'There is no distress, that I know of, in the case,' cried Lady Clonbrony. 'Where is your imagination running, Colambre? But merely for your establishment, your independence.'

'Establishment, I want none – independence I do desire, and will preserve. Assure my father, my *dear mother*, that I will not be an expense to him. I will live within the allowance he made me at Cambridge – I will give up half of it – I will do anything for his convenience – but marry for money, that I cannot do.'

'Then, Colambre, you are very disobliging,' said Lady Clonbrony, with an expression of disappointment and displeasure; 'for your father says, if you don't marry Miss Broadhurst, we can't live in Lon'on another winter.'

This said – which, had she been at the moment mistress of herself, she would not have let out – Lady Clonbrony abruptly quitted the room. Her son stood motionless, saying to himself –

'Is this my mother? – How altered!'

The next morning he seized an opportunity of speaking to his father, whom he caught, with difficulty, just when he was going out, as usual, for the day. Lord Colambre, with all the respect due to his father, and with that affectionate manner by which he always knew how to soften the strength of his expressions, made nearly the same declarations of his resolution, by which his mother had been so much surprised and offended. Lord Clonbrony seemed more embarrassed, but not so much displeased. When Lord Colambre adverted, as delicately as he could, to the selfishness of desiring from him the sacrifice of liberty for life, to say nothing of his affections, merely to enable his family to make a splendid figure in London, Lord Clonbrony exclaimed, 'That's all nonsense! – cursed nonsense! That's the way we are obliged to state the thing to your mother, my dear boy, because I might talk her deaf before she would understand or listen to anything else. But, for my own share, I don't care a rush if London was sunk in the salt sea. Little Dublin for my money, as Sir Terence O'Fay says.'

'Who is Sir Terence O'Fay, may I ask, sir?'

'Why, don't you know Terry? Ay, you've been so long at Cambridge, I forgot. And did you never see Terry?'

'I have seen him, sir – I met him yesterday at Mr Mordicai's, the coachmaker's.'

'Mordicai's!' exclaimed Lord Clonbrony, with a sudden blush, which he endeavoured to hide by taking snuff. 'He is a damned rascal, that Mordicai! I hope you didn't believe a word he said – nobody does that knows him.'

'I am glad, sir, that you seem to know him so well, and to be upon your guard against him,' replied Lord Colambre; 'for, from what I heard of his conversation, when he was not aware who I was, I am convinced he would do you any injury in his power.'

'He shall never have me in his power, I promise him. We shall take care of that. But what did he say?'

Lord Colambre repeated the substance of what Mordicai had said, and Lord Clonbrony reiterated – 'Damned rascal! – damned rascal! I'll get out of his hands; I'll have no more to do with him.' But, as he spoke, he exhibited evident symptoms of uneasiness, moving continually, and shifting from leg to leg like a foundered horse.

He could not bring himself positively to deny that he had debts and difficulties; but he would by no means open the state of his affairs to his son – 'No father is called upon to do that,' said he to himself; 'none but a fool would do it.'

Lord Colambre, perceiving his father's embarrassment, withdrew his eyes, respectfully refrained from all further inquiries, and simply repeated the assurance he had made to his mother, that he would put his family to no additional expense; and that, if it was necessary, he would willingly give up half his allowance.

'Not at all – not at all, my dear boy,' said his father; 'I would rather cramp myself than that you should be cramped, a thousand times over. But it is all my Lady Clonbrony's nonsense. If people would but, as they ought, stay in their own country, live on their own estates, and kill their own mutton, money need never be wanting.'

For killing their own mutton, Lord Colambre did not see the indispensable necessity; but he rejoiced to hear his father assert that people should reside in their own country.

'Ay,' cried Lord Clonbrony, to strengthen his assertion, as he always thought it necessary to do, by quoting some other person's opinion. 'So Sir Terence O'Fay always says, and that's the reason your mother can't endure poor Terry. You don't know Terry? No, you have only seen him; but, indeed, to see him is to know him; for he is the most off-hand, good fellow in Europe.'

'I don't pretend to know him yet,' said Lord Colambre. 'I am not so presumptuous as to form my opinion at first sight.'

'Oh, curse your modesty!' interrupted Lord Clonbrony; 'you mean, you don't pretend to like him yet; but Terry will make you like him. I defy you not. I'll introduce you to him – him to you, I mean – most warm-hearted, generous dog upon earth – convivial – jovial – with wit and humour enough, in his own way, to split you – split me if he has not. You need not cast down your eyes, Colambre. What's your objection?'

'I have made none, sir; but, if you urge me, I can only say that, if he has all these good qualities, it is to be regretted that he does not look and speak a little more like a gentleman.'

'A gentleman! he is as much a gentleman as any of your formal prigs – not the exact Cambridge cut, maybe. Curse your English education! 'Twas none of my advice. I suppose you mean to take after your mother in the notion that nothing can be good, or genteel, but what's English.'

'Far from it, sir; I assure you, I am as warm a friend to Ireland as your heart could wish. You will have no reason, in that respect at least, nor, I hope, in any other, to curse my English education; and, if my gratitude and affection can avail, you shall never regret the kindness and liberality with which you have, I fear, distressed yourself to afford me the means of becoming all that a British nobleman ought to be.'

'Gad! you distress me now!' said Lord Clonbrony, 'and I didn't expect it, or I wouldn't make a fool of myself this way,' added he, ashamed of his emotion, and whiffling it off. 'You have an Irish heart, that I see, which no education can spoil. But you must like Terry. I'll give you time, as he said to me, when first he taught me to like usquebaugh. Good-morning to you!'

Whilst Lady Clonbrony, in consequence of her residence in London, had become more of a fine lady, Lord Clonbrony, since he left Ireland, had become less of a gentleman. Lady Clonbrony, born an Englishwoman, disclaiming and disencumbering herself of all the Irish in town, had, by giving splendid entertainments, at an enormous expense, made her way into a certain set of fashionable company. But Lord Clonbrony, who was somebody in Ireland, who was a great person in Dublin, found himself nobody in England, a mere cipher in London. Looked down upon by the fine people with whom his lady associated, and heartily weary of them, he retreated from them altogether, and sought entertainment and self-complacency in society beneath him – indeed, both in rank and education, but in which he had the satisfaction of feeling himself the first person in company. Of these associates, the first in talents, and in jovial profligacy, was Sir Terence O'Fay – a man of low extraction, who had been knighted by an Irish lord-lieutenant in some convivial frolic. No one could tell a good story, or sing a good song better than Sir Terence; he exaggerated his native brogue, and his natural propensity to blunder, caring little whether the company laughed at him or with him, provided they laughed. 'Live and laugh – laugh and live,' was his motto; and certainly he lived on laughing, as well as many better men can contrive to live on a thousand a year.

Lord Clonbrony brought Sir Terence home with him next day to introduce him to Lord Colambre; and it happened that on this occasion Terence appeared to peculiar disadvantage, because, like many other people, '*Il gâtoit l'esprit qu'il avoit en voulant avoir celui qu'il n'avoit pas.*'

Having been apprised that Lord Colambre was a fine scholar, fresh from Cambridge, and being conscious of his own deficiencies of literature, instead of trusting to his natural talents, he summoned to his aid, with no small effort, all the scraps of learning he had acquired in early days, and even brought before the company all the gods and goddesses with whom he had formed an acquaintance at school. Though embarrassed by this unusual encumbrance of learning, he endeavoured to make all subservient to his immediate design, of paying his court to Lady Clonbrony, by forwarding the object she had most anxiously in view – the match between her son and Miss Broadhurst.

'And so, Miss Nugent,' said he, not daring, with all his assurance, to address himself directly to Lady Clonbrony – 'and so, Miss Nugent, you are going to have great doings, I'm told, and a wonderful grand gala. There's nothing in the wide world equal to being in a good, handsome crowd. No later now than the last ball at the Castle – that was before I left Dublin, Miss Nugent – the apartments, owing to the popularity of my lady-lieutenant, was so throng – so throng – that I remember very well, in the doorway, a lady – and a very genteel woman she was too, though a stranger to me – saying to me, "Sir, your finger's in my ear." "I know it, madam," says I, "but I can't take it out till the crowd give me elbow room."

'But it's gala I'm thinking of now. I hear you are to have the golden Venus, my Lady Clonbrony, won't you?'

'Sir!'

This freezing monosyllable notwithstanding, Sir Terence pursued his course fluently. 'The golden Venus! – Sure, Miss Nugent, you, that are so quick, can't but know I would apostrophise Miss Broadhurst that is, but that won't be long so, I hope. My Lord Colambre, have you seen much yet of that young lady?'

'No, sir.'

'Then I hope you won't be long so. I hear great talk now of the Venus of Medicis, and the Venus of this and that, with the Florence Venus, and the sable Venus, and that other Venus, that's washing of her hair, and a hundred other Venuses, some good, some bad. But, be that as it will, my lord, trust a fool – ye may, when he tells you truth – the golden Venus is the only one on earth that can stand, or that will stand, through all ages and temperatures; for gold rules the court, gold rules the camp, and men below, and heaven above.'

'Heaven above! Take care, Terry! Do you know what you're saying?' interrupted Lord Clonbrony.

'Do I? Don't I?' replied Terry. 'Deny, if you please, my lord, that it was for a golden pippin that the three goddesses *fit* – and that the *Hippomenes* was about golden apples – and did not Hercules rob a garden for golden apples? – and did not the pious Eneas himself take a golden branch with him, to make himself welcome to his father in hell?' said Sir Terence, winking at Lord Colambre.

'Why, Terry, you know more about books than I should have suspected,' said Lord Clonbrony.

'Nor you would not have suspected me to have such a great acquaintance among the goddesses neither, would you, my lord? But, apropos, before we quit, of what material, think ye, was that same Venus's famous girdle, now, that made roses and lilies so quickly appear? Why, what was it, but a girdle of sterling gold, I'll engage? – for gold is the only true thing for a young man to look after in a wife.'

Sir Terence paused, but no applause ensued.

'Let them talk of Cupids and darts, and the mother of the Loves and

Graces. Minerva may sing odes and *dythambrics*, or whatsoever her wisdomship pleases. Let her sing, or let her say she'll never get a husband in this world or the other, without she had a good thumping *fortin*, and then she'd go off like wildfire.'

'No, no, Terry, there you're out; Minerva has too bad a character for learning to be a favourite with gentlemen,' said Lord Clonbrony.

'Tut – Don't tell me! – I'd get her off before you could say Jack Robinson, and thank you too, if she had fifty thousand down, or a thousand a year in land. Would you have a man so d——d nice as to balk when house and land is a-going – a-going – a-going! – because of the encumbrance of a little learning? I never heard that Miss Broadhurst was anything of a learned lady.'

'Miss Broadhurst!' said Grace Nugent; 'how did you get round to Miss Broadhurst?'

'Oh! by the way of Tipperary,' said Lord Colambre.

'I beg your pardon, my lord, it was apropos to a good fortune, which, I hope, will not be out of your way, even if you went by Tipperary. She has, besides £100,000 in the funds, a clear landed property of £10,000 per annum. *Well! some people talk of morality, and some of religion, but give me a little snug* PROPERTY. But, my lord, I've a little business to transact this morning, and must not be idling and indulging myself here.' So, bowing to the ladies, he departed.

'Really, I am glad that man is gone,' said Lady Clonbrony. 'What a relief to one's ears! I am sure I wonder, my lord, how you can bear to carry that strange creature always about with you – so vulgar as he is.'

'He diverts me,' said Lord Clonbrony, 'while many of your correct-mannered fine ladies or gentlemen put me to sleep. What signifies what accent people speak in that have nothing to say – hey, Colambre?'

Lord Colambre, from respect to his father, did not express his opinion, but his aversion to Sir Terence O'Fay was stronger even than his mother's; though Lady Clonbrony's detestation of him was much increased by perceiving that his coarse hints about Miss Broadhurst had operated against her favourite scheme.

The next morning, at breakfast, Lord Clonbrony talked of bringing Sir Terence with him that night to her gala. She absolutely grew pale with horror.

'Good heavens! Lady Langdale, Mrs Dareville, Lady Pococke, Lady Chatterton, Lady D——, Lady G——, his Grace of V——; what would they think of him? And Miss Broadhurst to see him going about with my Lord Clonbrony!' – It could not be. No; her ladyship made the most solemn and desperate protestation, that she would sooner give up her gala altogether – tie up the knocker – say she was sick – rather be sick, or be dead, than be obliged to have such a creature as Sir Terence O'Fay at her gala.

'Have it your own way, my dear, as you have everything else!' cried Lord Clonbrony, taking up his hat, and preparing to decamp; 'but, take notice, if you won't receive him you need not expect me. So a good-morning to you, my Lady Clonbrony. You may find a worse friend in need, yet, than that same Sir Terence O'Fay.'

'I trust I shall never be in need, my lord,' replied her ladyship. 'It would be strange, indeed, if I were, with the fortune I brought.'

'Oh! that fortune of hers!' cried Lord Clonbrony, stopping both his ears as he ran out of the room; 'shall I never hear the end of that fortune, when I've seen the end of it long ago?'

During this matrimonial dialogue, Grace Nugent and Lord Colambre never once looked at each other. Grace was very diligently trying the changes that could be made in the positions of a china-mouse, a cat, a dog, a cup, and a Brahmin, on the mantelpiece; Lord Colambre as diligently reading the newspaper.

'Now, my dear Colambre,' said Lady Clonbrony, 'put down the paper, and listen to me. Let me entreat you not to neglect Miss Broadhurst tonight, as I know that the family come here chiefly on your account.'

'My dear mother, I never can neglect any deserving young lady, and particularly one of your guests; but I shall be careful not to do more than not to neglect, for I never will pretend what I do not feel.'

'But, my dear Colambre, Miss Broadhurst is everything you could wish, except being a beauty.'

'Perhaps, madam,' said Lord Colambre, fixing his eyes on Grace Nugent, 'you think that I can see no farther than a handsome face?'

The unconscious Grace Nugent now made a warm eulogium of Miss Broadhurst's sense, and wit, and independence of character.

'I did not know that Miss Broadhurst was a friend of yours, Miss Nugent?'

'She is, I assure you, a friend of mine; and, as a proof, I will not praise her at this moment. I will go farther still – I will promise that I never will praise her to you till you begin to praise her to me.'

Lord Colambre smiled, and now listened, as if he wished that Grace should go on speaking, even of Miss Broadhurst.

'That's my sweet Grace!' cried Lady Clonbrony. 'Oh! she knows how to manage these men – not one of them can resist her!'

Lord Colambre, for his part, did not deny the truth of this assertion.

'Grace,' added Lady Clonbrony, 'make him promise to do as we would have him.'

'No; promises are dangerous things to ask or to give,' said Grace. 'Men and naughty children never make promises, especially promises to be good, without longing to break them the next minute.'

'Well, at least, child, persuade him, I charge you, to make my gala go off well. That's the first thing we ought to think of now. Ring the bell! And all heads and hands I put in requisition for the gala.'

Chapter 3

THE OPENING OF HER GALA, the display of her splendid reception-rooms, the Turkish tent, the Alhambra, the pagoda, formed a proud moment to Lady Clonbrony. Much did she enjoy, and much too naturally, notwithstanding all her efforts to be stiff and stately, much too naturally did she show her enjoyment of the surprise excited in some and affected by others on their first entrance.

One young, very young lady expressed her astonishment so audibly as to attract the notice of all the bystanders. Lady Clonbrony, delighted, seized both her hands, shook them, and laughed heartily; then, as the young lady with her party passed on, her ladyship recovered herself, drew up her head, and said to the company near her –

'Poor thing! I hope I covered her little *naïveté* properly? How NEW she must be!'

Then, with well-practised dignity, and half-subdued self-complacency of aspect, her ladyship went gliding about – most importantly busy, introducing my lady *this* to the sphynx candelabra, and my lady *that* to the Trebisond trellice; placing some delightfully for the perspective of the Alhambra; establishing others quite to her satisfaction on seraglio ottomans; and honouring others with a seat under the statira canopy. Receiving and answering compliments from successive crowds of select friends, imagining herself the mirror of fashion, and the admiration of the whole world, Lady Clonbrony was, for her hour, as happy certainly as ever woman was in similar circumstances.

Her son looked at her, and wished that this happiness could last. Naturally inclined to sympathy, Lord Colambre reproached himself for not feeling as gay at this instant as the occasion required. But the festive scene, the blazing lights, the 'universal hubbub,' failed to raise his spirits. As a dead weight upon them hung the remembrance of Mordicai's denunciations; and, through the midst of this Eastern magnificence, this unbounded profusion, he thought he saw future domestic misery and ruin to those he loved best in the world.

The only object present on which his eye rested with pleasure was Grace Nugent. Beautiful – in elegant and dignified simplicity – thoughtless of herself – yet with a look of thought, and with an air of melancholy, which accorded exactly with his own feelings, and which he believed to arise from the same reflections that had passed in his own mind.

'Miss Broadhurst, Colambre! all the Broadhursts!' said his mother, wakening him, as she passed by, to receive them as they entered. Miss Broadhurst appeared, plainly dressed – plainly, even to singularity – without any diamonds or ornament.

'Brought Philippa to you, my dear Lady Clonbrony, this figure, rather than not bring her at all,' said puffing Mrs Broadhurst; 'and had all the difficulty in the world to get her out at all, and now I've promised she shall stay but half an hour. Sore throat – terrible cold she took in the morning. I'll swear for her, she'd not have come for any one but you.'

The young lady did not seem inclined to swear, or even to say this for herself; she stood wonderfully unconcerned and passive, with an expression of humour lurking in her eyes, and about the corners of her mouth; whilst Lady Clonbrony was 'shocked,' and 'gratified,' and 'concerned,' and 'flattered'; and whilst everybody was hoping, and fearing, and busying themselves about her – 'Miss Broadhurst, you'd better sit here!' – 'Oh, for Heaven's sake! Miss Broadhurst, not there!' 'Miss Broadhurst, if you'll take my opinion;' and 'Miss Broadhurst, if I may advise – '

'Grace Nugent!' cried Lady Clonbrony – 'Miss Broadhurst always listens to you. Do, my dear, persuade Miss Broadhurst to take care of herself, and let us take her to the inner little pagoda, where she can be so warm and so retired – the very thing for an invalid. Colambre! pioneer the way for us, for the crowd's immense.'

Lady Anne and Lady Catharine H— , Lady Langdale's daughters, were at this time leaning on Miss Nugent's arm, and moved along with this party to the inner pagoda. There was to be cards in one room, music in another, dancing in a third, and, in this little room, there were prints and chess-boards, etc.

'Here you will be quite to yourselves,' said Lady Clonbrony; let me establish you comfortably in this, which I call my sanctuary – my *snuggery* – Colambre, that little table! – Miss Broadhurst, you play chess? Colambre, you'll play with Miss Broadhurst – '

'I thank your ladyship,' said Miss Broadhurst, 'but know nothing of chess, but the moves. Lady Catharine, you will play, and I will look on.'

Miss Broadhurst drew her seat to the fire; Lady Catharine sat down to play with Lord Colambre; Lady Clonbrony withdrew, again recommending Miss Broadhurst to Grace Nugent's care. After some commonplace conversation, Lady Anne! H— , looking at the company in the adjoining apartment, asked her sister how old Miss Somebody was, who passed by. This led to reflections upon the comparative age and youthful appearance of several of their acquaintance, and upon the care with which mothers concealed the age of their daughters. Glances passed between Lady Catharine and Lady Anne.

'For my part,' said Miss Broadhurst, 'my mother would labour that point of secrecy in vain for me; for I am willing to tell my age, even if my face did not tell it for me, to all whom it may concern. I am past three-and-twenty – shall be four-and-twenty the 5th of next July.'

'Three-and-twenty! Bless me! I thought you were not twenty!' cried Lady Anne.

'Four-and-twenty next July! – impossible!' cried Lady Catherine.

'Very possible,' said Miss Broadhurst, quite unconcerned.

'Now, Lord Colambre, would you believe it? Can you believe it?' asked Lady Catharine.

'Yes, he can,' said Miss Broadhurst. 'Don't you see that he believes it as firmly as you and I do? Why should you force his lordship to pay a compliment contrary to his better judgment, or to extort a smile from him under false pretences? I am sure he sees that you, ladies, and I trust he perceives that I, do not think the worse of him for this.'

Lord Colambre smiled now without any false pretence; and, relieved at once from all apprehension of her joining in his mother's views, or of her expecting particular attention from him, he became at ease with Miss Broadhurst, showed a desire to converse with her, and listened eagerly to what she said. He recollected that Grace Nugent had told him that this young lady had no common character; and, neglecting his move at chess, he looked up at Grace as much as to say, '*Draw her out*, pray.'

But Grace was too good a friend to comply with that request; she left Miss Broadhurst to unfold her own character.

'It is your move, my lord,' said Lady Catharine.

'I beg your ladyship's pardon – '

'Are not these rooms beautiful, Miss Broadhurst?' said Lady Catharine, determined, if possible, to turn the conversation into a commonplace, safe channel; for she had just felt, what most of Miss Broadhurst's acquaintance had in their turn felt, that she had an odd way of startling people, by setting their own secret little motives suddenly before them.

'Are not these rooms beautiful?'

'Beautiful! – Certainly.'

The beauty of the rooms would have answered Lady Catharine's purpose for some time, had not Lady Anne imprudently brought the conversation back again to Miss Broadhurst.

'Do you know, Miss Broadhurst,' said she, 'that if I had fifty sore throats, I could not have refrained from my diamonds on this GALA night; and such diamonds as you have! Now, really, I could not believe you to be the same person we saw blazing at the opera the other night!'

'Really! could not you, Lady Anne? That is the very thing that entertains me. I only wish that I could lay aside my fortune sometimes, as well as my diamonds, and see how few people would know me then. Might not I, Grace, by the golden rule, which, next to practice, is the best rule in the world, calculate and answer that question?'

'I am persuaded,' said Lord Colambre, 'that Miss Broadhurst has friends on whom the experiment would make no difference.'

'I am convinced of it,' said Miss Broadhurst; 'and that is what makes me tolerably happy, though I have the misfortune to be an heiress.'

'That is the oddest speech,' said Lady Anne. 'Now I should so like to be a great heiress, and to have, like you, such thousands and thousands at command.'

'And what can the thousands upon thousands do for me? Hearts, you know, Lady Anne, are to be won only by radiant eyes. Bought hearts your ladyship certainly would not recommend. They're such poor things – no wear at all. Turn them which way you will, you can make nothing of them.'

'You've tried then, have you?' said Lady Catharine.

'To my cost. Very nearly taken in by them half a dozen times; for they are brought to me by dozens; and they are so made up for sale, and the people do so swear to you that it's real, real love, and it looks so like it; and, if you stoop to examine it, you hear it pressed upon you by such elegant oaths – By all that's lovely! – By all my hopes of happiness! – By your own charming self! Why, what can one do but look like a fool, and believe; for these men, at the time, all look so like gentlemen, that one cannot bring oneself flatly to tell them that they are cheats and swindlers, that they are perjuring their precious souls. Besides, to call a lover a perjured creature is to encourage him. He would have a right to complain if you went back after that.'

'Oh dear! what a move was there!' cried Lady Catharine. 'Miss Broadhurst is so entertaining tonight, notwithstanding her sore throat, that one can positively attend to nothing else. And she talks of love and lovers too with such *connoissance de fait* – counts her lovers by dozens, tied up in true-lovers' knots!'

'Lovers! – no, no! Did I say lovers? – suitors I should have said.

There's nothing less like a lover, a true lover, than a suitor, as all the world knows, ever since the days of Penelope. Dozens! – never had a lover in my life! And fear, with much reason, I never shall have one to my mind.'

'My lord, you've given up the game,' cried Lady Catharine; 'but you make no battle.'

'It would be so vain to combat against your ladyship,' said Lord Colambre, rising, and bowing politely to Lady Catharine, but turning the next instant to converse with Miss Broadhurst.

'But when I talked of liking to be an heiress,' said Lady Anne, 'I was not thinking of lovers.'

'Certainly. One is not always thinking of lovers, you know,' added Lady Catharine.

'Not always,' replied Miss Broadhurst. 'Well, lovers out of the question on all sides, what would your ladyship buy with the thousands upon thousands?'

'Oh, everything, if I were you,' said Lady Anne.

'Rank, to begin with,' said Lady Catharine.

'Still my old objection – bought rank is but a shabby thing.'

'But there is so little difference made between bought and hereditary rank in these days,' said Lady Catharine.

'I see a great deal still,' said Miss Broadhurst; 'so much, that I would never buy a title.'

'A title without birth, to be sure,' said Lady Anne, 'would not be so well worth buying; and as birth certainly is not to be bought – '

'And even birth, were it to be bought, I would not buy,' said Miss Broadhurst, 'unless I could be sure to have with it all the politeness, all the noble sentiments, all the magnanimity – in short, all that should grace and dignify high birth.'

'Admirable!' said Lord Colambre. Grace Nugent smiled.

'Lord Colambre, will you have the goodness to put my mother in mind I must go away?'

'I am bound to obey, but I am very sorry for it,' said his lordship.

'Are we to have any dancing tonight, I wonder?' said Lady Catharine. 'Miss Nugent, I am afraid we have made Miss Broadhurst talk so much, in spite of her hoarseness, that Lady Clonbrony will be quite angry with us. And here she comes!'

My Lady Clonbrony came to hope, to beg, that Miss Broadhurst would not think of running away; but Miss Broadhurst could not be prevailed upon to stay. Lady Clonbrony was delighted to see that her son assisted Grace Nugent most carefully in *shawling* Miss Broadhurst; his lordship conducted her to her carriage, and his mother drew many happy auguries from the gallantry of his manner, and from the young lady's having stayed three-quarters, instead of half an hour – a circumstance which Lady Catharine did not fail to remark.

The dancing, which, under various pretences, Lady Clonbrony had delayed till Lord Colambre was at liberty, began immediately after Miss Broadhurst's departure; and the chalked mosaic pavement of the Alhambra was, in a few minutes, effaced by the dancers' feet. How transient are all human joys, especially those of vanity! Even on this long meditated, this long desired, this gala night, Lady Clonbrony found her triumph incomplete – inadequate to her expectations. For the first hour all had been compliment, success, and smiles; presently came the *buts*, and the hesitated objections, and the damning with faint praise. All *that* could be borne. Everybody has his taste – and one person's taste is as good as another's; and while she had Mr Soho to cite, Lady Clonbrony thought she might be well satisfied. But she could not be satisfied with Colonel Heathcock, who, dressed in black, had stretched his 'fashionable length of limb' under the statira canopy upon the snow-white swan-down couch. When, after having monopolised attention, and been the subject of much bad wit, about black swans and rare birds, and swans being geese and geese being swans, the colonel condescended to rise, and, as Mrs Dareville said, to vacate his couch, that couch was no longer white – the black impression of the colonel remained on the sullied snow.

'Eh, now! really didn't recollect I was in black,' was all the apology he made. Lady Clonbrony was particularly vexed that the appearance of the statira canopy should be spoiled before the effect had been seen by Lady Pococke, and Lady Chatterton, and Lady G—, Lady P—, and the Duke of V—, and a party of superlative fashionables, who had promised *to look in upon her*, but who, late as it was, had not yet arrived. They came in at last. But Lady Clonbrony had no reason to regret for their sake the statira couch. It would have been lost upon them, as was everything else which she had prepared with so much pains and cost to excite their admiration. They came resolute not to admire. Skilled in the art of making others unhappy, they just looked round with an air of apathy. 'Ah I you've had Soho! – Soho has done wonders for you here! – Vastly well! – Vastly well! – Soho's very clever in his way!'

Others of great importance came in, full of some slight accident that had happened to themselves, or their horses, or their carriages; and, with privileged selfishness, engrossed the attention of all within their sphere of conversation. Well, Lady Clonbrony got over all this, and got over the history of a letter about a chimney that was on fire, a week ago, at the Duke of V—'s old house, in Brecknockshire. In gratitude

for the smiling patience with which she listened to him, his Grace of
V— fixed his glass to look at the Alhambra, and had just pronounced it
to be 'Well! – very well!' when the Dowager Lady Chatterton made a
terrible discovery – a discovery that filled Lady Clonbrony with
astonishment and indignation – Mr Soho had played her false! What
was her mortification when the dowager assured her that these
identical Alhambra hangings had not only been shown by Mr Soho to
the Duchess of Torcaster, but that her grace had had the refusal of
them, and had actually rejected them, in consequence of Sir Horace
Grant the great traveller's objecting to some of the proportions of the
pillars. Soho had engaged to make a new set, vastly improved, by Sir
Horace's suggestions, for her Grace of Torcaster.

Now Lady Chatterton was the greatest talker extant; and she went
about the rooms telling everybody of her acquaintance – and she was
acquainted with everybody – how shamefully Soho had imposed upon
poor Lady Clonbrony, protesting she could not forgive the man. 'For,'
said she, 'though the Duchess of Torcaster has been his constant
customer for ages, and his patroness, and all that, yet this does not
excuse him – and Lady Clonbrony's being a stranger, and from Ireland,
makes the thing worse.' From Ireland! – that was the unkindest cut of
all – but there was no remedy.

In vain poor Lady Clonbrony followed the dowager about the
rooms, to correct this mistake, and to represent, in justice to Mr Soho,
though he had used her so ill, that he knew she was an Englishwoman.
The dowager was deaf, and no whisper could reach her ear. And when
Lady Clonbrony was obliged to bawl an explanation in her ear, the
dowager only repeated –

'In justice to Mr Soho! – No, no; he has not done you justice, my
dear Lady Clonbrony! and I'll expose him to everybody. Englishwoman! – no, no, no! – Soho could not take you for an Englishwoman!'

All who secretly envied or ridiculed Lady Clonbrony enjoyed this
scene. The Alhambra hangings, which had been, in one short hour
before, the admiration of the world, were now regarded by every eye
with contempt, as *cast* hangings, and every tongue was busy declaiming
against Mr Soho; everybody declared that, from the first, the want of
proportion had 'struck them, but that they would not mention it till
others found it out.'

People usually revenge themselves for having admired too much, by
afterwards despising and depreciating without mercy – in all great
assemblies the perception of ridicule is quickly caught, and quickly too
revealed. Lady Clonbrony, even in her own house, on her gala night,
became an object of ridicule – decently masked, indeed, under the

appearance of condolence with her ladyship, and of indignation against 'that abominable Mr Soho!'

Lady Langdale, who was now, for reasons of her own, upon her good behaviour, did penance, as she said, for her former imprudence, by abstaining even from whispered sarcasms. She looked on with penitential gravity, said nothing herself, and endeavoured to keep Mrs Dareville in order; but that was no easy task. Mrs Dareville had no daughters, had nothing to gain from the acquaintance of my Lady Clonbrony; and, conscious that her ladyship would bear a vast deal from her presence, rather than forego the honour of her sanction, Mrs Dareville, without any motives of interest, or good-nature of sufficient power to restrain her talent and habit of ridicule, free from hope or fear, gave full scope to all the malice of mockery, and all the insolence of fashion. Her slings and arrows, numerous as they were and outrageous, were directed against such petty objects, and the mischief was so quick, in its aim and its operation, that, felt but not seen, it is scarcely possible to register the hits, or to describe the nature of the wounds.

Some hits sufficiently palpable, however, were recorded for the advantage of posterity. When Lady Clonbrony led her to look at the Chinese pagoda, the lady paused, with her foot on the threshold, as if afraid to enter this porcelain Elysium, as she called it – Fool's Paradise, she would have said; and, by her hesitation, and by the half-pronounced word, suggested the idea – 'None but belles without petticoats can enter here,' said she, drawing her clothes tight round her; 'fortunately, I have but two, and Lady Langdale has but one.' Prevailed upon to venture in, she walked on with prodigious care and trepidation, affecting to be alarmed at the crowd of strange forms and monsters by which she was surrounded.

'Not a creature here that I ever saw before in nature! Well, now I may boast I've been in a real Chinese pagoda!'

'Why yes, everything is appropriate here, I flatter myself,' said Lady Clonbrony.

'And how good of you, my dear Lady Clonbrony, in defiance of bulls and blunders, to allow us a comfortable English fireplace and plenty of Newcastle coal, in China! – And a white marble – no! white velvet hearthrug, painted with beautiful flowers – oh, the delicate, the *useful thing*!'

Vexed by the emphasis on the word *useful*, Lady Clonbrony endeavoured to turn off the attention of the company. 'Lady Langdale, your ladyship's a judge of china – this vase is an unique, I am told.'

'I am told,' interrupted Mrs Dareville, 'this is the very vase in which

B— , the nabob's father, who was, you know, a China captain, smuggled his dear little Chinese wife and all her fortune out of Canton – positively, actually put the lid on, packed her up, and sent her off on shipboard! – True! true! upon my veracity! I'll tell you my authority!'

With this story Mrs Dareville drew all attention from the jar, to Lady Clonbrony's infinite mortification.

Lady Langdale at length turned to look at a vast range of china jars.

'Ali Baba and the forty thieves!' exclaimed Mrs Dareville; 'I hope you have boiling oil ready!'

Lady Clonbrony was obliged to laugh, and to vow that Mrs Dareville was uncommon pleasant tonight. 'But now,' said her ladyship, 'let me take you on to the Turkish tent.'

Having with great difficulty got the malicious wit out of the pagoda and into the Turkish tent, Lady Clonbrony began to breathe more freely; for here she thought she was upon safe ground: 'Everything, I flatter myself,' said she, 'is correct and appropriate, and quite picturesque.' The company, dispersed in happy groups, or reposing on seraglio ottomans, drinking lemonade and sherbet – beautiful Fatimas admiring, or being admired – 'Everything here quite correct, appropriate, and picturesque,' repeated Mrs Dareville.

This lady's powers as a mimic were extraordinary, and she found them irresistible. Hitherto she had imitated Lady Clonbrony's air and accent only behind her back; but, bolder grown, she now ventured, in spite of Lady Langdale's warning pinches, to mimic her kind hostess before her face, and to her face. Now, whenever Lady Clonbrony saw anything that struck her fancy in the dress of her fashionable friends, she had a way of hanging her head aside, and saying, with a peculiar sentimental drawl –

'How pretty! – how elegant! Now that quite suits my *teeste*!' This phrase, precisely in the same accent, and with the head set to the same angle of affectation, Mrs Dareville had the assurance to address to her ladyship, apropos to something which she pretended to admire in Lady Clonbrony's *costume* – a costume which, excessively fashionable in each of its parts, was, all together, so extraordinarily unbecoming as to be fit for a print-shop. The perception of this, added to the effect of Mrs Dareville's mimicry, was almost too much for Lady Langdale; she could not possibly have stood it, but for the appearance of Miss Nugent at this instant behind Lady Clonbrony. Grace gave one glance of indignation which seemed suddenly to strike Mrs Dareville. Silence for a moment ensued, and afterwards the tone of the conversation was changed.

'Salisbury! – explain this to me,' said a lady, drawing Mr Salisbury aside. 'If you are in the secret, do explain this to me; for unless I had seen it, I could not have believed it. Nay, though I have seen it, I do not believe it. How was that daring spirit laid? By what spell?'

'By the spell which superior minds always cast on inferior spirits.'

'Very fine,' said the lady, laughing, 'but as old as the days of Leonora de Galigai, quoted a million times. Now tell me something new and to the purpose, and better suited to modern days.'

'Well, then, since you will not allow me to talk of superior minds in the present days, let me ask you if you have never observed that a wit, once conquered in company by a wit of a higher order, is thenceforward in complete subjection to the conqueror, whenever and wherever they meet.'

'You would not persuade me that yonder gentle-looking girl could ever be a match for the veteran Mrs Dareville? She may have the wit, but has she the courage?'

'Yes; no one has more courage, more civil courage, where her own dignity, or the interests of her friends are concerned. I will tell you an instance or two tomorrow.'

'Tomorrow! – Tonight! – tell it me now.'

'Not a safe place.'

'The safest in the world, in such a crowd as this. Follow my example. Take a glass of orgeat – sip from time to time, thus – speak low, looking innocent all the while straight forward, or now and then up at the lamps – keep on in an even tone – use no names – and you may tell anything.'

'Well, then, when Miss Nugent first came to London, Lady Langdale – '

'Two names already – did not I warn ye?'

'But how can I make myself intelligible?'

'Initials – can't you use – or genealogy? What stops you? – It is only Lord Colambre, a very safe person, I have a notion, when the eulogium is of Grace Nugent.'

Lord Colambre, who had now performed his arduous duties as a dancer, and had disembarrassed himself of all his partners, came into the Turkish tent just at this moment to refresh himself, and just in time to hear Mr Salisbury's anecdotes.

'Now go on.'

'Lady Langdale, you know, sets an inordinate value upon her curtsies in public, and she used to treat Miss Nugent, as her ladyship treats many other people, sometimes noticing, and sometimes pretending not to know her, according to the company she happened to be with. One day they met in some fine company – Lady Langdale looked as if she was afraid of committing herself by a curtsy. Miss Nugent waited for a good opportunity; and, when all the world was silent, leant forward, and called to Lady Langdale, as if she had something to communicate of the greatest consequence, skreening her whisper with her hand, as in an aside on the stage, – 'Lady Langdale, you may curtsy to me now – nobody is looking.'

'The retort courteous!' said Lord Colambre – 'the only retort for a woman.'

'And her ladyship deserved it so well. But Mrs Dareville, what happened about her?'

'Mrs Dareville, you remember, some years ago, went to Ireland with some lady-lieutenant to whom she was related. There she was most hospitably received by Lord and Lady Clonbrony – went to their country house – was as intimate with Lady Clonbrony and with Miss Nugent as possible – stayed at Clonbrony Castle for a month; and yet, when Lady Clonbrony came to London, never took the least notice of her. At last, meeting at the house of a common friend, Mrs Dareville could not avoid recognising her ladyship; but, even then, did it in the least civil manner and most cursory style possible. "Ho! Lady Clonbrony! – didn't know you were in England! – When did you come? – How long shall you stay in town? – Hope, before you leave England, your ladyship and Miss Nugent will give us a day?" *A day!* – Lady Clonbrony was so astonished by this impudence of ingratitude, that she hesitated how to *take it*; but Miss Nugent, quite coolly, and with a smile, answered, 'A day! – certainly – to you, who gave us a month!'

'Admirable! Now I comprehend perfectly why Mrs Dareville declines insulting Miss Nugent's friends in her presence.'

Lord Colambre said nothing, but thought much. 'How I wish my mother,' thought he, 'had some of Grace Nugent's proper pride! She would not then waste her fortune, spirits, health, and life, in courting such people as these.'

He had not seen – he could not have borne to have beheld – the manner of her guests; but he observed that she now looked harassed and vexed; and he was provoked and mortified by hearing her begging and beseeching some of these saucy leaders of the ton to oblige her, to do her the favour, to do her the honour, to stay to supper. It was just ready – actually announced. 'No, they would not – they could not; they were obliged to run away – engaged to the Duchess of Torcaster.'

'Lord Colambre, what is the matter?' said Miss Nugent, going up to him, as he stood aloof and indignant: 'Don't look so like a chafed lion; others may perhaps read your countenance as well as I do.'

'None can read my mind as well,' replied he. 'Oh, my dear Grace!'

'Supper! – supper!' cried she; 'your duty to your neighbour, your hand to your partner.'

Lady Catherine, as they went downstairs to supper, observed that Miss Nugent had not been dancing, that she had kept quite in the background all night – quite in the shade.

'Those,' said Lord Colambre, 'who are contented in the shade are the best able to bear the light; and I am not surprised that one so interesting in the background should not desire to be the foremost figure in a piece.'

The supper room, fitted up at great expense, with scenery to imitate Vauxhall, opened into a superb greenhouse, lighted with coloured lamps, a band of music at a distance – every delicacy, every luxury that could gratify the senses, appeared in profusion. The company ate and drank – enjoyed themselves – went away – and laughed at their hostess. Some, indeed, who thought they had been neglected, were in too bad humour to laugh, but abused in sober earnest; for the Lady Clonbrony had offended half, nay three-quarters of her guests, by what they termed her exclusive attention to those very leaders of the ton, from whom she had suffered so much, and who had made it obvious to all that they thought they did her too much honour in appearing at her gala. So ended the gala for which she had lavished such sums; for which she had laboured so indefatigably; and from which she had expected such triumph.

'Colambre, bid the musicians stop; they are playing to empty benches,' said Lady Clonbrony. 'Grace, my dear, will you see that these lamps are safely put out? I am so tired, so *worn out*, I must go to bed; and I am sure I have caught cold too! What a *nervous business* it is to manage theses things! I wonder how one gets through it, or *why* one does it!'

Chapter 4

LADY CLONBRONY was taken ill the day after her gala; she had caught cold by standing, when much overheated, in a violent draught of wind, paying her parting compliments to the Duke of V—, who thought her a *bore*, and wished her in heaven all the time for keeping his horses standing. Her ladyship's illness was severe and long; she was confined to her room for some weeks by a rheumatic fever, and an inflammation in her eyes. Every day, when Lord Colambre went to see his mother, he found Miss Nugent in her apartment, and every hour he found fresh reason to admire this charming girl. The affectionate tenderness, the indefatigable patience, the strong attachment she showed for her aunt, actually raised Lady Clonbrony in her son's opinion. He was persuaded she must surely have some good or great qualities, or she could not have excited such strong affection. A few foibles out of the question, such as her love of fine people, her affectation of being English, and other affectations too tedious to mention, Lady Clonbrony was really a good woman, had good principles, moral and religious, and, selfishness not immediately interfering, she was good-natured; and though her soul and attention were so completely absorbed in the duties of acquaintanceship that she did not know it, she really had affections – they were concentrated upon a few near relations. She was extremely fond and extremely proud of her son. Next to her son, she was fonder of her niece than of any other creature. She had received Grace Nugent into her family when she was left an orphan, and deserted by some of her other relations. She had bred her up, and had treated her with constant kindness. This kindness and these obligations had raised the warmest gratitude in Miss Nugent's heart; and it was the strong principle of gratitude which rendered her capable of endurance and exertions seemingly far above her strength. This young lady was not of a robust appearance, though she now underwent extraordinary fatigue. Her aunt could scarcely bear that she should leave her for a moment: she could not close her eyes unless Grace sat up with her many hours every night. Night after night she bore this fatigue; and yet, with little sleep or rest, she preserved her health, at least supported her spirits; and every morning, when Lord Colambre came into his mother's room, he saw Miss Nugent look as blooming as if she had enjoyed the most refreshing sleep. The bloom was, as he observed, not permanent; it came and went, with every emotion of her feeling heart; and he soon learned to fancy her almost as handsome when she was pale as when she had a colour. He had thought her beautiful when he beheld her in all the radiance of light, and with all the advantages of dress at the gala, but he found her infinitely more lovely and interesting now, when he saw her in a sick-room – a half-darkened chamber – where often he could but just discern her form, or distinguish her, except by her graceful motion as she passed, or when, but for a moment, a window-curtain drawn aside let the sun shine upon her face, or on the unadorned ringlets of her hair.

Much must be allowed for an inflammation in the eyes, and something for a rheumatic fever; yet it may seem strange that Lady Clonbrony should be so blind and deaf as neither to see nor hear all this time; that, having lived so long in the world, it should never occur to her that it was rather imprudent to have a young lady, not eighteen, nursing her – and such a young lady! – when her son, not one-and-twenty – and such a son! – came to visit her daily. But, so it was. Lady Clonbrony knew nothing of love – she had read of it, indeed, in novels, which sometimes for fashion's sake she had looked at, and over which she had been obliged to doze; but this was only love in books – love in real life she had never met with – in the life she led, how should she? She had heard of its making young people, and old people even, do foolish things; but those were foolish people; and if they were worse than foolish, why it was shocking, and nobody visited them. But Lady Clonbrony had not, for her own part, the slightest notion how people could be brought to this pass, nor how anybody out of Bedlam could prefer to a good house, a decent equipage, and a proper establishment, what is called love in a cottage. As to Colambre, she had too good an opinion of his understanding – to say nothing of his duty to his family, his pride, his rank, and his being her son – to let such an idea cross her imagination. As to her niece; in the first place, she was her niece, and first cousins should never marry, because they form no new connections to strengthen the family interest, or raise its consequence. This doctrine her ladyship had repeated for years so often and so dogmatically, that she conceived it to be incontrovertible, and of as full force as any law of the land, or as any moral or religious obligation. She would as soon have suspected her niece of an intention of stealing her diamond necklace as of purloining Colambre's heart, or marrying this heir of the house of Clonbrony.

Miss Nugent was so well apprised, and so thoroughly convinced of all this, that she never for one moment allowed herself to think of Lord Colambre as a lover. Duty, honour, and gratitude – gratitude, the strong feeling and principle of her mind – forbade it; she had so prepared and habituated herself to consider him as a person with whom she could not possibly be united that, with perfect ease and simplicity, she behaved towards him exactly as if he was her brother – not in the equivocating sentimental romance style in which ladies talk of treating men as their brothers, whom they are all the time secretly thinking of and endeavouring to please as lovers – not using this phrase as a convenient pretence, a safe mode of securing herself from suspicion or scandal, and of enjoying the advantages of confidence and the intimacy of friendship, till the propitious moment, when it should be time to declare or avow *the secret of the heart*. No; this young lady was quite above all double-dealing; she had no mental reservation – no metaphysical subtleties – but, with plain, unsophisticated morality, in good faith and simple truth, acted as she professed, thought what she said, and was that which she seemed to be.

As soon as Lady Clonbrony was able to see anybody, her niece sent to Mrs Broadhurst, who was very intimate with the family; she used to come frequently, almost every evening, to sit with the invalid. Miss Broadhurst accompanied her mother, for she did not like to go out with any other chaperon – it was disagreeable to spend her time alone at home, and most agreeable to spend it with her friend Miss Nugent. In this she had no design, no coquetry; Miss Broadhurst had too lofty and independent a spirit to stoop to coquetry: she thought that, in their interview at the gala, she understood Lord Colambre, and that he understood her – that he was not inclined to court her for her fortune – that she would not be content with any suitor who was not a lover. She was two or three years older than Lord Colambre, perfectly aware of her want of beauty, yet with a just sense of her own merit, and of what was becoming and due to the dignity of her sex. This, she trusted, was visible in her manners, and established in Lord Colambre's mind; so that she ran no risk of being misunderstood by him; and as to what the rest of the world thought, she was so well used to hear weekly and daily reports of her going to be married to fifty different people, that she cared little for what was said on this subject. Indeed, conscious of rectitude, and with an utter contempt for mean and commonplace gossiping, she was, for a woman, and a young woman, rather too disdainful of the opinion of the world. Mrs Broadhurst, though her daughter had fully explained herself respecting Lord Colambre, before she began this course of visiting, yet rejoiced that, even on this footing, there should be constant intercourse between them. It was Mrs Broadhurst's warmest wish that her daughter should obtain rank, and connect herself with an ancient family: she was sensible that the young lady's being older than the gentleman might be an obstacle; and very sorry she was to find that her daughter had so imprudently, so unnecessarily, declared her age; but still this little obstacle might be overcome; much greater difficulties in the marriage of inferior heiresses were every day got over, and thought nothing of. Then, as to the young lady's own sentiments, her mother knew them better than she did herself; she understood her daughter's pride, that she dreaded to be made an object of bargain and sale; but Mrs Broadhurst, who, with all her coarseness of mind, had rather a better notion of love matters than Lady Clonbrony, perceived, through her daughter's horror of being offered to Lord Colambre, through her anxiety that nothing approaching to an advance on the part of her family should be made, that if Lord Colambre should himself advance, he would stand a better chance of being accepted than any other of the numerous persons who had yet aspired to the favour of this heiress. The very circumstance of his having paid no court to her at first, operated in his favour; for it proved that he was not mercenary, and that, whatever attention he might afterwards show, she must be sure would be sincere and disinterested.

'And now, let them but see one another in this easy, intimate kind of way, and you will find, my dear Lady Clonbrony, things will go on of their own accord, all the better for our – minding our cards – and never minding anything else. I remember, when I was young – but let that pass – let the young people see one another, and manage their own affairs their own way – let them be together – that's all I say. Ask half the men you are acquainted with why they married, and their answer, if they speak truth, will be: "Because I met Miss such-a-one at such a place, and we were continually together." Propinquity! propinquity! – as my father used to say – and he was married five times, and twice to heiresses.'

In consequence of this plan of leaving things to themselves, every evening Lady Clonbrony made out her own little card-table with Mrs Broadhurst, and a Mr and Miss Pratt, a brother and sister, who were the most obliging, convenient neighbours imaginable. From time to time, as Lady Clonbrony gathered up her cards, she would direct an inquiring glance to the group of young people at the other table; whilst the more prudent Mrs Broadhurst sat plump with her back to them, pursing up her lips, and contracting her brows in token of deep calculation, looking down impenetrable at her cards, never even noticing Lady Clonbrony's glances, but inquiring from her partner, 'How many they were by honours?'

The young party generally consisted of Miss Broadhurst, Lord Colambre, Miss Nugent, and her admirer, Mr Salisbury. Mr Salisbury was a middle-aged gentleman, very agreeable, and well informed; he had travelled; had seen a great deal of the world; had lived in the best company; had acquired what is called good *tact*; was full of anecdote, not mere gossiping anecdotes that lead to nothing, but anecdotes characteristic of national manners, of human nature in general, or of those illustrious individuals who excite public curiosity and interest. Miss Nugent had seen him always in large companies, where he was admired for his *savoir-vivre*, and for his entertaining anecdotes, but where he had no opportunity of producing any of the higher powers of his understanding, or showing character. She found that Mr Salisbury appeared to her quite a different person when conversing with Lord Colambre. Lord Colambre, with that ardent thirst for knowledge which it is always agreeable to gratify, had an air of openness and generosity, a frankness, a warmth of manner, which, with good breeding, but with something beyond it and superior to its established forms, irresistibly won the confidence and attracted the affection of those with whom he conversed. His manners were peculiarly agreeable to a person like Mr Salisbury, tired of the sameness and egotism of men of the world.

Miss Nugent had seldom till now had the advantage of hearing much conversation on literary subjects. In the life she had been compelled to lead she had acquired accomplishments, had exercised her understanding upon everything that passed before her, and from circumstances had formed her judgment and her taste by observations on real life; but the ample page of knowledge had never been unrolled to her eyes. She had never had opportunities of acquiring literature herself, but she admired it in others, particularly in her friend Miss Broadhurst. Miss Broadhurst had received all the advantages of education which money could procure, and had profited by them in a manner uncommon among those for whom they are purchased in such abundance; she not only had had many masters, and read many books, but had thought of what she read, and had supplied, by the strength and energy of her own mind, what cannot be acquired by the assistance of masters. Miss Nugent, perhaps overvaluing the information that she did not possess, and free from all idea of envy, looked up to her friend as to a superior being, with a sort of enthusiastic admiration; and now, with 'charmed attention,' listened, by turns, to her, to Mr Salisbury, and to Lord Colambre, whilst they conversed on literary subjects – listened, with a countenance so full of intelligence, of animation so expressive of every good and kind affection, that the gentlemen did not always know what they were saying.

'Pray go on,' said she, once, to Mr Salisbury; 'you stop, perhaps, from politeness to me – from compassion to my ignorance; but, though I am ignorant, you do not tire me, I assure you. Did you ever condescend to read the Arabian tales? Like him whose eyes were touched by the magical application from the dervise, I am enabled at once to see the riches of a new world – Oh! how unlike, how superior to that in which I have lived! – the GREAT world, as it is called.'

Lord Colambre brought down a beautiful edition of the Arabian tales, looked for the story to which Miss Nugent had alluded, and showed it to Miss Broadhurst, who was also searching for it in another volume.

Lady Clonbrony, from her card-table, saw the young people thus engaged.

'I profess not to understand these things so well as you say you do, my dear Mrs Broadhurst,' whispered she; 'but look there now; they are at their books! What do you expect can come of that sort of thing? So ill-bred, and downright rude of Colambre, I must give him a hint.'

'No, no, for mercy's sake! my dear Lady Clonbrony, no hints, no hints, no remarks! What would you have? – she reading, and my lord at the back of her chair, leaning over – and allowed, mind, to lean over to read the same thing. Can't be better! Never saw any man yet allowed to come so near her! Now, Lady Clonbrony, not a word, not a look, I beseech.'

'Well, well! – but if they had a little music.'

'My daughter's tired of music. How much do I owe your ladyship now? – three rubbers, I think. Now, though you would not believe it of a young girl,' continued Mrs Broadhurst, 'I can assure your ladyship, my daughter would often rather go to a book than a ball.'

'Well, now, that's very extraordinary, in the style in which she has been brought up; yet books and all that are so fashionable now, that it's very natural,' said Lady Clonbrony.

About this time, Mr Berryl, Lord Colambre's Cambridge friend, for whom his lordship had fought the battle of the curricle with Mordicai, came to town. Lord Colambre introduced him to his mother, by whom he was graciously received; for Mr Berryl was a young gentleman of good figure, good address, good family, heir to a good fortune, and in every respect a fit match for Miss Nugent. Lady Clonbrony thought that it would be wise to secure him for her niece before he should make his appearance in the London world, where mothers and daughters would soon make him feel his own consequence. Mr Berryl, as Lord Colambre's intimate friend, was admitted to the private evening parties at Lady Clonbrony's, and he contributed to render them still more agreeable. His information, his habits of thinking, and his views, were all totally different from Mr Salisbury's; and their collision continually struck out that sparkling novelty which pleases peculiarly in conversation. Mr Berryl's education, disposition, and tastes, fitted him exactly for the station which he was destined to fill in society – that of *a country gentleman*; not meaning by that expression a mere eating, drinking, hunting, shooting, ignorant country squire of the old race, which is now nearly extinct; but a cultivated, enlightened, independent English country gentleman – the happiest, perhaps, of human beings. On the comparative felicity of the town and country life; on the dignity, utility, elegance, and interesting nature of their different occupations, and general scheme of passing their time, Mr Berryl and Mr Salisbury had one evening a playful, entertaining, and, perhaps, instructive conversation; each party, at the end, remaining, as frequently happens, of their own opinion. It was observed that Miss Broadhurst ably and warmly defended Mr Berryl's side of the question; and in their views, plans, and estimates of life, there appeared a remarkable, and as Lord Colambre thought, a happy coincidence. When she was at last called upon to give her decisive judgment between a town and a country life, she declared that 'if she were condemned to the extremes of either, she should prefer a country life, as much as she should prefer Robinson Crusoe's diary to the journal of the idle man in the *Spectator*.'

'Lord bless me! Mrs Broadhurst, do you hear what your daughter is saying?' cried Lady Clonbrony, who, from the card-table, lent an attentive ear to all that was going forward. 'Is it possible that Miss Broadhurst, with her fortune, and pretensions, and sense, can really be serious in saying she would be content to live in the country?'

'What's that you say, child, about living in the country?' said Mrs Broadhurst.

Miss Broadhurst repeated what she had said.

'Girls always think so who have lived in town,' said Mrs Broadhurst. 'They are always dreaming of sheep and sheep-hooks; but the first winter the country cures them; a shepherdess, in winter, is a sad and sorry sort of personage, except at a masquerade.'

'Colambre,' said Lady Clonbrony, 'I am sure Miss Broadhurst's sentiments about town life, and all that, must delight you; for do you know, ma'am, he is always trying to persuade me to give up living in town? Colambre and Miss Broadhurst perfectly agree.'

'Mind your cards, my dear Lady Clonbrony,' interrupted Mrs Broadhurst, 'in pity to your partner. Mr Pratt has certainly the patience of Job – your ladyship has revoked twice this hand.'

Lady Clonbrony begged a thousand pardons, fixed her eyes and endeavoured to fix her mind on the cards; but there was something said at the other end of the room, about an estate in Cambridgeshire, which soon distracted her attention again. Mr Pratt certainly had the patience of Job. She revoked, and lost the game, though they had four by honours.

As soon as she rose from the card-table, and could speak to Mrs Broadhurst apart, she communicated her apprehensions.

'Seriously, my dear madam,' said she, 'I believe I have done very wrong to admit Mr Berryl just now, though it was on Grace's account I did it. But, ma'am, I did not know Miss Broadhurst had an estate in Cambridgeshire; their two estates just close to one another, I heard them say. Lord bless me, ma'am! there's the danger of propinquity indeed!'

'No danger, no danger,' persisted Mrs Broadhurst. 'I know my girl better than you do, begging your ladyship's pardon. No one thinks less of estates than she does.'

'Well, I only know I heard her talking of them, and earnestly too.'

'Yes, very likely; but don't you know that girls never think of what they are talking about, or rather never talk of what they are thinking about? And they have always ten times more to say to the man they don't care for, than to him they do.'

'Very extraordinary!' said Lady Clonbrony. 'I only hope you are right.'

'I am sure of it,' said Mrs Broadhurst. 'Only let things go on, and mind your cards, I beseech you, tomorrow night better than you did tonight; and you will see that things will turn out just as I prophesied. Lord Colambre will come to a point-blank proposal before the end of the week, and will be accepted, or my name's not Broadhurst. Why in plain English, I am clear my girl likes him; and when that's the case, you know, can you doubt how the thing will end?'

Mrs Broadhurst was perfectly right in every point of her reasoning but one. From long habit of seeing and considering that such an heiress as her daughter might marry whom she pleased – from constantly seeing that she was the person to decide and to reject – Mrs Broadhurst had literally taken it for granted that everything was to depend upon her daughter's inclinations: she was not mistaken, in the present case, in opining that the young lady would not be averse to Lord Colambre, if he came to what she called a point-blank proposal. It really never occurred to Mrs Broadhurst that any man, whom her daughter was the least inclined to favour, could think of anybody else. Quick-sighted in these affairs as the matron thought herself, she saw but one side of the question: blind and dull of comprehension as she thought Lady Clonbrony on this subject, she was herself so completely blinded by her own prejudices, as to be incapable of discerning the plain thing that was before her eyes; *videlicet*, that Lord Colambre preferred Grace Nugent. Lord Colambre made no proposal before the end of the week, but this Mrs Broadhurst attributed to an unexpected occurrence, which prevented things from going on in the train in which they had been proceeding so smoothly. Sir John Berryl, Mr Berryl's father, was suddenly seized with a dangerous illness. The news was brought to Mr Berryl one evening whilst he was at Lady Clonbrony's. The circumstances of domestic distress, which afterwards occurred in the family of his friend, entirely occupied Lord Colambre's time and attention. All thoughts of love were suspended, and his whole mind was given up to the active services of friendship. The sudden illness of Sir John Berryl spread an alarm among his creditors which brought to light at once the disorder of his affairs, of which his son had no knowledge or suspicion. Lady Berryl had been a very expensive woman, especially in equipages; and Mordicai, the coachmaker, appeared at this time the foremost and the most inexorable of their creditors. Conscious that the charges in his account were exorbitant, and that they would not be allowed if examined by a court of justice; that it was a debt which only ignorance and extravagance could have in the first instance incurred, swelled afterwards to an amazing amount by interest, and interest upon interest; Mordicai was impatient to obtain payment whilst Sir John yet lived, or at least to obtain legal security for the whole sum from the heir. Mr Berryl offered his bond for the amount of the reasonable charges in his account; but this Mordicai absolutely refused, declaring that now he had the power in his own hands, he would use it to obtain the utmost penny of his debt; that he would not let the thing slip through his fingers; that a debtor never yet escaped him, and never should; that a man's lying upon his deathbed was no excuse to a creditor; that he was not a whiffler, to stand upon ceremony about disturbing a gentleman in his last moments; that he was not to be cheated out of his due by such niceties; that he was prepared to go all lengths the law would allow; for that, as to what people said of him, he did not care a doit – 'Cover your face with your hands, if you like it, Mr Berryl; you may be ashamed for me, but I feel no shame for myself – I am not so weak.' Mordicai's countenance said more than his words; livid with malice, and with atrocious determination in his eyes, he stood. 'Yes, sir,' said he, 'you may look at me as you please – it is possible – I am in earnest. Consult what you'll do now, behind my back or before my face, it comes to the same thing; for nothing will do but my money or your bond, Mr Berryl. The arrest is made on the person of your father, luckily made while the breath is still in the body. Yes – start forward to strike me, if you dare – your father, Sir John Berryl, sick or well, is my prisoner.'

Lady Berryl and Mr Berryl's sisters, in an agony of grief, rushed into the room.

'It's all useless,' cried Mordicai, turning his back upon the ladies; 'these tricks upon creditors won't do with me; I'm used to these scenes; I'm not made of such stuff as you think. Leave a gentleman in peace in his last moments. No! he ought not, nor shan't die in peace, if he don't pay his debts; and if you are all so mighty sorry, ladies, there's the gentleman you may kneel to; if tenderness is the order of the day, it's for the son to show it, not me. Ay, now, Mr Berryl,' cried he, as Mr Berryl took up the bond to sign it, 'you're beginning to know I'm not a fool to be trifled with. Stop your hand, if you choose it, sir – it's all the same to me; the person, or the money, I'll carry with me out of this house.'

Mr Berryl signed the bond, and threw it to him.

'There, monster! – quit the house!'

'*Monster* is not actionable – I wish you had called me *rascal*,' said Mordicai, grinning a horrible smile; and taking up the bond deliberately, returned it to Mr Berryl. 'This paper is worth nothing to me, sir – it is not witnessed.'

Mr Berryl hastily left the room, and returned with Lord Colambre. Mordicai changed countenance and grew pale, for a moment, at sight of Lord Colambre.

'Well, my lord, since it so happens, I am not sorry that you should be witness to this paper,' said he; 'and indeed not sorry that you should witness the whole proceeding; for I trust I shall be able to explain to you my conduct.'

'I do not come here, sir,' interrupted Lord Colambre, 'to listen to any explanations of your conduct, which I perfectly understand; – I come to witness a bond for my friend Mr Berryl, if you think proper to extort from him such a bond.'

'I extort nothing, my lord. Mr Berryl, it is quite a voluntary act, take notice, on your part; sign or not, witness or not, as you please, gentlemen,' said Mordicai, sticking his hands in his pockets, and recovering his look of black and fixed determination.

'Witness it, witness it, my dear lord,' said Mr Berryl, looking at his mother and weeping sisters; 'witness it, quick!'

'Mr Berryl must just run over his name again in your presence, my lord, with a dry pen,' said Mordicai, putting the pen into Mr Berryl's hand.

'No, sir,' said Lord Colambre, 'my friend shall never sign it.'

'As you please, my lord – the bond or the body, before I quit this house,' said Mordicai.

'Neither, sir, shall you have; and you quit this house directly.'

'How! how! – my lord, how's this?'

'Sir, the arrest you have made is as illegal as it is inhuman.'

'Illegal, my lord!' said Mordicai, startled.

'Illegal, sir. I came into this house at the moment when your bailiff asked and was refused admittance. Afterwards, in the confusion of the family above stairs, he forced open the house door with an iron bar – I saw him – I am ready to give evidence of the fact. Now proceed at your peril.'

Mordicai, without reply snatched up his hat, and walked towards the door; but Lord Colambre held the door open – the door was immediately at the head of the stairs – and Mordicai, seeing his indignant look and proud form, hesitated to pass; for he had always heard that Irishmen are 'quick in the executive part of justice.'

'Pass on, sir,' repeated Lord Colambre, with an air of ineffable contempt: 'I am a gentleman – you have nothing to fear.'

Mordicai ran downstairs; Lord Colambre, before he went back into the room, waited to see Mordicai and his bailiff out of the house. When Mordicai was fairly at the bottom of the stairs, he turned, and, white with rage, looked up at Lord Colambre.

'Charity begins at home, my lord,' said he. 'Look at home – you shall pay for this,' added he, standing half-shielded by the house door, for Lord Colambre moved forward as he spoke the last words; 'and I give you this warning, because I know it will be of no use to you – Your most obedient, my lord.'

The house door closed after Mordicai.

'Thank Heaven!' thought Lord Colambre, 'that I did not horsewhip that mean wretch! This warning shall be of use to me. But it is not time to think of that yet.'

Lord Colambre turned from his own affairs to those of his friend, to offer all the assistance and consolation in his power. Sir John Berryl died that night. His daughters, who had lived in the highest style in London, were left totally unprovided for. His widow had mortgaged her jointure. Mr Berryl had an estate now left to him, but without any income. He could not be so dishonest as to refuse to pay his father's just debts; he could not let his mother and sisters starve. The scene of distress to which Lord Colambre was witness in this family made a still greater impression upon him than had been made by the warning or the threats of Mordicai. The similarity between the circumstances of his friend's family and of his own struck him forcibly.

All this evil had arisen from Lady Berryl's passion for living in London and at watering-places. She had made her husband an ABSENTEE – an absentee from his home, his affairs, his duties, and his estate. The sea, the Irish Channel, did not, indeed, flow between him and his estate; but it was of little importance whether the separation was effected by land or water – the consequences, the negligence, the extravagance, were the same.

Of the few people of his age who are capable of profiting by the experience of others, Lord Colambre was one. 'Experience,' as an elegant writer has observed, 'is an article that may be borrowed with safety, and is often dearly bought.'

Chapter 5

IN THE MEANTIME, Lady Clonbrony had been occupied with thoughts very different from those which passed in the mind of her son. Though she had never completely recovered from her rheumatic pains, she had become inordinately impatient of confinement to her own house, and weary of those dull evenings at home, which had, in her son's absence, become insupportable. She told over her visiting tickets regularly twice a day, and gave to every card of invitation a heartfelt sigh. Miss Pratt alarmed her ladyship, by bringing intelligence of some parties given by persons of consequence, to which she was not invited. She feared that she should be forgotten in the world, well knowing how soon the world forgets those they do not see every day and everywhere. How miserable is the fine lady's lot who cannot forget the world, and who is forgot by the world in a moment! How much more miserable still is the condition of a would-be fine lady, working her way up in the world with care and pains! By her, every the slightest failure of attention, from persons of rank and fashion, is marked and felt with jealous anxiety, and with a sense of mortification the most acute – an invitation omitted is a matter of the most serious consequence, not only as it regards the present, but the future; for if she be not invited by Lady A, it will lower her in the eyes of Lady B, and of all the ladies of the alphabet. It will form a precedent of the most dangerous and inevitable application. If she has nine invitations, and the tenth be wanting, the nine have no power to make her happy. This was precisely Lady Clonbrony's case – there was to be a party at Lady St James's, for which Lady Clonbrony had no card.

'So ungrateful, so monstrous, of Lady St James! – What! was the gala so soon forgotten, and all the marked attentions paid that night to Lady St James! – attentions, you know, Pratt, which were looked upon with a jealous eye, and made me enemies enough, I am told, in another quarter! Of all people, I did not expect to be slighted by Lady St James!'

Miss Pratt, who was ever ready to undertake the defence of any person who had a title, pleaded, in mitigation of censure, that perhaps Lady St James might not be aware that her ladyship was yet well enough to venture out.

'Oh, my dear Miss Pratt, that cannot be the thing; for, in spite of my rheumatism, which really was bad enough last Sunday, I went on purpose to the Royal Chapel, to show myself in the closet, and knelt close to her ladyship. And, my dear, we curtsied, and she congratulated me, after church, upon my being abroad again, and was so happy to see me look so well, and all that – Oh! it is something very extraordinary and unaccountable!'

'But, I daresay, a card will come yet,' said Miss Pratt.

Upon this hint, Lady Clonbrony's hope revived; and, staying her anger, she began to consider how she could manage to get herself invited. Refreshing tickets were left next morning at Lady St James's with their corners properly turned up; to do the thing better, separate tickets for herself and for Miss Nugent were left for each member of the family; and her civil messages, left with the footman, extended to the utmost possibility of remainder. It had occurred to her ladyship that for Miss Somebody, *the companion*, of whom she had never in her life thought before, she had omitted to leave a card last time, and she now left a note of explanation; she further, with her rheumatic head and arm out of the coach-window, sat, the wind blowing keen upon her, explaining to the porter and the footman, to discover whether her former tickets had gone safely up to Lady St James; and on the present occasion, to make assurance doubly sure, she slid handsome expedition money into the servant's hand – 'Sir, you will be sure to remember.' – 'Oh certainly, your ladyship!'

She well knew what dire offence has frequently been taken, what sad disasters have occurred, in the fashionable world, from the neglect of a porter in delivering, or of a footman in carrying up one of those talismanic cards. But, in spite of all her manœuvres, no invitation to the party arrived next day. Pratt was next set to work. Miss Pratt was a most convenient go-between, who, in consequence of doing a thousand little services, to which few others of her rank in life would stoop, had obtained the *entrée* to a number of great houses, and was behind the scenes in many fashionable families. Pratt could find out, and Pratt could hint, and Pratt could manage to get things done cleverly – and hints were given, in all directions, to *work round* to Lady St James. But still they did not take effect. At last Pratt suggested that, perhaps, though everything else had failed, dried salmon might be tried with success. Lord Clonbrony had just had some uncommonly good from Ireland, which Pratt knew Lady St James would like to have at her supper, because a certain personage, whom she would not name, was particularly fond of it. – Wheel within wheel in the fine world, as well as in the political world! – Bribes for all occasions, and for all ranks! The timely present was sent, accepted with many thanks, and under-stood as it was meant. Per favour of this propitiatory offering, and of a promise of half a dozen pair of real Limerick gloves to Miss Pratt – a promise which Pratt clearly comprehended to be a conditional promise – the grand object was at length accomplished. The very day before the party was to take place came cards of invitation to Lady Clonbrony and to Miss Nugent, with Lady St James's apologies; her ladyship was concerned to find that, by some negligence of her servants, these cards were not sent in proper time. 'How slight an apology will do from some people!' thought Miss Nugent; 'how eager to forgive, when it is for our interest or our pleasure; how well people act the being deceived, even when all parties know that they see the whole truth; and how low pride will stoop to gain its object!'

Ashamed of the whole transaction, Miss Nugent earnestly wished that a refusal should be sent, and reminded her aunt of her rheumatism; but rheumatism and all other objections were overruled – Lady Clonbrony would go. It was just when this affair was thus, in her opinion, successfully settled, that Lord Colambre came in, with a countenance of unusual seriousness, his mind full of the melancholy scenes he had witnessed in his friend's family.

'What is the matter, Colambre?'

He related what had passed; he described the brutal conduct of Mordicai; the anguish of the mother and sisters; the distress of Mr Berryl. Tears rolled down Miss Nugent's cheeks. Lady Clonbrony declared it was very *shocking*; listened with attention to all the particulars; but never failed to correct her son, whenever he said Mr Berryl.

'*Sir Arthur* Berryl, you mean.'

She was, however, really touched with compassion when he spoke of Lady Berryl's destitute condition; and her son was going on to repeat what Mordicai had said to him, but Lady Clonbrony interrupted –

'Oh, my dear Colambre! don't repeat that detestable man's impertinent speeches to me. If there is anything really about business, speak to your father. At any rate, don't tell us of it now, because I've a hundred things to do,' said her ladyship, hurrying out of the room. 'Grace – Grace Nugent! I want you!'

Lord Colambre sighed deeply.

'Don't despair,' said Miss Nugent, as she followed to obey her aunt's summons. 'Don't despair; don't attempt to speak to her again till tomorrow morning. Her head is now full of Lady St James's party. When it is emptied of that, you will have a better chance. Never despair.'

'Never, while you encourage me to hope – that any good can be done.'

Lady Clonbrony was particularly glad that she had carried her point

about this party at Lady St James's; because, from the first private
intimation that the Duchess of Torcaster was to be there, her ladyship
flattered herself that the long-desired introduction might then be
accomplished. But of this hope Lady St James had likewise received
intimation from the double-dealing Miss Pratt; and a warning note was
despatched to the duchess to let her grace know that circumstances had
occurred which had rendered it impossible not to ask *the Clonbronies*. An
excuse, of course, for not going to this party was sent by the duchess –
her grace did not like large parties – she would have the pleasure of
accepting Lady St James's invitation for her select party on Wednesday
the 10th. Into these select parties Lady Clonbrony had never been
admitted. In return for her great entertainments she was invited to great
entertainments, to large parties; but farther she could never penetrate.

At Lady St James's, and with her set, Lady Clonbrony suffered a
different kind of mortification from that which Lady Langdale and Mrs
Dareville made her endure. She was safe from the witty raillery, the sly
innuendo, the insolent mimicry; but she was kept at a cold, impassable
distance, by ceremony – 'So far shalt thou go, and no farther' was
expressed in every look, in every word, and in a thousand different ways.

By the most punctilious respect and nice regard to precedency, even
by words of courtesy – 'Your ladyship does me honour,' etc. – Lady St
James contrived to mortify and to mark the difference between those
with whom she was, and with whom she was not, upon terms of
intimacy and equality. Thus the ancient grandees of Spain drew a line
of demarcation between themselves and the newly-created nobility.
Whenever or wherever they met, they treated the new nobles with the
utmost respect, never addressed them but with all their titles, with low
bows, and with all the appearance of being, with the most perfect
consideration, anything but their equals; whilst towards one another
the grandees laid aside their state, and omitting their titles, it was,
'Alcalà – Medina – Sidonia – Infantado,' and a freedom and familiarity
which marked equality. Entrenched in etiquette in this manner, and
mocked with marks of respect, it was impossible either to intrude or to
complain of being excluded.

At supper at Lady St James's, Lady Clonbrony's present was
pronounced by some gentleman to be remarkably high flavoured. This
observation turned the conversation to Irish commodities and Ireland.
Lady Clonbrony, possessed by the idea that it was disadvantageous to
appear as an Irishwoman, or as a favourer of Ireland, began to be
embarrassed by Lady St James's repeated thanks. Had it been in her
power to offer anything else with propriety, she would not have
thought of sending her ladyship anything from Ireland. Vexed by the

questions that were asked her about *her country*, Lady Clonbrony, as usual, denied it to be her country, and went on to depreciate and abuse everything Irish; to declare that there was no possibility of living in Ireland; and that, for her own part, she was resolved never to return thither. Lady St James, preserving perfect silence, let her go on. Lady Clonbrony, imagining that this silence arose from coincidence of opinion, proceeded with all the eloquence she possessed, which was very little, repeating the same exclamations, and reiterating her vow of perpetual expatriation; till at last an elderly lady, who was a stranger to her, and whom she had till this moment scarcely noticed, took up the defence of Ireland with much warmth and energy: the eloquence with which she spoke, and the respect with which she was heard, astonished Lady Clonbrony.

'Who is she?' whispered her ladyship.

'Does not your ladyship know Lady Oranmore – the Irish Lady Oranmore?'

'Lord bless me! – what have I said! – what have I done! Oh! why did not you give me a hint, Lady St James?'

'I was not aware that your ladyship was not acquainted with Lady Oranmore,' replied Lady St James, unmoved by her distress.

Everybody sympathised with Lady Oranmore, and admired the honest zeal with which she abided by her country, and defended it against unjust aspersions and affected execrations. Every one present enjoyed Lady Clonbrony's confusion, except Miss Nugent, who sat with her eyes bowed down by penetrative shame during the whole of this scene; she was glad that Lord Colambre was not witness to it; and comforted herself with the hope that, upon the whole, Lady Clonbrony would be benefited by the pain she had felt. This instance might convince her that it was not necessary to deny her country to be received in any company in England; and that those who have the courage and steadiness to be themselves, and to support what they feel and believe to be the truth, must command respect. Miss Nugent hoped that in consequence of this conviction Lady Clonbrony would lay aside the little affectations by which her manners were painfully constrained and ridiculous; and, above all, she hoped that what Lady Oranmore had said of Ireland might dispose her aunt to listen with patience to all Lord Colambre might urge in favour of returning to her home. But Miss Nugent hoped in vain. Lady Clonbrony never in her life generalised any observations, or drew any but a partial conclusion from the most striking facts.

'Lord! my dear Grace!' said she, as soon as they were seated in their carriage, 'what a scrape I got into tonight at supper, and what disgrace I came to! – and all this because I did not know Lady Oranmore. Now you see the inconceivable disadvantage of not knowing everybody – everybody of a certain rank, of course, I mean.'

Miss Nugent endeavoured to slide in her own moral on the occasion, but it would not do.

'Yes, my dear, Lady Oranmore may talk in that kind of style of Ireland, because, on the other hand, she is so highly connected in England; and, besides, she is an old lady, and may take liberties; in short, she is Lady Oranmore, and that's enough.'

The next morning, when they all met at breakfast, Lady Clonbrony complained bitterly of her increased rheumatism, of the disagreeable, stupid party they had had the preceding night, and of the necessity of going to another formal party that night, the next, and the next, and, in the true fine lady style, deplored her situation, and the impossibility of avoiding those things,

> Which felt they curse, yet covet still to feel.

Miss Nugent determined to retire as soon as she could from the breakfast-room, to leave Lord Colambre an opportunity of talking over his family affairs at full liberty. She knew by the seriousness of his countenance that his mind was intent upon doing so, and she hoped that his influence with his father and mother would not be exerted in vain. But just as she was rising from the breakfast-table, in came Sir Terence O'Fay, and, seating himself quite at his ease, in spite of Lady Clonbrony's repulsive looks, his awe of Lord Colambre having now worn off –

'I'm tired,' said he, 'and have a right to be tired; for it's no small walk I've taken for the good of this noble family this morning. And, Miss Nugent, before I say more, I'll take a cup of *ta* from you, if you please.'

Lady Clonbrony rose, with great stateliness, and walked to the farthest end of the room, where she established herself at her writing-table, and began to write notes.

Sir Terence wiped his forehead deliberately.

'Then I've had a fine run – Miss Nugent, I believe you never saw me run; but I can run, I promise you, when it's to serve a friend. And, my lord (turning to Lord Clonbrony), what do you think I run for this morning – to buy a bargain – and of what? – a bargain of a bad debt – a debt of yours, which I bargained for, and up just in time – and Mordicai's ready to hang himself this minute. For what do you think but that rascal was bringing upon you – but an execution? – he was.'

'An execution!' repeated everybody present, except Lord Colambre.

'And how has this been prevented, sir?' said Lord Colambre.

'Oh! let me alone for that,' said Sir Terence. 'I got a hint from my little friend, Paddy Brady, who would not be paid for it either, though he's as poor as a rat. Well! as soon as I got the hint, I dropped the thing I had in my hand, which was the *Dublin Evening*, and ran for the bare life – for there wasn't a coach – in my slippers, as I was, to get into the prior creditor's shoes, who is the little solicitor that lives in Crutched Friars, which Mordicai never dreamt of, luckily; so he was very genteel, though he was taken on a sudden, and from his breakfast, which an Englishman don't like particularly – I popped him a douceur of a draught, at thirty-one days, on Garraghty, the agent; of which he must get notice; but I won't descant on the law before the ladies – he handed me over his debt and execution, and he made me prior creditor in a trice. Then I took coach in state, the first I met, and away with me to Long Acre – saw Mordicai. "Sir," says I, "I hear you're meditating an execution on a friend of mine." "Am I?" said the rascal; "who told you so?" "No matter," said I; "but I just called in to let you know there's no use in life of your execution; for there's a prior creditor with his execution to be satisfied first." So he made a great many black faces, and said a great deal, which I never listened to, but came off here clean to tell you all the story.'

'Not one word of which do I understand,' said Lady Clonbrony.

'Then, my dear, you are very ungrateful,' said Lord Clonbrony.

Lord Colambre said nothing, for he wished to learn more of Sir Terence O'Fay's character, of the state of his father's affairs, and of the family methods of proceeding in matters of business.

'Faith! Terry, I know I'm very thankful to you – but an execution's an ugly thing – and I hope there's no danger – '

'Never fear!' said Sir Terence: 'haven't I been at my wits' ends for myself or my friends ever since I come to man's estate – to years of discretion, I should say, for the deuce a foot of estate have I! But use has sharpened my wits pretty well for your service; so never be in dread, my good lord; for look ye!' cried the reckless knight, sticking his arms akimbo – 'look ye here! in Sir Terence O'Fay stands a host that desires no better than to encounter, single witted, all the duns in the united kingdoms, Mordicai the Jew inclusive.'

'Ah! that's the devil, that Mordicai,' said Lord Clonbrony; 'that's the only man on earth I dread.'

'Why, he is only a coachmaker, is not he?' said Lady Clonbrony: 'I can't think how you can talk, my lord, of dreading such a low man. Tell him, if he's troublesome, we won't bespeak any more carriages; and, I'm sure, I wish you would not be so silly, my lord, to employ him any more, when you know he disappointed me the last birthday about the landau, which I have not got yet.'

'Nonsense, my dear,' said Lord Clonbrony; 'you don't know what you are talking of. Terry, I say, even a friendly execution is an ugly thing.'

'Phoo! phoo! – an ugly thing! So is a fit of the gout – but one's all the better for it after. 'Tis just a renewal of life, my lord, for which one must pay a bit of a fine, you know. Take patience, and leave me to manage all properly – you know I'm used to these things. Only you recollect, if you please, how I managed my friend Lord — ; it's bad to be mentioning names – but Lord *everybody-knows-who* – didn't I bring him through cleverly, when there was that rascally attempt to seize the family plate? I had notice, and what did I do, but broke open a partition between that lord's house and my lodgings, which I had taken next door; and so, when the sheriff's officers were searching below on the ground floor, I just shoved the plate easy through to my bedchamber at a moment's warning, and then bid the gentlemen walk in, for they couldn't set a foot in my paradise, the devils! So they stood looking at it through the wall, and cursing me, and I holding both my sides with laughter at their fallen faces.'

Sir Terence and Lord Clonbrony laughed in concert.

'This is a good story,' said Miss Nugent, smiling; 'but surely, Sir Terence, such things are never done in real life?'

'Done! ay, are they; and I could tell you a hundred better strokes, my dear Miss Nugent.'

'Grace!' cried Lady Clonbrony, 'do pray have the goodness to seal and send these notes; for really,' whispered she, as her niece came to the table, 'I *cawnt stea*, I cawnt bear that man's *vice*, his accent grows horrider and horrider!'

Her ladyship rose, and left the room.

'Why, then,' continued Sir Terence, following up Miss Nugent to the table, where she was sealing letters, 'I must tell you how I *sarved* that same man on another occasion, and got the victory too.'

No general officer could talk of his victories, or fight his battles o'er again, with more complacency than Sir Terence O'Fay recounted his *civil* exploits.

'Now I'll tell Miss Nugent. There was a footman in the family, not an Irishman, but one of your powdered English scoundrels that ladies are so fond of having hanging to the backs of their carriages; one Fleming he was, that turned spy, and traitor, and informer, went privately and gave notice to the creditors where the plate was hid in the thickness of the chimney; but if he did, what happened? Why, I had my counter-spy, an honest little Irish boy, in the creditor's shop, that I had secured with a little douceur of usquebaugh; and he outwitted, as was natural, the English lying valet, and gave us notice just in the nick, and I got ready for their reception; and, Miss Nugent, I only wish you'd seen the excellent sport we had, letting them follow the scent they got; and when they were sure of their game, what did they find? – Ha! ha! ha! – dragged out, after a world of labour, a heavy box of – a load of brickbats; not an item of my friend's plate – that was all snug in the coal-hole, where them dunces never thought of looking for it. Ha! ha! ha!'

'But come, Terry,' cried Lord Clonbrony, 'I'll pull down your pride. How finely, another time, your job of the false ceiling answered in the hall. I've heard that story, and have been told how the sheriff's fellow thrust his bayonet up through your false plaster, and down came tumbling the family plate – hey, Terry? That hit cost your friend, Lord everybody-knows-who, more than your head's worth, Terry.'

'I ask your pardon, my lord, it never cost him a farthing.'

'When he paid £7000 for the plate, to redeem it?'

'Well! and did not I make up for that at the races of — ? The creditors learned that my lord's horse, Naboclish, was to run at — races; and, as the sheriff's officer knew he dare not touch him on the race-ground, what does he do, but he comes down early in the morning on the mail-coach, and walks straight down to the livery stables. He had an exact description of the stables, and the stall, and the horse's body-clothes.

'I was there, seeing the horse taken care of; and, knowing the cut of the fellow's jib, what does I do, but whips the body-clothes off Naboclish, and claps them upon a garrone that the priest would not ride.

'In comes the bailiff – "Good morrow to you, sir," says I, leading out of the stable my lord's horse, with an *ould* saddle and bridle on.

' "Tim Neal," says I to the groom, who was rubbing down the garrone's heels, "mind your hits today, and *wee'l* wet the plate tonight."

' "Not so fast, neither," says the bailiff – "here's my writ for seizing the horse."

' "Och," says I, "you wouldn't be so cruel." '

' "That's all my eye," says he, seizing the garrone, while I mounted Naboclish, and rode him off deliberately to —'

'Ha! ha! ha! – That *was* neat, I grant you, Terry,' said Lord Clonbrony. 'But what a dolt of a born ignoramus must that sheriff's fellow have been, not to know Naboclish when he saw him!'

'But stay, my lord – stay, Miss Nugent – I have more for you,' following her wherever she moved. 'I did not let him off so, even. At the cant, I bid and bid against them for the pretended Naboclish, till I left him on their hands for 500 guineas. Ha! ha! ha! – was not that famous?'

'But,' said Miss Nugent, 'I cannot believe you are in earnest, Sir Terence. Surely this would be –'

'What? – out with it, my dear Miss Nugent.'

'I am afraid of offending you.'

'You can't, my dear, I defy you – say the word that came to the tongue's end; it's always the best.'

'I was going to say, swindling,' said the young lady, colouring deeply.

'Oh! you was going to say wrong, then! It's not called swindling amongst gentlemen who know the world – it's only jockeying – fine sport – and very honourable to help a friend at a dead lift. Anything to get a friend out of a present pressing difficulty.'

'And when the present difficulty is over, do your friends never think of the future?'

'The future! leave the future to posterity,' said Sir Terence; 'I'm counsel only for the present; and when the evil comes, it's time enough to think of it. I can't bring the guns of my wits to bear till the enemy's alongside of me, or within sight of me at the least. And besides, there never was a good commander yet, by sea or land, that would tell his little expedients beforehand, or before the very day of battle.'

'It must be a sad thing,' said Miss Nugent, sighing deeply, 'to be reduced to live by little expedients – daily expedients.'

Lord Colambre struck his forehead, but said nothing.

'But if you are beating your brains about your own affairs, my Lord Colambre, my dear,' said Sir Terence, 'there's an easy way of settling your family affairs at once; and, since you don't like little daily expedients, Miss Nugent, there's one great expedient, and an expedient for life, that will settle it all to your satisfaction – and ours. I hinted it delicately to you before, but, between friends, delicacy is impertinent; so I tell you, in plain English, you've nothing to do but go and propose yourself, just as you stand, to the heiress Miss B—, that desires no better –'

'Sir!' cried Lord Colambre, stepping forward, red with sudden anger. Miss Nugent laid her hand upon his arm –

'Oh, my lord!'

'Sir Terence O'Fay,' continued Lord Colambre, in a moderated tone, 'you are wrong to mention that young lady's name in such a manner.'

'Why, then, I said only Miss B—, and there are a whole hive of *bees*. But I'll engage she'd thank me for what I suggested, and think herself the queen bee if my expedient was adopted by you.'

'Sir Terence,' said his lordship, smiling, 'if my father thinks proper that you should manage his affairs, and devise expedients for him, I have nothing to say on that point; but I must beg you will not trouble yourself to suggest expedients for me, and that you will have the goodness to leave me to settle my own affairs.'

Sir Terence made a low bow, and was silent for five seconds; then turning to Lord Clonbrony, who looked much more abashed than he did –

'By the wise one, my good lord, I believe there are some men – noblemen, too – that don't know their friends from their enemies. It's my firm persuasion, now, that if I had served you as I served my friend I was talking of, your son there would, ten to one, think I had done him an injury by saving the family plate.'

'I certainly should, sir. The family plate, sir, is not the first object in my mind,' replied Lord Colambre; 'family honour – Nay, Miss Nugent, I must speak,' continued his lordship, perceiving, by her countenance, that she was alarmed.

'Never fear, Miss Nugent dear,' said Sir Terence; 'I'm as cool as a cucumber. Faith! then, my Lord Colambre, I agree with you, that family honour's a mighty fine thing, only troublesome to one's self and one's friends, and expensive to keep up with all the other expenses and debts a gentleman has nowadays. So I, that am under no natural obligations to it by birth or otherwise, have just stood by through life, and asked myself, before I would volunteer being bound to it, what could this same family honour do for a man in this world? And, first and foremost, I never remember to see family honour stand a man in much stead in a court of law – never saw family honour stand against an execution, or a custodiam, or an injunction even. 'Tis a rare thing, this same family honour, and a very fine thing; but I never knew it yet, at a pinch, pay for a pair of boots even,' added Sir Terence, drawing up his own with much complacency.

At this moment Sir Terence was called out of the room by one who wanted to speak to him on particular business.

'My dear father,' cried Lord Colambre, 'do not follow him; stay for one moment, and hear your son – your true friend.'

Miss Nugent went out of the room, that she might leave the father and son at liberty.

'Hear your natural friend for one moment,' cried Lord Colambre. 'Let me beseech you, father, not to have recourse to any of these paltry expedients, but trust your son with the state of your affairs, and we shall find some honourable means –'

'Yes, yes, yes, very true; when you're of age, Colambre, we'll talk of it; but nothing can be done till then. We shall get on, we shall get through, very well, till then, with Terry's assistance. And I must beg you will not say a word more against Terry – I can't bear it – I can't hear it – I can't do without him. Pray don't detain me – I can say no more – except,' added he, returning to his usual concluding sentence, 'that there need, at all events, be none of this, if people would but live upon their own estates, and kill their own mutton.' He stole out of the room, glad to escape, however shabbily, from present explanation and present pain. There are persons without resource who in difficulties return always to the same point, and usually to the same words.

While Lord Colambre was walking up and down the room, much vexed and disappointed at finding that he could make no impression on his father's mind, nor obtain his confidence as to his family affairs, Lady Clonbrony's woman, Mrs Petito, knocked at the door, with a message from her lady, to beg, if Lord Colambre was *by himself*, he would go to her dressing-room, as she wished to have a conference with him. He obeyed her summons.

'Sit down, my dear Colambre – ' And she began precisely with her old sentence –

'With the fortune I brought your father, and with my lord's estate, I *cawnt* understand the meaning of all these pecuniary difficulties; and all that strange creature Sir Terence says is algebra to me, who speak English. And I am particularly sorry he was let in this morning – but he's such a brute that he does not think anything of forcing one's door, and he tells my footman he does not mind *not at home* a pinch of snuff. Now what can you do with a man who could say that sort of thing, you know – the world's at an end.'

'I wish my father had nothing to do with him, ma'am, as much as you can wish it,' said Lord Colambre; 'but I have said all that a son can with propriety say, and without effect.'

'What particularly provokes me against him,' continued Lady Clonbrony, 'is what I have just heard from Grace, who was really hurt by it, too, for she is the warmest friend in the world: I allude to the creature's indelicate way of touching upon a tender *pint*, and mentioning an amiable young heiress's name. My dear Colambre, I trust you have given me credit for my inviolable silence all this time upon the *pint* nearest my heart. I am rejoiced to hear you *was* so warm when she was mentioned inadvertently by that brute, and I trust you now see the advantages of the projected union in as strong and agreeable a *pint* of view as I do, my own Colambre; and I should leave things to themselves, and let you prolong the *dees* of courtship as you please, only for what I now hear incidentally from my lord and the brute, about pecuniary embarrassments, and the necessity of something being done before next winter. And indeed I think now, in propriety, the proposal cannot be delayed much longer; for the world begins to talk of the thing as done; and even Mrs Broadhurst, I know, had no doubt that, if this *contretemps* about the poor Berryls had not occurred, your proposal would have been made before the end of last week.'

Our hero was not a man to make a proposal because Mrs Broadhurst expected it, or to marry because the world said he was going to be married. He steadily said that, from the first moment the subject had been mentioned, he had explained himself distinctly; that the young lady's friends could not, therefore, be under any doubt as to his intentions; that, if they had voluntarily deceived themselves, or exposed the lady in situations from which the world was led to make false conclusions, he was not answerable: he felt his conscience at ease – entirely so, as he was convinced that the young lady herself, for whose merit, talents, independence, and generosity of character he professed high respect, esteem, and admiration, had no doubts either of the extent or the nature of his regard.

'Regard, respect, esteem, admiration! – Why, my dearest Colambre! this is saying all I want; satisfies me, and I am sure would satisfy Mrs Broadhurst and Miss Broadhurst too.'

'No doubt it will, ma'am; but not if I aspired to the honour of Miss Broadhurst's hand, or professed myself her lover.'

'My dear, you are mistaken; Miss Broadhurst is too sensible a girl, a vast deal, to look for love, and a dying lover, and all that sort of stuff; I am persuaded – indeed I have it from good, from the best authority – that the young lady – you know one must be delicate in these cases, where a young lady of such fortune, and no despicable family too is concerned; therefore I cannot speak quite plainly – but I say I have it from the best authority, that you would be preferred to any other suitor, and, in short, that – '

'I beg your pardon, madam, for interrupting you,' cried Lord Colambre, colouring a good deal; 'but you must excuse me if I say, that the only authority on which I could believe this is one from which I am morally certain I shall never hear it – from Miss Broadhurst herself.'

'Lord, child! if you would only ask her the question, she would tell you it is truth, I daresay.'

'But as I have no curiosity on the subject, ma'am – '

'Lord bless me! I thought everybody had curiosity. But still, without curiosity, I am sure it would gratify you when you did hear it; and can't you just put the simple question?'

'Impossible!'

'Impossible! – now that is so very provoking when the thing is all but done. Well, take your own time; all I will ask of you then is, to let things go on as they are going – smoothly and pleasantly; and I'll not press you farther on the subject at present. Let things go on smoothly, that's all I ask, and say nothing.'

'I wish I could oblige you, mother; but I cannot do this. Since you tell me that the world and Miss Broadhurst's friends have already misunderstood my intentions, it becomes necessary, in justice to the young lady and to myself, that I should make all further doubt impossible. I shall, therefore, put an end to it at once, by leaving town tomorrow.'

Lady Clonbrony, breathless for a moment with surprise, exclaimed, 'Bless me! leave town tomorrow! Just at the beginning of the season! Impossible! – I never saw such a precipitate, rash young man. But stay only a few weeks, Colambre; the physicians advise Buxton for my rheumatism, and you shall take us to Buxton early in the season – you cannot refuse me that. Why, if Miss Broadhurst was a dragon, you could not be in a greater hurry to run away from her. What are you afraid of?'

'Of doing what is wrong – the only thing, I trust, of which I shall ever be afraid.'

Lady Clonbrony tried persuasion and argument – such argument as she could use – but all in vain – Lord Colambre was firm in his resolution; at last, she came to tears; and her son, in much agitation, said –

'I cannot bear this, mother! I would do anything you ask, that I could do with honour; but this is impossible.'

'Why impossible? I will take all blame upon myself; and you are sure that Miss Broadhurst does not misunderstand you, and you esteem her, and admire her, and all that; and all I ask is, that you'll go on as you are, and see more of her; and how do you know but you may fall in love with her, as you call it, tomorrow?'

'Because, madam, since you press me so far, my affections are engaged to another person. Do not look so dreadfully shocked, my dear mother – I have told you truly, that I think myself too young, much too young, yet to marry. In the circumstances in which I know my family are, it is probable that I shall not for some years be able to marry as I wish. You may depend upon it that I shall not take any step, I shall not even declare my attachment to the object of my affection, without your knowledge; and, far from being inclined to follow headlong my own passions – strong as they are – be assured that the honour of my family, your happiness, my mother, my father's, are my first objects: I shall never think of my own till these are secured.'

Of the conclusion of this speech, Lady Clonbrony heard only the sound of the words; from the moment her son had pronounced that his affections were engaged, she had been running over in her head every probable and improbable person she could think of; at last, suddenly starting up, she opened one of the folding-doors into the next apartment, and called –

'Grace! – Grace Nugent! – put down your pencil, Grace, this minute, and come here!'

Miss Nugent obeyed with her usual alacrity; and the moment she entered the room, Lady Clonbrony, fixing her eyes full upon her, said –

'There's your cousin Colambre tells me his affections are engaged.'

'Yes, to Miss Broadhurst, no doubt,' said Miss Nugent, smiling, with a simplicity and openness of countenance which assured Lady Clonbrony that all was safe in that quarter: a suspicion which had darted into her mind was dispelled.

'No doubt. Ay, do you hear that *no doubt*, Colambre? – Grace, you see, has no doubt; nobody has any doubt but yourself, Colambre.'

'And are your affections engaged, and not to Miss Broadhurst?' said Miss Nugent, approaching Lord Colambre.

'There now! you see how you surprise and disappoint everybody, Colambre.'

'I am sorry that Miss Nugent should be disappointed,' said Lord Colambre.

'But because I am disappointed, pray do not call me Miss Nugent, or turn away from me, as if you were displeased.'

'It must, then, be some Cambridgeshire lady,' said Lady Clonbrony. 'I am sure I am very sorry he ever went to Cambridge, – Oxford I advised: one of the Miss Berryls, I presume, who have nothing. I'll have nothing more to do with those Berryls – there was the reason of the son's vast intimacy. Grace, you may give up all thoughts of Sir Arthur.'

'I have no thoughts to give up, ma'am,' said Miss Nugent, smiling. 'Miss Broadhurst,' continued she, going on eagerly with what she was saying to Lord Colambre – 'Miss Broadhurst is my friend, a friend I love and admire; but you will allow that I strictly kept my promise, never to praise her to you, till you should begin to praise her to me. Now recollect, last night, you did praise her to me, so justly, that I thought you liked her, I confess; so that it is natural I should feel a little disappointed. Now you know the whole of my mind; I have no intention to encroach on your confidence; therefore, there is no occasion to look so embarrassed. I give you my word, I will never speak to you again upon the subject,' said she, holding out her hand to him, 'provided you will never again call me Miss Nugent. Am I not your own cousin Grace? – Do not be displeased with her.'

'You are my own dear cousin Grace; and nothing can be farther from my mind than any thought of being displeased with her; especially just at this moment, when I am going away, probably for a considerable time.'

'Away! – when? – where?'

'Tomorrow morning, for Ireland.'

'Ireland! of all places,' cried Lady Clonbrony. 'What upon earth puts it into your head to go to Ireland? You do very well to go out of the way of falling in love ridiculously, since that is the reason of your going; but what put Ireland into your head, child?'

'I will not presume to ask my mother what put Ireland out of her head,' said Lord Colambre, smiling; 'but she will recollect that it is my native country.'

'That was your father's fault, not mine,' said Lady Clonbrony; 'for I wished to have been confined in England; but he would have it to say that his son and heir was born at Clonbrony Castle – and there was a great argument between him and my uncle, and something about the Prince of Wales and Caernarvon Castle was thrown in, and that turned the scale, much against my will; for it was my wish that my son should be an Englishman born – like myself. But, after all, I don't see that having the misfortune to be born in a country should tie one to it in any sort of way; and I should have hoped your English *edication*, Colambre, would have given you too liberal *idears* for that – so I *reely* don't see why you should go to Ireland merely because it's your native country.'

'Not merely because it is my native country; but I wish to go thither – I desire to become acquainted with it – because it is the country in which my father's property lies, and from which we draw our subsistence.'

'Subsistence! Lord bless me, what a word! fitter for a pauper than a nobleman – subsistence! Then, if you are going to look after your father's property, I hope you will make the agents do their duty, and send us remittances. And pray how long do you mean to stay?'

'Till I am of age, madam, if you have no objection. I will spend the ensuing months in travelling in Ireland; and I will return here by the time I am of age, unless you and my father should, before that time, be in Ireland.'

'Not the least chance of that, if I can prevent it, I promise you,' said Lady Clonbrony.

Lord Colambre and Miss Nugent sighed.

'And I am sure I shall take it very unkindly of you, Colambre, if you go and turn out a partisan for Ireland, after all, like Grace Nugent.'

'A partisan! no; – I hope not a partisan, but a friend,' said Miss Nugent.

'Nonsense, child! – I hate to hear people, women especially, and young ladies particularly, talk of being friends to this country or that country. What can they know about countries? Better think of being friends to themselves, and friends to their friends.'

'I was wrong,' said Miss Nugent, 'to call myself a friend to Ireland; I meant to say, that Ireland had been a friend to me; that I found Irish friends, when I had no other; an Irish home, when I had no other; that my earliest and happiest years, under your kind care, had been spent there; and that I can never forget *that*, my dear aunt – I hope you do not wish that I should.'

'Heaven forbid, my sweet Grace!' said Lady Clonbrony, touched by her voice and manner – 'Heaven forbid! I don't wish you to do or be anything but what you are; for I am convinced there's nothing I could ask you would not do for me; and, I can tell you, there's few things you could ask, love, I would not do for you.'

A wish was instantly expressed in the eyes of her niece.

Lady Clonbrony, though not usually quick at interpreting the wishes of others, understood and answered, before she ventured to make her request in words.

'Ask anything but *that*, Grace. Return to Clonbrony, while I am able to live in London? That I never can or will do for you or anybody!' looking at her son in all the pride of obstinacy; 'so there is an end of the matter. Go you where you please, Colambre; and I shall stay where I please: – I suppose, as your mother, I have a right to say this much?'

Her son, with the utmost respect, assured her that he had no design to infringe upon her undoubted liberty of judging for herself; that he had never interfered, except so far as to tell her circumstances of her affairs, with which she seemed to be totally unacquainted, and of which it might be dangerous to her to continue in ignorance.

'Don't talk to me about affairs,' cried she, drawing her hand away from her son. 'Talk to my lord, or my lord's agents, since you are going to Ireland, about business – I know nothing about business; but this I know, I shall stay in England, and be in London, every season, as long as I can afford it; and when I cannot afford to live here, I hope I shall not live anywhere. That's my notion of life; and that's my determination, once for all; for, if none of the rest of the Clonbrony family have any, I thank Heaven I have some spirit.' Saying this, with her most stately manner she walked out of the room. Lord Colambre instantly followed her; for, after the resolution and the promise he had made, he did not dare to trust himself at this moment with Miss Nugent.

There was to be a concert this night at Lady Clonbrony's, at which Mrs and Miss Broadhurst were, of course, expected. That they might not be quite unprepared for the event of her son's going to Ireland, Lady Clonbrony wrote a note to Mrs Broadhurst, begging her to come half an hour earlier than the time mentioned in the cards, 'that she might talk over something *particular* that had just occurred.'

What passed at this cabinet council, as it seems to have had no immediate influence on affairs, we need not record. Suffice it to observe, that a great deal was said, and nothing done. Miss Broadhurst, however, was not a young lady who could be easily deceived, even where her passions were concerned. The moment her mother told her of Lord Colambre's intended departure, she saw the whole truth. She had a strong mind – was capable of drawing aside, at once, the curtain of self-delusion, and looking steadily at the skeleton of truth – she had a generous, perhaps because a strong mind; for, surrounded, as she had been from her childhood, by every means of self-indulgence which wealth and flattery could bestow, she had discovered early, what few persons in her situation discover till late in life, that selfish gratifications may render us incapable of other happiness, but can never, of themselves, make us happy. Despising flatterers, she had determined to make herself friends – to make them in the only possible way – by deserving them. Her father made his immense fortune by the power and habit of constant, bold, and just calculation. The power and habit which she had learned from him she applied on a far larger scale; with him, it was confined to speculations for the acquisition of money; with her, it extended to the attainment of happiness. He was calculating and mercenary: she was estimative and generous.

Miss Nugent was dressing for the concert, or, rather, was sitting half-dressed before her glass, reflecting, when Miss Broadhurst came into her room. Miss Nugent immediately sent her maid out of the room.

'Grace,' said Miss Broadhurst, looking at Grace with an air of open, deliberate composure, 'you and I are thinking of the same thing – of the same person.'

'Yes, of Lord Colambre,' said Miss Nugent, ingenuously and sorrowfully.

'Then I can put your mind at ease, at once, my dear friend, by assuring you that I shall think of him no more. That I have thought of him, I do not deny – I have thought, that if, notwithstanding the difference in our ages, and other differences, he had preferred me, I should have preferred him to any person who has ever yet addressed me. On our first acquaintance, I clearly saw that he was not disposed to pay court to my fortune; and I had also then coolness of judgment sufficient to perceive that it was not probable he should fall in love with my person. But I was too proud in my humility, too strong in my honesty, too brave, too ignorant; in short, I knew nothing of the matter. We are all of us, more or less, subject to the delusions of vanity, or hope, or love – I – even I! – who thought myself so clear-sighted, did not know how, with one flutter of his wings, Cupid can set the whole atmosphere in motion; change the proportions, size, colour, value, of every object; lead us into a *mirage*, and leave us in a dismal desert.'

'My dearest friend!' said Miss Nugent, in a tone of true sympathy.

'But none but a coward, or a fool would sit down in the desert and weep, instead of trying to make his way back before the storm rises, obliterates the track, and overwhelms everything. Poetry apart, my dear Grace, you may be assured that I shall think no more of Lord Colambre.'

'I believe you are right. But I am sorry, very sorry, it must be so.'

'Oh, spare me your sorrow!'

'My sorrow is for Lord Colambre,' said Miss Nugent. 'Where will he find such a wife? – Not in Miss Berryl, I am sure – pretty as she is; a mere fine lady! Is it possible that Lord Colambre! Lord Colambre! should prefer such a girl – Lord Colambre!'

Miss Broadhurst looked at her friend as she spoke, and saw truth in her eyes; saw that she had no suspicion that she was herself the person beloved.

'Tell me, Grace, are you sorry that Lord Colambre is going away?'

'No, I am glad. I was sorry when I first heard it; but now I am glad, very glad; it may save him from a marriage unworthy of him, restore him to himself, and reserve him for – the only woman I ever saw who is suited to him, who is equal to him, who would value and love him, as he deserves to be valued and loved.'

'Stop, my dear; if you mean me, I am not, and I never can be, that woman. Therefore, as you are my friend, and wish my happiness, as I sincerely believe you do, never, I conjure you, present such an idea before my mind again – it is out of my mind, I hope, for ever. It is important to me that you should know and believe this. At least I will preserve my friends. Now let this subject never be mentioned or alluded to again between us, my dear. We have subjects enough of conversation; we need not have recourse to pernicious sentimental gossipings. There is a great difference between wanting *a confidante*, and treating a friend with confidence. My confidence you possess; all that ought, all that is to be known of my mind, you know, and – Now I will leave you in peace to dress for the concert.'

'Oh, don't go! you don't interrupt me. I shall be dressed in a few minutes; stay with me, and you may be assured, that neither now, nor at any other time, shall I ever speak to you on the subject you desire me to avoid. I entirely agree with you about *confidantes* and sentimental gossipings. I love you for not loving them.'

A thundering knock at the door announced the arrival of company.

'Think no more of love, but as much as you please of friendship – dress yourself as fast as you can,' said Miss Broadhurst. 'Dress, dress is the order of the day.'

'Order of the day and order of the night, and all for people I don't care for in the least,' said Grace. 'So life passes!'

'Dear me, Miss Nugent,' cried Petito, Lady Clonbrony's woman, coming in with a face of alarm, 'not dressed yet! My lady is gone down, and Mrs Broadhurst and my Lady Pococke's come, and the Honourable Mrs Trembleham; and signor, the Italian singing gentleman, has been walking up and down the apartments there by himself, disconsolate, this half-hour, and I wondering all the time nobody rang for me – but my lady dressed, Lord knows how! without anybody. Oh, merciful! Miss Nugent, if you could stand still for one single particle of a second. So then I thought of stepping in to Miss Nugent; for the young ladies are talking so fast, says I to myself, at the door, they will never know how time goes, unless I give 'em a hint. But now my lady is below, there's no need, to be sure, to be nervous, so we may take the thing quietly, without being in a flustrum. Dear ladies, is not this now a very sudden motion of our young lord's for Ireland? – Lud a mercy! Miss Nugent, I'm sure your motions is sudden enough; and your dress behind is all, I'm sure, I can't tell how.' – 'Oh, never mind,' said the young lady, escaping from her; 'it will do very well, thank you, Petito.'

'It will do very well, never mind,' repeated Petito muttering to herself, as she looked after the ladies, whilst they ran downstairs. 'I can't abide to dress any young lady who says never mind, and it will do very well. That, and her never talking to one confi*dant*ially, or trusting one with the least bit of her secrets, is the thing I can't put up with from Miss Nugent; and Miss Broadhurst holding the pins to me, as much as to say, Do your business, Petito, and don't talk. – Now, that's so impertinent, as if one wasn't the same flesh and blood, and had not as good a right to talk of everything, and hear of everything, as themselves. And Mrs Broadhurst, too, cabinet-councilling with my lady, and pursing up her city mouth when I come in, and turning off the discourse to snuff, forsooth; as if I was an ignoramus, to think they closeted themselves to talk of snuff. Now, I think a lady of quality's woman has as good a right to be trusted with her lady's secrets as with her jewels; and if my Lady Clonbrony was a real lady of quality, she'd know that, and consider the one as much my paraphernalia as the other. So I shall tell my lady tonight, as I always do when she vexes me, that I never lived in an Irish family before, and don't know the ways of it – then she'll tell me she was born in Hoxfordshire – then I shall say, with my saucy look, "Oh, was you, my lady? – I always forget that you was an Englishwoman:" then maybe she'll say, "Forget! – you forget yourself strangely, Petito." Then I shall say, with a great deal of dignity, "If your ladyship thinks so, my lady, I'd better go." And I'd desire no better than that she would take me at my word; for my Lady Dashfort's is a much better place, I'm told, and she's dying to have me, I know.'

And having formed this resolution, Petito concluded her apparently interminable soliloquy, and went with my lord's gentleman into the antechamber, to hear the concert, and give her judgment on everything; as she peeped in through the vista of heads into the Apollo saloon – for tonight the Alhambra was transformed into the Apollo saloon – she saw that whilst the company, rank behind rank, in close semicircles, had crowded round the performers to hear a favourite singer, Miss Broadhurst and Lord Colambre were standing in the outer semicircle, talking to one another earnestly. Now would Petito have given up her reversionary chance of the three nearly new gowns she expected from Lady Clonbrony, in case she stayed; or, in case she went, the reversionary chance of any dress of Lady Dashfort's except her scarlet velvet, merely to hear what Miss Broadhurst and Lord Colambre were saying. Alas! she could only see their lips move; and of what they were talking, whether of music or love, and whether the match was to be on or off, she could only conjecture. But the diplomatic style having now descended to waiting-maids, Mrs Petito talked to her friends in the antechamber with as mysterious and consequential an air and tone, as a *chargé d'affaires*, or as the lady of a *chargé d'affaires*, could have assumed. She spoke of her *private belief*; of *the impression left upon her mind*; and her *confidential* reasons for thinking as she did; of her 'having had it from the *fountain's* head;' and of 'her fear of any *committal* of her authorities.'

Notwithstanding all these authorities, Lord Colambre left London next day, and pursued his way to Ireland, determined that he would see and judge of that country for himself, and decide whether his mother's dislike to residing there was founded on caprice or reasonable causes.

In the meantime, it was reported in London that his lordship was gone to Ireland to make out the title to some estate, which would be necessary for his marriage settlement with the great heiress, Miss

Broadhurst. Whether Mrs Petito or Sir Terence O'Fay had the greater share in raising and spreading this report, it would be difficult to determine; but it is certain, however or by whomsoever raised, it was most useful to Lord Clonbrony, by keeping his creditors quiet.

Chapter 6

THE TIDE did not permit the packet to reach the Pigeon-house, and the impatient Lord Colambre stepped into a boat, and was rowed across the bay of Dublin. It was a fine summer morning. The sun shone bright on the Wicklow mountains. He admired, he exulted in the beauty of the prospect; and all the early associations of his childhood, and the patriotic hopes of his riper years, swelled his heart as he approached the shores of his native land. But scarcely had he touched his mother earth, when the whole course of his ideas was changed; and if his heart swelled, it swelled no more with pleasurable sensations, for instantly he found himself surrounded and attacked by a swarm of beggars and harpies, with strange figures and stranger tones: some craving his charity, some snatching away his luggage, and at the same time bidding him 'never trouble himself,' and 'never fear.' A scramble in the boat and on shore for bags and parcels began, and an amphibious fight betwixt men, who had one foot on sea and one on land, was seen; and long and loud the battle of trunks and portmanteaus raged! The vanquished departed, clinching their empty hands at their opponents, and swearing inextinguishable hatred; while the smiling victors stood at ease, each grasping his booty – bag, basket, parcel, or portmanteau: 'And, your honour, where *will* these go? – Where *will* we carry 'em all to, for your honour?' was now the question. Without waiting for an answer, most of the goods were carried at the discretion of the porters to the custom-house, where, to his lordship's astonishment, after this scene of confusion, he found that he had lost nothing but his patience; all his goods were safe, and a few *tinpennies* made his officious porters happy men and boys; blessings were showered upon his honour, and he was left in peace at an excellent hotel in — Street, Dublin. He rested, refreshed himself, recovered his good-humour, and walked into the coffee-house, where he found several officers – English, Irish, and Scotch. One English officer, a very gentleman-like, sensible-looking man, of middle age, was sitting reading a little pamphlet, when Lord Colambre entered; he looked up from time to time, and in a few minutes rose and joined the conversation; it turned upon the beauties and defects of the city of Dublin. Sir James Brooke, for that was the name of the gentleman, showed one of his brother officers the book which he had been reading, observing that, in his opinion, it contained one of the best views of Dublin which he had ever seen, evidently drawn by the hand of a master, though in a slight, playful, and ironical style: it was '*An intercepted Letter from China.*' The conversation extended from Dublin to various parts of Ireland, with all which Sir James Brooke showed that he was well acquainted. Observing that this conversation was particularly interesting to Lord Colambre, and quickly perceiving that he was speaking to one not ignorant of books, Sir James spoke of different representations and misrepresentations of Ireland. In answer to Lord Colambre's inquiries, he named the works which had afforded him most satisfaction; and with discriminative, not superficial celerity, touched on all ancient and modern authors, from Spenser and Davies to Young and Beaufort. Lord Colambre became anxious to cultivate the acquaintance of a gentleman who appeared so able and willing to afford him information. Sir James Brooke, on his part, was flattered by this eagerness of attention, and pleased by our hero's manners and conversation; so that, to their mutual satisfaction, they spent much of their time together whilst they were at this hotel; and, meeting frequently in society in Dublin, their acquaintance every day increased and grew into intimacy – an intimacy which was highly advantageous to Lord Colambre's views of obtaining a just idea of the state of manners in Ireland. Sir James Brooke had at different periods been quartered in various parts of the country – had resided long enough in each to become familiar with the people, and had varied his residence sufficiently to form comparisons between different counties, their habits, and characteristics. Hence he had it in his power to direct the attention of our young observer at once to the points most worthy of his examination, and to save him from the common error of travellers – the deducing general conclusions from a few particular cases, or arguing from exceptions as if they were rules. Lord Colambre, from his family connections, had of course immediate introduction into the best society in Dublin, or rather into all the good society of Dublin. In Dublin there is positively good company, and positively bad; but not, as in London, many degrees of comparison: not innumerable luminaries of the polite world, moving in different orbits of fashion, but all the bright planets of note and name move and revolve in the same narrow limits. Lord Colambre did not find that either his father's or his mother's representations of society in Dublin resembled the reality, which he now beheld. Lady Clonbrony had, in terms of detestation, described Dublin such as it appeared to her soon after the Union; Lord Clonbrony had painted it with convivial enthusiasm, such as he saw it long and long before the

Union, when *first* he drank claret at the fashionable clubs. This picture, unchanged in his memory, and unchangeable by his imagination, had remained, and ever would remain, the same. The hospitality of which the father boasted, the son found in all its warmth, but meliorated and refined; less convivial, more social; the fashion of hospitality had improved. To make the stranger eat or drink to excess, to set before him old wine and old plate, was no longer the sum of good breeding. The guest now escaped the pomp of grand entertainments; was allowed to enjoy ease and conversation, and to taste some of that feast of reason and that flow of soul so often talked of, and so seldom enjoyed. Lord Colambre found a spirit of improvement, a desire for knowledge, and a taste for science and literature, in most companies, particularly among gentlemen belonging to the Irish bar; nor did he in Dublin society see any of that confusion of ranks or predominance of vulgarity of which his mother had complained. Lady Clonbrony had assured him that, the last time she had been at the drawing-room at the Castle, a lady, whom she afterwards found to be a grocer's wife, had turned angrily when her ladyship had accidentally trodden on her train, and had exclaimed with a strong brogue, 'I'll thank you, ma'am, for the rest of my tail.'

Sir James Brooke, to whom Lord Colambre, without *giving up his authority*, mentioned the fact, declared that he had no doubt the thing had happened precisely as it was stated; but that this was one of the extraordinary cases which ought not to pass into a general rule – that it was a slight instance of that influence of temporary causes, from which no conclusions, as to national manners, should be drawn.

'I happened,' continued Sir James, 'to be quartered in Dublin soon after the Union took place; and I remember the great but transient change that appeared. From the removal of both Houses of Parliament, most of the nobility, and many of the principal families among the Irish commoners, either hurried in high hopes to London, or retired disgusted and in despair to their houses in the country. Immediately, in Dublin, commerce rose into the vacated seats of rank; wealth rose into the place of birth. New faces and new equipages appeared; people, who had never been heard of before, started into notice, pushed themselves forward, not scrupling to elbow their way even at the Castle; and they were presented to my lord-lieutenant and to my lady-lieutenant; for their excellencies, for the time being, might have played their vice-regal parts to empty benches, had they not admitted such persons for the moment to fill their court. Those of former times, of hereditary pretensions and high-bred minds and manners, were scandalised at all this; and they complained, with justice, that the whole *tone* of society was altered; that the decorum, elegance, polish, and charm of society was gone; and I among the rest (said Sir James) felt and deplored their change. But, now it is all over, we may acknowledge that, perhaps, even those things which we felt most disagreeable at the time were productive of eventual benefit.

'Formerly, a few families had set the fashion. From time immemorial everything had, in Dublin, been submitted to their hereditary authority; and conversation, though it had been rendered polite by their example, was, at the same time, limited within narrow bounds. Young people, educated upon a more enlarged plan, in time grew up; and, no authority or fashion forbidding it, necessarily rose to their just place, and enjoyed their due influence in society. The want of manners, joined to the want of knowledge in the new set, created universal disgust: they were compelled, some by ridicule, some by bankruptcies, to fall back into their former places, from which they could never more emerge. In the meantime, some of the Irish nobility and gentry who had been living at an unusual expense in London – an expense beyond their incomes – were glad to return home to refit; and they brought with them a new stock of ideas, and some taste for science and literature, which, within these latter years, have become fashionable, indeed indispensable, in London. That part of the Irish aristocracy, who, immediately upon the first incursions of the vulgarians, had fled in despair to their fastnesses in the country, hearing of the improvements which had gradually taken place in society, and assured of the final expulsion of the barbarians, ventured from their retreats, and returned to their posts in town. So that now,' concluded Sir James, 'you find a society in Dublin composed of a most agreeable and salutary mixture of birth and education, gentility and knowledge, manner and matter; and you see pervading the whole new life and energy, new talent, new ambition, a desire and a determination to improve and be improved – a perception that higher distinction can now be obtained in almost all company, by genius and merit, than by airs and dress ... So much for the higher order. Now, among the class of tradesmen and shopkeepers, you may amuse yourself, my lord, with marking the difference between them and persons of the same rank in London.'

Lord Colambre had several commissions to execute for his English friends, and he made it his amusement in every shop to observe the manners and habits of the people. He remarked that there are in Dublin two classes of tradespeople: one, who go into business with intent to make it their occupation for life, and as a slow but sure means of providing for themselves and their families; another class, who take up trade merely as a temporary resource, to which they condescend for a few years, trusting that they shall, in that time, make a fortune, retire, and commence or recommence gentlemen. The Irish regular men of business are like all other men of business – punctual, frugal, careful, and so forth; with the addition of more intelligence, invention, and enterprise than are usually found in Englishmen of the same rank. But the Dublin tradesmen *pro tempore* are a class by themselves; they begin without capital, buy stock upon credit in hopes of making large profits, and, in the same hopes, sell upon credit. Now, if the credit they can obtain is longer than that which they are forced to give, they go on and prosper; if not, they break, turn bankrupts, and sometimes, as bankrupts, thrive. By such men, of course, every *short cut* to fortune is followed; whilst every habit, which requires time to prove its advantage, is disregarded; nor with such views can a character for *punctuality* have its just value. In the head of a man who intends to be a tradesman today, and a gentleman tomorrow, the ideas of the honesty and the duties of a tradesman, and of the honour and the accomplishments of a gentleman, are oddly jumbled together, and the characteristics of both are lost in the compound.

He will *oblige* you, but he will not obey you; he will do you a favour, but he will not do you *justice*; he will do *anything to serve you*, but the particular thing you order he neglects; he asks your pardon, for he would not, for all the goods in his warehouse, *disoblige* you; not for the sake of your custom, but he has a particular regard for your family. Economy, in the eyes of such a tradesman, is, if not a mean vice, at least a shabby virtue, which he is too polite to suspect his customers of, and particularly proud to prove himself superior to. Many London tradesmen, after making their thousands and their tens of thousands, feel pride in still continuing to live like plain men of business; but from the moment a Dublin tradesman of this style has made a few hundreds, he sets up his gig, and then his head is in his carriage, and not in his business; and when he has made a few thousands, he buys or builds a country-house – and then, and thenceforward, his head, heart, and soul are in his country-house, and only his body in the shop with his customers.

Whilst he is making money, his wife, or rather his lady, is spending twice as much out of town as he makes in it. At the word country-house, let no one figure to himself a snug little box, like that in which a *warm* London citizen, after long years of toil, indulges himself, one day out of seven, in repose – enjoying from his gazebo the smell of the dust, and the view of passing coaches on the London road. No: these Hibernian villas are on a much more magnificent scale; some of them formerly belonged to Irish members of Parliament, who are at a distance from their country-seats. After the Union these were bought by citizens and tradesmen, who spoiled, by the mixture of their own fancies, what had originally been designed by men of good taste.

Some time after Lord Colambre's arrival in Dublin, he had an opportunity of seeing one of these villas, which belonged to Mrs Raffarty, a grocer's lady, and sister to one of Lord Clonbrony's agents, Mr Nicholas Garraghty. Lord Colambre was surprised to find that his father's agent resided in Dublin: he had been used to see agents, or stewards, as they are called in England, live in the country, and usually on the estate of which they have the management. Mr Nicholas Garraghty, however, had a handsome house in a fashionable part of Dublin. Lord Colambre called several times to see him, but he was out of town, receiving rents for some other gentlemen, as he was agent for more than one property.

Though our hero had not the honour of seeing Mr Garraghty, he had the pleasure of finding Mrs Raffarty one day at her brother's house. Just as his lordship came to the door, she was going, on her jaunting-car, to her villa, called Tusculum, situate near Bray. She spoke much of the beauties of the vicinity of Dublin; found his lordship was going with Sir James Brooke and a party of gentlemen to see the county of Wicklow; and his lordship and party were entreated to do her the honour of taking in his way a little collation at Tusculum.

Our hero was glad to have an opportunity of seeing more of a species of fine lady with which he was unacquainted.

The invitation was verbally made, and verbally accepted; but the lady afterwards thought it necessary to send a written invitation in due form, and the note she sent directed to the *most right honourable* the Lord Viscount Colambre. On opening it he perceived that it could not have been intended for him. It ran as follows:

My dear Juliana O'Leary,

I have got a promise from Colambre, that he will be with us at Tusculum on Friday the 20th, in his way from the county of Wicklow, for the collation I mentioned; and expect a large party of officers; so pray come early, with your house, or as many as the jaunting-car can bring. And pray, my dear, be *elegant*. You need not let it transpire to Mrs O'G— ; but make my apologies to Miss O'G— , if she says anything, and tell her I'm quite concerned I can't ask her for that day; because, tell her, I'm so crowded, and am to have none that day but *real quality*. – Yours ever and ever,

Anastasia Raffarty.

P.S. – And I hope to make the gentlemen stop the night with me; so will not have beds. Excuse haste, and compliments, etc.

Tusculum, Sunday 15.

After a charming tour in the county of Wicklow, where the beauty of the natural scenery, and the taste with which those natural beauties had been cultivated, far surpassed the sanguine expectations Lord Colambre had formed, his lordship and his companions arrived at Tusculum, where he found Mrs Raffarty, and Miss Juliana O'Leary, very elegant, with a large party of the ladies and gentlemen of Bray, assembled in a drawing-room, fine with bad pictures and gaudy gilding; the windows were all shut, and the company were playing cards with all their might. This was the fashion of the neighbourhood. In compliment to Lord Colambre and the officers, the ladies left the card-tables; and Mrs Raffarty, observing that his lordship seemed *partial* to walking, took him out, as she said, 'to do the honours of nature and art.'

His lordship was much amused by the mixture, which was now exhibited to him, of taste and incongruity, ingenuity and absurdity, genius and blunder; by the contrast between the finery and vulgarity, the affectation and ignorance of the lady of the villa. We should be obliged to *stop* too long at Tusculum were we to attempt to detail all the odd circumstances of this visit; but we may record an example or two which may give a sufficient idea of the whole.

In the first place, before they left the drawing-room, Miss Juliana O'Leary pointed out to his lordship's attention a picture over the drawing-room chimney-piece. 'Is not it a fine piece, my lord?' said she, naming the price Mrs Raffarty had lately paid for it at an auction. – 'It has a right to be a fine piece, indeed; for it cost a fine price!' Nevertheless this *fine* piece was a vile daub; and our hero could only avoid the sin of flattery, or the danger of offending the lady, by protesting that he had no judgment in pictures.

'Indeed, I don't pretend to be a connoisseur or conoscenti myself; but I'm told the style is undeniably modern. And was not I lucky, Juliana, not to let that *Medona* be knocked down to me? I was just going to bid, when I heard such smart bidding; but fortunately the auctioneer let out that it was done by a very old master – a hundred years old. Oh! your most obedient, thinks I! – if that's the case, it's not for my money; so I bought this, in lieu of the smoke-dried thing, and had it a bargain.'

In architecture, Mrs Raffarty had as good a taste and as much skill as in painting. There had been a handsome portico in front of the house; but this interfering with the lady's desire to have a veranda, which she said could not be dispensed with, she had raised the whole portico to the second story, where it stood, or seemed to stand, upon a tarpaulin roof. But Mrs Raffarty explained that the pillars, though they looked so properly substantial, were really hollow and as light as feathers, and were supported with cramps, without *disobliging* the front wall of the house at all to signify.

'Before she showed the company any farther,' she said, 'she must premise to his lordship, that she had been originally stinted in room for her improvements, so that she could not follow her genius liberally; she had been reduced to have some things on a confined scale, and occasionally to consult her pocket-compass; but she prided herself upon having put as much into a light pattern as could well be; that had been her whole ambition, study, and problem, for she was determined to have at least the honour of having a little *taste* of everything at Tusculum.'

So she led the way to a little conservatory, and a little pinery, and a little grapery, and a little aviary, and a little pheasantry, and a little dairy for show, and a little cottage for ditto, with a grotto full of shells, and a little hermitage full of earwigs, and a little ruin full of looking-glass, 'to enlarge and multiply the effect of the Gothic.' 'But you could only put your head in, because it was just fresh painted, and though there had been a fire ordered in the ruin all night, it had only smoked.'

In all Mrs Raffarty's buildings, whether ancient or modern, there was a studied crookedness.

'Yes,' she said, 'she hated everything straight, it was so formal and *unpicturesque*. Uniformity and conformity, she observed, had their day; but now, thank the stars of the present day, irregularity and difformity bear the bell, and have the majority.'

As they proceeded and walked through the grounds, from which Mrs Raffarty, though she had done her best, could not take that which nature had given, she pointed out to my lord 'a happy moving termination,' consisting of a Chinese bridge, with a fisherman leaning over the rails. On a sudden, the fisherman was seen to tumble over the bridge into the water. The gentlemen ran to extricate the poor fellow, while they heard Mrs Raffarty bawling to his lordship to beg he would never mind, and not trouble himself.

When they arrived at the bridge, they saw the man hanging from part of the bridge, and apparently struggling in the water; but when they attempted to pull him up, they found it was only a stuffed figure which had been pulled into the stream by a real fish, which had seized hold of the bait.

Mrs Raffarty, vexed by the fisherman's fall, and by the laughter it occasioned, did not recover herself sufficiently to be happily ridiculous during the remainder of the walk, nor till dinner was announced, when she apologised for 'having changed the collation, at first intended, into a dinner, which she hoped would be found no bad substitute, and which she flattered herself might prevail on my lord and the gentlemen to sleep, as there was no moon.'

The dinner had two great faults – profusion and pretension. There was, in fact, ten times more on the table than was necessary; and the entertainment was far above the circumstances of the person by whom it was given; for instance, the dish of fish at the head of the table had been brought across the island from Sligo, and had cost five guineas; as the lady of the house failed not to make known. But, after all, things were not of a piece; there was a disparity between the entertainment and the attendants; there was no proportion or fitness of things – a painful endeavour at what could not be attained, and a toiling in vain to conceal and repair deficiencies and blunders. Had the mistress of the house been quiet; had she, as Mrs Broadhurst would say, but let things alone, let things take their course, all would have passed off with well-bred people; but she was incessantly apologising, and fussing, and fretting inwardly and outwardly, and directing and calling to her servants – striving to make a butler who was deaf, a boy who was hare-brained, do the business of five accomplished footmen of *parts and figure*. The mistress of the house called for 'plates, clean plates! – hot plates!'

'But none did come, when she did call for them.'

Mrs Raffarty called 'Larry! Larry! My lord's plate, there! – James! bread to Captain Bowles! – James! port wine to the major! – James! James Kenny! James!'

'And panting James toiled after her in vain.'

At length one course was fairly got through, and after a torturing half-hour, the second course appeared, and James Kenny was intent upon one thing, and Larry upon another, so that the wine-sauce for the hare was spilt by their collision; but, what was worse, there seemed little chance that the whole of this second course should ever be placed altogether rightly upon the table. Mrs Raffarty cleared her throat, and nodded, and pointed, and sighed, and set Larry after Kenny, and Kenny after Larry; for what one did, the other undid; and at last the lady's anger kindled, and she spoke:

'Kenny! James Kenny! set the sea-cale at this corner, and put down the grass cross-corners; and match your macaroni yonder with *them* puddens, set – Ogh! James! the pyramid in the middle, can't ye?'

The pyramid, in changing places, was overturned. Then it was that the mistress of the feast, falling back in her seat, and lifting up her hands and eyes in despair, ejaculated, 'Oh, James! James!'

The pyramid was raised by the assistance of the military engineers, and stood trembling again on its base; but the lady's temper could not be so easily restored to its equilibrium.

The comedy of errors, which this day's visit exhibited, amused all the spectators. But Lord Colambre, after he had smiled, sometimes sighed. – Similar foibles and follies in persons of different rank, fortune, and manner, appear to common observers so unlike, that they laugh without scruples of conscience in one case, at what in another ought to touch themselves most nearly. It was the same desire to appear what they were not, the same vain ambition to vie with superior rank and fortune, or fashion, which actuated Lady Clonbrony and Mrs Raffarty; and whilst this ridiculous grocer's wife made herself the sport of some of her guests, Lord Colambre sighed, from the reflection that what she was to them, his mother was to persons in a higher rank of fashion. – He sighed still more deeply, when he considered, that, in whatever station or with whatever fortune, extravagance, that is the living beyond our income, must lead to distress and meanness, and end in shame and ruin. In the morning, as they were riding away from Tusculum and talking over their visit, the officers laughed heartily, and rallying Lord Colambre upon his seriousness, accused him of having fallen in love with Mrs Raffarty, or with the *elegant* Miss Juliana. Our hero, who wished never to be nice overmuch, or serious out of season, laughed with those that laughed, and endeavoured to catch the spirit of the jest. But Sir James Brooke, who now was well acquainted with his countenance, and who knew something of the history of his family, understood his real feelings, and, sympathising in them, endeavoured to give the conversation a new turn.

'Look there, Bowles,' said he, as they were just riding into the town of Bray; 'look at the barouche, standing at that green door, at the farthest end of the town. Is not that Lady Dashfort's barouche?'

'It looks like what she sported in Dublin last year,' said Bowles; 'but you don't think she'd give us the same two seasons? Besides, she is not in Ireland, is she? I did not hear of her intending to come over again.'

'I beg your pardon,' said another officer; 'she will come again to so good a market, to marry her other daughter. I hear she said, or swore, that she will marry the young widow, Lady Isabel, to an Irish nobleman.'

'Whatever she says, she swears, and whatever she swears, she'll do,' replied Bowles. 'Have a care, my Lord Colambre; if she sets her heart upon you for Lady Isabel, she has you. Nothing can save you. Heart she has none, so there you're safe, my lord,' said the other officer; 'but if Lady Isabel sets her eye upon you, no basilisk's is surer.'

'But if Lady Dashfort had landed I am sure we should have heard of it, for she makes noise enough wherever she goes; especially in Dublin, where all she said and did was echoed and magnified, till one could hear of nothing else. I don't think she has landed.'

'I hope to Heaven they may never land again in Ireland!' cried Sir James Brooke; 'one worthless woman, especially one worthless Englishwoman of rank, does incalculable mischief in a country like this, which looks up to the sister country for fashion. For my own part, as a warm friend to Ireland, I would rather see all the toads and serpents, and venomous reptiles, that St Patrick carried off in his bag, come back to this island, than these two *dashers*. Why, they would bite half the women and girls in the kingdom with the rage for mischief, before half the husbands and fathers could turn their heads about. And, once bit, there's no cure in nature or art.'

'No horses to this barouche!' cried Captain Bowles. – 'Pray, sir, whose carriage is this?' said the captain to a servant who was standing beside it.

'My Lady Dashfort, sir, it belongs to,' answered the servant, in rather a surly English tone; and turning to a boy who was lounging at the door – 'Pat, bid them bring out the horses, for my ladies is in a hurry to get home.'

Captain Bowles stopped to make his servant alter the girths of his horse, and to satisfy his curiosity; and the whole party halted. Captain Bowles beckoned to the landlord of the inn, who was standing at his door.

'So, Lady Dashfort is here again? – This is her barouche, is not it?'

'Yes, sir, she is – it is.'

'And has she sold her fine horses?'

'Oh no, sir – this is not her carriage at all – she is not here. That is, she is here, in Ireland; but down in the county of Wicklow, on a visit. And this is not her own carriage at all; – that is to say, not that which she has with herself, driving; but only just the cast barouche like, as she keeps for the lady's maids.'

'For the lady's maids! that is good! that is new, faith! – Sir James, do you hear that?'

'Indeed, then, and it's true, and not a word of a lie!' said the honest landlord. 'And this minute, we've got a directory of five of them abigails, sitting within in our house; as fine ladies, as great dashers, too, every bit as their principals; and kicking up as much dust on the road, every grain! – Think of them, now! The likes of them, that must have four horses, and would not stir a foot with one less! – As the gentleman's gentleman there was telling and boasting to me about now, when the barouche was ordered for them, there at the lady's house, where Lady Dashfort is on a visit – they said they would not get in till they'd get four horses; and their ladies backed them; and so the four horses was got; and they just drove out here, to see the points of view for fashion's sake, like their betters; and up with their glasses, like their ladies; and then out with their watches, and "Isn't it time to lunch?" So there they have been lunching within on what they brought with them; for nothing in our house could they touch, of course! They brought themselves a *picknick* lunch, with Madeira and Champagne to wash it down. Why, gentlemen, what do you think, but a set of them, as they were bragging to me, turned out of a boarding-house at Cheltenham, last year, because they had not peach-pies to their lunch! – But here they come! shawls, and veils, and all! – streamers flying! But mum is my cue! – Captain, are these girths to your fancy now?' said the landlord, aloud; then, as he stooped to alter a buckle, he said, in a voice meant to be heard only by Captain Bowles, 'If there's a tongue, male or female, in the three kingdoms, it's in that foremost woman, Mrs Petito.'

'Mrs Petito!' repeated Lord Colambre, as the name caught his ear; and, approaching the barouche in which the five abigails were now seated, he saw the identical Mrs Petito, who, when he left London, had been in his mother's service.

She recognised his lordship with very gracious intimacy; and, before he had time to ask any questions, she answered all she conceived he was going to ask, and with a volubility which justified the landlord's eulogium of her tongue.

'Yes, my lord! I left my Lady Clonbrony some time back – the day after you left town; and both her ladyship and Miss Nugent was charmingly, and would have sent their loves to your lordship, I'm sure, if they'd any notion I should have met you, my lord, so soon. And I was very sorry to part with them; but the fact was, my lord,' said Mrs Petito, laying a detaining hand upon Lord Colambre's whip, one end of which he unwittingly trusted within her reach, – 'I and my lady had a little difference, which the best friends, you know, sometimes have; so my Lady Clonbrony was so condescending to give me up to my Lady Dashfort – and I knew no more than the child unborn that her ladyship had it in contemplation to cross the seas. But, to oblige my lady, and as Colonel Heathcock, with his regiment of militia, was coming for purtection in the packet at the same time, and we to have the government-yacht, I waived my objections to Ireland. And, indeed, though I was greatly frighted at first, having heard all we've heard, you know, my lord, from Lady Clonbrony, of there being no living in Ireland, and expecting to see no trees nor accommodation, nor anything but bogs all along; yet I declare, I was very agreeably surprised; for, as far as I've seen at Dublin and in the vicinity, the accommodations, and everything of that nature, now is vastly put-up-able with!' – 'My lord,' said Sir James Brooke, 'we shall be late.' Lord Colambre, shortly withdrawing his whip from Mrs Petito, turned his horse away. She, stretching over the back of the barouche as he rode off, bawled to him –

'My lord, we're at Stephen's Green, when we're at Dublin.' But as he did not choose to hear, she raised her voice to its highest pitch, adding –

'And where are you, my lord, to be found? – as I have a parcel of Miss Nugent's for you.'

Lord Colambre instantly turned back, and gave his direction.

'Cleverly done, faith!' said the major. 'I did not hear her say when Lady Dashfort is to be in town,' said Captain Bowles.

'What, Bowles! have you a mind to lose more of your guineas to Lady Dashfort, and to be jockied out of another horse by Lady Isabel?'

'Oh! confound it – no! I'll keep out of the way of that – I have had enough,' said Captain Bowles; 'it is my Lord Colambre's turn now; you hear that Lady Dashfort would be very *proud* to see him. His lordship is in for it, and with such an auxiliary as Mrs Petito, Lady Dashfort has him for Lady Isabel, as sure as he has a heart or hand.'

'My compliments to the ladies, but my heart is engaged,' said Lord Colambre; 'and my hand shall go with my heart, or not at all.'

'Engaged! engaged to a very amiable, charming woman, no doubt,' said Sir James Brooke. 'I have an excellent opinion of your taste; and if you can return the compliment to my judgment, take my advice: don't trust to your heart's being engaged, much less plead that engagement; for it would be Lady Dashfort's sport, and Lady Isabel's joy, to make you break your engagement, and break your mistress's heart; the fairer, the more amiable, the more beloved, the greater the triumph, the greater the delight in giving pain. All the time love would be out of the question; neither mother nor daughter would care if you were hanged, or, as Lady Dashfort would herself have expressed it, if you were d—d.'

'With such women, I should think a man's heart could be in no great danger,' said Lord Colambre.

'There you might be mistaken, my lord; there's a way to every man's heart, which no man in his own case is aware of, but which every woman knows right well, and none better than these ladies – by his vanity.'

'True,' said Captain Bowles.

'I am not so vain as to think myself without vanity,' said Lord Colambre; 'but love, I should imagine, is a stronger passion than vanity.'

'You should imagine! Stay till you are tried, my lord. Excuse me,' said Captain Bowles, laughing.

Lord Colambre felt the good sense of this, and determined to have nothing to do with these dangerous ladies; indeed, though he had talked, he had scarcely yet thought of them; for his imagination was intent upon that packet from Miss Nugent, which Mrs Petito said she had for him. He heard nothing of it, or of her, for some days. He sent his servant every day to Stephen's Green to inquire if Lady Dashfort had returned to town. Her ladyship at last returned; but Mrs Petito could not deliver the parcel to any hand but Lord Colambre's own, and she would not stir out, because her lady was indisposed. No longer able to restrain his impatience, Lord Colambre went himself – knocked at Lady Dashfort's door – inquired for Mrs Petito – was shown into her parlour. The parcel was delivered to him; but to his utter disappointment, it was a parcel *for*, not *from* Miss Nugent. It contained merely an odd volume of some book of Miss Nugent's which Mrs Petito said she had put up along with her things *in a mistake*, and she thought it her duty to return it by the first opportunity of a safe conveyance.

Whilst Lord Colambre, to comfort himself for his disappointment, was fixing his eyes upon Miss Nugent's name, written by her own hand, in the first leaf of the book, the door opened, and the figure of an interesting-looking woman, in deep mourning, appeared – appeared for one moment, and retired.

'Only my Lord Colambre, about a parcel I was bringing for him from England, my lady – my Lady Isabel, my lord,' said Mrs Petito. Whilst Mrs Petito was saying this, the entrance and retreat had been made, and made with such dignity, grace, and modesty; with such innocence, dove-like eyes had been raised upon him, fixed and withdrawn; with such a gracious bend the Lady Isabel had bowed to him as she retired; with such a smile, and with so soft a voice, had repeated 'Lord Colambre!' that his lordship, though well aware that all this was mere acting, could not help saying to himself as he left the house:

'It is a pity it is only acting. There is certainly something very engaging in this woman. It is a pity she is an actress. And so young! A much younger woman than I expected. A widow before most women are wives. So young, surely she cannot be such a fiend as they described her to be!' A few nights afterwards Lord Colambre was with some of his acquaintance at the theatre, when Lady Isabel and her mother came into the box, where seats had been reserved for them, and where their appearance instantly made that *sensation* which is usually created by the entrance of persons of the first notoriety in the fashionable world. Lord Colambre was not a man to be dazzled by fashion, or to mistake

notoriety for deference paid to merit, and for the admiration com-
manded by beauty or talents. Lady Dashfort's coarse person, loud voice,
daring manners, and indelicate wit, disgusted him almost past endurance. He saw Sir James Brooke in the box opposite to him; and twice
determined to go round to him. His lordship had crossed the benches,
and once his hand was upon the lock of the door; but attracted as much
by the daughter as repelled by the mother, he could move no farther.
The mother's masculine boldness heightened, by contrast, the charms of
the daughter's soft sentimentality. The Lady Isabel seemed to shrink
from the indelicacy of her mother's manners, and seemed peculiarly
distressed by the strange efforts Lady Dashfort made, from time to time,
to drag her forward, and to fix upon her the attention of gentlemen.
Colonel Heathcock, who, as Mrs Petito had informed Lord Colambre,
had come over with his regiment to Ireland, was beckoned into their box
by Lady Dashfort, by her squeezed into a seat next to Lady Isabel; but
Lady Isabel seemed to feel sovereign contempt, properly repressed by
politeness, for what, in a low whisper to a female friend on the other side
of her, she called, 'the self-sufficient inanity of this sad coxcomb.' Other
coxcombs, of a more vivacious style, who stationed themselves round her
mother, or to whom her mother stretched from box to box to talk,
seemed to engage no more of Lady Isabel's attention than just what she
was compelled to give by Lady Dashfort's repeated calls of –
    'Isabel! Isabel! Colonel G— Isabel! Lord D— bowing to you. Belle!
Belle! Sir Harry B— Isabel, child, with your eyes on the stage? Did you
never see a play before? Novice! Major P— waiting to catch your eye
this quarter of an hour; and now her eyes gone down to her play-bill!
Sir Harry, do take it from her.

    Were eyes so radiant only made to read?

Lady Isabel appeared to suffer so exquisitely and so naturally from
this persecution, that Lord Colambre said to himself –
    'If this be acting, it is the best acting I ever saw. If this be art, it
deserves to be nature.'
    And with this sentiment he did himself the honour of handing Lady
Isabel to her carriage this night, and with this sentiment he awoke next
morning; and by the time he had dressed and breakfasted he determined that it was impossible all that he had seen could be acting. 'No
woman, no young woman, could have such art. Sir James Brooke had
been unwarrantably severe; he would go and tell him so.'
    But Sir James Brooke this day received orders for his regiment to
march to quarters in a distant part of Ireland. His head was full of arms,

and ammunition, and knapsacks, and billets, and routes; and there was no possibility, even in the present chivalrous disposition of our hero, to enter upon the defence of the Lady Isabel. Indeed, in the regret he felt for the approaching and unexpected departure of his friend, Lord Colambre forgot the fair lady. But just when Sir James had his foot in the stirrup, he stopped.

'By the bye, my dear lord, I saw you at the play last night. You seemed to be much interested. Don't think me impertinent, if I remind you of our conversation when we were riding home from Tusculum; and if I warn you,' said he, mounting his horse, 'to beware of counterfeits – for such are abroad.' Reining in his impatient steed, Sir James turned again and added, '*Deeds not words*, is my motto. Remember, we can judge better by the conduct of people towards others than by their manner towards ourselves.'

Chapter 7

OUR HERO was quite convinced of the good sense of his friend's last remark, that it is safer to judge of people by their conduct to others than by their manners towards ourselves; but as yet, he felt scarcely any interest on the subject of Lady Dashfort or Lady Isabel's characters; however, he inquired and listened to all the evidence he could obtain respecting this mother and daughter.

He heard terrible reports of the mischief they had done in families; the extravagance into which they had led men; the imprudence, to say no worse, into which they had betrayed women. Matches broken off, reputations ruined, husbands alienated from their wives, and wives made jealous of their husbands. But in some of these stories he discovered exaggeration so flagrant as to make him doubt the whole; in others, it could not be positively determined whether the mother or daughter had been the person most to blame.

Lord Colambre always followed the charitable rule of believing only half what the world says, and here he thought it fair to believe which half he pleased. He further observed, that, though all joined in abusing these ladies in their absence, when present they seemed universally admired. Though everybody cried 'shame!' and 'shocking!' yet everybody visited them. No parties so crowded as Lady Dashfort's; no party deemed pleasant or fashionable where Lady Dashfort or Lady Isabel was not. The *bons mots* of the mother were everywhere repeated; the dress and air of the daughter everywhere imitated. Yet Lord Colambre could not help being surprised at their popularity in Dublin, because, independently of all moral objections, there were causes of a different sort, sufficient, he thought, to prevent Lady Dashfort from being liked by the Irish; indeed by any society. She in general affected to be ill-bred, and inattentive to the feelings and opinions of others; careless whom she offended by her wit or by her decided tone. There are some persons in so high a region of fashion, that they imagine themselves above the thunder of vulgar censure. Lady Dashfort felt herself in this exalted situation, and fancied she might 'hear the innocuous thunder roll below.' Her rank was so high that none could dare to call her vulgar; what would have been gross in any one of meaner note, in her was freedom, or originality, or Lady Dashfort's way. It was Lady Dashfort's pleasure and pride to show her power in perverting the public taste. She often said to those English companions with whom she was intimate, 'Now see what follies I can lead these fools into. Hear the nonsense I can make them repeat as wit.' Upon some occasion, one of her friends *ventured* to fear that something she had said was *too strong.* 'Too strong, was it? Well, I like to be strong – woe be to the weak.' On another occasion she was told that certain visitors had seen her ladyship yawning. 'Yawn, did I? – glad of it – the yawn sent them away, or I should have snored; – rude, was I? they won't complain. To say I was rude to them would be to say, that I did not think it worth my while to be otherwise. Barbarians! are not we the civilised English, come to teach them manners and fashions? Whoever does not conform, and swear allegiance too, we shall keep out of the English pale.'

Lady Dashfort forced her way, and she set the fashion: fashion, which converts the ugliest dress into what is beautiful and charming, governs the public mode in morals and in manners; and thus, when great talents and high rank combine, they can debase or elevate the public taste.

With Lord Colambre she played more artfully; she drew him out in defence of his beloved country, and gave him opportunities of appearing to advantage; this he could not help feeling, especially when the Lady Isabel was present. Lady Dashfort had dealt long enough with human nature to know, that to make any man pleased with her, she should begin by making him pleased with himself.

Insensibly the antipathy that Lord Colambre had originally felt to Lady Dashfort wore off; her faults, he began to think, were assumed; he pardoned her defiance of good breeding, when he observed that she could, when she chose it, be most engagingly polite. It was not that she did not know what was right, but that she did not think it always for her interest to practise it.

The party opposed to Lady Dashfort affirmed that her wit depended merely on unexpectedness; a characteristic which may be applied to any impropriety of speech, manner, or conduct. In some of her ladyship's repartees, however, Lord Colambre now acknowledged there was more than unexpectedness; there was real wit; but it was of a sort utterly unfit for a woman, and he was sorry that Lady Isabel should hear it. In short, exceptionable as it was altogether, Lady Dashfort's conversation had become entertaining to him; and though he could never esteem or feel in the least interested about her, he began to allow that she could be agreeable.

'Ay, I knew how it would be,' said she, when some of her friends told her this. 'He began by detesting me, and did I not tell you that, if I thought it worth my while to make him like me, he must, sooner or later. I delight in seeing people begin with me as they do with olives, making all manner of horrid faces and silly protestations that they will never touch an olive again as long as they live; but, after a little time, these very folk grow so desperately fond of olives, that there is no dessert without them. Isabel, child, you are in the sweet line – but sweets cloy. You never heard of anybody living on marmalade, did ye?' – Lady Isabel answered by a sweet smile. – 'To do you justice, you play Lydia Languish vastly well,' pursued the mother; 'but Lydia, by herself, would soon tire; somebody must keep up the spirit and bustle, and carry on the plot of the piece; and I am that somebody – as you shall see. Is not that our hero's voice, which I hear on the stairs?'

It was Lord Colambre. His lordship had by this time become a constant visitor at Lady Dashfort's. Not that he had forgotten, or that he meant to disregard his friend Sir James Brooke's parting words. He promised himself faithfully, that if anything should occur to give him reason to suspect designs, such as those to which the warning pointed, he would be on his guard, and would prove his generalship by an able retreat. But to imagine attacks where none were attempted, to suspect ambuscades in the open country, would be ridiculous and cowardly.

'No,' thought our hero; 'Heaven forfend I should be such a coxcomb as to fancy every woman who speaks to me has designs upon my precious heart, or on my more precious estate!' As he walked from his hotel to Lady Dashfort's house, ingeniously wrong, he came to this conclusion, just as he ascended the stairs, and just as her ladyship had settled her future plan of operations.

After talking over the nothings of the day, and after having given two or three *cuts* at the society of Dublin, with two or three compliments to individuals, who, she knew, were favourites with his lordship, she suddenly turned to him –

'My lord, I think you told me, or my own sagacity discovered, that you want to see something of Ireland, and that you don't intend, like most travellers, to turn round, see nothing, and go home content.'

Lord Colambre assured her ladyship that she had judged him rightly, for, that nothing would content him but seeing all that was possible to be seen of his native country. It was for this special purpose he came to Ireland.

'Ah! – well – very good purpose – can't be better; but now, how to accomplish it. You know the Portuguese proverb says, "You go to hell for the good things you intend to do, and to heaven for those you do." Now let us see what you will do. Dublin, I suppose, you've seen enough of by this time; through and through – round and round – this makes me first giddy and then sick. Let me show you the country – not the face of it, but the body of it – the people. Not Castle this, or Newtown that, but their inhabitants. I know them; I have the key, or the picklock to their minds. An Irishman is as different an animal on his guard, and off his guard, as a miss in school from a miss out of school. A fine country for game, I'll show you; and, if you are a good marksman, you may have plenty of shots "at folly as it flies." '

Lord Colambre smiled. 'As to Isabel,' pursued her ladyship, 'I shall put her in charge of Heathcock, who is going with us. She won't thank me for that, but you will. Nay, no fibs, man; you know, I know, as who does not that has seen the world, that though a pretty woman is a mighty pretty thing, yet she is confoundedly in one's way, when anything else is to be seen, heard – or understood.'

Every objection anticipated and removed, and so far a prospect held out of attaining all the information he desired, with more than all the amusement he could have expected, Lord Colambre seemed much tempted to accept the invitation; but he hesitated, because, as he said, her ladyship might be going to pay visits where he was not acquainted.

'Bless you! don't let that be a stumbling-block in the way of your tender conscience. I am going to Killpatrickstown, where you'll be as welcome as light. You know them, they know you; at least you shall have a proper letter of invitation from my Lord and my Lady Killpatrick, and all that. And as to the rest, you know a young man is always welcome everywhere, a young nobleman kindly welcome, – I won't say such a young man, and such a young nobleman, for that might put you to your bows or your blushes – but *nobilitas* by itself, nobility is enough in all parties, in all families, where there are girls, and of course balls, as there are always at Killpatrickstown. Don't be alarmed; you shall not be forced to dance, or asked to marry. I'll be your security. You shall be at full liberty; and it is a house where you

can do just what you will. Indeed, I go to no others. These Killpatricks
are the best creatures in the world; they think nothing good or grand
enough for me. If I'd let them, they would lay down cloth of gold over
their bogs for me to walk upon. – Good-hearted beings!' added Lady
Dashfort, marking a cloud gathering on Lord Colambre's countenance. 'I laugh at them, because I love them. I could not love anything I
might not laugh at – your lordship excepted. So you'll come – that's
settled.'

And so it was settled. Our hero went to Killpatrickstown.

'Everything here sumptuous and unfinished, you see,' said Lady
Dashfort to Lord Colambre, the day after their arrival. 'All begun as if
the projectors thought they had the command of the mines of Peru, and
ended as if the possessors had not sixpence; *des arrangemens provisatoires*,
temporary expedients; in plain English, *make-shifts*. Luxuries, enough
for an English prince of the blood; comforts, not enough for an English
woman. And you may be sure that great repairs and alterations have
gone on to fit this house for our reception, and for our English eyes! –
Poor people! – English visitors, in this point of view, are horribly
expensive to the Irish. Did you ever hear that, in the last century, or in
the century before the last, to put my story far enough back, so that it
shall not touch anybody living; when a certain English nobleman, Lord
Blank A— , sent to let his Irish friend, Lord Blank B— , know that he
and all his train were coming over to pay him a visit; the Irish nobleman,
Blank B— , knowing the deplorable condition of his castle, sat down
fairly to calculate whether it would cost him most to put the building in
good and sufficient repair, fit to receive these English visitors, or to
burn it to the ground. He found the balance to be in favour of burning,
which was wisely accomplished next day. Perhaps Killpatrick would
have done well to follow this example. Resolve me which is worst, to be
burnt out of house and home, or to be eaten out of house and home. In
this house, above and below stairs, including first and second table,
housekeeper's room, lady's maids' room, butler's room, and gentleman's, one hundred and four people sit down to dinner every day,
as Petito informs me, beside kitchen boys, and what they call *char*-
women – who never sit down, but who do not eat or waste the less for
that; and retainers and friends, friends to the fifth and sixth generation,
who "must get their bit and their sup;" for, "sure, it's only Biddy," they
say,' continued Lady Dashfort, imitating their Irish brogue. 'And, "sure,
'tis nothing at all, out of all his honour, my lord, has. How could he *feel*
it! – Long life to him! – He's not that way: not a couple in all Ireland,
and that's saying a great dale, looks less after their own, nor is more off-
handeder, or open-hearteder, or greater open-house-keepers, *nor* my

Lord and my Lady Killpatrick." Now there's encouragement for a lord and a lady to ruin themselves.'

Lady Dashfort imitated the Irish brogue in perfection; boasted that 'she was mistress of fourteen different brogues, and had brogues for all occasions.' By her mixture of mimickry, sarcasm, exaggeration, and truth, she succeeded continually in making Lord Colambre laugh at everything at which she wished to make him laugh; at every *thing*, but not every *body*; whenever she became personal, he became serious, or at least endeavoured to become serious; and if he could not instantly resume the command of his risible muscles, he reproached himself.

'It is shameful to laugh at these people, indeed, Lady Dashfort, in their own house – these hospitable people, who are entertaining us.'

'Entertaining us! true, and if we are *entertained*, how can we help laughing?'

All expostulation was thus turned off by a jest, as it was her pride to make Lord Colambre laugh in spite of his better feelings and princi-ples. This he saw, and this seemed to him to be her sole object; but there he was mistaken. *Off-handed* as she pretended to be, none dealt more in the *impromptu fait à loisir*; and mentally short-sighted as she affected to be, none had more *longanimity* for their own interest.

It was her settled purpose to make the Irish and Ireland ridiculous and contemptible to Lord Colambre; to disgust him with his native country; to make him abandon the wish of residing on his own estate. To confirm him an absentee was her object previously to her ultimate plan of marrying him to her daughter. Her daughter was poor, she would therefore be glad to *get* an Irish peer for her; but would be very sorry, she said, to see Isabel banished to Ireland; and the young widow declared she could never bring herself to be buried alive in Clonbrony Castle.

In addition to these considerations, Lady Dashfort received certain hints from Mrs Petito, which worked all to the same point.

'Why, yes, my lady; I heard a great deal about all that when I was at Lady Clonbrony's,' said Petito, one day, as she was attending at her lady's toilette, and encouraged to begin chattering. 'And I own I was originally under the universal error, that my Lord Colambre was to be married to the great heiress, Miss Broadhurst; but I have been converted and reformed on that score, and am at present quite in another way and style of thinking.'

Petito paused, in hopes that her lady would ask, what was her present way of thinking? But Lady Dashfort, certain that she would tell her without being asked, did not take the trouble to speak, particularly as she did not choose to appear violently interested on the subject. – 'My present way of thinking,' resumed Petito, 'is in consequence of my having, with my own eyes and ears, witnessed and overheard his lordship's behaviour and words, the morning he was coming away from *Lunnun* for Ireland; when he was morally certain nobody was up, nor overhearing, nor overseeing him, there did I notice him, my lady, stopping in the antechamber, ejaculating over one of Miss Nugent's gloves, which he had picked up. "Limerick!" said he, quite loud to himself; for it was a Limerick glove, my lady, – "Limerick! – dear Ireland! she loves you as well as I do!" – or words to that effect; and then a sigh, and downstairs and off. So, thinks I, now the cat's out of the bag. And I wouldn't give much myself for Miss Broadhurst's chance of that young lord, with all her bank stock, scrip, and *omnum*. Now, I see how the land lies, and I'm sorry for it; for she's no *fortin*; and she's so proud, she never said a hint to me of the matter; but my Lord Colambre is a sweet gentleman; and – '

'Petito! don't run on so; you must not meddle with what you don't understand: the Miss Killpatricks, to be sure, are sweet girls, particularly the youngest.' – Her ladyship's toilette was finished; and she left Petito to go down to my Lady Killpatrick's woman, to tell, as a very great secret, the schemes that were in contemplation among the higher powers, in favour of the youngest of the Miss Killpatricks.

'So Ireland is at the bottom of his heart, is it?' repeated Lady Dashfort to herself; 'it shall not be long so.' From this time forward, not a day, scarcely an hour passed, but her ladyship did or said something to depreciate the county, or its inhabitants, in our hero's estimation. With treacherous ability, she knew and followed all the arts of misrepresentation; all those injurious arts which his friend, Sir James Brooke, had, with such honest indignation, reprobated. She knew how, not only to seize the ridiculous points, to make the most respectable people ridiculous, but she knew how to select the worst instances, the worst exceptions; and to produce them as examples, as precedents, from which to condemn whole classes, and establish general false conclusions respecting a nation.

In the neighbourhood of Killpatrickstown, Lady Dashfort said, there were several *squireens*, or little squires; a race of men who have succeeded to the *buckeens*, described by Young and Crumpe. *Squireens* are persons who, with good long leases, or valuable farms, possess incomes from three to eight hundred a year; who keep a pack of hounds; *take out* a commission of the peace, sometimes before they can spell (as her ladyship said), and almost always before they know anything of law or justice! Busy and loud about small matters; *jobbers at assizes*; combining with one another, and trying upon every occasion, public or private, to push themselves forward, to the annoyance of their superiors, and the terror of those below them.

In the usual course of things, these men are not often to be found in the society of gentry; except, perhaps, among those gentlemen or noblemen who like to see hangers-on at their tables; or who find it for their convenience to have underling magistrates, to *protect* their favourites, or to propose and *carry* jobs for them on grand juries. At election times, however, these persons rise into sudden importance with all who have views upon the county. Lady Dashfort hinted to Lord Killpatrick, that her private letters from England spoke of an approaching dissolution of Parliament; she knew that, upon this hint, a round of invitations would be sent to the squireens; and she was morally certain that they would be more disagreeable to Lord Colambre, and give him a worse idea of the country, than any other people who could be produced. Day after day some of these personages made their appearance; and Lady Dashfort took care to draw them out upon the subjects on which she knew that they would show the most self-sufficient ignorance, and the most illiberal spirit. This succeeded beyond her most sanguine expectations. 'Lord Colambre! how I pity you, for being compelled to these permanent sittings after dinner!' said Lady Isabel to him one night, when he came late to the ladies from the dining-room. 'Lord Killpatrick insisted upon my staying to help him to push about that never-ending, still-beginning electioneering bottle,' said Lord Colambre. 'Oh! if that were all; if these gentlemen would only drink; – but their conversation! I don't wonder my mother dreads returning to Clonbrony Castle, if my father must have such company as this. But, surely, it cannot be necessary.'

'Oh, indispensable! positively indispensable!' cried Lady Dashfort; 'no living in Ireland without it. You know, in every country in the world, you must live with the people of the country, or be torn to pieces; for my part, I should prefer being torn to pieces.'

Lady Dashfort and Lady Isabel knew how to take advantage of the contrast between their own conversation, and that of the persons by whom Lord Colambre was so justly disgusted; they happily relieved his fatigue with wit, satire, poetry, and sentiment; so that he every day became more exclusively fond of their company; for Lady Killpatrick and the Miss Killpatricks were mere commonplace people. In the mornings, he rode or walked with Lady Dashfort and Lady Isabel: Lady Dashfort, by way of fulfilling her promise of showing him the people, used frequently to take him into the cabins, and talk to their inhabitants. Lord and Lady Killpatrick, who had lived always for the fashionable world, had taken little pains to improve the condition of their tenants; the few attempts they had made were injudicious. They had built ornamented, picturesque cottages, within view of their demesne; and favourite followers of the family, people with half a century's habit of indolence and dirt, were *promoted* to these fine dwellings. The consequences were such as Lady Dashfort delighted to point out; everything let to go to ruin for the want of a moment's care, or pulled to pieces for the sake of the most trifling surreptitious profit; the people most assisted always appearing proportionally wretched and discontented. No one could, with more ease and more knowledge of her ground, than Lady Dashfort, do the *dishonour* of a country. In every cabin that she entered, by the first glance of her eye at the head, kerchiefed in no comely guise, or by the drawn-down corners of the mouth, or by the bit of a broken pipe, which in Ireland never characterises *stout labour*, or by the first sound of the voice, the drawling accent on 'your honour,' or, 'my lady,' she could distinguish the proper objects of her charitable designs, that is to say, those of the old uneducated race, whom no one can help, because they will never help themselves. To these she constantly addressed herself, making them give, in all their despairing tones, a history of their complaints and grievances; then asking them questions, aptly contrived to expose their habits of self-contradiction, their servility and flattery one moment, and their litigious and encroaching spirit the next: thus giving Lord Colambre the most unfavourable idea of the disposition and character of the lower class of the Irish people.

Lady Isabel the while standing by, with the most amiable air of pity, with expressions of the finest moral sensibility, softening all her mother said, finding ever some excuse for the poor creatures, and following with angelic sweetness to heal the wounds her mother inflicted.

When Lady Dashfort thought she had sufficiently worked upon Lord Colambre's mind to weaken his enthusiasm for his native country, and when Lady Isabel had, by the appearance of every virtue, added to a delicate preference, if not partiality, for our hero, ingratiated herself into his good opinion and obtained an interest in his mind, the wily mother ventured an attack of a more decisive nature; and so contrived it was, that, if it failed, it should appear to have been made without design to injure, and in total ignorance.

One day, Lady Dashfort, who in fact was not proud of her family, though she pretended to be so, had herself prevailed on, though with much difficulty, by Lady Killpatrick, to do the very thing she wanted to do, to show her genealogy, which had been beautifully blazoned, and which was to be produced as evidence in the lawsuit that brought her to Ireland. Lord Colambre stood politely looking on and listening, while her ladyship explained the splendid intermarriages of her family, pointing to each medallion that was filled gloriously with noble, and even with royal names, till at last she stopped short, and covering one medallion with her finger, she said –

'Pass over that, dear Lady Killpatrick. You are not to see that, Lord Colambre – that's a little blot in our scutcheon. You know, Isabel, we never talk of that prudent match of great-uncle John's; what could he expect by marrying into *that* family, where you know all the men were not *sans peur*, and none of the women *sans reproche*.'

'Oh mamma!' cried Lady Isabel, 'not one exception?'

'Not one, Isabel,' persisted Lady Dashfort; 'there was Lady — , and the other sister, that married the man with the long nose; and the daughter again, of whom they contrived to make an honest woman, by getting her married in time to a *blue riband*, and who contrived to get herself into Doctors' Commons the very next year.'

'Well, dear mamma, that is enough, and too much. Oh! pray don't go on,' cried Lady Isabel, who had appeared very much distressed during her mother's speech. 'You don't know what you are saying; indeed, ma'am, you don't.'

'Very likely, child; but that compliment I can return to you on the spot, and with interest; for you seem to me, at this instant, not to know either what you are saying or what you are doing. Come, come, explain.'

'Oh no, ma'am – Pray say so no more; I will explain myself another time.'

'Nay, there you are wrong, Isabel; in point of good-breeding, anything is better than hints and mystery. Since I have been so unlucky as to touch upon the subject, better go through with it, and, with all the boldness of innocence ask the question, Are you, my Lord Colambre, or are you not, related or connected with any of the St Omars?'

'Not that I know of,' said Lord Colambre; 'but I really am so bad a genealogist, that I cannot answer positively.'

'Then I must put the substance of my question into a new form. Have you, or have you not, a cousin of the name of Nugent?'

'Miss Nugent! – Grace Nugent! – Yes,' said Lord Colambre, with as much firmness of voice as he could command, and with as little change of countenance as possible; but, as the question came upon him so unexpectedly, it was not in his power to answer with an air of absolute indifference and composure.

'And her mother was – ' said Lady Dashfort.

'My aunt, by marriage; her maiden name was Reynolds, I think. But she died when I was quite a child. I know very little about her. I never saw her in my life; but I am certain she was a Reynolds.'

'Oh, my dear lord,' continued Lady Dashfort; 'I am perfectly aware that she did take and bear the name of Reynolds; but that was not her maiden name – her maiden name was — ; but perhaps it is a family secret that has been kept, for some good reason from you, and from the poor girl herself; the maiden name was St Omar, depend upon it. Nay, I would not have told this to you, my lord, if I could have conceived that it would affect you so violently,' pursued Lady Dashfort, in a tone of raillery; 'you see you are no worse off than we are. We have an intermarriage with the St Omars. I did not think you would be so much shocked at a discovery, which proves that our family and yours have some little connection.'

Lord Colambre endeavoured to answer, and mechanically said something about, 'happy to have the honour.' Lady Dashfort, truly happy to see that her blow had hit the mark so well, turned from his lordship without seeming to observe how seriously he was affected; and Lady Isabel sighed, and looked with compassion on Lord Colambre, and then reproachfully at her mother. But Lord Colambre heeded not her looks, and heard not of her sighs; he heard nothing, saw nothing, though his eyes were intently fixed on the genealogy, on which Lady Dashfort was still descanting to Lady Killpatrick. He took the first opportunity he could of quitting the room, and went out to take a solitary walk.

'There he is, departed, but not in peace, to reflect upon what has been said,' whispered Lady Dashfort to her daughter. 'I hope it will do him a vast deal of good.'

'None of the women *sans reproche*! None! – without one exception,' said Lord Colambre to himself; 'and Grace Nugent's mother a St Omar! – Is it possible? Lady Dashfort seems certain. She could not assert a positive falsehood – no motive. She does not know that Miss Nugent is the person to whom I am attached – she spoke at random. And I have heard it first from a stranger – not from my mother. Why was it kept secret from me? Now I understand the reason why my mother evidently never wished that I should think of Miss Nugent – why she always spoke so vehemently against the marriages of relations, of cousins. Why not tell me the truth? It would have had the strongest effect, had she known my mind.'

Lord Colambre had the greatest dread of marrying any woman whose mother had conducted herself ill. His reason, his prejudices, his pride, his delicacy, and even his limited experience, were all against it. All his hopes, his plans of future happiness, were shaken to their very foundation; he felt as if he had received a blow that stunned his mind, and from which he could not recover his faculties. The whole of that day he was like one in a dream. At night the painful idea continually recurred to him; and whenever he was falling asleep, the sound of Lady Dashfort's voice returned upon his ear, saying the words, 'What could he expect when he married one of the St Omars? None of the women *sans reproche.*'

In the morning he rose early; and the first thing he did was to write a letter to his mother, requesting (unless there was some important reason for her declining to answer the question) that she would immediately relieve his mind from a great *uneasiness* (he altered the word four times, but at last left it *uneasiness*). He stated what he had heard, and besought his mother to tell him the whole truth, without reserve.

Chapter 8

ONE MORNING Lady Dashfort had formed an ingenious scheme for leaving Lady Isabel and Lord Colambre *tête-à-tête*; but the sudden entrance of Heathcock disconcerted her intentions. He came to beg Lady Dashfort's interest with Count O'Halloran, for permission to hunt and shoot on his grounds. – 'Not for myself, 'pon honour, but for two officers who are quartered at the next *town* here, who will indubitably hang or drown themselves if they are debarred from sporting.'

'Who is this Count O'Halloran?' said Lord Colambre. Miss White, Lady Killpatrick's companion, said 'he was a great oddity;' Lady Dashfort, 'that he was singular;' and the clergyman of the parish, who was at breakfast, declared 'that he was a man of uncommon knowledge, merit, and politeness.'

'All I know of him,' said Heathcock, 'is, that he is a great sportsman, with a long queue, a gold-laced hat, and long skirts to a laced waistcoat.' Lord Colambre expressed a wish to see this extraordinary personage; and Lady Dashfort, to cover her former design, and, perhaps, thinking absence might be as effectual as too much propinquity, immediately offered to call upon the officers in their way, and carry them with Heathcock and Lord Colambre to Halloran Castle.

Lady Isabel retired with much mortification, but with becoming grace; and Captain Benson and Captain Williamson were taken to the count's. Captain Benson, who was a famous *whip*, took his seat on the box of the barouche, and the rest of the party had the pleasure of her ladyship's conversation for three or four miles: of her ladyship's conversation – for Lord Colambre's thoughts were far distant; Captain Williamson had not anything to say; and Heathcock nothing but, 'Eh! re'lly now! – 'pon honour!'

They arrived at Halloran Castle – a fine old building, part of it in ruins, and part repaired with great judgment and taste. When the carriage stopped, a respectable-looking man-servant appeared on the steps, at the open hall-door.

Count O'Halloran was out a-hunting; but his servant said 'that he would be at home immediately, if Lady Dashfort and the gentlemen would be pleased to walk in.'

On one side of the lofty and spacious hall stood the skeleton of an elk; on the other side, the perfect skeleton of a moose-deer, which, as the servant said, his master had made out, with great care, from the different bones of many of this curious species of deer, found in the lakes in the neighbourhood. The brace of officers witnessed their wonder with sundry strange oaths and exclamations. – 'Eh! 'pon honour – re'lly now!' said Heathcock; and, too genteel to wonder at or admire anything in the creation, dragged out his watch with some difficulty, saying, 'I wonder now whether they are likely to think of giving us anything to eat in this place?' And, turning his back upon the moose-deer, he straight walked out again upon the steps, called to his groom, and began to make some inquiry about his led horse. Lord Colambre surveyed the prodigious skeletons with rational curiosity, and with that sense of awe and admiration, by which a superior mind is always struck on beholding any of the great works of Providence.

'Come, my dear lord!' said Lady Dashfort; 'with our sublime sensations, we are keeping my old friend, Mr Alick Brady, this venerable person, waiting, to show us into the reception-room.'

The servant bowed respectfully – more respectfully than servants of modern date.

'My lady, the reception-room has been lately painted – the smell of paint may be disagreeable; with your leave, I will take the liberty of showing you into my master's study.'

He opened the door, went in before her, and stood holding up his finger, as if making a signal of silence to some one within. Her ladyship entered, and found herself in the midst of an odd assembly: an eagle, a goat, a dog, an otter, several gold and silver fish in a glass globe, and a white mouse in a cage. The eagle, quick of eye but quiet of demeanour, was perched upon his stand; the otter lay under the table, perfectly harmless; the Angora goat, a beautiful and remarkably little creature of its kind, with long, curling, silky hair, was walking about the room with the air of a beauty and a favourite; the dog, a tall Irish greyhound – one of the few of that fine race which is now almost extinct – had been given to Count O'Halloran by an Irish nobleman, a relation of Lady Dashfort's. This dog, who had formerly known her ladyship, looked at her with ears erect, recognised her, and went to meet her the moment she entered. The servant answered for the peaceable behaviour of all the rest of the company of animals, and retired. Lady Dashfort began to feed the eagle from a silver plate on his stand; Lord Colambre examined the inscription on his collar; the other men stood in amaze. Heathcock, who came in last, astonished out of his constant 'Eh! re'lly now!' the moment he put himself in at the door, exclaimed, 'Zounds! what's all this live lumber?' and he stumbled over the goat, who was at that moment crossing the way. The colonel's spur caught in the goat's curly beard; the colonel shook his foot, and entangled the spur worse and worse; the goat struggled and butted; the colonel skated forward on the polished oak floor, balancing himself with outstretched arms.

The indignant eagle screamed, and, passing by, perched on Heathcock's shoulders. Too well-bred to have recourse to the terrors of his beak, he scrupled not to scream, and flap his wings about the colonel's ears. Lady Dashfort, the while, threw herself back in her chair, laughing, and begging Heathcock's pardon. 'Oh, take care of the dog, my dear colonel!' cried she; 'for this kind of dog seizes his enemy by the back, and shakes him to death.' The officers, holding their sides, laughed, and begged – no pardon; while Lord Colambre, the only person who was not absolutely incapacitated, tried to disentangle the spur, and to liberate the colonel from the goat, and the goat from the colonel; an attempt in which he at last succeeded, at the expense of a considerable portion of the goat's beard. The eagle, however, still kept his place; and, yet mindful of the wrongs of his insulted friend the goat, had stretched his wings to give another buffet. Count O'Halloran entered; and the bird, quitting his prey, flew down to greet his master. The count was a fine old military-looking gentleman, fresh from the chace: his hunting accoutrements hanging carelessly about him, he advanced, unembarrassed, to the lady; and received his other guests with a mixture of military ease and gentleman-like dignity.

Without adverting to the awkward and ridiculous situation in which he had found poor Heathcock, he apologised in general for his troublesome favourites. 'For one of them,' said he, patting the head of the dog, which lay quiet at Lady Dashfort's feet, 'I see I have no need to apologise; he is where he ought to be. Poor fellow! he has never lost his taste for the good company to which he was early accustomed. As to the rest,' said he, turning to Lady Dashfort, 'a mouse, a bird, and a fish, are, you know, tribute from earth, air, and water, for my conqueror – '

'But from no barbarous Scythian!' said Lord Colambre, smiling. The count looked at Lord Colambre, as at a person worthy his attention; but his first care was to keep the peace between his loving subjects and his foreign visitors. It was difficult to dislodge the old settlers, to make room for the newcomers; but he adjusted these things with admirable facility; and, with a master's hand and master's eye, compelled each favourite to retreat into the back settlements. With becoming attention, he stroked and kept quiet old Victory, his eagle, who eyed Colonel Heathcock still, as if he did not like him; and whom the colonel eyed, as if he wished his neck fairly wrung off. The little goat had nestled himself close up to his liberator, Lord Colambre, and lay perfectly quiet, with his eyes closed, going very wisely to sleep, and submitting philosophically to the loss of one half of his beard. Conversation now commenced, and was carried on by Count O'Halloran with much ability and spirit, and with such quickness of discrimination and delicacy of taste, as quite surprised and delighted our hero. To the lady, the count's attention was first directed: he listened to her as she spoke, bending with an air of deference and devotion. She made her request for permission for Major Benson and Captain Williamson to hunt and shoot in his grounds; this was instantly granted.

'Her ladyship's requests were to him commands,' the count said. 'His gamekeeper should be instructed to give the gentlemen, her friends, every liberty, and all possible assistance.'

Then turning to the officers, he said he had just heard that several regiments of English militia had lately landed in Ireland; that one regiment was arrived at Killpatrickstown. He rejoiced in the advantages Ireland, and he hoped he might be permitted to add, England, would probably derive from the exchange of the militia of both countries; habits would be improved, ideas enlarged. The two countries have the same interest; and, from the inhabitants discovering more of each other's good qualities, and interchanging little good offices in common life, their esteem and affection for each other would increase, and rest upon the firm basis of mutual utility.'

To all this Major Benson and Captain Williamson made no reply.

'The major looks so like a stuffed man of straw,' whispered Lady Dashfort to Lord Colambre; 'and the captain so like the knave of clubs, putting forth one manly leg.'

Count O'Halloran now turned the conversation to field sports, and then the captain and major opened at once.

'Pray now, sir?' said the major, 'you fox-hunt in this country, I suppose; and now do you manage the thing here as we do? Over night, you know, before the hunt, when the fox is out, stopping up the earths of the cover we mean to draw, and all the rest for four miles round. Next morning we assemble at the cover's side, and the huntsman throws in the hounds. The gossip here is no small part of the entertainment; but as soon as we hear the hounds give tongue – '

'The favourite hounds,' interposed Williamson.

'The favourite hounds, to be sure,' continued Benson; 'there is a dead silence, till pug is well out of cover, and the whole pack well in; then cheer the hounds with tally-ho! till your lungs crack. Away he goes in gallant style, and the whole field is hard up, till pug takes a stiff country; then they who haven't pluck lag, see no more of him, and, with a fine blazing scent, there are but few of us in at the death.'

'Well, we are fairly in at the death, I hope,' said Lady Dashfort; 'I was thrown out sadly at one time in the chace.'

Lord Colambre, with the count's permission, took up a book in which the count's pencil lay, *Pasley on the Military Policy of Great Britain*; it was marked with many notes of admiration, and with hands pointing to remarkable passages.

'That is a book that leaves a strong impression on the mind,' said the count.

Lord Colambre read one of the marked passages, beginning with, 'All that distinguishes a soldier in outward appearance from a citizen is so trifling – ' but at this instant our hero's attention was distracted by seeing in a black-letter book this title of a chapter:

'Burial-place of the Nugents.'

'Pray now, sir,' said Captain Williamson, 'if I don't interrupt you, as you are such a famous fox-hunter, maybe, you nay be a fisherman too; and now in Ireland do you, *Mr* — '

A smart pinch on his elbow from his major, who stood behind him, stopped the captain short, as he pronounced the word *Mr*. Like all awkward people, he turned directly to ask, by his looks, what was the matter?

The major took advantage of his discomfiture, and, stepping before him, determined to have the fishing to himself, and went on with –

'Count O'Halloran, I presume you understand fishing too, as well as hunting?'

The count bowed: 'I do not presume to say that, sir.'

'But pray, count, in this country, do you arm your hook this ways? Give me leave;' taking the whip from Williamson's reluctant hand, 'this ways, laying the outermost part of your feather this fashion next to your hook, and the point next to your shank, this wise, and that wise; and then, sir, – count, you take the hackle of a cock's neck – '

'A plover's topping's better,' said Williamson.

'And work your gold and silver thread,' pursued Benson, 'up to your wings, and when your head's made, you fasten all.'

'But you never showed how your head's made,' interrupted Williamson.

'The gentleman knows how a head's made; any man can make a head, I suppose; so, sir, you fasten all.'

'You'll never get your head fast on that way, while the world stands,' cried Williamson.

'Fast enough for all purposes; I'll bet you a rump and dozen, captain; and then, sir, – count, you divide your wings with a needle.'

'A pin's point will do,' said Williamson.

The count, to reconcile matters, produced from an Indian cabinet, which he had opened for the lady's inspection, a little basket containing a variety of artificial flies of curious construction, which, as he spread them on the table, made Williamson and Benson's eyes almost sparkle with delight. There was the *dun-fly*, for the month of March; and the *stone-fly*, much in vogue for April; and the *ruddy-fly*, of red wool black silk, and red capon's feathers.

Lord Colambre, whose head was in the burial-place of the Nugents, wished them all at the bottom of the sea.

'And the *green-fly*, and the *moorish-fly*!' cried Benson, snatching them up with transport; 'and, chief, the *sad-yellow-fly*, in which the fish delight in June; the *sad-yellow-fly*, mad with the buzzard's wings, bound with black braked hemp, and, the *shell-fly*, for the middle of July, made of greenish wool wrapped about with the herle of a peacock's tail, famous for creating excellent sport.' All these and more were spread upon the table before the sportsmen's wondering eyes.

'Capital flies! capital, faith!' cried Williamson.

'Treasures, faith, real treasures, by G— !' cried Benson.

'Eh! 'pon honour! re'lly now,' were the first words which Heathcock had uttered since his battle with the goat.

'My dear Heathcock, are you alive still?' said Lady Dashfort; 'I had really forgotten your existence.'

So had Count O'Halloran, but he did not say so.

'Your ladyship has the advantage of me there,' said Heathcock, stretching himself; 'I wish I could forget my existence, for, in my mind, existence is a horrible *bore*.'

'I thought you *was* a sportsman,' said Williamson.

'Well, sir?'

'And a fisherman?'

'Well, sir?'

'Why, look you there, sir,' pointing to the flies, 'and tell a body life's a bore.'

'One can't *always* fish, or shoot, I apprehend, sir,' said Heathcock.

'Not always – but sometimes,' said Williamson, laughing; 'for I suspect shrewdly you've forgot some of your sporting in Bond Street.'

'Eh! 'pon honour! re'lly now!' said the colonel, retreating again to his safe entrenchment of affectation, from which he never could venture without imminent danger.

' 'Pon honour,' cried Lady Dashfort, 'I can swear for Heathcock, that I have eaten excellent hares and ducks of his shooting, which, to my knowledge,' added she, in a loud whisper, 'he bought in the market.'

'*Emptum aprum*!' said Lord Colambre to the count, without danger of being understood by those whom it concerned.

The count smiled a second time; but politely turning the attention of the company from the unfortunate colonel by addressing himself to the laughing sportsmen, 'Gentlemen, you seem to value these,' said he, sweeping the artificial flies from the table into the little basket from which they had been taken; 'would you do me the honour to accept of them? They are all of my own making, and consequently of Irish manufacture.' Then, ringing the bell, he asked Lady Dashfort's permission to have the basket put into her carriage.

Benson and Williamson followed the servant, to prevent them from being tossed into the boot. Heathcock stood still in the middle of the room taking snuff.

Count O'Halloran turned from him to Lord Colambre, who had just got happily to *the burial-place of the Nugents*, when Lady Dashfort, coming between them, and spying the title of the chapter, exclaimed –

'What have you there? – Antiquities! my delight! – but I never look at engravings when I can see realities.'

Lord Colambre was then compelled to follow, as she led the way into the hall, where the count took down golden ornaments, and brass-headed spears, and jointed horns of curious workmanship, that had been found on his estate; and he told of spermaceti wrapped in carpets, and he showed small urns, enclosing ashes; and from among these urns he selected one, which he put into the hands of Lord Colambre, telling him that it had been lately found in an old abbey-ground in his neighbourhood, which had been the burial-place of some of the Nugent family.

'I was just looking at the account of it, in the book which you saw open on my table. – And as you seem to take an interest in that family, my lord, perhaps,' said the count, 'you may think this urn worth your acceptance.'

Lord Colambre said, 'It would be highly valuable to him – as the Nugents were his near relations.'

Lady Dashfort little expected this blow; she, however, carried him off to the moose-deer, and from moose-deer to round-towers, to various architectural antiquities, and to the real and fabulous history of Ireland, on all which the count spoke with learning and enthusiasm. But now, to Colonel Heathcock's great joy and relief, a handsome collation appeared in the dining-room, of which Ulick opened the folding-doors.

'Count, you have made an excellent house of your castle,' said Lady Dashfort.

'It will be, when it is finished,' said the count. 'I am afraid,' added he, smiling, 'I live like many other Irish gentlemen, who never are, but always to be, blest with a good house. I began on too large a scale, and can never hope to live to finish it.'

' 'Pon honour! here's a good thing, which I hope we shall live to finish,' said Heathcock, sitting down before the collation; and heartily did he eat of grouse pie, and of Irish ortolans, which, as Lady Dashfort observed, 'afforded him indemnity for the past, and security for the future.'

'Eh! re'lly now! your Irish ortolans are famous good eating,' said Heathcock.

'Worth being quartered in Ireland, faith! to taste 'em,' said Benson.

The count recommended to Lady Dashfort some of 'that delicate sweetmeat, the Irish plum.'

'Bless me, sir – count!' cried Williamson, 'it's by far the best thing of the kind I ever tasted in all my life: where could you get this?'

'In Dublin, at my dear Mrs Godcy's; where *only*, in his Majesty's dominions, it is to be had,' said the count. The whole dish vanished in a few seconds. – ' 'Pon honour! I do believe this is the thing the queen's so fond of,' said Heathcock.

Then heartily did he drink of the count's excellent Hungarian wines; and, by the common bond of sympathy between those who have no other tastes but eating and drinking, the colonel, the major, and the captain were now all the best companions possible for one another.

Whilst 'they prolonged the rich repast,' Lady Dashfort and Lord Colambre went to the window to admire the prospect; Lady Dashfort asked the count the name of some distant hill.

'Ah!' said the count, 'that hill was once covered with fine wood; but it was all cut down two years ago.'

'Who could have been so cruel?' said her ladyship.

'I forget the present proprietor's name,' said the count, 'but he is one of those who, according to the *clause of distress* in their leases, *lead, drive, and carry away*, but never enter their lands; one of those enemies to Ireland – these cruel absentees!' Lady Dashfort looked through her glass at the mountain; – Lord Colambre sighed, and, endeavouring to pass it off with a smile, said frankly to the count –

'You are not aware, I am sure, count, that you are speaking to the son of an Irish absentee family. – Nay, do not be shocked, my dear sir; I tell you only, because I thought it fair to do so; but let me assure you, that nothing you could say on that subject could hurt me personally, because I feel that I am not, that I never can be, an enemy to Ireland. An absentee, voluntarily, I never yet have been; and as to the future, I declare – '

'I declare you know nothing of the future,' interrupted Lady Dashfort, in a half-peremptory, half-playful tone – 'you know nothing; make no rash vows, and you will break none.'

The undaunted assurance of Lady Dashfort's genius for intrigue gave her an air of frank imprudence, which prevented Lord Colambre from suspecting that more was meant than met the ear. The count and he took leave of one another with mutual regard; and Lady Dashfort rejoiced to have got our hero out of Halloran Castle.

Chapter 9

Lord Colambre had waited with great impatience for an answer to the letter of inquiry which he had written about Miss Nugent's mother. A letter from Lady Clonbrony arrived; he opened it with the greatest eagerness – passed over

'Rheumatism – warm weather – warm bath – Buxton balls – Miss Broadhurst – your *friend*, Sir Arthur Berryl, very assiduous!' The name of Grace Nugent he found at last, and read as follows:

Her mother's maiden name was *St Omar*; and there was a *faux pas*, certainly. She was, I am told (for it was before my time), educated at a convent abroad; and there was an affair with a Captain Reynolds, a young officer, which her friends were obliged to hush up. She brought an infant to England with her, and took the name of Reynolds – but none of that family would acknowledge her; and she lived in great obscurity, till your uncle Nugent saw, fell in love with her, and (knowing her whole history) married her. He adopted the child, gave her his name, and, after some years, the whole story was forgotten. Nothing could be more disadvantageous to Grace than to have it revived: this is the reason we kept it secret.

Lord Colambre tore the letter to bits.

From the perturbation which Lady Dashfort saw in his countenance, she guessed the nature of the letter which he had been reading, and for the arrival of which he had been so impatient.

'It has worked!' said she to herself. '*Pour le coup Philippe je te tiens!*'

Lord Colambre appeared this day more sensible, than he had ever yet seemed, to the charms of the fair Isabel.

'Many a tennis-ball, and many a heart is caught at the rebound,' said Lady Dashfort. 'Isabel! now is your time!'

And so it was – or so, perhaps, it would have been, but for a circumstance which her ladyship, with all her genius for intrigue, had never taken into her consideration. Count O'Halloran came to return the visit which had been paid to him; and, in the course of conversation, he spoke of the officers who had been introduced to him, and told Lady Dashfort that he had heard a report which shocked him much – he hoped it could not be true – that one of these officers had introduced his mistress as his wife to Lady Oranmore, who lived in the neighbourhood. This officer, it was said, had let Lady Oranmore send her carriage for this woman; and that she had dined at Oranmore with her ladyship and her daughters. 'But I cannot believe it! I cannot believe it to be possible, that any gentleman, that any *officer*, could do such a thing!' said the count.

'And is this all?' exclaimed Lady Dashfort. 'Is this all the terrible affair, my good count, which has brought your face to this prodigious length?'

The count looked at Lady Dashfort with astonishment.

'Such a look of virtuous indignation,' continued she, 'did I never behold, on or off the stage. Forgive me for laughing, count; but, believe me, comedy goes through the world better than tragedy, and, take it all in all, does rather less mischief. As to the thing in question, I know nothing about it: I dare say, it is not true; but, now, suppose it was – it is only a silly *quiz*, of a raw young officer, upon a prudish old dowager. I know nothing about it, for my part; but, after all, what irreparable mischief has been done? Laugh at the thing, and then it is a jest – a bad one, perhaps, but still only a jest – and there's an end of it; but take it seriously, and there is no knowing where it might end – in half a dozen duels, maybe.'

'Of that, madam,' said the count, 'Lady Oranmore's prudence and presence of mind have prevented all danger. Her ladyship *would* not understand the insult. She said, or she acted as if she said, "*Je ne veux rien voir, rien écouter, rien savoir*." Lady Oranmore is one of the most respectable – '

'Count, I beg your pardon!' interrupted Lady Dashfort; 'but I must tell you that your favourite, Lady Oranmore, has behaved very ill to me; purposely omitted to invite Isabel to her ball; offended and insulted me: – her praises, therefore, cannot be the most agreeable subject of conversation you can choose for my amusement; and as to the rest, you, who have such variety and so much politeness, will, I am sure, have the goodness to indulge my caprice in this instance.'

'I shall obey your ladyship, and be silent, whatever pleasure it might give me to speak on that subject,' said the count; 'and I trust Lady Dashfort will reward me by the assurance that, however playfully she may have just now spoken, she seriously disapproves and is shocked.'

'Oh, shocked! shocked to death! if that will satisfy you, my dear count.'

The count, obviously, was not satisfied; he had civil, as well as military courage, and his sense of right and wrong could stand against the raillery and ridicule of a fine lady.

The conversation ended: Lady Dashfort thought it would have no further consequences; and she did not regret the loss of a man like Count O'Halloran, who lived retired in his castle, and who could not have any influence upon the opinion of the fashionable world. However, upon turning from the count to Lord Colambre, who she thought had been occupied with Lady Isabel, and to whom she imagined all this dispute was uninteresting, she perceived, by his countenance, that she had made a great mistake. Still she trusted that her power over Lord Colambre was sufficient easily to efface whatever unfavourable impression this conversation had made upon his mind. He had no personal interest in the affair; and she had generally found that people are easily satisfied about any wrong or insult, public or private, in which they have no immediate concern. But all the charms of her conversation were now tried in vain to reclaim him from the reverie into which he had fallen.

His friend Sir James Brooke's parting advice occurred to our hero; his eyes began to open to Lady Dashfort's character; and he was, from this moment, freed from her power. Lady Isabel, however, had taken no part in all this – she was blameless; and, independently of her mother, and in pretended opposition of sentiment, she might have continued to retain the influence she had gained over Lord Colambre, but that a slight accident revealed to him *her* real disposition.

It happened, on the evening of this day, that Lady Isabel came into the library with one of the young ladies of the house, talking very eagerly, without perceiving Lord Colambre, who was sitting in one of the recesses reading.

'My dear creature, you are quite mistaken,' said Lady Isabel, 'he was never a favourite of mine; I always detested him; I only flirted with him to plague his wife. Oh that wife, my dear Elizabeth, I do hate!' cried she, clasping her hands, and expressing hatred with all her soul and with all her strength. 'I detest that Lady de Cresey to such a degree, that, to purchase the pleasure of making her feel the pangs of jealousy for one hour, look, I would this moment lay down this finger and let it be cut off.'

The face, the whole figure of Lady Isabel at this moment I appeared to Lord Colambre suddenly metamorphosed; instead of the soft, gentle, amiable female, all sweet charity and tender sympathy, formed to love and to be loved, he beheld one possessed and convulsed by an evil spirit – her beauty, if beauty it could be called, the beauty of a fiend. Some ejaculation, which he unconsciously uttered, made Lady Isabel start. She saw him – saw the expression of his countenance, and knew that all was over.

Lord Colambre, to the utter astonishment and disappointment of Lady Dashfort, and to the still greater mortification of Lady Isabel, announced this night that it was necessary he should immediately pursue his tour in Ireland. We pass over all the castles in the air which the young ladies of the family had built, and which now fell to the ground. We pass all the civil speeches of Lord and Lady Killpatrick; all the vehement remonstrances of Lady Dashfort; and the vain sighs of Lady Isabel. To the last moment Lady Dashfort said –

'He will not go.'

But he went; and, when he was gone, Lady Dashfort exclaimed, 'That man has escaped from me.' And after a pause, turning to her daughter, she, in the most taunting and contemptuous terms, reproached her as the cause of this failure, concluding by a declaration that she must in future manage her own affairs, and had best settle her mind to marry Heathcock; since every one else was too wise to think of her.

Lady Isabel of course retorted. But we leave this amiable mother and daughter to recriminate in appropriate terms, and we follow our hero, rejoiced that he has been disentangled from their snares. Those who have never been in similar peril will wonder much that he did not escape sooner; those who have ever been in like danger will wonder more that he escaped at all. Those who are best acquainted with the heart or imagination of man will be most ready to acknowledge that the combined charms of wit, beauty, and flattery, may, for a time, suspend the action of right reason in the mind of the greatest philosopher, or operate against the resolutions of the greatest of heroes.

Lord Colambre pursued his way to Castle Halloran, desirous, before he quitted this part of the country, to take leave of the count, who had shown him much civility, and for whose honourable conduct, and generous character, he had conceived a high esteem, which no little peculiarities of antiquated dress or manner could diminish. Indeed, the old-fashioned politeness of what was formerly called a well-bred gentleman pleased him better than the indolent or insolent selfishness of modern men of the ton. Perhaps, notwithstanding our hero's determination to turn his mind from everything connected with the idea of Miss Nugent, some latent curiosity about the burial-place of the Nugents might have operated to make him call upon the count. In this hope he was disappointed; for a cross miller, to whom the abbey-ground was set, on which the burial-place was found, had taken it into his head to refuse admittance, and none could enter his ground.

Count O'Halloran was much pleased by Lord Colambre's visit. The very day of Lord Colambre's arrival at Halloran Castle, the count was going to Oranmore; he was dressed, and his carriage was waiting; therefore Lord Colambre begged that he might not detain him, and the count requested his lordship to accompany him.

'Let me have the honour of introducing you, my lord, to a family, with whom, I am persuaded, you will be pleased; by whom you will be appreciated; and at whose house you will have an opportunity of seeing the best manner of living of the Irish nobility.' Lord Colambre accepted the invitation, and was introduced at Oranmore. The dignified appearance and respectable character of Lady Oranmore; the charming unaffected manners of her daughters; the air of domestic happiness and comfort in her family; the becoming magnificence, free from ostentation, in her whole establishment; the respect and affection with which she was treated by all who approached her, delighted and touched Lord Colambre; the more, perhaps, because he had heard this family so unjustly abused; and because he saw Lady Oranmore and her daughter, in immediate contrast to Lady Dashfort and Lady Isabel.'

A little circumstance which occurred during this visit increased his interest for the family. When Lady de Cresey's little boys came in after dinner, one of them was playing with a seal, which had just been torn from a letter. The child showed it to Lord Colambre, and asked him to read the motto. The motto was, 'Deeds, not words' – his friend Sir James Brooke's motto, and his arms. Lord Colambre eagerly inquired if this family was acquainted with Sir James, and he soon perceived that they were not only acquainted with him, but that they were particularly interested about him.

Lady Oranmore's second daughter, Lady Harriet, appeared particularly pleased by the manner in which Lord Colambre spoke of Sir James. And the child, who had now established himself on his lordship's knee, turned round, and whispered in his ear, 'Twas Aunt Harriet gave me the seal; Sir James is to be married to Aunt Harriet, and then he will be my uncle.'

Some of the principal gentry of this part of the country happened to dine at Oranmore one of the days Lord Colambre was there. He was surprised at the discovery, that there were so many agreeable, well-informed, and well-bred people, of whom, while he was at Killpatrickstown, he had seen nothing. He now discerned how far he had been deceived by Lady Dashfort.

Both the count, and Lord and Lady Oranmore, who were warmly attached to their country, exhorted him to make himself amends for the time he had lost, by seeing with his own eyes, and judging with his own understanding, of the country and its own inhabitants, during the remainder of the time he was to stay in Ireland. The higher classes, in most countries, they observed were generally similar; but, in the lower class, he would find many characteristic differences.

When he first came to Ireland, he had been very eager to go and see his father's estate, and to judge of the conduct of his agents, and the condition of his tenantry; but this eagerness had subsided, and the design had almost faded from his mind, whilst under the influence of Lady Dashfort's misrepresentations. A mistake, relative to some remittance from his banker in Dublin, obliged him to delay his journey a few days, and during that time Lord and Lady Oranmore showed him the neat cottages, the well-attended schools, in their neighbourhood. They showed him not only what could be done, but what had been done, by the influence of great proprietors residing on their own estates, and encouraging the people by judicious kindness.

He saw, he acknowledged the truth of this; but it did not come home to his feelings now as it would have done a little while ago. His views and plans were altered; he looked forward to the idea of marrying and settling in Ireland, and then everything in the country was interesting to him; but since he had forbidden himself to think of a union with Miss Nugent, his mind had lost its object and its spring; he was not sufficiently calm to think of the public good; his thoughts were absorbed by his private concern. He knew, and repeated to himself, that he ought to visit his own and his father's estates, and to see the condition of his tenantry; he desired to fulfil his duties, but they ceased to appear to him easy and pleasurable, for hope and love no longer brightened his prospects.

That he might see and hear more than he could as heir-apparent to the estate, he sent his servant to Dublin to wait for him there. He travelled *incognito*, wrapped himself in a shabby greatcoat, and took the name of Evans. He arrived at a village, or, as it was called, a town, which bore the name of Colambre. He was agreeably surprised by the air of neatness and finish in the houses and in the street, which had a nicely-swept paved footway. He slept at a small but excellent inn – excellent, perhaps, because it was small, and proportioned to the situation and business of the place. Good supper, good bed, good attendance; nothing out of repair; no things pressed into services for what they were never intended by nature or art; none of what are vulgarly called *make-shifts*. No chambermaid slipshod, or waiter smelling of whiskey; but all tight and right, and everybody doing their own business, and doing it as if it was their everyday occupation, not as if it was done by particular desire, for first or last time this season. The landlord came in at supper to inquire whether anything was wanted. Lord Colambre took this opportunity of entering into conversation with him, and asked him to whom the town belonged, and who were the proprietors of the neighbouring estates.

'The town belongs to an absentee lord – one Lord Clonbrony, who lives always beyond the seas, in London; and never seen the town since it was a town, to call a town.'

'And does the land in the neighbourhood belong to this Lord Clonbrony?'

'It does, sir; he's a great proprietor, but knows nothing of his property, nor of us. Never set foot among us, to my knowledge, since I was as high as the table. He might as well be a West India planter, and we negroes, for anything he knows to the contrary – has no more care, nor thought about us, than if he were in Jamaica, or the other world. Shame for him! – But there's too many to keep him in countenance.'

Lord Colambre asked him what wine he could have; and then inquired who managed the estate for this absentee.

'Mr Burke, sir. And I don't know why God was so kind to give so good an agent to an absentee like Lord Clonbrony, except it was for the sake of us, who is under him, and knows the blessing, and is thankful for the same.'

'Very good cutlets,' said Lord Colambre.

'I am happy to hear it, sir. They have a right to be good, for Mrs Burke sent her own cook to teach my wife to dress cutlets.'

'So the agent is a good agent, is he?'

'He is, thanks be to Heaven! And that's what few can boast, especially when the landlord's living over the seas: we have the luck to have got a good agent over us, in Mr Burke, who is a right bred gentleman; a snug little property of his own, honestly made; with the good will and good wishes, and respect of all.'

'Does he live in the neighbourhood?'

'Just *convanient*. At the end of the town; in the house on the hill, as you passed, sir; to the left, with the trees about it, all of his planting, finely grown too – for there's a blessing on all he does, and he has done a deal. – There's salad, sir, if you are *partial* to it. Very fine lettuce. Mrs Burke sent us the plants herself.'

'Excellent salad! So this Mr Burke has done a great deal, has he? In what way?'

'In every way, sir – sure was not it he that had improved, and fostered, and *made* the town of Colambre? – no thanks to the proprietor, nor to the young man whose name it bears, neither!'

'Have you any porter, pray, sir?'

'We have, sir, as good, I hope, as you'd drink in London, for it's the same you get there, I understand, from Cork. And I have some of my own brewing, which, they say, you could not tell the difference between it and Cork quality – if you'd be pleased to try. Harry, the corkscrew.'

The porter of his own brewing was pronounced to be extremely good; and the landlord observed it was Mr Burke encouraged him to learn to brew, and lent him his own brewer for a time to teach him.

'Your Mr Burke, I find, is *apropos* to porter, *apropos* to salad, *apropos* to cutlets, *apropos* to everything,' said Lord Colambre, smiling; 'he seems to be a *non-pareil* of an agent. I suppose you are a great favourite of his, and you do what you please with him?'

'Oh no, sir, I could not say that; Mr Burke does not have favourites anyway; but according to my deserts, I trust, I stand well enough with him, for, in truth, he is a right good agent.'

Lord Colambre still pressed for particulars; he was an Englishman, and a stranger, he said, and did not exactly know what was meant in Ireland by a good agent.

'Why, he is the man that will encourage the improving tenant; and show no favour or affection, but justice, which comes even to all, and does best for all at the long run; and, residing always in the country, like Mr Burke, and understanding country business, and going about continually among the tenantry, he knows when to press for the rent, and when to leave the money to lay out upon the land; and, according as they would want it, can give a tenant a help or a check properly. Then no duty-work called for, no presents, nor *glove-money*, nor *sealing-money* even, taken or offered; no underhand hints about proposals, when land would be out of lease, but a considerable preference, if deserved, to the old tenant, and if not, a fair advertisement, and the best offer and tenant accepted; no screwing of the land to the highest penny, just to please the head landlord for the minute, and ruin him at the end, by the tenant's racking the land, and running off with the year's rent; nor no bargains to his own relations or friends did Mr Burke ever give or grant, but all fair between landlord and tenant; and that's the thing that will last; and that's what I call the good agent.'

Lord Colambre poured out a glass of wine, and begged the inn-keeper to drink the good agent's health, in which he was heartily pledged. 'I thank your honour; – Mr Burke's health! and long may he live over and amongst us; he saved me from drink and ruin, when I was once inclined to it, and made a man of me and all my family.'

The particulars we cannot stay to detail: this grateful man, however, took pleasure in sounding the praises of his benefactor, and in raising him in the opinion of the traveller.

'As you've time, and are curious about such things, sir, perhaps you'd walk up to the school that Mrs Burke has for the poor children; and look at the market-house, and see how clean he takes a pride to keep the town; and any house in the town, from the priest to the parson's, that you'd go into, will give you the same character as I do of Mr Burke: from the brogue to the boot, all speak the same of him, and can say no other. God for ever bless and keep him over us!'

Upon making further inquiries, everything the innkeeper had said was confirmed by different inhabitants of the village. Lord Colambre conversed with the shopkeepers, with the cottagers; and, without making any alarming inquiries, he obtained all the information he wanted. He went to the village school – a pretty, cheerful house, with a neat garden and a play-green; met Mrs Burke; introduced himself to her as a traveller. The school was shown to him: it was just what it ought to be – neither too much nor too little had been attempted; there was neither too much interference nor too little attention. Nothing for exhibition; care to teach well, without any vain attempt to teach in a wonderfully short time. All that experience proves to be useful, in both Dr Bell's and Mr Lancaster's modes of teaching, Mrs Burke had adopted; leaving it to 'graceless zealots' to fight about the rest. That no attempts at proselytism had been made, and that no illiberal distinc-tions had been made in this school, Lord Colambre was convinced, in the best manner possible, by seeing the children of Protestants and Catholics sitting on the same benches, learning from the same books, and speaking to one another with the same cordial familiarity. Mrs Burke was an unaffected, sensible woman, free from all party prejudices, and, without ostentation, desirous and capable of doing good. Lord Colambre was much pleased with her, and very glad that she invited him to dinner.

Mr Burke did not come in till late; for he had been detained portioning out some meadows, which were of great consequence to the inhabitants of the town. He brought home to dine with him the clergyman and the priest of the parish, both of whom he had taken successful pains to accommodate with the land which suited their respective convenience. The good terms on which they seemed to be with each other, and with him, appeared to Lord Colambre to do honour to Mr Burke. All the favourable accounts his lordship had received of this gentleman were confirmed by what he saw and heard. After the clergyman and priest had taken leave, upon Lord Colambre's expressing some surprise, mixed with satisfaction, at seeing the harmony which subsisted between them, Mr Burke assured him that this was the same in many parts of Ireland. He observed, that 'as the suspicion of ill-will never fails to produce it,' so he had often found, that taking it for granted that no ill-will exists has the most conciliating effect. He said, to please opposite parties, he used no arts; but he tried to make all his neighbours live comfortably together, by making them acquainted with each other's good qualities; by giving them opportunities of meeting sociably, and, from time to time, of doing each other little services and good offices. 'Fortunately, he had so much to do,' he said, 'that he had no time for controversy. He was a plain man, made it a rule not to meddle with speculative points, and to avoid all irritating discussions; he was not to rule the country, but to live in it, and make others live as happily as he could.'

Having nothing to conceal in his character, opinions, or circumstances, Mr Burke was perfectly open and unreserved in his manner and conversation; freely answered all the traveller's inquiries, and took pains to show him everything he desired to see. Lord Colambre said he had thoughts of settling in Ireland; and declared, with truth, that he had not seen any part of the country he should like better to live in than this neighbourhood. He went over most of the estate with Mr Burke, and had ample opportunities of convincing himself that this gentleman was indeed, as the innkeeper had described him, 'a right good gentleman, and a right good agent.'

He paid Mr Burke some just compliments on the state of the tenantry, and the neat and flourishing appearance of the town of Colambre.

'What pleasure it will give the proprietor when he sees all you have done!' said Lord Colambre.

'Oh, sir, don't speak of it! – that breaks my heart; he never has shown the least interest in anything I have done; he is quite dissatisfied with me, because I have not ruined his tenantry, by forcing them to pay more than the land is worth; because I have not squeezed money from them by fining down rents; and – but all this, as an Englishman, sir, must be unintelligible to you. The end of the matter is, that, attached as I am to this place and the people about me, and, as I hope, the tenantry are to me – I fear I shall be obliged to give up the agency.'

'Give up the agency! How so? – you must not,' cried Lord Colambre, and, for the moment, he forgot himself; but Mr Burke took this only for an expression of good-will.

'I must, I am afraid,' continued he. 'My employer, Lord Clonbrony, is displeased with me – continual calls for money come upon me from England, and complaints of my slow remittances.'

'Perhaps Lord Clonbrony is in embarrassed circumstances,' said Lord Colambre.

'I never speak of my employer's affairs, sir,' replied Mr Burke; now for the first time assuming an air of reserve.

'I beg pardon, sir – I seem to have asked an indiscreet question.' Mr Burke was silent.

'Lest my reserve should give you a false impression, I will add, sir,' resumed Mr Burke, 'that I really am not acquainted with the state of his lordship's affairs in general. I know only what belongs to the estate under my own management. The principal part of his lordship's property, the Clonbrony estate, is under another agent, Mr Garraghty.'

'Garraghty!' repeated Lord Colambre; 'what sort of a person is he? But I may take it for granted, that it cannot fall to the lot of one and the same absentee to have two such agents as Mr Burke.'

Mr Burke bowed, and seemed pleased by the compliment, which he knew he deserved – but not a word did he say of Mr Garraghty; and Lord Colambre, afraid of betraying himself by some other indiscreet question, changed the conversation.

That very night the post brought a letter to Mr Burke, from Lord Clonbrony, which Mr Burke gave to his wife as soon as he had read it, saying –

'See the reward of all my services!'

Mrs Burke glanced her eye over the letter, and, being extremely fond of her husband, and sensible of his deserving far different treatment, burst into indignant exclamations –

'See the reward of all your services, indeed! – What an unreasonable, ungrateful man! – So, this is the thanks for all you have done for Lord Clonbrony!'

'He does not know what I have done, my dear. He never has seen what I have done.'

'More shame for him!'

'He never, I suppose, looks over his accounts, or understands them.'

'More shame for him!'

'He listens to foolish reports, or misrepresentations, perhaps. He is at a distance, and cannot find out the truth.'

'More shame for him!'

'Take it quietly, my dear; we have the comfort of a good conscience. The agency may be taken from me by this lord; but the sense of having done my duty, no lord or man upon earth can give or take away.'

'Such a letter!' said Mrs Burke, taking it up again. 'Not even the civility to write with his own hand! – only his signature to the scrawl – looks as if it was written by a drunken man, does not it, Mr Evans?' said she, showing the letter to Lord Colambre, who immediately recognised the writing of Sir Terence O'Fay.

'It does not look like the hand of a gentleman, indeed,' said Lord Colambre.

'It has Lord Clonbrony's own signature, let it be what it will,' said Mr Burke, looking closely at it; 'Lord Clonbrony's own writing the signature is, I am clear of that.'

Lord Clonbrony's son was clear of it also; but he took care not to give any opinion on that point.

'Oh, pray, read it, sir, read it,' said Mrs Burke, pleased by his tone of indignation; 'read it, pray; a gentleman may write a bad hand, but no *gentleman* could write such a letter as that to Mr Burke – pray read it, sir; you who have seen something of what Mr Burke has done for the town of Colambre, and what he has made of the tenantry and the estate of Lord Clonbrony.'

Lord Colambre read, and was convinced that his father had never written or read the letter, but had signed it, trusting to Sir Terence O'Fay's having expressed his sentiments properly.

Sir,

As I have no further occasion for your services, you will take notice, that I hereby request you will forthwith hand over, on or before the 1st of November next, your accounts, with the balance due of the *hanging-gale* (which, I understand, is more than ought to be at this season) to Nicholas O'Garraghty, Esq., College Green, Dublin, who in future will act as agent, and shall get, by post, immediately, a power of attorney for the same, entitling him to receive and manage the Colambre as well as the Clonbrony estate, for, Sir, your obedient humble servant,   CLONBRONY.

Grosvenor Square.

Though misrepresentation, caprice, or interest, might have induced Lord Clonbrony to desire to change his agent, yet Lord Colambre knew that his father never could have announced his wishes in such a style; and, as he returned the letter to Mrs Burke, he repeated, he was convinced that it was impossible that any nobleman could have written such a letter; that it must have been written by some inferior person; and that his lordship had signed it without reading it.

'My dear, I'm sorry you showed that letter to Mr Evans,' said Mr Burke; 'I don't like to expose Lord Clonbrony; he is a well-meaning gentleman, misled by ignorant or designing people; at all events, it is not for us to expose him.'

'He has exposed himself,' said Mrs Burke; 'and the world should know it.'

'He was very kind to me when I was a young man,' said Mr Burke; 'we must not forget that now, because we are angry, my love.'

'Why, no, my love, to be sure we should not; but who could have recollected it just at this minute but yourself? – And now, sir,' turning to Lord Colambre, 'you see what kind of a man this is: now is it not difficult for me to bear patiently to see him ill-treated?'

'Not only difficult, but impossible, I should think, madam,' said Lord Colambre; 'I know, even I, who am a stranger, cannot help feeling for both of you, as you must see I do.'

'And half the world, who don't know him,' continued Mrs Burke, 'when they hear that Lord Clonbrony's agency is taken from him, will think, perhaps, that he is to blame.'

'No, madam,' said Lord Colambre; 'that you need not fear; Mr Burke may safely trust to his character; from what I have within these two days seen and heard, I am convinced that such is the respect he has deserved and acquired, that no blame can touch him.'

'Sir, I thank you,' said Mrs Burke, the tears coming into her eyes; 'you can judge – you do him justice; but there are so many who don't know him, and who will decide without knowing any of the facts.'

'That, my dear, happens about everything to everybody,' said Mr Burke; 'but we must have patience; time sets all judgments right, sooner or later.'

'But the sooner the better,' said Mrs Burke. 'Mr Evans, I hope you will be so kind, if ever you hear this business talked of – '

'Mr Evans lives in Wales, my dear.'

'But he is travelling through Ireland, my dear, and he said he should return to Dublin, and, you know, there he certainly will hear it talked of; and I hope he will do me the favour to state what he has seen and knows to be the truth.'

'Be assured that I will do Mr Burke justice – as far as it is in my power,' said Lord Colambre, restraining himself much, that he might not say more than became his assumed character. He took leave of this worthy family that night, and, early the next morning, departed.

'Ah!' thought he, as he drove away from this well-regulated and flourishing place, 'how happy I might be, settled here with such a wife as – her of whom I must think no more.'

He pursued his way to Clonbrony, his father's other estate, which was at a considerable distance from Colambre; he was resolved to know what kind of agent Mr Nicholas Garraghty might be, who was to supersede Mr Burke, and by power of attorney to be immediately entitled to receive and manage the Colambre as well as the Clonbrony estate.

Chapter 10

TOWARDS THE EVENING of the second day's journey, the driver of Lord Colambre's hackney chaise stopped, and jumping off the wooden bar, on which he had been seated, exclaimed –

'We're come to the bad step, now. The bad road's beginning upon us, please your honour.'

'Bad road! that is very uncommon in this country. I never saw such fine roads as you have in Ireland.'

'That's true; and God bless your honour, that's sensible of that same, for it's not what all the foreign quality I drive have the manners to notice. God bless your honour! I heard you're a Welshman, but whether or no, I am sure you are a gentleman, anyway, Welsh or other.'

Notwithstanding the shabby greatcoat, the shrewd postillion perceived, by our hero's language, that he was a gentleman. After much dragging at the horses' heads, and pushing and lifting, the carriage was got over what the postillion said was the worst part of *the bad step*; but as the road 'was not yet to say good,' he continued walking beside the carriage.

'It's only bad just hereabouts, and that by accident,' said he, 'on account of there being no jantleman resident in it, nor near; but only a bit of an under-agent, a great little rogue, who gets his own turn out of the roads, and of everything else in life. I, Larry Brady, that am telling your honour, have a good right to know, for myself, and my father, and my brother, Pat Brady, the wheelwright, had once a farm under him; but was ruined, horse and foot, all along with him, and cast out, and my brother forced to fly the country, and is now working in some coachmaker's yard, in London; banished he is! – and here am – and now that I'm reduced to drive a hack, the agents a curse to me still, with these bad roads, killing my horses and wheels – and a shame to the country, which I think more of – Bad luck to him!'

'I know your brother; he lives with Mr Mordicai, in Long Acre, in London.'

'Oh, God bless you for that!'

They came at this time within view of a range of about four-and-twenty men and boys, sitting astride on four-and-twenty heaps of broken stones, on each side of the road; they were all armed with hammers, with which they began to pound with great diligence and noise as soon as they saw the carriage. The chaise passed between these batteries, the stones flying on all sides.

'How are you, Jem? – How are you, Phil?' said Larry. 'But hold your hand, can't ye, while I stop and get the stones out of the horses' *feet*. So you're making up the rent, are you, for St Dennis?'

'Whoosh!' said one of the pounders, coming close to the postillion, and pointing his thumb back towards the chaise. 'Who have you in it?'

'Oh, you need not scruple, he's a very honest man; – he's only a man from North Wales, one Mr Evans, an innocent jantleman, that's sent over to travel up and down the country, to find is there any copper mines in it.'

'How do you know, Larry?'

'Because I know very well, from one that was tould, and I *seen* him tax the man of the King's Head, with a copper half-crown, at first sight, which was only lead to look at, you'd think, to them that was not skilful in copper. So lend me a knife, till I cut a linch-pin out of the hedge, for this one won't go far.'

Whilst Larry was making the linch-pin, all scruple being removed, his question about St Dennis and the rent was answered.

'Ay, it's the rint, sure enough, we're pounding out for him; for he sent the driver round last-night-was-eight days, to warn us old Nick would be down a'-Monday, to take a sweep among us; and there's only six clear days, Saturday night, before the assizes, sure; so we must see and get it finished anyway, to clear the presentment again' the swearing day, for he and Paddy Hart is the overseers themselves, and Paddy is to swear to it.'

'St Dennis, is it? Then you've one great comfort and security – that he won't be *particular* about the swearing; for since ever he had his head on his shoulders, an oath never stuck in St Dennis's throat, more than in his own brother, old Nick's.'

'His head upon his shoulders!' repeated Lord Colambre. 'Pray, did you ever hear that St Dennis's head was off his shoulders?'

'It never was, plase your honour, to my knowledge.'

'Did you never, among your saints, hear of St Dennis carrying his head in his hand?' said Colambre.

'The *rael* saint!' said the postillion, suddenly changing his tone, and looking shocked. 'Oh, don't be talking that way of the saints, plase your honour.'

'Then of what St Dennis were you talking just now? – Whom do you mean by St Dennis, and whom do you call old Nick?'

'Old Nick,' answered the postillion, coming close to the side of the carriage, and whispering – 'Old Nick, plase your honour, is our nickname for one Nicholas Garraghty, Esq., of College Green, Dublin, and St Dennis is his brother Dennis, who is old Nick's brother in all things, and would fain be a saint, only he is a sinner. He lives just by here, in the country, under-agent to Lord Clonbrony, as old Nick is upper-agent – it's only a joke among the people, that are not fond of them at all. Lord Clonbrony himself is a very good jantleman, if he was not an absentee, resident in London, leaving us and everything to the likes of them.'

Lord Colambre listened with all possible composure and attention; but the postillion having now made his linch-pin of wood, and *fixed himself*, he mounted his bar, and drove on, saying to Lord Colambre, as he looked at the road-makers –

'Poor *cratures*! They couldn't keep their cattle out of pound, or themselves out of jail, but by making this road.'

'Is road-making, then, a very profitable business? – Have road-makers higher wages than other men in this part of the country?'

'It is, and it is not – they have, and they have not – plase your honour.'

'I don't understand you.'

'No, becaase you're an Englishman – that is, a Welshman – I beg your honour's pardon. But I'll tell you how that is, and I'll go slow over these broken stones, – for I can't go fast: it is where there's no jantleman over these under-agents, as here, they do as they plase; and when they have set the land they get rasonable from the head landlords, to poor cratures at a rack-rent, that they can't live and pay the rent, they say – '

'Who says?'

'Them under-agents, that have no conscience at all. Not all – but *some*, like Dennis, says, says he, "I'll get you a road to make up the rent:" that is, plase your honour, the agent gets them a presentment for so many perches of road from the grand jury, at twice the price that would make the road. And tenants are, by this means, as they take the road by contract, at the price given by the county, able to pay all they get by the job, over and above potatoes and salt, back again to the agent, for the arrear on the land. Do I make your honour *sensible?*'

'You make me much more sensible than I ever was before,' said Lord Colambre; 'but is not this cheating the county?'

'Well, and suppose,' replied Larry, 'is not it all for my good, and yours too, plase your honour?' said Larry, looking very shrewdly.

'My good!' said Lord Colambre, startled. 'What have I to do with it?'

'Haven't you to do with the roads as well as me, when you're travelling upon them, plase your honour? And sure, they'd never be got made at all, if they weren't made this ways; and it's the best way in the wide world, and the finest roads we have. And when the *rael* jantlemen's resident in the country, there's no jobbing can be, because they're then the leading men on the grand jury; and these journeymen jantlemen are then kept in order, and all's right.'

Lord Colambre was much surprised at Larry's knowledge of the manner in which county business is managed, as well as by his shrewd good sense: he did not know that this is not uncommon in his rank of life in Ireland.

Whilst Larry was speaking, Lord Colambre was looking from side to side at the desolation of the prospect.

'So this is Lord Clonbrony's estate, is it?'

'Ay, all you see, and as far and farther than you can see. My Lord Clonbrony wrote, and ordered plantations here, time back; and enough was paid to labourers for ditching and planting. And, what next? – Why, what did the under-agent do, but let the goats in through gaps, left o' purpose, to bark the trees, and then the trees was all banished. And next, the cattle was let in trespassing, and winked at, till the land was all poached; and then the land was waste, and cried down; and St Dennis wrote up to Dublin to old Nick, and he over to the landlord, how none would take it, or bid anything at all for it; so then it fell to him a cheap bargain. Oh, the tricks of them! who knows 'em, if I don't?'

Presently, Lord Colambre's attention was roused again, by seeing a man running, as if for his life, across a bog, near the roadside; he leaped over the ditch, and was upon the road in an instant. He seemed startled at first, at the sight of the carriage; but, looking at the postillion, Larry nodded, and he smiled and said –

'All's safe!'

'Pray, my good friend, may I ask what that is you have on your shoulder?' said Lord Colambre.

'*Plase* your honour, it is only a private still, which I've just caught out yonder in the bog; and I'm carrying it in with all speed to the gauger, to make a discovery, that the *jantleman* may benefit by the reward; I expect he'll make me a compliment.'

'Get up behind, and I'll give you a lift,' said the postillion.

'Thank you kindly – but better my legs!' said the man; and turning down a lane, off he ran again as fast as possible.

'Expect he'll make me a compliment,' repeated Lord Colambre, 'to make a discovery!'

'Ay, plase your honour; for the law is,' said Larry, 'that, if an unlawful still, that is, a still without licence for whiskey, is found, half the benefit of the fine that's put upon the parish goes to him that made the discovery; that's what that man is after, for he's an informer.'

'I should not have thought, from what I see of you,' said Lord Colambre, smiling, 'that you, Larry, would have offered an informer a lift.'

'Oh, plase your honour!' said Larry, smiling archly, 'would not I give the laws a lift, when in my power?'

Scarcely had he uttered these words, and scarcely was the informer out of sight, when across the same bog, and over the ditch, came another man, a half kind of gentleman, with a red silk handkerchief about his neck, and a silver-handled whip in his hand.

'Did you see any man pass the road, friend?' said he to the postillion.

'Oh! who would I see? or why would I tell?' replied Larry, in a sulky tone.

'Come, come, be smart!' said the man with the silver whip, offering to put half a crown into the postillion's hand; 'point me which way he took.'

'I'll have none o' your silver! don't touch me with it!' said Larry. 'But, if you'll take my advice, you'll strike across back, and follow the fields, out to Killogenesawee.'

The exciseman set out again immediately, in an opposite direction to that which the man who carried the still had taken. Lord Colambre now perceived that the pretended informer had been running off to conceal a still of his own.

'The gauger, plase your honour,' said Larry, looking back at Lord Colambre; 'the gauger is a *still-hunting*!'

'And you put him on a wrong scent!' said Lord Colambre.

'Sure, I told him no lie; I only said, "If you'll take my advice." And why was he such a fool as to take my advice, when I wouldn't take his fee?'

'So this is the way, Larry, you give a lift to the laws!'

'If the laws would give a lift to me, plase your honour, maybe I'd do as much by them. But it's only these revenue laws I mean; for I never, to my knowledge, broke another commandment; but it's what no honest poor man among his neighbours would scruple to take – a glass of *potsheen*.'

'A glass of what, in the name of Heaven?' said Lord Colambre.

'*Potsheen*, plase your honour; – becaase it's the little whiskey that's made in the private still or pot; and *sheen*, becaase it's a fond word for whatsoever we'd like, and for what we have little of, and would make much of: after taking the glass of it, no man could go and inform to ruin the *cratures*; for they all shelter on that estate under favour of them that go shares, and make rent of 'em – but I'd never inform again' 'em. And, after all, if the truth was known, and my Lord Clonbrony should be informed against, and presented, for it's his neglect is the bottom of the nuisance – '

'I find all the blame is thrown upon this poor Lord Clonbrony,' said Lord Colambre.

'Becaase he is absent,' said Larry. 'It would not be so was he *prisint*. But your honour was talking to me about the laws. Your honour's a stranger in this country, and astray about them things. Sure, why would I mind the laws about whiskey, more than the quality, or the judge on the bench?'

'What do you mean?'

'Why! was not I *prisint* in the court-house myself, when the *jidge* was on the bench judging a still, and across the court came in one with a sly jug of *potsheen* for the *jidge* himself, who *prefarred* it, when the right thing, to claret; and when I *seen* that, by the laws! a man might talk himself dumb to me after again' potsheen, or in favour of the revenue, or revenue-officers. And there they may go on, with their gaugers, and their surveyors, and their supervisors, and their *watching-officers*, and their coursing-officers, setting 'em one after another, or one over the head of another, or what way they will – we can baffle and laugh at 'em. Didn't I know, next door to our inn, last year, ten *watching-officers* set upon one distiller, and he was too cunning for them; and it will always be so, while ever the people think it no sin. No, till then, not all their dockets and permits signify a rush, or a turf. And the gauging rod even! who fears it? They may spare that rod, for it will never mend the child.'

How much longer Larry's dissertation on the distillery laws would have continued, had not his ideas been interrupted, we cannot guess;

but he saw he was coming to a town, and he gathered up the reins, and plied the whip, ambitious to make a figure in the eyes of its inhabitants.

This *town* consisted of one row of miserable huts, sunk beneath the side of the road, the mud walls crooked in every direction; some of them opening in wide cracks, or zigzag fissures, from top to bottom, as if there had just been an earthquake – all the roofs sunk in various places – thatch off, or overgrown with grass – no chimneys, the smoke making its way through a hole in the roof, or rising in clouds from the top of the open door – dunghills before the doors, and green standing puddles – squalid children, with scarcely rags to cover them, gazing at the carriage.

'Nugent's town,' said the postillion, 'once a snug place, when my Lady Clonbrony was at home to whitewash it, and the like.'

As they drove by, some men and women put their heads through the smoke out of the cabins; pale women with long, black, or yellow locks – men with countenances and figures bereft of hope and energy.

'Wretched, wretched people!' said Lord Colambre.

'Then it's not their fault neither,' said Larry; 'for my own uncle's one of them, and as thriving and hard a working man as could be in all Ireland, he was, *afore* he was tramped under foot, and his heart broke. I was at his funeral, this time last year; and for it, may the agent's own heart, if he has any, burn – '

Lord Colambre interrupted this denunciation by touching Larry's shoulder, and asking some question, which, as Larry did not distinctly comprehend, he pulled up the reins, and the various noises of the vehicle stopped suddenly.

'I did not hear well, plase your honour.'

'What are those people?' pointing to a man and woman, curious figures, who had come out of a cabin, the door of which the woman, who came out last, locked, and carefully hiding the key in the thatch, turned her back upon the man, and they walked away in different directions: the woman bending under a huge bundle on her back, covered by a yellow petticoat turned over her shoulders; from the top of this bundle the head of an infant appeared; a little boy, almost naked, followed her with a kettle, and two girls, one of whom could but just walk, held her hand and clung to her ragged petticoat; forming, altogether, a complete group of beggars. The woman stopped, and looked back after the man.

The man was a Spanish-looking figure, with gray hair; a wallet hung at the end of a stick over one shoulder, a reaping-hook in the other hand; he walked off stoutly, without ever casting a look behind him.

'A kind harvest to you, John Dolan,' cried the postillion, 'and success to ye, Winny, with the quality. There's a luck-penny for the child to begin with,' added he, throwing the child a penny. 'Your honour, they're only poor *cratures going* up the country to beg, while the man goes over to reap the harvest in England. Nor this would not be, neither, if the lord was in it to give 'em *employ*. That man, now, was a good and a willing *slave* in his day: I mind him working with myself in the shrubberies at Clonbrony Castle, when I was a boy – but I'll not be detaining your honour, now the road's better.'

The postillion drove on at a good rate for some time, till he came to a piece of the road freshly covered with broken stones, where he was obliged again to go slowly.

They overtook a string of cars, on which were piled up high, beds, tables, chairs, trunks, boxes, bandboxes.

'How are you, Finnucan? you've fine loading there – from Dublin, are you?'

'From Bray.'

'And what news?'

'*Great* news and bad, for old Nick, or some belonging to him, thanks be to Heaven! for myself hates him.'

'What's happened him?'

'His sister's husband that's failed, the great grocer that was, the man that had the wife that *ow'd* the fine house near Bray, that they got that time the Parliament *flitted*, and that I seen in her carriage flaming – well, it's all out; they're all *done up*.'

'Tut! is that all? then they'll thrive, and set up again grander than ever, I'll engage; have not they old Nick for an attorney at their back? a good warrant!'

'Oh, trust him for that! he won't *go security* nor pay a farthing for his *shister*, nor wouldn't was she his father; I heard him telling her so, which I could not have done in his place at that time, and she crying as if her heart would break, and I standing by in the parlour.'

'The *neger*! And did he speak that way, and you by?'

'Ay did he; and said, "Mrs Raffarty," says he, "it's all your own fault; you're an extravagant fool, and ever was, and I wash my hands of you;" that was the word he spoke; and she answered, and said, "And mayn't I send the beds and blankets," said she, "and what I can, by the cars, out of the way of the creditors, to Clonbrony Castle; and won't you let me hide there from the shame, till the bustle's over?" – "You may do that," says he, "for what I care; but remember," says he, "that I've the first claim to them goods;" and that's all he would grant. So they are coming down all o' Monday – them are her bandboxes and all – to settle it; and faith it was a pity of her! to hear her sobbing, and to see her own brother speak and look so hard! and she a lady.'

'Sure she's not a lady born, no more than himself,' said Larry; 'but that's no excuse for him. His heart's as hard as that stone,' said Larry; 'and my own people knew that long ago, and now his own know it; and what right have we to complain, since he's as bad to his own flesh and blood as to us?'

With this consolation, and with a 'God speed you,' given to the carman, Larry was driving off; but the carman called to him, and pointed to a house, at the corner of which, on a high pole, was swinging an iron sign of three horse-shoes, set in a crooked frame, and at the window hung an empty bottle, proclaiming whiskey within.

'Well, I don't care if I do,' said Larry; 'for I've no other comfort left me in life now. I beg your honour's pardon, sir, for a minute,' added he, throwing the reins into the carriage to Lord Colambre, as he leaped down. All remonstrance and power of lungs to reclaim him vain! He darted into the whiskey-house with the carman – reappeared before Lord Colambre could accomplish getting out, remounted his seat, and, taking the reins, 'I thank your honour,' said he; 'and I'll bring you into Clonbrony before it's pitch-dark yet, though it's nightfall, and that's four good miles, but "a spur in the head is worth two in the heel." '

Larry, to demonstrate the truth of his favourite axiom, drove off at such a furious rate over great stones left in the middle of the road by carmen, who had been driving in the gudgeons of their axle-trees to hinder them from lacing, that Lord Colambre thought life and limb in imminent danger; and feeling that at all events the jolting and bumping was past endurance, he had recourse to Larry's shoulder, and shook and pulled, and called to him to go slower, but in vain; at last the wheel struck full against a heap of stones at a turn of the road, the wooden linch-pin came off, and the chaise was overset: Lord Colambre was a little bruised, but glad to escape without fractured bones.

'I beg your honour's pardon,' said Larry, completely sobered; 'I'm as glad as the best pair of boots ever I see, to see your honour nothing the worse for it. It was the linch-pin, and them barrows of loose stones, that ought to be fined anyway, if there was any justice in the country.'

'The pole is broke; how are we to get on?' said Lord Colambre.

'Murder! murder! – and no smith nearer than Clonbrony; nor rope even. It's a folly to talk, we can't get to Clonbrony, nor stir a step backward or forward the night.'

'What, then, do you mean to leave me all night in the middle of the road?' cried Lord Colambre, quite exasperated.

'Is it me! please your honour? I would not use any jantleman so ill, *barring* I could do no other,' replied the postillion, coolly; then, leaping across the ditch, or, as he called it, the *gripe* of the ditch, he scrambled up, and while he was scrambling, said, 'If your honour will lend me your hand till I pull you up the back of the ditch, the horses will stand while we go. I'll find you as pretty a lodging for the night, with a widow of a brother of my shister's husband that was, as ever you slept in your life; for old Nick or St Dennis has not found 'em out yet; and your honour will be, no compare, snugger than the inn at Clonbrony, which has no roof, the devil a stick. But where will I get your honour's hand; for it's coming on so dark, I can't see rightly. There, you're up now safe. Yonder candle's the house.'

'Go and ask whether they can give us a night's lodging.'

'Is it *ask*? when I see the light! – Sure they'd be proud to give the traveller all the beds in the house, let alone one. Take care of the potato furrows, that's all, and follow me straight. I'll go on to meet the dog, who knows me and might be strange to your honour.'

'Kindly welcome,' were the first words Lord Colambre heard when he approached the cottage; and 'kindly welcome' was in the sound of the voice and in the countenance of the old woman who came out, shading her rush-candle from the wind, and holding it so as to light the path. When he entered the cottage, he saw a cheerful fire and a neat pretty young woman making it blaze: she curtsied, put her spinning-wheel out of the way, set a stool by the fire for the stranger, and repeating, in a very low tone of voice, 'Kindly welcome, sir,' retired.

'Put down some eggs, dear, there's plenty in the bowl,' said the old woman, calling to her; 'I'll do the bacon. Was not we lucky to be up? – The boy's gone to bed, but waken him,' said she, turning to the postillion; 'and he'll help you with the chay, and put your horses in the bier for the night.'

No; Larry chose to go on to Clonbrony with the horses, that he might get the chaise mended betimes for his honour. The table was set; clean trenchers, hot potatoes, milk, eggs, bacon, and 'kindly welcome to all.'

'Set the salt, dear; and the butter, love; where's your head, Grace, dear?'

'Grace!' repeated Lord Colambre, looking up; and, to apologise for his involuntary exclamation, he added, 'Is Grace a common name in Ireland?'

'I can't say, plase your honour, but it was give her by Lady Clonbrony, from a niece of her own that was her foster-sister, God bless her! and a very kind lady she was to us and to all when she was living in it; but those times are gone past,' said the old woman, with a sigh. The young woman sighed too; and, sitting down by the fire, began to count the notches in a little bit of stick, which she held in her hand; and, after she had counted them, sighed again.

'But don't be sighing, Grace, now,' said the old woman; 'sighs is bad sauce for the traveller's supper; and we won't be troubling him with more,' added she, turning to Lord Colambre with a smile.

'Is your egg done to your liking?'

'Perfectly, thank you.'

'Then I wish it was a chicken for your sake, which it should have been, and roast too, had we time. I wish I could see you eat another egg.'

'No more, thank you, my good lady; I never ate a better supper, nor received a more hospitable welcome.'

'Oh, the welcome is all we have to offer.'

'May I ask what that is?' said Lord Colambre, looking at the notched stick, which the young woman held in her hand, and on which her eyes were still fixed.

'It's a *tally*, plase your honour. Oh, you're a foreigner; – it's the way the labourers do keep the account of the day's work with the overseer, the bailiff; a notch for every day the bailiff makes on his stick, and the labourer the like on his stick, to tally; and when we come to make up the account, it's by the notches we go. And there's been a mistake, and is a dispute here between our boy and the overseer; and she was counting the boy's tally, that's in bed, tired, for in troth he's over-worked.'

'Would you want anything more from me, mother?' said the girl, rising and turning her head away.

'No, child; get away, for your heart's full.'

She went instantly.

'Is the boy her brother?' said Lord Colambre.

'No; he's her bachelor,' said the old woman, lowering her voice.

'Her bachelor?'

'That is, her sweetheart: for she is not my daughter, though you heard her call me mother. The boy's my son; but I am *afeard* they must give it up; for they're too poor, and the times is hard, and the agent's harder than the times; there's two of them, the under and the upper; and they grind the substance of one between them, and then blow one away like chaff: but we'll not be talking of that to spoil your honour's night's rest. The room's ready, and here's the rushlight.'

She showed him into a very small but neat room. 'What a comfortable-looking bed!' said Lord Colambre.

'Ah, these red check curtains,' said she, letting them down; 'these have lasted well; they were give me by a good friend, now far away, over the seas – my Lady Clonbrony; and made by the prettiest hands

ever you see, her niece's, Miss Grace Nugent's, and she a little child
that time; sweet love! all gone!'

The old woman wiped a tear from her eye, and Lord Colambre did
what he could to appear indifferent. She set down the candle, and left
the room; Lord Colambre went to bed, but he lay awake, 'revolving
sweet and bitter thoughts.'

Chapter 11

THE KETTLE was on the fire, tea-things set, everything prepared for
her guest by the hospitable hostess, who, thinking the gentleman
would take tea to his breakfast, had sent off a *gossoon* by the *first light* to
Clonbrony, for an ounce of tea, a *quarter of sugar*, and a loaf of white
bread; and there was on the little table good cream, milk, butter, eggs –
all the promise of an excellent breakfast. It was a *fresh* morning, and
there was a pleasant fire on the hearth, neatly swept up. The old
woman was sitting in her chimney corner, behind a little skreen of
whitewashed wall, built out into the room, for the purpose of keeping
those who sat at the fire from the *blast of the door*. There was a loophole
in this wall, to let the light in, just at the height of a person's head, who
was sitting near the chimney. The rays of the morning sun now came
through it, shining across the face of the old woman, as she sat knitting;
Lord Colambre thought he had seldom seen a more agreeable countenance, intelligent eyes, benevolent smile, a natural expression of
cheerfulness, subdued by age and misfortune.

'A good-morrow to you kindly, sir, and I hope you got the night
well? – A fine day for us this Sunday morning; my Grace is gone to
early prayers, so your honour will be content with an old woman to
make your breakfast. Oh, let me put in plenty, or it will never be good;
and if your honour takes stir-about, an old hand will engage to make
that to your liking, anyway; for, by great happiness, we have what will
just answer for you of the nicest meal the miller made my Grace a
compliment of, last time she went to the mill.'

Lord Colambre observed, that this miller had good taste; and his
lordship paid some compliment to Grace's beauty, which the old
woman received with a smile, but turned off the conversation. 'Then,'
said she, looking out of the window, 'is not that there a nice little
garden the boy dug for her and me, at his breakfast and dinner hours?
Ah! he's a good boy, and a good warrant to work; and the good son
desarves the good wife, and it's he that will make the good husband; and

with my goodwill he, and no other, shall get her, and with her goodwill the same; and I bid 'em keep up their heart, and hope the best, for there's no use in fearing the worst till it comes.'

Lord Colambre wished very much to know the worst.

'If you would not think a stranger impertinent for asking,' said he, 'and if it would not be painful to you to explain.'

'Oh, impertinent, your honour! it's very kind – and, sure, none's a stranger to one's heart, that feels for one. And for myself, I can talk of my troubles without thinking of them. So, I'll tell you all – if the worst comes to the worst – all that is, is, that we must quit, and give up this little snug place, and house, and farm, and all, to the agent – which would be hard on us, and me a widow, when my husband did all that is done to the land; and if your honour was a judge, you could see, if you stepped out, there has been a deal done, and built the house, and all – but it plased Heaven to take him. Well, he was too good for this world, and I'm satisfied – I'm not saying a word again' that – I trust we shall meet in heaven, and be happy, surely. And, meantime, here's my boy, that will make me as happy as ever widow was on earth – if the agent will let him. And I can't think the agent, though they that know him best call him old Nick, would be so wicked to take from us that which he never gave us. The good lord himself granted us the *lase*; the life's dropped, and the years is out; but we had a promise of renewal in writing from the landlord. God bless him! if he was not away, he'd be a good gentleman, and we'd be happy and safe.'

'But if you have a promise in writing of a renewal, surely you are safe, whether your landlord is absent or present?'

'Ah, no! that makes a great *differ*, when there's no eye or hand over the agent. I would not wish to speak or think ill of him or any man; but was he an angel, he could not know to do the tenantry justice, the way he is living always in Dublin, and coming down to the country only the receiving days, to make a sweep among us, and gather up the rents in a hurry, and he in such haste back to town – can just stay to count over our money, and give the receipts. Happy for us, if we get that same! – but can't expect he should have time to see or hear us, or mind our improvements, any more than listen to our complaints! Oh, there's great excuse for the gentleman, if that was any comfort for us,' added she, smiling.

'But, if he does not live amongst you himself, has not he some under-agent, who lives in the country?' said Lord Colambre.

'He has so.'

'And he should know your concerns: does he mind them?'

'He should know – he should know better; but as to minding our

concerns, your honour knows,' continued she, smiling again, 'every
one in this world must mind their own concerns; and it would be a
good world, if it was even so. There's a great deal in all things, that
don't appear at first sight. Mr Dennis wanted Grace for a wife for his
bailiff, but she would not have him; and Mr Dennis was very sweet to
her himself – but Grace is rather high with him as proper, and he has a
grudge *again* us ever since. Yet, indeed, there,' added she, after another
pause, 'as you say, I think we are safe; for we have that memorandum in
writing, with a pencil, given under his own hand, on the back of the
lase, to me, by the same token when my good lord had his foot on the
step of the coach, going away; and I'll never forget the smile of her that
got that good turn done for me, Miss Grace. And just when she was
going to England and London, and, young as she was, to have the
thought to stop and turn to the likes of me! Oh, then, if you could
see her, and know her, as I did! *That* was the comforting angel upon
earth – look and voice, and heart and all! Oh, that she was here present,
this minute! – But did you scald yourself?' said the widow to Lord
Colambre. 'Sure you must have scalded yourself; for you poured the
kettle straight over your hand, and it boiling! – O *deear*! to think of so
young a gentleman's hand shaking so like my own.'

Luckily, to prevent her pursuing her observations from the hand to
the face, which might have betrayed more than Lord Colambre wished
she should know, her own Grace came in at this instant.

'There it's for you, safe, mother dear – the *lase*!' said Grace, throwing
a packet into her lap. The old woman lifted up her hands to heaven,
with the lease between them. – 'Thanks be to Heaven!' Grace passed
on, and sunk down on the first seat she could reach. Her face flushed,
and, looking much fatigued, she loosened the strings of her bonnet and
cloak – 'Then, I'm tired;' but, recollecting herself, she rose, and
curtsied to the gentleman.

'What tired ye, dear?'

'Why, after prayers, we had to go – for the agent was not at prayers,
nor at home for us, when we called – we had to go all the way up to the
castle; and there, by great good luck, we found Mr Nick Garraghty
himself, come from Dublin, and the *lase* in his hands; and he sealed it
up that way, and handed it to me very civil. I never saw him so good –
though he offered me a glass of spirits, which was not manners to a
decent young woman, in a morning – as Brian noticed after. Brian
would not take any either, nor never does. We met Mr Dennis and the
driver coming home; and he says, the rent must be paid tomorrow, or,
instead of renewing, he'll seize and sell all. Mother dear, I would have
dropped with the walk, but for Brian's arm.' – 'It's a wonder, dear, what

makes you so weak, that used to be so strong.' – 'But if we can sell the cow for anything at all to Mr Dennis, since his eye is set upon her, better let him have her, mother dear; and that and my yarn, which Mrs Garraghty says she'll allow me for, will make up the rent – and Brian need not talk of America. But it must be in golden guineas, the agent will take the rent no other way; and you won't get a guinea for less than five shillings. Well, even so, it's easy selling my new gown to one that covets it, and that will give me in exchange the price of the gold; or, suppose that would not do, add this cloak, – it's handsome, and I know a friend would be glad to take it, and I'd part it as ready as look at it – Anything at all, sure, rather than that he should be forced to talk of emigrating; or, oh, worse again, listing for the bounty – to save us from the cant or the jail, by going to the hospital, or his grave, maybe – Oh, mother!'

'Oh, child! This is what makes you weak, fretting. Don't be that way. Sure here's the *lase*, and that's good comfort; and the soldiers will be gone out of Clonbrony tomorrow, and then that's off your mind. And as to America, it's only talk – I won't let him, he's dutiful; and would sooner sell my dresser and down to my bed, dear, than see you sell anything of yours, love. Promise me you won't. Why didn't Brian come home all the way with you, Grace?'

'He would have seen me home,' said Grace, 'only that he went up a piece of the mountain for some stones or ore for the gentleman – for he had the manners to think of him this morning, though, shame for me, I had not, when I come in, or I would not have told you all this, and he himself by. See, there he is, mother.'

Brian came in very hot, out of breath, with his hat full of stones. 'Good morrow to your honour. I was in bed last night; and sorry they did not call me up to be of *sarvice*. Larry was telling us, this morning, your honour's from Wales, and looking for mines in Ireland, and I heard talk that there was one on our mountain – maybe, you'd be *curous* to see, and so I brought the best I could, but I'm no judge.'

'Nor I, neither,' thought Lord Colambre; but he thanked the young man, and determined to avail himself of Larry's misconception or false report; examined the stones very gravely, and said, 'This promises well. Lapis caliminaris, schist, plum-pudding stone, rhomboidal, crystal, blend, garrawachy,' and all the strange names he could think of, jumbling them together at a venture.

'The *lase*! – Is it?' cried the young man, with joy sparkling in his eyes, as his mother held up the packet. 'Then all's safe! and he's an honest man, and shame on me, that could suspect he meant us wrong. Lend me the papers.'

He cracked the seals, and taking off the cover, – 'It's the *lase*, sure enough. Shame on me! – But stay, where's the memorandum?'

'It's there, sure,' said his mother, 'where my lord's pencil writ it. I don't read. – Grace, dear, look.'

The young man put it into her hands, and stood without power to utter a syllable.

'It's not here! It's gone! – no sign of it.'

'Gracious Heaven! that can't be,' said the old woman, putting on her spectacles; 'let me see – I remember the very spot.'

'It's taken away – it's rubbed clean out! – Oh, wasn't I fool? But who could have thought he'd be the villain!' The young man seemed neither to see nor hear; but to be absorbed in thought.

Grace, with her eyes fixed upon him, grew as pale as death – 'He'll go – he's gone.'

'She's gone!' cried Lord Colambre, and the mother just caught her in her arms as she was falling.

'The chaise is ready, *plase* your honour,' said Larry, coming into the room. 'Death! what's here?'

'Air! – she's coming to,' said the young man – 'Take a drop of water, my own Grace.'

'Young man, I promise you,' cried Lord Colambre (speaking in the tone of a master), striking the young man's shoulder, who was kneeling at Grace's feet; but recollecting and restraining himself, he added, in a quiet voice – 'I promise you I shall never forget the hospitality I have received in this house, and I am sorry to be obliged to leave you in distress.'

These words uttered with difficulty, he hurried out of the house, and into his carriage. 'Go back to them,' said he to the postillion; 'go back and ask whether, if I should stay a day or two longer in this country, they would let me return at night and lodge with them. And here, man, stay, take this,' putting money into his hands, 'for the good woman of the house.'

The postillion went in, and returned.

'She won't at all – I knew she would not.'

'Well, I am obliged to her for the night's lodging she did give me; I have no right to expect more.'

'What is it? – Sure she bid me tell you – "and welcome to the lodging; for," said she, "he is a kind-hearted gentleman;" but here's the money; it's that I was telling you she would not have at all.'

'Thank you. Now, my good friend Larry, drive me to Clonbrony, and do not say another word, for I'm not in a talking humour.'

Larry nodded, mounted, and drove to Clonbrony. Clonbrony was now a melancholy scene. The houses, which had been built in a better style of architecture than usual, were in a ruinous condition; the dashing was off the walls, no glass in the windows, and many of the roofs without slates. For the stillness of the place Lord Colambre in some measure accounted, by considering that it was Sunday; therefore, of course, all the shops were shut up, and all the people at prayers. He alighted at the inn, which completely answered Larry's representation of it. Nobody to be seen but a drunken waiter, who, as well as he could articulate, informed Lord Colambre that 'his mistress was in her bed since Thursday-was-a-week; the hostler at the *wash-woman's*, and the cook at second prayers.'

Lord Colambre walked to the church, but the church gate was locked and broken – a calf, two pigs, and an ass, in the churchyard; and several boys (with more of skin apparent than clothes) were playing at hustlecap upon a tombstone, which, upon nearer observation, he saw was the monument of his own family. One of the boys came to the gate, and told Lord Colambre 'there was no use in going into the church, becaase there was no church there; nor had not been this twelvemonth; becaase there was no curate; and the parson was away always, since the lord was at home – that is, was not at home – he nor the family.'

Lord Colambre returned to the inn, where, after waiting a considerable time, he gave up the point – he could not get any dinner – and in the evening he walked out again into the town. He found several ale-houses, however, open, which were full of people; all of them as busy and as noisy as possible. He observed that the interest was created by an advertisement of several farms on the Clonbrony estate, to be set by Nicholas Garraghty, Esq. He could not help smiling at his being witness *incognito* to various schemes for outwitting the agents and defrauding the landlord; but, on a sudden, the scene was changed; a boy ran in, crying out, that 'St Dennis was riding down the hill into the town; and, if you would not have the licence,' said the boy, 'take care of yourself.'

'*If you wouldn't have the licence*,' Lord Colambre perceived, by what followed, meant, '*If you have not a licence*.' Brannagan immediately snatched an untasted glass of whiskey from a customer's lips (who cried, Murder!) gave it and the bottle he held in his hand to his wife, who swallowed the spirits, and ran away with the bottle and glass into some back hole; whilst the bystanders laughed, saying, 'Well thought of, Peggy!'

'Clear out all of you at the back door, for the love of heaven, if you wouldn't be the ruin of me,' said the man of the house, setting a ladder to a corner of the shop. 'Phil, hoist me up the keg to the loft,' added he, running up the ladder; 'and one of *yees* step up street, and give Rose M'Givney notice, for she's selling too.'

The keg was hoisted up; the ladder removed; the shop cleared of all the customers; the shutters shut; the door barred; the counter cleaned. 'Lift your stones, sir, if you plase,' said the wife, as she rubbed the counter, 'and say nothing of what you *seen* at all; but that you're a stranger and a traveller seeking a lodging, if you're questioned, or waiting to see Mr Dennis. There's no smell of whiskey in it now, is there, sir?'

Lord Colambre could not flatter her so far as to say this – he could only hope no one would perceive it.

'Oh, and if *he* would, the smell of whiskey was nothing,' as the wife affirmed, 'for it was everywhere in nature, and no proof again' any one, good or bad.'

'Now St Dennis may come when he will, or old Nick himself!' So she tied up a blue handkerchief over her head, and had the toothache, 'very bad.'

Lord Colambre turned to look for the man of the house.

'He's safe in bed,' said the wife.

'In bed! When?'

'Whilst you turned your head, while I was tying the handkerchief over my face. Within the room, look, he is snug.'

And there he was in bed certainly, and his clothes on the chest.

A knock, a loud knock at the door.

'St Dennis himself! – Stay, till I unbar the door,' said the woman; and, making a great difficulty, she let him in, groaning, and saying –

'We was all done up for the night, *plase* your honour, and myself with the toothache, very bad – And the lodger, that's going to take an egg only, before he'd go into his bed. My man's in it, and asleep long ago.'

With a magisterial air, though with a look of blank disappointment, Mr Dennis Garraghty walked on, looked into *the room*, saw the good man of the house asleep, heard him snore, and then, returning, asked Lord Colambre 'who he was, and what brought him there?'

Our hero said he was from England, and a traveller; and now, bolder grown as a geologist, he talked of his specimens, and his hopes of finding a mine in the neighbouring mountains; then adopting, as well as he could, the servile tone and abject manner in which he found Mr Dennis was to be addressed, 'he hoped he might get encouragement from the gentleman at the head of the estate.'

'To bore, is it? – Well, don't *bore* me about it. I can't give you any answer now, my good friend; I'm engaged.'

Out he strutted. 'Stick to him up the town, if you have a mind to get your answer,' whispered the woman. Lord Colambre followed, for he wished to see the end of this scene.

'Well, sir, what are you following and sticking to me, like my shadow, for?' said Mr Dennis, turning suddenly upon Lord Colambre.

His lordship bowed low. 'Waiting for my answer, sir, when you are at leisure. Or, may I call upon you tomorrow?'

'You seem to be a civil kind of fellow; but, as to boring, I don't know – if you undertake it at your own expense. I dare say there may be minerals in the ground. Well, you may call at the castle tomorrow, and when my brother has done with the tenantry, I'll speak to him *for* you, and we'll consult together, and see what we think. It's too late tonight. In Ireland, nobody speaks to a gentleman about business after dinner – your servant, sir; anybody can show you the way to the castle in the morning.' And, pushing by his lordship, he called to a man on the other side of the street, who had obviously been waiting for him; he went under a gateway with this man, and gave him a bag of guineas. He then called for his horse, which was brought to him by a man whom Colambre had heard declaring that he would bid for the land that was advertised; whilst another, who had the same intentions, most respectfully held St Dennis's stirrup, whilst he mounted without thanking either of these men.. St Dennis clapped spurs to his steed, and rode away. No thanks, indeed, were deserved; for the moment he was out of hearing, both cursed him after the manner of their country.

'Bad luck go with you, then! – And may you break your neck before you get home, if it was not for the *lase* I'm to get, and that's paid for.'

Lord Colambre followed the crowd into a public-house, where a new scene presented itself to his view.

The man to whom St Dennis gave the bag of gold was now selling this very gold to the tenants, who were to pay their rent next day at the castle.

The agent would take nothing but gold. The same guineas were bought and sold several times over, to the great profit of the agent and loss of the poor tenants; for, as the rents were paid, the guineas were resold to another set, and the remittances made through bankers to the landlord; who, as the poor man who explained the transaction to Lord Colambre expressed it, 'gained nothing by the business, bad or good, but the ill-will of the tenantry.'

The higgling for the price of the gold; the time lost in disputing about the goodness of the notes, among some poor tenants, who could not read or write, and who were at the mercy of the man with the bag in his hand; the vexation, the useless harassing of all who were obliged to submit ultimately – Lord Colambre saw; and all this time he endured the smell of tobacco and whiskey, and of the sound of various brogues, the din of men wrangling, brawling, threatening, whining, drawling, cajoling, cursing, and every variety of wretchedness.

'And is this my father's town of Clonbrony?' thought Lord Colambre. 'Is this Ireland? – No, it is not Ireland. Let me not, like most of those who forsake their native country, traduce it. Let me not, even to my own mind, commit the injustice of taking a speck for the whole. What I have just seen is the picture only of that to which an Irish estate and Irish tenantry may be degraded in the absence of those whose duty and interest it is to reside in Ireland to uphold justice by example and authority; but who, neglecting this duty, commit power to bad hands and bad hearts – abandon their tenantry to oppression, and their property to ruin.'

It was now fine moonlight, and Lord Colambre met with a boy, who said he could show him a short way across the fields to the widow O'Neill's cottage.

Chapter 12

ALL WERE ASLEEP at the cottage, when Lord Colambre arrived, except the widow, who was sitting up, waiting for him; and who had brought her dog into the house, that he might not fly at him, or bark at his return. She had a roast chicken ready for her guest, and it was – but this she never told him – the only chicken she had left; all the others had been sent with the *duty fowl*, as a present to the under-agent's lady. While he was eating his supper, which he ate with the better appetite, as he had had no dinner, the good woman took down from the shelf a pocket-book, which she gave him: 'Is not that your book?' said she. 'My boy Brian found it after you in the potato furrow, where you dropped it.'

'Thank you,' said Lord Colambre; 'there are bank notes in it, which I could not afford to lose.'

'Are there?' said she; 'he never opened it – nor I.'

Then, in answer to his inquiries about Grace and the young man, the widow answered, 'They are all in heart now, I thank ye kindly, sir, for asking; they'll sleep easy tonight anyway, and I'm in great spirits for them and myself – for all's smooth now. After we parted you, Brian saw Mr Dennis himself about the *lase* and memorandum, which he never denied, but knew nothing about. "But, be that as it may," says he, "you're improving tenants, and I'm confident my brother will consider ye; so what you'll do is, you'll give up the possession tomorrow to myself, that will call for it by cock-crow, just for form's sake; and then go up to the castle with the new *lase* ready drawn, in your hand, and if all's paid off clear of the rent, and all that's due, you'll get the new *lase* signed; I'll promise you that upon the word and honour of a gentleman." And there's no going beyond that, you know, sir. So my boy came home as light as a feather, and as gay as a lark, to bring us the good news; only he was afraid we might not make up the rent, guineas and all; and because he could not get paid for the work he done, on account of the mistake in the overseer's tally, I sold the cow to a neighbour – dog-cheap; but needs must, as they say, when old Nick *drives*,' said the widow, smiling. 'Well, still it was but paper we got for the cow; then that must be gold before the agent would take or touch it – so I was laying out to sell the dresser, and had taken the plates and cups, and little things off it, and my boy was lifting it out with Andy the carpenter, that was agreeing for it, when in comes Grace, all rosy, and out of breath – it's a wonder I minded her run out, and not missed her. "Mother," says she, "here's the gold for you! don't be stirring your dresser." – "And where's your gown and cloak, Grace?" says I. But I beg your pardon, sir; maybe I'm tiring you?'

Lord Colambre encouraged her to go on.

' "Where's your gown and cloak, Grace?" says I. – "Gone," says she. "The cloak was too warm and heavy, and I don't doubt, mother, but it was that helped to make me faint this morning. And as to the gown, sure I've a very nice one here, that you spun for me yourself, mother; and that I prize above all the gowns ever came out of a loom; and that Brian said become me to his fancy above any gown ever he see me wear; and what could I wish for more?" Now I'd a mind to scold her for going to sell the gown unknown'st to me, but I don't know how it was, I couldn't scold her just then, so kissed her, and Brian the same, and that was what no man ever did before. And she had a mind to be angry with him, but could not, nor ought not, says I; "for he's as good as your husband now, Grace; and no man can part yees now," says I, putting their hands together. Well, I never saw her look so pretty; nor there was not a happier boy that minute on God's earth than my son, nor a happier mother than myself; and I thanked God that had given them to me; and down they both fell on their knees for my blessing, little worth as it was; and my heart's blessing they had, and I laid my hands upon them. "It's the priest you must get to do this for you tomorrow," says I. And Brian just held up the ring, to show me all was ready on his part, but could not speak. "Then there's no America any more!" said Grace, low to me, and her heart was on her lips; but the colour came and went, and I was a *feard* she'd have swooned again, but not for sorrow, so I carried her off. Well, if she was not my own – but she is not my own born, so I may say it – there never was a better girl, nor a more kind-hearted, nor generous; never thinking anything she could do, or give, too much for them she loved, and anything at all would do for herself; the sweetest natured and tempered both, and always was, from this high; the bond that held all together, and joy of the house.'

'Just like her namesake,' cried Lord Colambre.

'Plase your honour?'

'Is not it late?' said Lord Colambre, stretching himself and gaping; 'I've walked a great way today.'

The old woman lighted his rushlight, showed him to his red check bed, and wished him a very good night; not without some slight sentiment of displeasure at his gaping thus at the panegyric on her darling Grace. Before she left the room, however, her short-lived resentment vanished, upon his saying that he hoped, with her permission, to be present at the wedding of the young couple.

Early in the morning Brian went to the priest, to ask his reverence when it would be convenient to marry him; and, whilst he was gone, Mr Dennis Garraghty came to the cottage, to receive the rent and possession. The rent was ready, in gold, and counted into his hand.

'No occasion for a receipt; for a new *lase* is a receipt in full for everything.'

'Very well, sir,' said the widow; 'I know nothing of law. You know best – whatever you direct – for you are acting as a friend to us now. My son got the attorney to draw the pair of new *lases* yesterday, and here they are ready, all to signing.'

Mr Dennis said his brother must settle that part of the business, and that they must carry them up to the castle; 'but first give me the possession.'

Then, as he instructed her, she gave up the key of the door to him, and a bit of the thatch of the house; and he raked out the fire, and said every living creature must go out. 'It's only form of law,' said he.

'And must my lodger get up and turn out, sir?' said she.

'He must turn out, to be sure – not a living soul must be left in it, or it's no legal possession properly. Who is you lodger?'

On Lord Colambre's appearing, Mr Dennis showed some surprise, and said, 'I thought you were lodging at Brannagan's; are not you the man who spoke to me at his house about the gold mines?'

'No, sir, he never lodged at Brannagan's,' said the widow.

'Yes, sir, I am the person who spoke to you about the gold mines at

Brannagan's; but I did not like to lodge –'

'Well, no matter where you liked to lodge; you must walk out of this lodging now, if you please, my good friend.'

So Mr Dennis pushed his lordship out by the shoulders, repeating, as the widow turned back and looked with some surprise and alarm, 'only for form sake, only for form sake! then locking the door, took the key, and put it into his pocket The widow held out her hand for it: 'The form's gone through now, sir, is not it? Be plased to let us in again.'

'When the new lease is signed, I'll give you possession again; but not till then – for that's the law. So make away with you to the castle; and mind,' added he, winking slily, – 'mind you take sealing-money with you, and something to buy gloves.'

'Oh, where will I find all that?' said the widow.

'I have it, mother; don't fret,' said Grace. 'I have it – the price of – what I can want. So let us go off to the castle without delay. Brian will meet us on the road, you know.'

They set off for Clonbrony Castle, Lord Colambre accompanying them. Brian met them on the road. 'Father Tom is ready, dear mother; bring her in, and he'll marry us. I'm not my own man till she's mine. Who knows what may happen?'

'Who knows? that's true,' said the widow.

'Better go to the castle first,' said Grace.

'And keep the priest waiting! You can't use his reverence so,' said Brian.

So she let him lead her into the priest's house, and she did not make any of the awkward draggings back, or ridiculous scenes of grimace sometimes exhibited on these occasions but blushing rosy red, yet with more self-possession than could have been expected from her timid nature, she gave her hand to the man she loved, and listened with attentive devotion to the holy ceremony.

'Ah!' thought Lord Colambre, whilst he congratulated the bride, 'shall I ever be as happy as these poor people are at this moment?' He longed to make them some little present, but all he could venture at this moment was to pay the priest's *dues*.

The priest positively refused to take anything. 'They are the best couple in my parish,' said he; 'and I'll take nothing, sir, from you, a stranger and my guest.'

'Now, come what will, I'm a match for it. No trouble can touch me,' said Brian.

'Oh, don't be bragging,' said the widow.

'Whatever trouble God sends, He has given one now will help to bear it, and sure I may be thankful,' said Grace.

'Such good hearts must be happy – shall be happy!' said Lord Colambre.

'Oh, you're very kind,' said the widow, smiling; 'and I wouldn't doubt you, if you had the power. I hope, then, the agent will give you encouragement about them mines, that we may keep you among us.'

'I am determined to settle among you, warm-hearted, generous people!' cried Lord Colambre, 'whether the agent gives me encouragement or not,' added he.

It was a long walk to Clonbrony Castle; the old woman, as she said herself, would not have been able for it, but for a *lift* given to her by a friendly carman, whom they met on the road with an empty car. This carman was Finnucan, who dissipated Lord Colambre's fears of meeting and being recognised by Mrs Raffarty; for he, in answer to the question of, 'Who is at the castle?' replied, 'Mrs Raffarty will be in it afore night; but she's on the road still. There's none but old Nick in it yet; and he's more of a *neger* than ever; for think, that he would not pay me a farthing for the carriage of his *shister's* boxes and bandboxes down. If you're going to have any dealings with him, God grant ye a safe deliverance!'

'Amen!' said the widow, and her son and daughter.

Lord Colambre's attention was now engaged by the view of the castle and park of Clonbrony. He had not seen it since he was six years old. Some faint reminiscence from his childhood made him feel or fancy that he knew the place. It was a fine castle, spacious park; but all about it, from the broken piers at the great entrance, to the mossy gravel and loose steps at the hall-door, had an air of desertion and melancholy. Walks overgrown, shrubberies wild, plantations run up into bare poles; fine trees cut down, and lying on the gravel in lots to be sold. A hill that had been covered with an oak wood, in which, in his childhood, our hero used to play, and which he called the black forest, was gone; nothing to be seen but the white stumps of the trees, for it had been freshly cut down, to make up the last remittances. – 'And how it went, when sold! – but no matter,' said Finnucan; 'it's all alike. – It's the back way into the yard, I'll take you, I suppose.'

And such a yard! 'But it's no matter,' repeated Lord Colambre to himself; 'it's all alike.'

In the kitchen a great dinner was dressing for Mr Garraghty's friends, who were to make merry with him when the business of the day was over.

'Where's the keys of the cellar, till I get out the claret for after dinner,' says one; 'and the wine for the cook – sure there's venison,' cries another. – 'Venison! – That's the way my lord's deer goes,' says a third, laughing. – 'Ay, sure! and very proper, when he's not here to eat 'em.' – 'Keep your nose out of the kitchen, young man, if you *plase*,' said the agent's cook, shutting the door in Lord Colambre's face. 'There's the way to the office, if you've money to pay, up the back stairs.'

'No; up the grand staircase they must – Mr Garraghty ordered,' said the footman; 'because the office is damp for him, and it's not there he'll see anybody today; but in my lady's dressing-room.'

So up the grand staircase they went, and through the magnificent apartments, hung with pictures of great value, spoiling with damp. 'Then, isn't it a pity to see them? There's my lady, and all spoiling,' said the widow.

Lord Colambre stopped before a portrait of Miss Nugent. – 'Shamefully damaged!' cried he. 'Pass on, or let me pass, if you *plase*,' said one of the tenants; 'and don't be stopping the doorway.' 'I have business more nor you with the agent,' said the surveyor; 'where is he?'

'In the *presence-chamber*,' replied another; 'where should the viceroy be but in the *presence-chamber*?'

There was a full levee, and fine smell of greatcoats. – 'Oh! would you put your hats on the silk cushions?' said the widow to some men in the doorway, who were throwing off their greasy hats on a damask sofa. – 'Why not? where else?' 'If the lady was in it, you wouldn't,' said she, sighing. – 'No, to be sure, I wouldn't; great news! would I make no *differ* in the presence of old Nick and my lady?' said he, in Irish. 'Have I no sense or manners, good woman, think ye?' added he, as he shook the ink out of his pen on the Wilton carpet, when he had finished signing his name to a paper on his knee. 'You may wait long before you get to the speech of the great man,' said another, who was working his way through numbers. They continued pushing forward, till they came within sight of Mr Nicholas Garraghty, seated in state; and a worse countenance, or a more perfect picture of an insolent, petty tyrant in office, Lord Colambre had never beheld.

We forbear all further detail of this levee. 'It's all the same!' as Lord Colambre repeated to himself, on every fresh instance of roguery or oppression to which he was witness; and, having completely made up his mind on the subject, he sat down quietly in the background, waiting till it should come to the widow's turn to be dealt with, for he was now interested only to see how she would be treated. The room gradually thinned; Mr Dennis Garraghty came in, and sat down at the table, to help his brother to count the heaps of gold.

'Oh, Mr Dennis, I'm glad to see you as kind as your promise, meeting me here,' said the widow O'Neill, walking up to him; 'I'm sure you'll speak a good word for me; here's the *lases* – who will I offer this to?' said she, holding the *glove-money* and *sealing-money*, – 'for I'm strange and ashamed.'

'Oh, don't be ashamed – there's no strangeness in bringing money or taking it,' said Mr Nicholas Garraghty, holding out his hand. 'Is this the proper compliment?'

'I hope so, sir; your honour knows best.'

'Very well,' slipping it into his private purse. 'Now, what's your business?'

'The *lases* to sign – the rent's all paid up.'

'Leases! Why, woman, is the possession given up?'

'It was, *plase* your honour; and Mr Dennis has the key of our little place in his pocket.'

'Then I hope he'll keep it there. *Your* little place – it's no longer yours; I've promised it to the surveyor. You don't think I'm such a fool as to renew to you at this rent.'

'Mr Dennis named the rent. But anything your honour *plases* – anything at all that we can pay.'

'Oh, it's out of the question – put it out of your head. No rent you can offer would do, for I've promised it to the surveyor.'

'Sir, Mr Dennis knows my lord gave us his promise in writing of a renewal, on the back of the *ould lase*.'

'Produce it.'

'Here's the *lase*, but the promise is rubbed out.'

'Nonsense! coming to me with a promise that's rubbed out. Who'll listen to that in a court of justice, do you think?'

'I don't know, plase your honour; but this I'm sure of, my lord and Miss Nugent, though but a child at the time, God bless her! who was by when my lord wrote it with his pencil, will remember it.'

'Miss Nugent! what can she know of business? – What has she to do with the management of my Lord Clonbrony's estate, pray?'

'Management! – no, sir.'

'Do you wish to get Miss Nugent turned out of the house?'

'Oh, God forbid! – how could that be?'

'Very easily; if you set about to make her meddle and witness in what my lord does not choose.'

'Well then, I'll never mention Miss Nugent's name in it at all, if it was ever so with me. But be *plased*, sir, to write over to my lord, and ask him; I'm sure he'll remember it.'

'Write to my lord about such a trifle – trouble him about such nonsense!'

'I'd be sorry to trouble him. Then take it on my word, and believe me, sir; for I would not tell a lie, nor cheat rich or poor, if in my power, for the whole estate, nor the whole world: for there's an eye above.'

'Cant! nonsense! – Take those leases off the table; I never will sign them. Walk off, ye canting hag; it's an imposition – I will never sign them.'

'You *will* then, sir,' cried Brian, growing red with indignation; 'for the law shall make you, so it shall; and you'd as good have been civil to my mother, whatever you did – for I'll stand by her while I've life; and I know she has right, and shall have law. I saw the memorandum written before ever it went into your hands, sir, whatever became of it after; and will swear to it, too.'

'Swear away, my good friend; much your swearing will avail in your own case in a court of justice,' continued old Nick.

'And against a gentleman of my brother's established character and property,' said St Dennis. 'What's your mother's character against a gentleman's like his?'

'Character! take care how you go to that, anyway, sir,' cried Brian.

Grace put her hand before his mouth, to stop him.

'Grace, dear, I must speak, if I die for it; sure it's for my mother,' said the young man, struggling forward, while his mother held him back; 'I must speak.'

'Oh, he's ruin'd, I see it,' said Grace, putting her hand before her eyes, 'and he won't mind me.'

'Go on, let him go on, pray, young woman,' said Mr Garraghty, pale with anger and fear, his lips quivering; 'I shall be happy to take down his words.'

'Write them; and may all the world read it, and welcome!'

His mother and wife stopped his mouth by force.

'Write you, Dennis,' said Mr Garraghty, giving the pen to his brother; for his hand shook so he could not form a letter. 'Write the very words, and at the top' (pointing) after warning, *'with malice prepense.'*

'Write, then – mother, Grace – let me,' cried Brian, speaking in a smothered voice, as their hands were over his mouth. 'Write then, that, if you'd either of you a character like my mother, you might defy the world; and your word would be as good as your oath.'

'*Oath!* mind that, Dennis,' said Mr Garraghty.

'Oh, sir! sir! won't you stop him?' cried Grace, turning suddenly to Lord Colambre.

'Oh dear, dear, if you haven't lost your feeling for us,' cried the widow.

'Let him speak,' said Lord Colambre, in a tone of authority; 'let the voice of truth be heard.'

'*Truth!*' cried St Dennis, and dropped the pen.

'And who the devil are you, sir?' said old Nick.

'Lord Colambre, I protest!' exclaimed a female voice; and Mrs Raffarty at this instant appeared at the open door.

'Lord Colambre!' repeated all present, in different tones.

'My lord, I beg pardon,' continued Mrs Raffarty, advancing as if her legs were tied; 'had I known you was down here, I would not have presumed. I'd better retire; for I see you're busy.'

'You'd best; for you're mad, sister,' said St Dennis, pushing her back; 'and we *are* busy; go to your room, and keep quiet, if you can.'

'First, madam,' said Lord Colambre, going between her and the door, 'let me beg that you will consider yourself as at home in this house, whilst any circumstances make it desirable to you. The hospitality you showed me you cannot think that I now forget.'

'Oh, my lord, you're too good – how few – too kind – kinder than my own,' and bursting into tears, she escaped out of the room.

Lord Colambre returned to the party round the table, who were in various attitudes of astonishment, and with faces of fear, horror, hope, joy, doubt..

'Distress,' continued his lordship, 'however incurred, if not by vice, will always find a refuge in this house. I speak in my father's name, for I know I speak his sentiments. But never more shall vice,' said he, darting such a look at the brother agents as they felt to the backbone – 'never more shall vice, shall fraud enter here.'

He paused, and there was a momentary silence.

'There spoke the true thing! and the *rael* gentleman; my own heart's satisfied,' said Brian, folding his arms, and standing erect.

'Then so is mine,' said Grace, taking breath, with a deep sigh.

The widow advancing, put on her spectacles, and, looking up close at Lord Colambre's face – 'Then it's a wonder I didn't know the family likeness.'

Lord Colambre now recollecting that he still wore the old greatcoat, threw it off.

'Oh, bless him! Then now I'd know him anywhere. I'm willing to die now, for we'll all be happy.'

'My lord, since it is so – my lord, may I ask you,' said Mr Garraghty, now sufficiently recovered to be able to articulate, but scarcely to express his ideas; 'if what your lordship hinted just now – '

'I hinted nothing, sir; I spoke plainly.'

'I beg pardon, my lord,' said old Nick; – 'respecting vice, was levelled at me; because, if it was, my lord,' trying to stand erect; 'let me tell your lordship, if I could think it was – '

'If it did not hit you, sir, no matter at whom it was levelled.'

'And let me ask, my lord, if I may presume, whether, in what you suggested by the word fraud, your lordship had any particular meaning?' said St Dennis.

'A very particular meaning, sir, – feel in your pocket for the key of this widow's house, and deliver it to her.'

'Oh, if that's all the meaning, with all the pleasure in life. I never meant to detain it longer than till the leases were signed,' said St Dennis.

'And I'm ready to sign the leases this minute,' said the brother.

'Do it, sir, this minute; I have read them; I will be answerable to my father.'

'Oh, as to that, my lord, I have power to sign for your father.' He signed the leases; they were duly witnessed by Lord Colambre.

'I deliver this as my act and deed,' said Mr Garraghty; – 'my lord,' continued he, 'you see, at the first word from you; and had I known sooner the interest you took in the family, there would have been no difficulty; for I'd make it a principle to oblige you, my lord.'

'Oblige me!' said Lord Colambre, with disdain.

'But when gentlemen and noblemen travel *incognito*, and lodge in cabins,' added St Dennis, with a satanic smile, glancing his eye on Grace, 'they have good reasons, no doubt.'

'Do not judge my heart by your own, sir,' said Lord Colambre, coolly; 'no two things in nature can, I trust, be more different. My purpose in travelling *incognito* has been fully answered: I was determined to see and judge how my father's estates were managed; and I have seen, compared, and judged. I have seen the difference between the Clonbrony and the Colambre property; and I shall represent what I have seen to my father.'

'As to that, my lord, if we are to come to that – but I trust your lordship will suffer me to explain these matters. – Go about your business, my good friends; you have all you want; – and, my lord, after dinner, when you are cool, I hope I shall be able to make you sensible that things have been represented to your lordship in a mistaken light; and I flatter myself I shall convince you I have not only always acted the part of a friend to the family, but am particularly willing to conciliate your lordship's goodwill,' said he, sweeping the rouleaus of gold into a bag; 'any accommodation in my power, at any time.'

'I want no accommodation, sir, – were I starving, I would accept of none from you. Never can you conciliate my goodwill; for you can never deserve it.'

'If that be the case, my lord, I must conduct myself accordingly; but it's fair to warn you, before you make any representation to my Lord Clonbrony, that if he should think of changing his agent, there are accounts to be settled between us – that may be a consideration.'

'No, sir; no consideration – my father never shall be the slave of such a paltry consideration.'

'Oh, very well, my lord; you know best. If you choose to make an assumpsit, I'm sure I shall not object to the security. Your lordship will be of age soon, I know – I'm sure I'm satisfied – but,' added he with a malicious smile, 'I rather apprehend you don't know what you undertake; I only premise that the balance of accounts between us is not what can properly be called a paltry consideration.'

'On that point, perhaps, sir, you and I may differ.'

'Very well, my lord, you will follow your own principles, if it suits your convenience.'

'Whether it does or not, sir, I shall abide by my principles.'

'Dennis! the letters to the post. – When do you go to England, my lord?'

'Immediately, sir,' said Lord Colambre; his lordship saw new leases from his father to Mr Dennis Garraghty, lying on the table, unsigned.

'Immediately!' repeated Messrs. Nicholas and Dennis, with an air of dismay. Nicholas got up, looked out of the window, and whispered something to his brother, who instantly left the room.

Lord Colambre saw the post-chaise at the door, which had brought Mrs Raffarty to the castle, and Larry standing beside it; his lordship instantly threw up the sash, and holding between his finger and thumb a six-shilling piece, cried, 'Larry, my friend, let me have the horses!'

'You shall have 'em – your honour,' said Larry. Mr Dennis Garraghty appeared below, speaking in a magisterial tone. 'Larry, my brother must have the horses.'

'He can't, *plase* your honour – they're engaged.'

'Half a crown! – a crown! – half a guinea!' said Mr Dennis Garraghty, raising his voice, as he increased his proffered bribe. To each offer Larry replied, 'You can't, *plase* your honour, they're engaged;' – and, looking up to the window at Lord Colambre, he said, 'As soon as they have eaten their oats, you shall have 'em.'

No other horses were to be had. The agent was in consternation. Lord Colambre ordered that Larry should have some dinner, and whilst the postillion was eating, and the horses finishing their oats, his lordship wrote the following letter to his father, which, to prevent all possibility of accident, he determined to put, with his own hand, into the post-office at Clonbrony, as he passed through the town.

My dear Father,

I hope to be with you in a few days. Lest anything should detain me on the road, I write this, to make an earnest request to you, that you will not sign any papers, or transact any farther business wish Messrs. Nicholas or Dennis Garraghty, before you see your affectionate son,

COLAMBRE.

The horses came out. Larry sent word he was ready, and Lord Colambre, having first eaten a slice of his own venison, ran down to the carriage, followed by the thanks and blessings of the widow, her son, and daughter, who could hardly make their way after him to the chaise-door, so great was the crowd which had gathered on the report of his lordship's arrival.

'Long life to your honour! Long life to your lordship!' echoed on all sides. 'Just come, and going, are you?'

'Good-bye to you all, good people!'

'Then *good-bye* is the only word we wouldn't wish to hear from your honour.'

'For the sake both of landlord and tenant, I must leave you now, my good friends; but I hope to return to you at some future time.'

'God bless you! and speed ye! and a safe journey to your honour! – and a happy return to us, and soon!' cried a multitude of voices.

Lord Colambre stopped at the chaise-door, and beckoned to the widow O'Neill, before whom others had pressed. An opening was made for her instantly.

'There! that was the very way his father stood, with his feet on the steps. And Miss Nugent was *in it*.'

Lord Colambre forgot what he was going to say – with some difficulty recollected.

'This pocket-book,' said he, 'which your son restored to me – I intend it for your daughter – don't keep it, as your son kept it for me, without opening it. Let what is within-side,' added he, as he got into the carriage, 'replace the cloak and gown, and let all things necessary for a bride be bought; "for the bride that has all things to borrow has surely mickle to do." – Shut the door, and drive on.'

'Blessings be *wid* you,' cried the widow, 'and God give you grace!'

Chapter 13

LARRY DROVE OFF at full gallop, and kept on at a good rate, till he got out of the great gate, and beyond the sight of the crowd; then, pulling up, he turned to Lord Colambre – '*Plase* your honour, I did not know nor guess ye was my lord, when I let you have the horses; did not know who you was from Adam, I'll take my affidavit.'

'There's no occasion,' said Lord Colambre; 'I hope you don't repent letting me have the horses, now you do know who I am?'

'Oh! not at all, sure; I'm as glad as the best horse I ever crossed, that your honour is my lord – but I was only telling your honour, that you might not be looking upon me as a *time-sarver*.'

'I do not look upon you as a *time-sarver*, Larry; but keep on, that time may serve me.'

In two words, he explained his cause of haste; and no sooner explained than understood. Larry thundered away through the town of Clonbrony, bending over his horses, plying the whip, and lending his very soul at every lash. With much difficulty, Lord Colambre stopped him at the end of the town, at the post-office. The post was gone out – gone a quarter of an hour.

'Maybe we'll overtake the mail,' said Larry; and, as he spoke, he slid down from his seat, and darted into the public-house, reappearing, in a few moments, with a *copper* of ale and a horn in his hand; he and another man held open the horses' mouths, and poured the ale through the horn clown their throats.

'Now, they'll go with spirit!'

And, with the hope of overtaking the mail, Larry made them go 'for life or death,' as he said; but in vain! At the next stage, at his own inn-door, Larry roared for fresh horses till he got them, harnessed them with his own hands, holding the six-shilling piece, which Lord Colambre had given him, in his mouth, all the while; for he could not take time to put it into his pocket.

'Speed ye! I wish I was driving you all the way, then,' said he. The other postillion was not yet ready. 'Then your honour sees,' said he, putting his head into the carriage, '*consarning* of them Garraghties – old Nick and St Dennis – the best part, that is the worst part, of what I told you, proved true; and I'm glad of it, that is, I'm sorry for it – but glad your honour knows it in time. So Heaven prosper you! And may all the saints (*barring* St Dennis) have charge of you, and all belonging to you, till we see you here again! – And when will it be?'

'I cannot say when I shall return to you myself, but I will do my best to send your landlord to you soon. In the meantime, my good fellow, keep away from the sign of the Horse-shoe – a man of your sense to drink and make an idiot and a brute of yourself!'

'True! – And it was only when I had lost hope I took to it – but now! Bring me the book, one of *yees*, out of the landlady's parlour. – By the virtue of this book, and by all the books that ever was shut and opened, I won't touch a drop of spirits, good or bad, till I see your honour again, or some of the family, this time twelvemonth – that long I'll live on hope – but mind, if you disappoint me, I don't swear but I'll take to the whiskey, for comfort, all the rest of my days. But don't be staying here, wasting your time, advising me. Bartley! take the reins, can't ye?' cried he, giving them to the fresh postillion; 'and keep on, for your life, for there's thousands of pounds depending on the race – so, off, off, Bartley, with speed of light!'

Bartley did his best; and such was the excellence of the roads, that, notwithstanding the rate at which our hero travelled, he arrived safely in Dublin, and just in time to put his letter into the post-office, and to sail in that night's packet. The wind was fair when Lord Colambre went on board, but before they got out of the bay it changed; they made no way all night; in the course of the next day, they had the mortification to see another packet from Dublin sail past them, and when they landed at Holyhead, were told the packet, which had left Ireland twelve hours after them, had been in an hour before them. The passengers had taken their places in the coach, and engaged what horses could be had. Lord Colambre was afraid that Mr Garraghty was one of them; a person exactly answering his description had taken four horses, and set out half an hour before in great haste for London. Luckily, just as those who had taken their places in the mail were getting into the coach, Lord Colambre saw among them a gentleman, with whom he had been acquainted in Dublin, a barrister, who was come over during the long vacation, to make a tour of pleasure in England. When Lord Colambre explained the reason he had for being in haste to reach London, he had the good-nature to give up to him his place in the coach. Lord Colambre travelled all night, and delayed not one moment, till he reached his father's house in London.

'My father at home?'

'Yes, my lord, in his own room – the agent from Ireland with him, on particular business – desired not to be interrupted – but I'll go and tell him, my lord, you are come.'

Lord Colambre ran past the servant, as he spoke – made his way into

the room – found his father, Sir Terence O'Fay, and Mr Garraghty –
leases open on the table before them; a candle lighted; Sir Terence
sealing; Garraghty emptying a bag of guineas on the table, and Lord
Clonbrony actually with a pen in his hand, ready to sign.

As the door opened, Garraghty started back, so that half the contents
of his bag rolled upon the floor.

'Stop, my dear father, I conjure you,' cried Lord Colambre, springing forward, and kneeling to his father; at the same moment snatching
the pen from his hand.

'Colambre! God bless you, my dear boy! at all events. But how came
you here? – And what do you mean?' said his father.

'Burn it!' cried Sir Terence, pinching the sealing-wax; 'for I burnt
myself with the pleasure of the surprise.'

Garraghty, without saying a word, was picking up the guineas that
were scattered upon the floor.

'How fortunate I am,' cried Lord Colambre, 'to have arrived just in
time to tell you, my dear father, before you put your signature to these
papers, before you conclude this bargain, all I know, all I have seen, of
that man!'

'Nick Garraghty, honest old Nick; do you know him, my lord?' said
Sir Terence.

'Too well, sir.'

'Mr Garraghty, what have you done to offend my son? I did not
expect this,' said Lord Clonbrony.

'Upon my conscience, my lord, nothing to my knowledge,' said Mr
Garraghty, picking up the guineas; 'but showed him every civility, even
so far as offering to accommodate him with cash without security; and
where will you find the other agent, in Ireland or anywhere else, will do
that? To my knowledge, I never did anything, by word or deed, to
offend my Lord Colambre; nor could not, for I never saw him, but for
ten minutes, in my days; and then he was in such a foaming passion –
begging his lordship's pardon – owing to the misrepresentations he
met with of me, I presume, from a parcel of blackguards that he went
amongst, *incognito*, he would not let me or my brother Dennis say a
word to set him right; but exposed me before all the tenantry, and then
threw himself into a hack, and drove off here, to stop the signing of
these leases, I perceive. But I trust,' concluded he, putting the
replenished money-bag down with a heavy sound on the table,
opposite to Lord Clonbrony, – 'I trust, my Lord Clonbrony will do me
justice; that's all I have to say.'

'I comprehend the force of your last argument fully, sir,' said Lord
Colambre. 'May I ask how many guineas there are in the bag? I don't

ask whether they are my father's or not.'

'They are to be your lordship's father's, sir, if he thinks proper,' replied Garraghty. 'How many, I don't know that I can justly, positively say – five hundred, suppose.'

'And they would be my father's if he signed those leases – I understand that perfectly, and understand that my father would lose three times that sum by the bargain. – My dear father, you start but it is true. Is not this the rent, sir, at which you were going to let Mr Garraghty have the land?' placing a paper before Lord Clonbrony.

'It is – the very thing.'

'And here, sir, written with my own hand, are copies of the proposals I saw, from responsible, respectable tenants, offered and refused. – Is it so, or is it not, Mr Garraghty? – deny it, if you can.'

Mr Garraghty grew pale; his lips quivered; he stammered; and, after a shocking convulsion of face, could at last articulate – only –

'That there was a great difference between tenant and tenant, his lordship must be sensible, especially for so large a rent.' – 'As great a difference as between agent and agent, I am sensible – especially for so large a property!' said Lord Colambre, with cool contempt. 'You find, sir, I am well informed with regard to this transaction; you will find, also, that I am equally well informed with respect to every part of your conduct towards my father and his tenantry. If, in relating to him what I have seen and heard, I should make any mistakes, you are here; and I am glad you are, to set me right, and to do yourself justice.'

'Oh! as to that, I should not presume to contradict anything your lordship asserts from your own authority: where would be the use? I leave it all to your lordship. But, as it is not particularly agreeable to stay to hear one's self abused – Sir Terence! I'll thank you to hand me my hat! – And if you'll have the goodness, my Lord Clonbrony, to look over finally the accounts before morning, I'll call at your leisure to settle the balance, as you find convenient; as to the leases, I'm quite indifferent.'

So saying, he took up his money-bag.

'Well, you'll call again in the morning, Mr Garraghty!' said Sir Terence; 'and, by that time, I hope we shall understand this misunderstanding better.'

Sir Terence pulled Lord Clonbrony's sleeve: 'Don't let him go with the money – it's much wanted!'

'Let him go,' said Lord Colambre; 'money can be had by honourable means.'

'Wheugh! – He talks as if he had the Bank of England at his command, as every young man does,' said Sir Terence.

Lord Colambre deigned no reply. Lord Clonbrony walked

undecidedly between his agent and his son – looked at Sir Terence, and said nothing.

Mr Garraghty departed; Lord Clonbrony called after him from the head of the stairs –

'I shall be at home and at leisure in the morning.' Sir Terence ran downstairs after him; Lord Colambre waited quietly for their return.

'Fifteen hundred guineas, at a stroke of a goose-quill! – That was a neat hit, narrowly missed, of honest Nick's!' said Lord Clonbrony. 'Too bad! too bad, faith! – I am much, very much obliged to you, Colambre, for that hint; by tomorrow morning we shall have him in another tune.'

'And he must double the bag, or quit,' said Sir Terence.

'Treble it, if you please, Terry. Sure, three times five's fifteen; – fifteen hundred down, or he does not get my signature to those leases for his brother, nor get the agency of the Colambre estate. Colambre, what more have you to tell of him? for, since he is making out his accounts against me, it is no harm to have a *per contra* against him that may ease my balance.'

'Very fair! very fair!' said Sir Terence. 'My lord, trust me for remembering all the charges against him – every item; and when he can't clear himself, if I don't make him buy a good character dear enough, why, say I'm a fool, and don't know the value of character, good or bad!'

'If you know the value of character, Sir Terence,' said Lord Colambre, 'you know that it is not to be bought or sold.' Then, turning from Sir Terence to his father, he gave a full and true account of all he had seen in his progress through his Irish estates; and drew a faithful picture both of the bad and good agent. Lord Clonbrony, who had benevolent feelings, and was fond of his tenantry, was touched; and, when his son ceased speaking, repeated several times –

'Rascal! rascal! How dare he use my tenants so – the O'Neills in particular! – Rascal! bad heart! – I'll have no more to do with him.' But, suddenly recollecting himself, he turned to Sir Terence, and added, 'That's sooner said than done – I'll tell you honestly, Colambre, your friend Mr Burke may be the best man in the world – but he is the worst man to apply to for a remittance, or a loan, in a HURRY! He always tells me "he can't distress the tenants." ' – 'And he never, at coming into the agency even,' said Sir Terence, '*advanced* a good round sum to the landlord, by way of security for his good behaviour. Now honest Nick did that much for us at coming in.'

'And at going out is he not to be repaid?' said Lord Colambre.

'That's the devil!' said Lord Clonbrony; that's the very reason I can't conveniently turn him out.'

'I will make it convenient to you, sir, if you will permit me,' said Lord Colambre. 'In a few days I shall be of age, and will join with you in raising whatever sum you want, to free you from this man. Allow me to look over his account; and whatever the honest balance may be, let him have it.'

'My dear boy!' said Lord Clonbrony, 'you're a generous fellow. Fine Irish heart! – glad you're my son! But there's more, much more, that you don't know,' added he, looking at Sir Terence, who cleared his throat; and Lord Clonbrony, who was on the point of opening all his affairs to his son, stopped short.

'Colambre,' said he, 'we will not say anything more of this at present; for nothing effectual can be done till you are of age, and then we shall see all about it.'

Lord Colambre perfectly understood what his father meant, and what was meant by the clearing of Sir Terence's throat. Lord Clonbrony wanted his son to join him in opening the estate to pay his debts; and Sir Terence feared that, if Lord Colambre were abruptly told the whole sum total of the debts, he would never be persuaded to join in selling or mortgaging so much of his patrimony as would be necessary for their payment. Sir Terence thought that the young man, ignorant probably of business, and unsuspicious of the state of his father's affairs, might be brought, by proper management, to any measures they desired. Lord Clonbrony wavered between the temptation to throw himself upon the generosity of his son, and the immediate convenience of borrowing a sum of money from his agent, to relieve his present embarrassments.

'Nothing can be settled,' repeated he, 'till Colambre is of age; so it does not signify talking of it.'

'Why so, sir?' said Lord Colambre. 'Though my act, in law, may not be valid, till I am of age, my promise, as a man of honour, is binding now; and, I trust, would be as satisfactory to my father as any legal deed whatever.'

'Undoubtedly, my dear boy; but – '

'But what?' said Lord Colambre, following his father's eye, which turned to Sir Terence O'Fay, as if asking his permission to explain.

'As my father's friend, sir, you ought, permit me to say, at this moment to use your influence to prevail upon him to throw aside all reserve with a son, whose warmest wish is to serve him, and to see him at ease and happy.'

'Generous, dear boy,' cried Lord Clonbrony. 'Terence, I can't stand it; but how shall I bring myself to name the amount of the debts?'

'At some time or other, I must know it,' said Lord Colambre; 'I cannot be better prepared at any moment than the present; never more disposed to give my assistance to relieve all difficulties. Blindfold, I cannot be led to any purpose, sir,' said he, looking at Sir Terence; 'the attempt would be degrading and futile. Blindfolded I will not be – but, with my eyes open, I will see, and go straight and prompt as heart can go, to my father's interest, without a look or thought to my own.'

'By St Patrick! the spirit of a prince, and an Irish prince, spoke there,' cried Sir Terence; 'and if I'd fifty hearts, you'd have all in your hand this minute, at your service, and warm. Blindfold you! after that, the man that would attempt it *desarves* to be shot; and I'd have no sincerer pleasure in life than shooting him this moment, was he my best friend. But it's not Clonbrony, or your father, my lord, would act that way, no more than Sir Terence O'Fay – there's the schedule of the debts,' drawing a paper from his bosom; 'and I'll swear to the lot, and not a man on earth could do that but myself.'

Lord Colambre opened the paper. His father turned aside, covering his face with both his hands.

'Tut, man,' said Sir Terence; 'I know him now better than you; he will stand, you'll find, the shock of that regiment of figures – he is steel to the backbone, and proof spirit.'

'I thank you, my dear father,' said Lord Colambre, 'for trusting me thus at once with a view of the truth. At first sight it is, I acknowledge, worse than I expected; but I make no doubt that, when you allow me to examine Mr Garraghty's accounts and Mr Mordicai's claims, we shall be able to reduce this alarming total considerably, my dear father. You think we learn nothing but Latin and Greek at Cambridge; but you are mistaken.'

'The devil a pound, nor a penny,' said Sir Terence; 'for you have to deal with a Jew and old Nick; and I'm not a match for them. I don't know who is; and I have no hope of getting any abatement. I've looked over the accounts till I'm sick.'

'Nevertheless, you will observe that fifteen hundred guineas have been saved to my father, at one stroke, by his not signing those leases.'

'Saved to you, my lord; not your father, if you plase,' said Sir Terence. 'For now I'm upon the square with you, I must be straight as an arrow, and deal with you as the son and friend of my friend; before, I was considering you only as the son and heir, which is quite another thing, you know; accordingly, acting for your father here, I was making the best bargain against you I could; honestly, now, I tell you. I knew the value of the lands well enough; we were as sharp as Garraghty, and he knew it; we were to have had *the difference* from him, partly in cash and partly in balance of accounts – you comprehend – and you only would have been the loser, and never would have known it, maybe, till after we all were dead and buried; and then you might have set aside Garraghty's lease easy, and no harm done to any but a rogue that *desarved* it; and, in the meantime, an accommodation to my honest friend, my lord, your father, here. But, as fate would have it, you upset all by your progress *incognito* through them estates. Well, it's best as it is, and I am better pleased to be as we are, trusting all to a generous son's own heart. Now put the poor father out of pain, and tell us what you'll do, my dear.'

'In one word, then,' said Lord Colambre, 'I will, upon two conditions, either join my father in levying fines to enable him to sell or mortgage whatever portion of his estate is necessary for the payment of these debts; or I will, in whatever other mode he can point out, as more agreeable or more advantageous to him, join in giving security to his creditors.'

'Dear, noble fellow!' cried Sir Terence; 'none but an Irishman could do it.'

Lord Clonbrony, melted to tears, could not articulate, but held his arms open to embrace his son.

'But you have not heard my conditions yet,' said Lord Colambre.

'Oh, confound the conditions!' cried Sir Terence.

'What conditions could he ask that I could refuse at this minute?' said Lord Clonbrony.

'Nor I – was it my heart's blood, and were I to be hanged for it,' cried Sir Terence. 'And what are the conditions?'

'That Mr Garraghty shall be dismissed from the agency.'

'And welcome, and glad to get rid of him – the rogue, the tyrant,' said Lord Clonbrony; 'and, to be beforehand with you in your next wish, put Mr Burke into his place.'

'I'll write the letter for you to sign, my lord, this minute,' cried Terry, 'with all the pleasure in life. No; it's my Lord Colambre should do that in all justice.'

'But what's your next condition? I hope it's no worse,' said Lord Clonbrony.

'That you and my mother should cease to be absentees.'

'Oh murder!' said Sir Terence; 'maybe that's not so easy; for there are two words to that bargain.'

Lord Clonbrony declared that, for his own part, he was ready to return to Ireland next morning, and to promise to reside on his estate all the rest of his days; that there was nothing he desired more, provided Lady Clonbrony would consent to it; but that he could not promise for her; that she was as obstinate as a mule on that point; that he had often tried, but that there was no moving her; and that, in short, he could not promise on her part.

But it was on this condition, Lord Colambre said, he must insist. Without this condition was granted, he would not engage to do anything.

'Well, we must only see how it will be when she comes to town; she will come up from Buxton the day you're of age to sign some papers,' said Lord Clonbrony; 'but,' added he, with a very dejected look and voice, 'if all's to depend on my Lady Clonbrony's consenting to return to Ireland, I'm as far from all hope of being at ease as ever.'

'Upon my conscience, we're all at sea again,' said Sir Terence.

Lord Colambre was silent: but in his silence there was such an air of firmness, that both Lord Clonbrony and Sir Terence were convinced entreaties would on this point be fruitless – Lord Clonbrony sighed deeply.

'But when it's ruin or safety, and her husband and all belonging to her at stake, the woman can't persist in being a mule,' said Sir Terence.

'Of whom are you talking?' said Lord Colambre.

'Of whom? Oh, I beg your lordship's pardon – I thought I was talking to my lord; but, in other words, as you are her son, I'm persuaded her ladyship, your mother, will prove herself a reasonable woman – when she sees she can't help it. So, my Lord Clonbrony, cheer up; a great deal may be done by the fear of Mordicai, and an execution, especially now the prior creditor. Since there's no reserve between you and I now, my Lord Colambre,' said Sir Terence, 'I must tell you all, and how we shambled on those months while you were in Ireland. First, Mordicai went to law, to prove I was in a conspiracy with your father, pretending to be prior creditor, to keep him off and out of his own; which, after a world of swearing and law – law always takes time to do justice, that's one comfort – the villain proved at last to be true enough, and so cast us; and I was forced to be paid off last week. So there's no prior creditor, or any shield of pretence that way. Then his execution was coming down upon us, and nothing to stay it till I thought of a monthly annuity to Mordicai, in the shape of a wager. So, the morning after he cast us, I went to him: "Mr Mordicai," says I, "you must be *plased* to see a man you've beaten so handsomely; and though I'm sore, both for myself and my friend, yet you see I can laugh still; though an execution is no laughing matter, and I'm sinsible you've one in petto in your sleeve for my friend Lord Clonbrony. But I'll lay you a wager of a hundred guineas in paper that a marriage of his son with a certain heiress, before next Lady-day, will set all to rights, and pay you with a compliment too.'

'Good heavens, Sir Terence! surely you said no such thing?'

'I did – but what was it but a wager? which is nothing but a dream; and, when lost, as I am as sinsible as you are that it must be, why, what is it, after all, but a bonus, in a gentlemanlike form, to Mordicai? which, I grant you, is more than he deserves, for staying the execution till you be of age; and even for my Lady Clonbrony's sake, though I know she hates me like poison, rather than have her disturbed by an execution, I'd pay the hundred guineas this minute out of my own pocket, if I had 'em in it.'

A thundering knock at the door was heard at this moment.

'Never heed it; let 'em thunder,' said Sir Terence; 'whoever it is, they won't get in; for my lord bid them let none in for their life. It's necessary for us to be very particular about the street-door now; and I advise a double chain for it, and to have the footmen well tutored to look before they run to a double rap; for a double rap might be a double trap.'

'My lady and Miss Nugent, my lord,' said a footman, throwing open the door.

'My mother! Miss Nugent!' cried Lord Colambre, springing eagerly forward.

'Colambre! here!' said his mother; 'but it's all too late now, and no matter where you are.'

Lady Clonbrony coldly suffered her son to embrace her; and he, without considering the coldness of her manner, scarcely hearing, and not at all understanding the words she said, fixed his eyes on his cousin, who, with a countenance all radiant with affectionate joy, held out her hand to him.

'Dear cousin Colambre, what an unexpected pleasure!'

He seized the hand; but, as he was going to kiss it, the recollection of St Omar crossed his mind; he checked himself, and said something about joy and pleasure, but his countenance expressed neither; and Miss Nugent, much surprised by the coldness of his manner, withdrew her hand, and, turning away, left the room.

'Grace! darling!' called Lord Clonbrony, 'whither so fast, before you've given me a word or a kiss?'

She came back, and hastily kissed her uncle, who folded her in his arms. 'Why must I let you go? And what makes you so pale, my dear child?'

'I am a little – a little tired. I will be with you again soon.'

Her uncle let her go.

'Your famous Buxton baths don't seem to have agreed with her, by all I can see,' said Lord Clonbrony.

'My lord, the Buxton baths are no way to blame; but I know what is to blame, and who is to blame,' said Lady Clonbrony, in a tone of displeasure, fixing her eyes upon her son. 'Yes, you may well look confounded, Colambre; but it is too late now – you should have known your own mind in time. I see you have heard it, then – but I am sure I don't know how; for it was only decided the day I left Buxton. The news could hardly travel faster than I did. Pray, how did you hear it?'

'Hear what, ma'am?' said Lord Colambre.

'Why, that Miss Broadhurst is going to be married.'

'Oh, is that all, ma'am!' said our hero, much relieved.

'All! Now, Lord Colambre, you *reelly* are too much for my patience. But I flatter myself you will feel, when I tell you, that it is your friend, Sir Arthur Berryl, as I always prophesied, who has carried off the prize from you.'

'But for the fear of displeasing my dear mother, I should say, that I do feel sincere pleasure in this marriage – I always wished it: my friend, Sir Arthur, from the first moment, trusted me with the secret of his attachment; he knew that he had my warm good wishes for his success; he knew that I thought most highly of the young lady; but that I never thought of her as a wife for myself.'

'And why did not you? that is the very thing I complain of,' said Lady Clonbrony. 'But it is all over now. You may set your heart at ease, for they are to be married on Thursday; and poor Mrs Broadhurst is ready to break her heart, for she was set upon a coronet for her daughter; and you, ungrateful as you are, you don't know how she wished you to be the happy man. But only conceive, after all that had passed, Miss Broadhurst had the assurance to expect I would let my niece be her bridesmaid. Oh, I flatly refused; that is, I told Grace it could not be; and, that there might be no affront to Mrs Broadhurst, who did not deserve it, I pretended Grace had never mentioned it; but ordered my carriage, and left Buxton directly. Grace was hurt, for she is very warm in her friendships. I am sorry to hurt Grace. But *reelly* I could not let her be bridesmaid; – and that, if you must know, is what vexed her, and made the tears come in her eyes, I suppose – and I'm sorry for it; but one must keep up one's dignity a little. After all, Miss Broadhurst was only a citizen – and *reelly* now, a very odd girl; never did anything like anybody else; settled her marriage at last in the oddest way. Grace, can you tell the particulars? I own, I am tired of the subject, and tired of my journey. My lord, I shall take leave to dine in my own room today,' continued her ladyship, as she quitted the room.

'I hope her ladyship did not notice me,' said Sir Terence O'Fay, coming from behind a window-curtain.

'Why, Terry, what did you hide for?' said Lord Clonbrony.

'Hide! I didn't hide, nor wouldn't from any man living, *let alone* any woman. Hide! no; but I just stood looking out of the window, behind this curtain, that my poor Lady Clonbrony might not be discomfited and shocked by the sight of one whom she can't abide, the very minute she come home. Oh, I've some consideration – it would have put her out of humour worse with both of you too; and for that there's no need, as far as I see. So I'll take myself off to my coffee-house to dine, and maybe you may get her down and into spirits again. But, for your lives, don't touch upon Ireland the night, nor till she has fairly got the better of the marriage. *Apropos* – there's my wager to Mordicai gone at a slap. It's I that ought to be scolding you, my Lord Colambre; but I trust you will do as well yet, not in point of purse, maybe. But I'm not one of those that think that money's everything – though, I grant you, in this world, there's nothing to be had without it – love excepted – which most people don't believe in – but not I – in particular cases. So I leave you, with my blessing, and I've a notion, at this time, that is better than my company – your most devoted –'

The good-natured Sir Terence would not be persuaded by Lord Clonbrony to stay. Nodding at Lord Colambre as he went out of the room, he said, 'I've an eye, in going, to your heart's ease too. When I played myself, I never liked standers-by.'

Sir Terence was not deficient in penetration, but he never could help boasting of his discoveries.

Lord Colambre was grateful for his judicious departure; and followed his equally judicious advice, not to touch upon Ireland this night.

Lady Clonbrony was full of Buxton, and he was glad to be relieved from the necessity of talking; and he indulged himself in considering what might be passing in Miss Nugent's mind. She now appeared in remarkably good spirits; for her aunt had given her a hint that she thought her out of humour because she had not been permitted to be Miss Broadhurst's bridesmaid, and she was determined to exert herself to dispel this notion. This it was now easy for her to do, because she had, by this time, in her own imagination, found a plausible excuse for that coldness in Lord Colambre's reception of her, by which she had at first been hurt; she had settled it, that he had taken it for granted she was of his mother's sentiments respecting Miss Broadhurst's marriage, and that this idea, and perhaps the apprehension of her reproaches, had caused his embarrassment – she knew that she could easily set this misunderstanding right. Accordingly, when Lady Clonbrony had talked herself to sleep about Buxton, and was taking her afternoon's nap, as it was her custom to do when she had neither cards nor company to keep her awake, Miss Nugent began to explain her own sentiments, and to give Lord Colambre, as her aunt had desired, an account of the manner in which Miss Broadhurst's marriage had been settled.

'In the first place,' said she, 'let me assure you that I rejoice in this marriage; I think your friend, Sir Arthur Berryl, is every way deserving of my friend, Miss Broadhurst; and this from me,' said she, smiling, 'is no slight eulogium. I have marked the rise and progress of their attachment; and it has been founded on the perception of such excellent qualities on each side, that I have no fear for its permanence. Sir Arthur Berryl's honourable conduct in paying his father's debts, and his generosity to his mother and sisters, whose fortunes were left entirely dependent upon him, first pleased my friend. It was like what she would have done herself, and like – in short, it is what few young men, as she said, of the present day would do. Then his refraining from all personal expenses, his going without equipage and without horses, that he might do what he felt to be right, whilst it exposed him continually to the ridicule of fashionable young men, or to the charge of avarice, made a very different impression on Miss Broadhurst's mind; her esteem and admiration were excited by these proofs of strength of character, and of just and good principles.'

'If you go on, you will make me envious and jealous of my friend,' said Lord Colambre.

'You jealous! – Oh, it is too late now – besides, you cannot be jealous, for you never loved.'

'I never loved Miss Broadhurst, I acknowledge.'

'There was the advantage Sir Arthur Berryl had over you – he loved, and my friend saw it.'

'She was clear-sighted,' said Lord Colambre.

'She was clear-sighted,' repeated Miss Nugent; 'but if you mean that she was vain, and apt to fancy people in love with her, I can assure you that you are mistaken. Never was woman, young or old, more clear-sighted to the views of those by whom she was addressed. No flattery, no fashion, could blind her judgment.'

'She knew how to choose a friend well, I am sure,' said Lord Colambre.

'And a friend for life too, I am sure you will allow – and she had such numbers, such strange variety of admirers, as might have puzzled the choice and turned the brain of any inferior person. Such a succession of lovers as she has had this summer, ever since you went to Ireland – they appeared and vanished like figures in a magic-lantern. She had three noble admirers – rank in three different forms offered themselves. First came in, hobbling, rank and gout; next, rank and gaming; then rank, very high rank, over head and ears in debt. All of these were rejected; and, as they moved off, I thought Mrs Broadhurst would have broken her heart. Next came fashion, with his head, heart, and soul in his cravat – he quickly made his bow, or rather his nod, and walked off, taking a pinch of snuff. Then came a man of gallantry, but,' whispered Miss Nugent, 'there was a mistress in the wood; and my friend could have nothing to do with that gentleman.'

'Now, if she liked the man,' interrupted Lord Clonbrony, 'and I suppose she did, for all women, but yourself, Grace, like men of gallantry, Miss Broadhurst was a goose for refusing him on account of the mistress; because she might have been bought up, and settled with a few thousand pounds.'

'Be that as it may,' said Miss Nugent; 'my friend did not like, and would not accept, of the man of gallantry; so he retired and comforted himself with a copy of verses. Then came a man of wit – but still it was wit without worth; and presently came "worth without wit." She preferred "wit and worth united," which she fortunately at last found, Lord Colambre, in your friend, Sir Arthur Berryl.'

'Grace, my girl!' said her uncle,' I'm glad to see you've got up your spirits again, though you were not to be bridesmaid. Well, I hope you'll be bride soon – I'm sure you ought to be – and you should think of rewarding that poor Mr Salisbury, who plagues me to death, whenever he can catch hold of me, about you. He must have our definitive at last, you know, Grace.'

A silence ensued, which neither Miss Nugent nor Lord Colambre seemed willing, or able, to break.

'Very good company, faith, you three! – One of ye asleep, and the other two saying nothing, to keep one awake. Colambre, have you no Dublin news? Grace, have you no Buxton scandal? What was it Lady Clonbrony told us you'd tell us, about the oddness of Miss Broadhurst's settling her marriage? Tell me that, for I love to hear odd things.'

'Perhaps you will not think it odd,' said she. 'One evening – but I should begin by telling you that three of her admirers, beside Sir Arthur Berryl, had followed her to Buxton, and had been paying their court to her all the time we were there; and at last grew impatient for her decision.'

'Ay, for her definitive!' said Lord Clonbrony. Miss Nugent was put out again, but resumed –

'So one evening, just before the dancing began, the gentlemen were all standing round Miss Broadhurst; one of them said, "I wish Miss Broadhurst would decide – that whoever she dances with tonight should be her partner for life; what a happy man he would be!"

' "But how can I decide?" said Miss Broadhurst.

' "I wish I had a friend to plead for me!" said one of the suitors, looking at me.

' "Have you no friend of your own?" said Miss Broadhurst.

' "Plenty of friends," said the gentleman.

' "Plenty! – then you must be a very happy man," replied Miss Broadhurst. "Come," said she, laughing, "I will dance with that man who can convince me – that he has, near relations excepted, one true friend in the world! That man who has made the best friend, I dare say, will make the best husband!"

'At that moment,' continued Miss Nugent, 'I was certain who would be her choice. The gentlemen all declared at first that they had abundance of excellent friends – the best friends in the world! but when Miss Broadhurst cross-examined them, as to what their friends had done for them, or what they were willing to do, modern friendship dwindled into a ridiculously small compass. I cannot give you the particulars of the cross-examination, though it was conducted with great spirit and humour by Miss Broadhurst; but I can tell you the result – that Sir Arthur Berryl, by incontrovertible facts, and eloquence warm from the heart, convinced everybody present that he had the best friend in the world; and Miss Broadhurst, as he finished speaking, gave him her hand, and he led her off in triumph – So you see, Lord Colambre, you were at last the cause of my friend's marriage!'

She turned to Lord Colambre as she spoke these words, with such an affectionate smile, and such an expression of open, inmost tenderness in her whole countenance, that our hero could hardly resist the impulse of his passion – could hardly restrain himself from falling at her feet that instant, and declaring his love. 'But St Omar! St Omar! – It must not be!'

'I must be gone!' said Lord Clonbrony, pulling out his watch. 'It is time to go to my club; and poor Terry will wonder what has become of me.'

Lord Colambre instantly offered to accompany his father; much to Lord Clonbrony's, and more to Miss Nugent's surprise.

'What!' said she to herself, 'after so long an absence, leave me! – Leave his mother, with whom he always used to stay – on purpose to avoid me! What can I have done to displease him? It is clear it was not about Miss Broadhurst's marriage he was offended; for he looked pleased, and like himself, whilst I was talking of that; but the moment afterwards, what a constrained, unintelligible expression of countenance – and leaves me to go to a club which he detests!'

As the gentlemen shut the door on leaving the room, Lady Clonbrony wakened, and, starting up, exclaimed –

'What's the matter? Are they gone? Is Colambre gone?'

'Yes, ma'am, with my uncle.'

'Very odd! very odd of him to go and leave me! he always used to stay with me – what did he say about me?'

'Nothing, ma'am.'

'Well, then, I have nothing to say about him, or about anything, indeed, for I'm excessively tired and stupid – alone in Lon'on's as bad as anywhere else. Ring the bell, and we'll go to bed directly – if you have no objection, Grace.'

Grace made no objection; Lady Clonbrony went to bed and to sleep in ten minutes. Miss Nugent went to bed; but she lay awake, considering what could be the cause of her cousin Colambre's hard unkindness, and of 'his altered eye.' She was openness itself; and she determined that, the first moment she could speak to him alone, she would at once ask for an explanation. With this resolution, she rose in the morning, and went down to the breakfast-room, in hopes of meeting him, as it had formerly been his custom to be early; and she expected to find him reading in his usual place.

Chapter 14

No – Lord Colambre was not in his accustomed place, reading in the breakfast-room: nor did he make his appearance till both his father and mother had been some time at breakfast.

'Good-morning to you, my Lord Colambre,' said his mother, in a reproachful tone, the moment he entered; 'I am much obliged to you for your company last night.'

'Good-morning to you, Colambre,' said his father, in a more jocose tone of reproach; 'I am obliged to you for your good company last night.'

'Good-morning to you, Lord Colambre,' said Miss Nugent; and though she endeavoured to throw all reproach from her looks, and to let none be heard in her voice, yet there was a slight tremulous motion in that voice which struck our hero to the heart.

'I thank you, ma'am, for missing me,' said he, addressing himself to his mother; 'I stayed away but half an hour; I accompanied my father to St James's Street, and when I returned I found that every one had retired to rest.'

'Oh, was that the case?' said Lady Clonbrony; 'I own I thought it very unlike you to leave me in that sort of way.'

'And, lest you should be jealous of that half-hour when he was accompanying me,' said Lord Clonbrony, 'I must remark, that, though I had his body with me, I had none of his mind; that he left at home with you ladies, or with some fair one across the water, for the deuce of two words did he bestow upon me, with all his pretence of accompanying me.'

'Lord Colambre seems to have a fair chance of a pleasant breakfast,' said Miss Nugent, smiling; 'reproaches on all sides.'

'I have heard none on your side, Grace,' said Lord Clonbrony; 'and that's the reason, I suppose, he wisely takes his seat beside you. But, come, we will not badger you any more, my dear boy. We have given him as fine a complexion amongst us as if he had been out hunting these three hours; have not we, Grace?'

'When Colambre has been a season or two more in Lon'on, he'll not be so easily put out of countenance,' said Lady Clonbrony; 'you don't see young men of fashion here blushing about nothing.'

'No, nor about anything, my dear,' said Lord Clonbrony; 'but that's no proof they do nothing they ought to blush for.'

'What they do, there's no occasion for ladies to inquire,' said Lady Clonbrony; 'but this I know, that it's a great disadvantage to a young man of a certain rank to blush; for no people, who live in a certain set, ever do; and it is the most opposite thing possible to a certain air, which, I own, I think Colambre wants; and now that he has done travelling in Ireland, which is no use in *pint* of giving a gentleman a travelled air, or anything of that sort, I hope he will put himself under my conduct for next winter's campaign in town.'

Lord Clonbrony looked as if he did not know how to look; and, after drumming on the table for some seconds, said –

'Colambre, I told you how it would be. That's a fatal hard condition of yours.'

'Not a hard condition, I hope, my dear father,' said Lord Colambre.

'Hard it must be, since it can't be fulfilled, or won't be fulfilled, which comes to the same thing,' replied Lord Clonbrony, sighing.

'I am persuaded, sir, that it will be fulfilled,' said Lord Colambre; 'I am persuaded that, when my mother hears the truth, and the whole truth – when she finds that your happiness, and the happiness of her whole family, depend upon her yielding her taste on one subject – '

'Oh, I see now what you are about,' cried Lady Clonbrony; 'you are coming round with your persuasions and prefaces to ask me to give up Lon'on, and go back with you to Ireland, my lord. You may save yourselves the trouble, all of you, for no earthly persuasions shall make me do it. I will never give up my taste on that *pint*. My happiness has a right to be as much considered as your father's, Colambre, or anybody's; and, in one word, I won't do it,' cried she, rising angrily from the breakfast-table.

'There! did not I tell you how it would be?' cried Lord Clonbrony.

'My mother has not heard me, yet,' said Lord Colambre, laying his hand upon his mother's arm, as she attempted to pass; 'hear me, madam, for your own sake. You do not know what will happen, this very day – this very hour, perhaps – if you do not listen to me.'

'And what will happen?' said Lady Clonbrony, stopping short.

'Ay, indeed; she little knows,' said Lord Clonbrony, 'what's hanging over her head.'

'Hanging over my head?' said Lady Clonbrony, looking up; 'nonsense! – what?'

'An execution, madam!' said Lord Colambre.

'Gracious me! an execution!' said Lady Clonbrony, sitting down again; 'but I heard you talk of an execution months ago, my lord, before my son went to Ireland, and it blew over – I heard no more of it.'

'It won't blow over now,' said Lord Clonbrony; 'you'll hear more of it now. Sir Terence O'Fay it was, you may remember, that settled it then.'

'Well, and can't he settle it now? Send for him, since he understands these cases; and I will ask him to dinner myself, for your sake, and be very civil to him, my lord.'

'All your civility, either for my sake or your own, will not signify a straw, my dear, in this case – anything that poor Terry could do, he'd do, and welcome, without it; but he can do nothing.'

'Nothing! – that's very extraordinary. But I'm clear no one dare to bring a real execution against us in earnest; and you are only trying to frighten me to your purpose, like a child; but it shan't do.'

'Very well, my dear; you'll see – too late.'

A knock at the house door.

'Who is it? – What is it?' cried Lord Clonbrony, growing very pale.

Lord Colambre changed colour too, and ran downstairs. 'Don't let 'em let anybody in, for your life, Colambre; under any pretence,' cried Lord Clonbrony, calling from the head of the stairs; then running to the window, 'By all that's good, it's Mordicai himself! and the people with him.'

'Lean your head on me, my dear aunt,' said Miss Nugent. Lady Clonbrony leant back, trembling, and ready to faint.

'But he's walking off now; the rascal could not get in – safe for the present!' cried Lord Clonbrony, rubbing his hands, and repeating, 'safe for the present!'

'Safe for the present!' repeated Lord Colambre, coming again into the room. 'Safe for the present hour.'

'He could not get in, I suppose – oh, I warned all the servants well,' said Lord Clonbrony, 'and so did Terry. Ay, there's the rascal, Mordicai, walking off, at the end of the street; I know his walk a mile off. Gad! I can breathe again. I am glad he's gone. But he will come back and always lie in wait, and some time or other, when we're off our guard (unawares), he'll slide in.'

'Slide in! Oh, horrid!' cried Lady Clonbrony, sitting up, and wiping away the water which Miss Nugent had sprinkled on her face.

'Were you much alarmed?' said Lord Colambre, with a voice of tenderness, looking at his mother first, but his eyes fixing on Miss Nugent.

'Shockingly!' said Lady Clonbrony; 'I never thought it would *reelly* come to this.'

'It will really come to much more, my dear,' said Lord Clonbrony, 'that you may depend upon, unless you prevent it.'

'Lord! what can I do? – I know nothing of business, how should I, Lord Clonbrony; but I know there's Colambre – I was always told that when he was of age everything should be settled; and why can't he settle it when he's upon the spot?'

'And upon one condition, I will,' cried Lord Colambre; 'at what loss to myself, my dear mother, I need not mention.'

'Then I will mention it,' cried Lord Clonbrony; 'at the loss it will be of nearly half the estate he would have had, if we had not spent it.'

'Loss! Oh, I am excessively sorry my son's to be at such a loss – it must not be.'

'It cannot be otherwise,' said Lord Clonbrony; 'nor it can't be this way either, my Lady Clonbrony, unless you comply with his condition, and consent to return to Ireland.'

'I cannot – I will not,' replied Lady Clonbrony. 'Is this your condition, Colambre? – I take it exceedingly ill of you. I think it very unkind, and unhandsome, and ungenerous, and undutiful of you, Colambre; you, my son!' She poured forth a torrent of reproaches; then came to entreaties and tears. But our hero, prepared for this, had steeled his mind; and he stood resolved not to indulge his own feelings, or to yield to caprice or persuasion, but to do that which he knew was best for the happiness of hundreds of tenants who depended upon them – best for both his father and his mother's ultimate happiness and respectability.

'It's all in vain,' cried Lord Clonbrony; 'I have no resource but one, and I must condescend now to go to him this minute, for Mordicai will be back and seize all – I must sign and leave all to Garraghty.'

'Well, sign, sign, my lord, and settle with Garraghty. – Colambre, I've heard all the complaints you brought over against that man. My lord spent half the night telling them to me; but all agents are bad, I suppose; at any rate I can't help it – sign, sign, my lord; he has money – yes, do; go and settle with him, my lord.'

Lord Colambre and Miss Nugent, at onc and the same moment, stopped Lord Clonbrony as he was quitting the room, and then approached Lady Clonbrony with supplicating looks; but she turned her head to the other side, and, as if putting away their entreaties, made a repelling motion with both her hands, and exclaimed, 'No, Grace Nugent! – no, Colambre – no – no, Colambre! I'll never hear of leaving Lon'on – there's no living out of Lon'on – I can't, I won't live out of Lon'on, I say.'

Her son saw that the *Londonomania* was now stronger than ever upon her, but resolved to make one desperate appeal to her natural feelings, which, though smothered, he could not believe were wholly extinguished; he caught her repelling hands, and pressing them with respectful tenderness to his lips –

'Oh, my dear mother, you once loved your son,' said he; 'loved him better than anything in this world; if one spark of affection for him remains, hear him now, and forgive him, if he pass the bounds – bounds he never passed before – of filial duty. Mother, in compliance with your wishes my father left Ireland – left his home, his duties, his friends, his natural connexions, and for many years he has lived in England, and you have spent many seasons in London.'

'Yes, in the very best company – in the very first circles,' said Lady Clonbrony; 'cold as the high-bred English are said to be in general to strangers.'

'Yes,' replied Lord Colambre; 'the very best company (if you mean the most fashionable) have accepted of our entertainments. We have forced our way into their frozen circles; we have been permitted to breathe in these elevated regions of fashion; we have it to say, that the duke of *this*, and my lady *that*, are of our acquaintance. We may say more; we may boast that we have vied with those whom we could never equal. And at what expense have we done all this? For a single season, the last winter (I will go no farther), at the expense of a great part of your timber, the growth of a century – swallowed in the entertainments of one winter in London! Our hills to be bare for another half century to come! But let the trees go; I think more of your tenants – of those left under the tyranny of a bad agent, at the expense of every comfort, every hope they enjoyed! – tenants, who were thriving and prosperous;

who used to smile upon you, and to bless you both! In one cottage, I have seen – '

Here Lord Clonbrony, unable to restrain his emotion, hurried out of the room.

'Then I am sure it is not my fault,' said Lady Clonbrony; 'for I brought my lord a large fortune; and I am confident I have not, after all, spent more any season, in the best company, than he has among a set of low people, in his muddling, discreditable way.'

'And how has he been reduced to this?' said Lord Colambre. 'Did he not formerly live with gentlemen, his equals, in his own country; his contemporaries? Men of the first station and character, whom I met in Dublin, spoke of him in a manner that gratified the heart of his son; he was respectable and respected at his own home; but when he was forced away from that home, deprived of his objects, his occupations induced him to live in London, or at watering-places, where he could find no employments that were suitable to him – set down, late in life, in the midst of strangers, to him cold and reserved – himself too proud to bend to those who disdained him as an Irishman – is he not more to be pitied than blamed for – yes, I, his son, must say the word – the degradation which has ensued? And do not the feelings, which have this moment forced him to leave the room, show that he is capable? – Oh, mother!' cried Lord Colambre, throwing himself at Lady Clonbrony's feet, 'restore my father to himself! Should such feelings be wasted? – No; give them again to expand in benevolent, in kind, useful actions; give him again to his tenantry, his duties, his country, his home; return to that home yourself, dear mother! leave all the nonsense of high life – scorn the impertinence of these dictators of fashion, by whom, in return for all the pains we take to imitate, to court them – in return for the sacrifice of health, fortune, peace of mind, they bestow sarcasm, contempt, ridicule, and mimickry!'

'Oh, Colambre! Colambre! mimickry – I'll never believe it.'

'Believe me – believe me, mother; for I speak of what I know. Scorn them – quit them! Return to an unsophisticated people – to poor, but grateful hearts, still warm with the remembrance of your kindness, still blessing you for favours long since conferred, ever praying to see you once more. Believe me, for I speak of what I know – your son has heard these prayers, has felt these blessings. Here! at my heart felt, and still feel them, when I was not known to be your son, in the cottage of the widow O'Neill.'

'Oh, did you see the widow O'Neill? and does she remember me?' said Lady Clonbrony.

'Remember you! and you, Miss Nugent! I have slept in the bed – I would tell you more, but I cannot.'

'Well! I never should have thought they would have remembered me so long! – poor people!' said Lady Clonbrony. 'I thought all in Ireland must have forgotten me, it is now so long since I was at home.'

'You are not forgotten in Ireland by any rank, I can answer for that. Return home, my dearest mother – let me see you once more among your natural friends, beloved, respected, happy!'

'Oh, return! let us return home!' cried Miss Nugent, with a voice of great emotion. 'Return, let us return home! My beloved aunt, speak to us! – say that you grant our request!'

She kneeled beside Lord Colambre, as she spoke.

'Is it possible to resist that voice – that look?' thought Lord Colambre.

'If anybody knew,' said Lady Clonbrony, 'if anybody could conceive, how I detest the sight, the thoughts of that old yellow damask furniture, in the drawing-room at Clonbrony Castle – '

'Good heavens!' cried Lord Colambre, starting up, and looking at his mother in stupefied astonishment; 'is *that* what you are thinking of, ma'am?'

'The yellow damask furniture!' said her niece, smiling. 'Oh, if that's all, that shall never offend your eyes again. Aunt, my painted velvet chairs are finished; and trust the furnishing that room to me. The legacy lately left me cannot be better applied – you shall see how beautifully it will be furnished.'

'Oh, if I had money, I should like to do it myself; but it would take an immensity to new furnish Clonbrony Castle properly.'

'The furniture in this house – ' said Miss Nugent, looking round.

'Would do a great deal towards it, I declare,' cried Lady Clonbrony; 'that never struck me before, Grace, I protest – and what would not suit one might sell or exchange here – and it would be a great amusement to me – and I should like to set the fashion of something better in that country. And I declare, now, I should like to see those poor people, and that widow O'Neill. I do assure you, I think I was happier at home; only, that one gets, I don't know how, a notion, one's nobody out of Lon'on. But, after all, there's many drawbacks in Lon'on – and many people are very impertinent, I'll allow – and if there's a woman in the world I hate, it is Mrs Dareville – and, if I was leaving Lon'on, I should not regret Lady Langdale neither – and Lady St James is as cold as a stone. Colambre may well say *frozen circles* – these sort of people are really very cold, and have, I do believe, no hearts. I don't verily think there is one of them would regret me more – Hey! let me see, Dublin – the winter – Merrion Square – new furnished – and the summer – Clonbrony Castle!'

Lord Colambre and Miss Nugent waited in silence till her mind should have worked itself clear. One great obstacle had been removed; and now that the yellow damask had been taken out of her imagination, they no longer despaired.

Lord Clonbrony put his head into the room.

'What hopes? – any? if not, let me go.'

He saw the doubting expression of Lady Clonbrony's countenance – hope in the face of his son and niece.

'My dear, dear Lady Clonbrony, make us all happy by one word,' said he, kissing her.

'You never kissed me so since we left Ireland before,' said Lady Clonbrony. 'Well, since it must be so, let us go,' said she.

'Did I ever see such joy!' said Lord Clonbrony, clasping his hands; 'I never expected such joy in my life! I must go and tell poor Terry!' and off he ran.

'And now, since we are to go,' said Lady Clonbrony, 'pray let us go immediately, before the thing gets wind, else I shall have Mrs Dareville, and Lady Langdale, and Lady St James, and all the world, coming to condole with me, just to satisfy their own curiosity; and then Miss Pratt, who hears everything that everybody says, and more than they say, will come and tell me how it is reported everywhere that we are ruined. Oh! I never could bear to stay and hear all this. I'll tell you what I'll do – you are to be of age the day after tomorrow, Colambre – very well, there are some papers for me to sign – I must stay to put my name to them, and that done, that minute I'll leave you and Lord Clonbrony to settle all the rest; and I'll get into my carriage with Grace, and go down to Buxton again; where you can come for me, and take me up, when you're all ready to go to Ireland – and we shall be so far on our way. Colambre, what do you say to this?'

'That – if you like it, madam,' said he, giving one hasty glance at Miss Nugent, and withdrawing his eyes, 'it is the best possible arrangement.'

'So,' thought Grace, 'that is the best possible arrangement which takes us away.'

'If I like it!' said Lady Clonbrony; 'to be sure I do, or I should not propose it. What is Colambre thinking of? I know, Grace, at all events, what you and I must think of – of having the furniture packed up, and settling what's to go, and what's to be exchanged, and all that. Now, my dear, go and write a note directly to Mr Soho, and bid him come himself, immediately; and we'll go and make out a catalogue this instant of what furniture I will have packed.'

So, with her head full of furniture, Lady Clonbrony retired. 'I go to my business, Colambre; and I leave you to settle yours in peace.'

In peace! – Never was our hero's mind less at peace than at this moment. The more his heart felt that it was painful, the more his reason told him it was necessary that he should part from Grace Nugent. To his union with her there was an obstacle, which his prudence told him ought to be insurmountable; yet he felt that, during the few days he had been with her, the few hours he had been near her, he had, with his utmost power over himself, scarcely been master of his passion, or capable of concealing it from its object. It could not have been done but for her perfect simplicity and innocence. But how could this be supposed on his part? How could he venture to live with this charming girl? How could he settle at home? What resource?

His mind turned towards the army; he thought that abroad, and in active life, he should lose all the painful recollections, and drive from his heart all the resentments, which could now be only a source of unavailing regret. But his mother – his mother, who had now yielded her own taste to his entreaties, for the good of her family – she expected him to return and live with her in Ireland. Though not actually promised or specified, he knew that she took it for granted; that it was upon this hope, this faith, she consented; he knew that she would be shocked at the bare idea of his going into the army. There was one chance – our hero tried, at this moment, to think it the best possible chance – that Miss Nugent might marry Mr Salisbury, and settle in England. On this idea he relied as the only means of extricating him from difficulties.

It was necessary to turn his thoughts immediately to business, to execute his promises to his father. Two great objects were now to be accomplished – the payment of his father's debts, and the settlement of the Irish agent's accounts; and, in transacting this complicated business, he derived considerable assistance from Sir Terence O'Fay, and from Sir Arthur Berryl's solicitor, Mr Edwards. Whilst acting for Sir Arthur, on a former occasion, Lord Colambre had gained the entire confidence of this solicitor, who was a man of the first eminence. Mr Edwards took the papers and Lord Clonbrony's title-deeds home with him, saying that he would give an answer the next morning. He then waited upon Lord Colambre, and informed him, that he had just received a letter from Sir Arthur Berryl, who, with the consent and desire of his lady, requested that whatever money might be required by Lord Clonbrony should be immediately supplied on their account, without waiting till Lord Colambre should be of age, as the ready money might be of some convenience to him in accelerating the journey to Ireland, which Sir Arthur and Lady Berryl knew was his lordship's object. Sir Terence O'Fay now supplied Mr Edwards with accurate information as to the demands that were made upon Lord Clonbrony, and of the respective characters of the creditors. Mr Edwards undertook to settle with the fair claimants; Sir Terence with the rogues; so that by the advancement of ready money from *the Berryls*, and by the detection of false and exaggerated charges, which Sir Terence made among the inferior class, the debts were reduced nearly to one half of their former amount. Mordicai, who had been foiled in his vile attempt to become sole creditor, had, however, a demand of more than seven thousand pounds upon Lord Clonbrony, which he had raised to this enormous sum in six or seven years, by means well known to himself. He stood the foremost in the list, not from the greatness of the sum, but from the danger of his adding to it the expenses of law. Sir Terence undertook to pay the whole with five thousand pounds. Lord Clonbrony thought it impossible; the solicitor thought it improvident, because he knew that upon a trial a much greater abatement would be allowed; but Lord Colambre was determined, from the present embarrassments of his own situation, to leave nothing undone that could be accomplished immediately.

Sir Terence, pleased with his commission, immediately went to Mordicai.

'Well, Sir Terence,' said Mordicai, 'I hope you are come to pay me my hundred guineas; for Miss Broadhurst is married!'

'Well, Mister Mordicai, what then? The ides of March are come, but not gone! Stay, if you plase, Mister Mordicai, till Lady-day, when it becomes due; in the meantime, I have a handful, or rather an armful, of bank-notes for you, from my Lord Colambre.'

'Humph!' said Mordicai; 'how's that? he'll not be of age these three days.'

'Don't matter for that; he has sent me to look over your account, and to hope that you will make some small ABATEMENT in the total.'

'Harkee, Sir Terence – you think yourself very clever in things of this sort, but you've mistaken your man; I have an execution for the whole, and I'll be d—d if all your cunning shall MAKE me take up with part!'

'Be *asy*, Mister Mordicai! – you shan't make me break your bones, nor make me drop one actionable word against your high character; for I know your clerk there, with that long goose-quill behind his ear, would be ready evidence again' me. But I beg to know, in one word, whether you will take five thousand down, and GIVE Lord Clonbrony a discharge?'

'No, Mr Terence! nor six thousand nine hundred and ninety-nine pounds. My demand is £7130, odd shillings: if you have that money, pay it; if not, I know how to get it, and along with it complete revenge for all the insults I have received from that greenhorn, his son.'

'Paddy Brady!' cried Sir Terence, 'do you hear that? Remember that word, *revenge*! Mind, I call you to witness!'

'What, sir, will you raise a rebellion among my workmen?'

'No, Mr Mordicai, no rebellion; and I hope you won't cut the boy's ears off for listening to a little of the brogue – So listen, my good lad. Now, Mr Mordicai, I offer you here, before little goose-quill, £5000 ready penny – take it, or leave it; take your money, and leave your revenge; or, take your revenge, and lose your money.'

'Sir Terence, I value neither your threats nor your cunning. Good-morning to you.'

'Good-morning to you, Mr Mordicai – but not kindly! Mr Edwards, the solicitor, has been at the office to take off the execution; so now you may have law to your heart's content! And it was only to plase the young lord that the *ould* one consented to my carrying this bundle to you,' – showing the bank-notes.

'Mr Edwards employed!' cried Mordicai. 'Why, how the devil did Lord Clonbrony get into such hands as his? The execution taken off! Well, sir, go to law – I am ready for you; Jack Latitat IS A MATCH for your sober solicitor.'

'Good-morning again to you, Mr Mordicai; we're fairly out of your clutches, and we have enough to do with our money.'

'Well, Sir Terence, I must allow you have a very wheedling way – Here, Mr Thompson, make out a receipt for Lord Clonbrony: I never go to law with an old customer, if I can help it.'

This business settled, Mr Soho was next to be dealt with.

He came at Lady Clonbrony's summons; and was taking directions, with the utmost *sang froid*, for packing up and sending off the very furniture for which he was not paid.

Lord Colambre called him into his father's study; and, producing his bill, he began to point out various articles which were charged at prices that were obviously extravagant.

'Why, really, my lord, they are *abundantly* extravagant; if I charged vulgar prices, I should be only a vulgar tradesman. I, however, am not a broker, nor a Jew. Of the article superintendence, which is only £500, I cannot abate a doit; on the rest of the bill, if you mean to offer *ready*, I mean, without any negotiation, to abate thirty per cent; and I hope that is a fair and gentlemanly offer.'

'Mr Soho, there is your money!'

'My Lord Colambre! I would give the contents of three such bills to be sure of such noblemanly conduct as yours. Lady Clonbrony's furniture shall be safely packed, without costing her a farthing.'

With the help of Mr Edwards, the solicitor, every other claim was soon settled; and Lord Clonbrony, for the first time since he left Ireland, found himself out of debt, and out of danger.

Old Nick's account could not be settled in London. Lord Colambre had detected numerous false charges, and sundry impositions; the land, which had been purposely let to run wild, so far from yielding any rent, was made a source of constant expense, as remaining still unset: this was a large tract, for which St Dennis had at length offered a small rent.

Upon a fair calculation of the profits of the ground, and from other items in the account, Nicholas Garraghty, Esq., appeared at last to be, not the creditor, but the debtor to Lord Clonbrony. He was dismissed with disgrace, which perhaps he might not have felt, if it had not been accompanied by pecuniary loss, and followed by the fear of losing his other agencies, and by the dread of immediate bankruptcy.

Mr Burke was appointed agent in his stead to the Clonbrony as well as the Colambre estate. His appointment was announced to him by the following letter: –

To Mrs Burke, at Colambre

Dear Madam,

The traveller whom you so hospitably received some months ago was Lord Colambre – he now writes to you in his proper person. He promised you that he would, as far as it might be in his power, do justice to Mr Burke's conduct and character, by representing what he had done for Lord Clonbrony in the town of Colambre, and in the whole management of the tenantry and property under his care.

Happily for my father, my dear madam, he is now as fully convinced as you could wish him to be of Mr Burke's merits; and he begs me to express his sense of the obligations he is under to him and to you. He entreats that you will pardon the impropriety of a letter, which, as I assured you the moment I saw it, he never wrote or read. This will, he says, cure him, for life, of putting his signature to any paper without reading it.

He hopes that you will forget that such a letter was ever received, and that you will use your influence with Mr Burke to induce him to continue to our family his regard and valuable services. Lord Clonbrony encloses a power of attorney, enabling Mr Burke to act in future for him, if Mr Burke will do him that favour, in managing the Clonbrony as well as the Colambre estate.

Lord Clonbrony will be in Ireland in the course of next month, and intends to have the pleasure of soon paying his respects in

person to Mr Burke, at Colambre. – I am, dear madam, your
obliged guest, and faithful servant,   COLAMBRE.

Grosvenor Square, London.

Lord Colambre was so continually occupied with business during the
two days previous to his coming of age, every morning at his solicitor's
chambers, every evening in his father's study, that Miss Nugent never
saw him but at breakfast or dinner; and, though she watched for it most
anxiously, never could find an opportunity of speaking to him alone, or
of asking an explanation of the change and inconsistencies of his
manner. At last, she began to think that, in the midst of so much
business of importance, by which he seemed harassed, she should do
wrong to torment him, by speaking of any small disquietude that
concerned only herself. She determined to suppress her doubts, to keep
her feelings to herself, and to endeavour, by constant kindness, to
regain that place in his affections which she imagined that she had lost.
'Everything will go right again,' thought she, 'and we shall all be happy,
when he returns with us to Ireland – to that dear home which he loves
as well as I do!'

The day Lord Colambre was of age, the first thing he did was to sign
a bond for five thousand pounds, Miss Nugent's fortune, which had
been lent to his father, who was her guardian.

'This, sir, I believe,' said he, giving it to his father as soon as signed –
'this, I believe, is the first debt you would wish to have secured.'

'Well thought of, my dear boy! – God bless you! – that has weighed
more upon my conscience and heart than all the rest, though I never
said anything about it. I used, whenever I met Mr Salisbury, to wish
myself fairly down at the centre of the earth; not that he ever thought
of fortune, I'm sure; for he often told me, and I believed him, he would
rather have Miss Nugent without a penny, if he could get her, than the
first fortune in the empire. But I'm glad she will not go to him
penniless, for all that; and by my fault, especially. There, there's my
name to it – do witness it, Terry. But, Colambre, you must give it to
her – you must take it to Grace.'

'Excuse me, sir; it is no gift of mine – it is a debt of yours. I beg you
will take the bond to her yourself, my dear father.'

'My dear son, you must not always have your own way, and hide
everything good you do, or give me the honour of it – I won't be the jay
in borrowed feathers. I have borrowed enough in my life, and I've done
with borrowing now, thanks to you, Colambre – so come along with
me; for I'll be hanged if ever I give this joint bond to Miss Nugent,
without you along with me. Leave Lady Clonbrony here to sign these

papers. Terry will witness them properly, and you come along with me.'

'And pray, my lord,' said her ladyship, 'order the carriage to the door; for, as soon as you have my signature, I hope you'll let me off to Buxton.'

'Oh, certainly – the carriage is ordered – everything ready, my dear.'

'And pray tell Grace to be ready,' added Lady Clonbrony.

'That's not necessary; for she is always ready,' said Lord Clonbrony. 'Come, Colambre,' added he, taking his son under the arm, and carrying him up to Miss Nugent's dressing-room.

They knocked, and were admitted.

'Ready!' said Lord Clonbrony; 'ay, always ready – so I said. Here's Colambre, my darling,' continued he, 'has secured your fortune to you to my heart's content; but he would not condescend to come up to tell you so, till I made him. Here's the bond; put your hand to it, Colambre; you were ready enough to do that when it cost you something; and now, all I have to ask of you is, to persuade her to marry out of hand, that I may see her happy before I die. Now my heart's at ease! I can meet Mr Salisbury with a safe conscience. One kiss, my little Grace. If anybody can persuade you, I'm sure it's that man that's now leaning against the mantelpiece. It's Colambre's will, or your heart's not made like mine – so I leave you.'

And out of the room walked he, leaving his poor son in as awkward, embarrassing, and painful a situation, as could well be conceived. Half a dozen indistinct ideas crossed his mind; quick conflicting feelings made his heart beat and stop. And how it would have ended, if he had been left to himself, whether he would have stood or fallen, have spoken or have continued silent, can never now be known, for all was decided without the action of his will. He was awakened from his trance by these simple words from Miss Nugent –

'I'm much obliged to you, cousin Colambre – more obliged to you for your kindness in thinking of me first, in the midst of all your other business, than by your securing my fortune. Friendship – and your friendship – is worth more to me than fortune. May I believe that is secured?'

'Believe it! Oh, Grace, can you doubt it?'

'I will not; it would make me too unhappy. I will not.'

'You need not.'

'That is enough – I am satisfied – I ask no farther explanation. You are truth itself – one word from you is security sufficient. We are friends for life,' said she, taking his hand between both of hers; 'are not we?'

'We are – and therefore sit down, cousin Grace, and let me claim the privilege of friendship, and speak to you of him who aspires to be more than your friend for life, Mr — '

'Mr Salisbury!' said Miss Nugent; 'I saw him yesterday. We had a very long conversation; I believe he understands my sentiments perfectly, and that he no longer thinks of being *more* to me than a friend for life.'

'You have refused him!'

'Yes. I have a high opinion of Mr Salisbury's understanding, a great esteem for his character; I like his manners and conversation; but I do not love him, and therefore, you know, I could not marry him.'

'But, my dear Miss Nugent, with a high opinion, a great esteem, and liking his manners and conversation, in such a well-regulated mind as yours, can there be a better foundation for love?'

'It is an excellent foundation,' said she; 'but I never went any farther than the foundation; and, indeed, I never wished to proceed any farther.'

Lord Colambre scarcely dared to ask why; but, after some pause, he said –

'I don't wish to intrude upon your confidence.'

'You cannot intrude upon my confidence; I am ready to give it to you entirely, frankly; I hesitated only because another person was concerned. Do you remember, at my aunt's gala, a lady who danced with Mr Salisbury?'

'Not in the least.'

'A lady with whom you and Mr Salisbury were talking, just before supper, in the Turkish tent.'

'Not in the least.'

'As we went down to supper, you told me you had had a delightful conversation with her – that you thought her a charming woman.'

'A charming woman! – I have not the slightest recollection of her.'

'And you told me that she and Mr Salisbury had been praising me *à l'envie l'une et l'autre.*'

'Oh, I recollect her now perfectly,' said Lord Colambre; 'but what of her?'

'She is the woman who, I hope, will be Mrs Salisbury. Ever since I have been acquainted with them both, I have seen that they were suited to each other; and fancy, indeed I am almost sure, that she could love him, tenderly love him – and, I know, I could not. But my own sentiments, you may be sure, are all I ever told Mr Salisbury.'

'But of your own sentiments you may not be sure,' said Lord Colambre; 'and I see no reason why you should give him up from false generosity.'

'Generosity?' interrupted Miss Nugent; 'you totally misunderstand me; there is no generosity, nothing for me to give up in the case. I did not refuse Mr Salisbury from generosity, but because I did not love him. Perhaps my seeing this at first prevented me from thinking of him as a lover; but, from whatever cause, I certainly never felt love for Mr Salisbury, nor any of that pity which is said to lead to love; perhaps,' added she, smiling, 'because I was aware that he would be so much better off after I refused him – so much happier with one suited to him in age, talents, fortune, and love – "What bliss, did he but know his bliss," were *his*.'

'Did he but know his bliss,' repeated Lord Colambre; 'but is not he the best judge of his own bliss?'

'And am not I the best judge of mine?' said Miss Nugent; 'I go no farther.'

'You are; and I have no right to go farther. Yet, this much permit me to say, my dear Grace, that it would give me sincere pleasure, that is, real satisfaction, to see you happily – established.'

'Thank you, my dear Lord Colambre; but you spoke that like a man of seventy at least, with the most solemn gravity of demeanour.'

'I meant to be serious, not solemn,' said Lord Colambre, endeavouring to change his tone.

'There now,' said she, in a playful tone, 'you have *seriously* accomplished the task my good uncle set you; so I will report well of you to him, and certify that you did all that in you lay to exhort me to marry; that you have even assured me that it would give you sincere pleasure, that is, real satisfaction, to see me happily established.'

'Oh, Grace, if you knew how much I felt when I said that, you would spare this raillery.'

'I will be serious – I am most seriously convinced of the sincerity of your affection for me; I know my happiness is your object in all you have said, and I thank you from my heart for the interest you take about me. But really and truly, I do not wish to marry. This is not a mere commonplace speech; but I have not yet seen any man I could love. I like you, cousin Colambre, better than Mr Salisbury – I would rather live with you than with him; you know that is a certain proof that I am not likely to be in love with him. I am happy as I am, especially now we are all going to dear Ireland, home, to live together: you cannot conceive with what pleasure I look forward to that.'

Lord Colambre was not vain; but love quickly sees love where it exists, or foresees the probability, the possibility of its existence. He saw that Miss Nugent might love him tenderly, passionately; but that duty, habit, the prepossession that it was impossible she could marry her cousin Colambre – a prepossession instilled into her by his mother –

had absolutely prevented her from ever yet thinking of him as a lover. He saw the hazard for her, he felt the danger for himself. Never had she appeared to him so attractive as at this moment, when he felt the hope that he could obtain return of love.

'But St Omar! – Why! why is she a St Omar! – illegitimate! – "No St Omar *sans reproche*." My wife she cannot be – I will not engage her affections.'

Swift as thoughts in moments of strong feeling pass in the mind without being put into words, our hero thought all this, and determined, cost what it would, to act honourably.

'You spoke of my returning to Ireland, my dear Grace. I have not yet told you my plans.'

'Plans! are not you returning with us?' said she, precipitately; 'are not you going to Ireland – home – with us?'

'No – I am going to serve a campaign or two abroad. I think every young man in these times – '

'Good heavens! What does this mean? What can you mean?' cried she, fixing her eyes upon his, as if she would read his very soul. 'Why? what reason? – Oh, tell me the truth – and at once.'

His change of colour – his hand that trembled, and withdrew from hers – the expression of his eyes as they met hers – revealed the truth to her at once. As it flashed across her mind, she started back; her face grew crimson, and, in the same instant, pale as death.

'Yes – you see, you feel the truth now,' said Lord Colambre. 'You see, you feel, that I love you – passionately.'

'Oh, let me not hear it!' said she; 'I must not – ought not. Never, till this moment, did such a thought cross my mind – I thought it impossible – oh, make me think so still.'

'I will – it *is* impossible that we can ever be united.'

'I always thought so,' said she, taking breath with a deep sigh. 'Then why not live as we have lived?'

'I cannot – I cannot answer for myself – I will not run the risk; and therefore I must quit you – knowing, as I do, that there is an invincible obstacle to our union, of what nature I cannot explain; I beg you not to inquire.'

'You need not beg it – I shall not inquire – I have no curiosity – none,' said she, in a passive, dejected tone; 'that is not what I am thinking of in the least. I know there are invincible obstacles; I wish it to be so. But, if invincible, you who have so much sense, honour, and virtue – '

'I hope, my dear cousin, that I have honour and virtue. But there are temptations to which no wise, no good man will expose himself.

Innocent creature! you do not know the power of love. I rejoice that you have always thought it impossible – think so still – it will save you from – all I must endure. Think of me but as your cousin, your friend – give your heart to some happier man. As your friend, your true friend, I conjure you, give your heart to some more fortunate man. Marry, if you can feel love – marry, and be happy. Honour! virtue! Yes, I have both, and I will not forfeit them. Yes, I will merit your esteem and my own – by actions, not words; and I give you the strongest proof, by tearing myself from you at this moment. Farewell!'

'The carriage at the door, Miss Nugent, and my lady calling for you,' said her maid. 'Here's your key, ma'am, and here's your gloves, my dear ma'am.'

'The carriage at the door, Miss Nugent,' said Lady Clonbrony's woman, coming eagerly with parcels in her hand, as Miss Nugent passed her and ran downstairs; 'and I don't know where I laid my lady's *numbrella*, for my life – do you, Anne?'

'No, indeed – but I know here's my own young lady's watch that she has left. Bless me! I never knew her to forget anything on a journey before.'

'Then she is going to be married, as sure as my name's le Maistre, and to my Lord Colambre; for he has been here this hour, to my certain Bible knowledge. Oh, you'll see, she will be Lady Colambre.'

'I wish she may, with all my heart,' said Anne; 'but I must run down – they're waiting.'

'Oh no,' said Mrs le Maistre, seizing Anne's arm, and holding her fast; 'stay – you may safely – for they're all kissing and taking leave, and all that, you know; and *my* lady is talking on about Mr Soho, and giving a hundred directions about legs of *tables*, and so forth, I warrant – she's always an hour after she's ready before she gets in – and I'm looking for the *numbrella*. So stay, and tell me – Mrs Petito wrote over word it was to be Lady Isabel; and then a contradiction came – it was turned into the youngest of the Killpatricks; and now here he's in Miss Nugent's dressing-room to the last moment. Now, in my opinion, that am not censorious, this does not look so pretty; but, according to my verdict, he is only making a fool of Miss Nugent, like the rest; and his lordship seems too like what you might call a male *cocket*, or a masculine jilt.'

'No more like a masculine jilt than yourself, Mrs le Maistre,' cried Anne, taking fire. 'And my young lady is not a lady to be made a fool of, I promise you; nor is my lord likely to make a fool of any woman.'

'Bless us all! that's no great praise for any young nobleman, Miss Anne.'

'Mrs le Maistre! Mrs le Maistre! are you above?' cried a footman from the bottom of the stairs; 'my lady's calling for you.'

'Very well! very well!' said sharp Mrs le Maistre; 'very well! and if she is – manners, sir! – Come up for one, can't you, and don't stand bawling at the bottom of the stairs, as if one had no ears to be saved. I'm coming as fast as I conveniently can.' Mrs le Maistre stood in the doorway, so as to fill it up, and prevent Anne from passing.

'Miss Anne! Miss Anne! Mrs le Maistre!' cried another footman; 'my lady's in the carriage, and Miss Nugent.'

'Miss Nugent! – is she?' cried Mrs le Maistre, running downstairs, followed by Anne. 'Now, for the world in pocket-pieces wouldn't I have missed seeing him hand Miss Nugent in; for by that I could have judged definitively.'

'My lord, I beg pardon! – I'm *afeard* I'm late,' said Mrs le Maistre, as she passed Lord Colambre, who was standing motionless in the hall. 'I beg a thousand pardons; but I was hunting high and low, for my lady's *numbrella*.'

Lord Colambre did not hear or heed her; his eyes were fixed, and they never moved.

Lord Clonbrony was at the open carriage-door, kneeling on the step, and receiving Lady Clonbrony's 'more last words' for Mr Soho. The two waiting-maids stood together on the steps.

'Look at our young lord, how he stands,' whispered Mrs le Maistre to Anne, 'the image of despair! And she, the picture of death! – I don't know what to think.'

'Nor I; but don't stare if you can help it,' said Anne. 'Get in, get in, Mrs le Maistre,' added she, as Lord Clonbrony now rose from the step, and made way for them.

'Ay, in with you – in with you, Mrs le Maistre,' said Lord Clonbrony. 'Good-bye to you, Anne, and take care of your young mistress at Buxton; let me see her blooming when we meet again; I don't half like her looks, and I never thought Buxton agreed with her.'

'Buxton never did anybody harm,' said Lady Clonbrony; 'and as to bloom, I'm sure, if Grace has not bloom enough in her cheeks this moment to please you, I don't know what you'd have, my dear lord – Rouge? – Shut the door, John! Oh, stay! – Colambre! Where upon earth's Colambre?' cried her ladyship, stretching from the farthest side of the coach to the window. – 'Colambre!'

Colambre was forced to appear.

'Colambre, my dear! I forgot to say that, if anything detains you longer than Wednesday se'nnight, I beg you will not fail to write, or I shall be miserable.'

'I will write; at all events, my dearest mother, you shall hear from me.'

'Then I shall be quite happy. Go on!'

The carriage drove on.

'I do believe Colambre's ill; I never saw a man look so ill in my life – did you, Grace? – as he did the minute we drove on. He should take advice. I've a mind,' cried Lady Clonbrony, laying her hand on the cord to stop the coachman – 'I've a mind to turn about, tell him so, and ask what is the matter with him.'

'Better not!' said Miss Nugent; 'he will write to you, and tell you – if anything is the matter with him. Better go on now to Buxton!' continued she, scarcely able to speak. Lady Clonbrony let go the cord.

'But what is the matter with you, my dear Grace? for you are certainly going to die too!'

'I will tell you – as soon as I can; but don't ask me now, my dear aunt!'

'Grace, Grace! pull the cord!' cried Lady Clonbrony – 'Mr Salisbury's phaeton!– Mr Salisbury, I'm happy to see you! We're on our way to Buxton – as I told you.'

'So am I,' said Mr Salisbury. 'I hope to be there before your ladyship; will you honour me with any commands? – of course, I will see that everything is ready for your reception.'

Her ladyship had not any commands. Mr Salisbury drove on rapidly.

Lady Clonbrony's ideas had now taken the Salisbury channel.

'You didn't know that Mr Salisbury was going to Buxton to meet you, did you, Grace?' said Lady Clonbrony.

'No, indeed, I did not!' said Miss Nugent; 'and I am very sorry for it.'

'Young ladies, as Mrs Broadhurst says, "never know, or at least never tell, what they are sorry or glad for," ' replied Lady Clonbrony. 'At all events, Grace, my love, it has brought the fine bloom back to your cheeks; and I own I am satisfied.'

Chapter 15

'Gone! for ever gone from me!' said Lord Colambre to himself, as the carriage drove away. 'Never shall I see her more – never *will* I see her more, till she is married.'

Lord Colambre went to his own room, locked the door, and was relieved in some degree by the sense of privacy; by the feeling that he could now indulge his reflections undisturbed. He had consolation – he had done what was honourable – he had transgressed no duty, abandoned no principle – he had not injured the happiness of any human being – he had not, to gratify himself, hazarded the peace of the woman he loved – he had not sought to win her heart. Of her innocent, her warm, susceptible heart, he might perhaps have robbed her – he knew it – but he had left it untouched, he hoped entire, in her own power, to bless with it hereafter some man worthy of her. In the hope that she might be happy, Lord Colambre felt relief; and in the consciousness that he had made his parents happy, he rejoiced. But, as soon as his mind turned that way for consolation, came the bitter concomitant reflection, that his mother must be disappointed in her hopes of his accompanying her home, and of his living with her in Ireland; she would be miserable when she should hear that he was going abroad into the army – and yet it must be so – and he must write, and tell her so. 'The sooner this difficulty is off my mind, the sooner this painful letter is written, the better,' thought he. 'It must be done – I will do it immediately.'

He snatched up his pen, and began a letter.

'My dear mother – Miss Nugent – '

He was interrupted by a knock at his door.

'A gentleman below, my lord,' said a servant, 'who wishes to see you.'

'I cannot see any gentleman. Did you say I was at home?'

'No, my lord; I said you was not at home; for I thought you would not choose to be at home, and your own man was not in the way for me to ask – so I denied you; but the gentleman would not be denied; he said I must come and see if you was at home. So, as he spoke as if he was a gentleman not used to be denied, I thought it might be somebody of consequence, and I showed him into the front drawing-room. I think he said he was sure you'd be at home for a friend from Ireland.'

'A friend from Ireland! Why did not you tell me that sooner?' said Lord Colambre, rising, and running downstairs. 'Sir James Brooke, I daresay.'

No, not Sir James Brooke; but one he was almost as glad to see – Count O'Halloran!

'My dear count! the greater pleasure for being unexpected.'

'I came to London but yesterday,' said the count; 'but I could not be here a day, without doing myself the honour of paying my respects to Lord Colambre.'

'You do me not only honour, but pleasure, my dear count. People when they like one another, always find each other out, and contrive to meet even in London.'

'You are too polite to ask what brought such a superannuated militaire as I am,' said the count, 'from his retirement into this gay world again. A relation of mine, who is one of our Ministry, knew that I had some maps, and plans, and charts, which might be serviceable in an expedition they are planning. I might have trusted my charts across the channel, without coming myself to convoy them, you will say. But my relation fancied – young relations, you know, if they are good for anything, are apt to overvalue the heads of old relations – fancied that mine was worth bringing all the way from Halloran Castle to London, to consult with *tête-à-tête*. So you know, when this was signified to me by a letter from the secretary in office, *private, most confidential*, what could I do, but do myself the honour to obey? For though honour's voice cannot provoke the silent dust, yet "flattery soothes the dull cold ear of *age*." – But enough, and too much of myself,' said the count: 'tell me, my dear lord, something of yourself. I do not think England seems to agree with you so well as Ireland; for, excuse me, in point of health, you don't look like the same man I saw some weeks ago.'

'My mind has been ill at ease of late,' said Lord Colambre. 'Ay, there's the thing! The body pays for the mind – but those who have feeling minds, pain and pleasure altogether computed, have the advantage; or at least they think so; for they would not change with those who have them not, were they to gain by the bargain the most robust body that the most selfish coxcomb, or the heaviest dunce extant, ever boasted. For instance, would you now, my lord, at this moment change altogether with Major Benson, or Captain Williamson, or even our friend, "Eh, really now, 'pon honour " – would you? – I'm glad to see you smile.'

'I thank you for making me smile, for I assure you I want it. I wish – if you would not think me encroaching upon your politeness and kindness in honouring me with this visit – You see,' continued he, opening the doors of the back drawing-room, and pointing to large packages – 'you see we are all preparing for a march; my mother has left town half an hour ago – my father engaged to dine abroad – only I at home – and, in this state of confusion, could I even venture to ask Count O'Halloran to stay and dine with me, without being able to offer him Irish ortolans or Irish plums – in short, will you let me rob you of two or three hours of your time? I am anxious to have your opinion on a subject of some importance to me, and on one where you are peculiarly qualified to judge and decide for me.'

'My dear lord, frankly, I have nothing half so good or so agreeable to do with my time; command my hours. I have already told you how much it flatters me to be consulted by the most helpless clerk in office; how much more about the private concerns of an enlightened young – friend, will Lord Colambre permit me to say? I hope so; for though the length of our acquaintance might not justify the word, yet regard and intimacy are not always in proportion to the time people have known each other, but to their mutual perception of certain attaching qualities, a certain similarity and suitableness of character.'

The good count, seeing that Lord Colambre was in much distress of mind, did all he could to soothe him by kindness; far from making any difficulty about giving up a few hours of his time, he seemed to have no other object in London, and no purpose in life, but to attend to our hero. To put him at ease, and to give him time to recover and arrange his thoughts, the count talked of indifferent subjects.

'I think I heard you mention the name of Sir James Brooke.'

'Yes, I expected to have seen him when the servant first mentioned a friend from Ireland; because Sir James had told me that, as soon as he could get leave of absence, he would come to England.'

'He is come; is now at his estate in Huntingdonshire; doing, what do you think? I will give you a leading hint; recollect the seal which the little De Cresey put into your hands the day you dined at Oranmore. Faithful to his motto, "Deeds not words," he is this instant, I believe, at deeds, title-deeds; making out marriage settlements, getting ready to put his seal to the happy articles.'

'Happy man! I give him joy,' said Lord Colambre; 'happy man! going to be married to such a woman – daughter of such a mother.'

'Daughter of such a mother! That is indeed a great addition and a great security to his happiness,' said the count. 'Such a family to marry into; good from generation to generation; illustrious by character as well as by genealogy; "all the sons brave, and all the daughters chaste." '
– Lord Colambre with difficulty repressed his feelings. – 'If I could choose, I would rather that a woman I loved were of such a family than that she had for her dower the mines of Peru.'

'So would I,' cried Lord Colambre.

'I am glad to hear you say so, my lord, and with such energy; so few young men of the present day look to what I call good connection. In marrying, a man does not, to be sure, marry his wife's mother; and yet a prudent man, when he begins to think of the daughter, would look sharp at the mother; ay, and back to the grandmother too, and along the whole female line of ancestry.'

'True – most true – he ought – he must.'

'And I have a notion,' said the count, smiling, 'your lordship's practice has been conformable to your theory.'

'I! – mine!' said Lord Colambre, starting, and looking at the count with surprise.

'I beg your pardon,' said the count; 'I did not intend to surprise your confidence. But you forget that I was present, and saw the impression which was made on your mind by a mother's want of a proper sense of delicacy and propriety – Lady Dashfort.'

'Oh, Lady Dashfort! she was quite out of my head.'

'And Lady Isabel? – I hope she is quite out of your heart.'

'She never was in it,' said Lord Colambre.

'Only laid siege to it,' said the count. 'Well, I am glad your heart did not surrender at discretion, or rather without discretion. Then I may tell you, without fear or preface, that the Lady Isabel, who "talks of refinement, delicacy, sense," is going to stoop at once, and marry – Heathcock.'

Lord Colambre was not surprised, but concerned and disgusted, as he always felt, even when he did not care for the individual, from hearing anything which tended to lower the female sex in public estimation.

'As to myself,' said he, 'I cannot say I have had an escape, for I don't think I ever was in much danger.'

'It is difficult to measure danger when it is over – past danger, like past pain, is soon forgotten,' said the old general. 'At all events, I rejoice in your present safety.'

'But is she really going to be married to Heathcock?' said Lord Colambre.

'Positively; they all came over in the same packet with me, and they are all in town now, buying jewels, and equipages, and horses. Heathcock, you know, is as good as another man, *à peu près*, for all those purposes; his father is dead, and left him a large estate. *Que voulez vous?* as the French valet said to me on the occasion. *C'est que monsieur est un homme de bien: il a des biens, à ce qu'on dit.*'

Lord Colambre could not help smiling.

'How they got Heathcock to fall in love is what puzzles me,' said his lordship. 'I should as soon have thought of an oyster's falling in love as that being!'

'I own I should have sooner thought,' replied the count, 'of his falling in love with an oyster; and so would you, if you had seen him, as I did, devouring oysters on shipboard.

> Say, can the lovely *heroine* hope to vie
> With a fat turtle or a ven'son pie?

But that is not our affair; let the Lady Isabel look to it.'

Dinner was announced; and no farther conversation of any consequence passed between the count and Lord Colambre till the cloth was removed and the servants had withdrawn. Then our hero opened on the subject which was heavy at his heart.

'My dear count – to go back to the *burial-place of the Nugents*, where my head was lost the first time I had the pleasure of seeing you – you know, or, possibly,' said he, smiling, 'you do not know, that I have a cousin of the name of Nugent?'

'You told me,' replied the count, 'that you had near relations of that name; but I do not recollect that you mentioned any one in particular.'

'I never named Miss Nugent to you. No! it is not easy to me to talk of her, and impossible to me to describe her. If you had come one half-hour sooner this morning, you would have seen her: I know she is exactly suited to your excellent taste. But it is not at first sight she pleases most; she gains upon the affections, attaches the heart, and unfolds upon the judgment. In temper, manners, and good sense, in every quality a man can or should desire in a wife, I never saw her equal. Yet, there is an obstacle, an invincible obstacle, the nature of which I cannot explain to you, that forbids me to think of her as a wife. She lives with my father and mother: they are returning to Ireland. I wished, earnestly wished, on many accounts, to have accompanied them, chiefly on my mother's; but it cannot be. The first thing a man must do is to act honourably; and, that he may do so, he must keep out of the way of a temptation which he believes to be above his strength. I will never see Miss Nugent again till she is married; I must either stay in England, or go abroad. I have a mind to serve a campaign or two, if I could get a commission in a regiment going to Spain; but I understand so many are eager to go at this moment, that it is very difficult to get a commission in such a regiment.'

'It is difficult,' said the count. 'But,' added he, after thinking for a moment, 'I have it! I can get the thing done for you, and directly. Major Benson, in consequence of that affair, you know, about his mistress, is forced to quit the regiment. When the lieutenant-colonel came to quarters, and the rest of the officers heard the fact, they would not keep company with Benson, and would not mess with him. I know he wants to sell out; and that regiment is to be ordered immediately to Spain. I will have the thing done for you, if you request it.'

'First, give me your advice, Count O'Halloran; you are well acquainted with the military profession, with military life. Would you advise me – I won't speak of myself, because we judge better by general views than by particular cases – would you advise a young man at present to go into the army?'

The count was silent for a few minutes, and then replied: 'Since you seriously ask my opinion, my lord, I must lay aside my own prepossessions, and endeavour to speak with impartiality. To go into the army in these days, my lord, is, in my sober opinion, the most absurd and base, or the wisest and noblest thing a young man can do. To enter into the army, with the hope of escaping from the application necessary to acquire knowledge, letters, and science – I run no risk, my lord, in saying this to you – to go into the army, with the hope of escaping from knowledge, letters, science, and morality; to wear a red coat and an epaulette; to be called captain; to figure at a ball; to lounge away time in country sports, at country quarters, was never, even in times of peace, creditable; but it is now absurd and base. Submitting to a certain portion of ennui and contempt, this mode of life for an officer was formerly practicable – but now cannot be submitted to without utter, irremediable disgrace. Officers are now, in general, men of education and information; want of knowledge, sense, manners, must consequently be immediately detected, ridiculed, and despised in a military man. Of this we have not long since seen lamentable examples in the raw officers who have lately disgraced themselves in my neighbourhood in Ireland – that Major Benson and Captain Williamson. But I will not advert to such insignificant individuals, such are rare exceptions – I leave them out of the question – I reason on general principles. The life of an officer is not now a life of parade, of coxcombical, or of profligate idleness – but of active service, of continual hardship and danger. All the descriptions which we see in ancient history of a soldier's life – descriptions which, in times of peace, appeared like romance – are now realised; military exploits fill every day's newspapers, every day's conversation. A martial spirit is now essential to the liberty and the existence of our own country. In the present state of things, the military must be the most honourable profession, because the most useful. Every movement of an army is followed, wherever it goes, by the public hopes and fears. Every officer must now feel, besides this sense of collective importance, a belief that his only dependence must be on his own merit – and thus his ambition, his enthusiasm, are raised; and when once this noble ardour is kindled in the breast, it excites to exertion, and supports under endurance. But I forget myself,' said the count, checking his enthusiasm; 'I promised to speak soberly. If I have said too much, your own good sense, my lord, will correct me, and your good-nature will forgive the prolixity of an old man, touched upon his favourite subject – the passion of his youth.'

Lord Colambre, of course, assured the count that he was not tired. Indeed, the enthusiasm with which this old officer spoke of his profession, and the high point of view in which he placed it, increased our hero's desire to serve a campaign abroad. Good sense, politeness, and experience of the world preserved Count O'Halloran from that foible with which old officers are commonly reproached, of talking continually of their own military exploits. Though retired from the world, he had contrived, by reading the best books, and corresponding with persons of good information, to keep up with the current of modern affairs; and he seldom spoke of those in which he had been formerly engaged. He rather too studiously avoided speaking of himself; and this fear of egotism diminished the peculiar interest he might have inspired: it disappointed curiosity, and deprived those with whom he conversed of many entertaining and instructive anecdotes. However, he sometimes made exceptions to his general rule in favour of persons who peculiarly pleased him, and Lord Colambre was of this number.

He this evening, for the first time, spoke to his lordship of the years he had spent in the Austrian service; told him anecdotes of the emperor; spoke of many distinguished public characters whom he had known abroad; of those officers who had been his friends and companions. Among others he mentioned, with particular regard, a young English officer who had been at the same time with him in the Austrian service, a gentleman of the name of Reynolds.

The name struck Lord Colambre, it was the name of the officer who had been the cause of the disgrace of Miss St Omar – of Miss Nugent's mother. 'But there are so many Reynoldses.'

He eagerly asked the age – the character of this officer.

'He was a gallant youth,' said the count, 'but too adventurous – too rash. He fell, after distinguishing himself in a glorious manner, in his twentieth year – died in my arms.'

'Married or unmarried?' cried Lord Colambre.

'Married – he had been privately married, less than a year before his death, to a very young English lady, who had been educated at a convent in Vienna. He was heir to a considerable property, I believe, and the young lady had little fortune; and the affair was kept secret from the fear of offending his friends, or for some other reason – I do not recollect the particulars.'

'Did he acknowledge his marriage?' said Lord Colambre.

'Never till he was dying – then he confided his secret to me.'

'Do you recollect the name of the young lady he married?'

'Yes – a Miss St Omar.'

'St Omar!' repeated Lord Colambre, with an expression of lively joy in his countenance. 'But are you certain, my dear count, that she was really married, legally married, to Mr Reynolds? Her marriage has been denied by all his friends and relations – hers have never been able to establish it – her daughter is – My dear count, were you present at the marriage?'

'No,' said the count, 'I was not present at the marriage; I never saw the lady, nor do I know anything of the affair, except that Mr Reynolds, when he was dying, assured me that he was privately married to a Miss St Omar, who was then boarding at a convent in Vienna. The young man expressed great regret at leaving her totally unprovided for; but said that he trusted his father would acknowledge her, and that her friends would be reconciled to her. He was not of age, he said, to make a will; but I think he told me that his child, who at that time was not born, would, even if it should be a girl, inherit a considerable property. With this, I cannot, however, charge my memory positively; but he put a packet into my hands which, he told me, contained a certificate of his marriage, and, I think he said, a letter to his father; this he requested that I would transmit to England by some safe hand. Immediately after his death, I went to the English ambassador, who was then leaving Vienna, and delivered the packet into his hands; he promised to have it safely delivered. I was obliged to go the next day, with the troops, to a distant part of the country. When I returned, I inquired at the convent what had become of Miss St Omar – I should say Mrs Reynolds; and I was told that she had removed from the convent to private lodgings in the town, some time previous to the birth of her child. The abbess seemed much scandalised by the whole transaction; and I remember I relieved her mind by assuring her that there had been a regular marriage. For poor young Reynolds' sake, I made farther inquiries about the widow, intending, of course, to act as a friend, if she was in any difficulty or distress. But I found, on inquiry at her lodgings, that her brother had come from England for her, and had carried her and her infant away. The active scenes,' continued the count, 'in which I was immediately afterwards engaged, drove the whole affair from my mind. Now that your questions have recalled them, I feel certain of the facts I have mentioned; and I am ready to establish them by my testimony.'

Lord Colambre thanked him with an eagerness that showed how much he was interested in the event. It was clear, he said, either that the packet left with the ambassador had not been delivered, or that the father of Mr Reynolds had suppressed the certificate of the marriage, as it had never been acknowledged by him or by any of the family. Lord Colambre now frankly told the count why he was so anxious about this affair; and Count O'Halloran, with all the warmth of youth, and with all the ardent generosity characteristic of his country, entered into his feelings, declaring that he would never rest till he had established the truth.

'Unfortunately,' said the count, 'the ambassador who took the packet in charge is dead. I am afraid we shall have difficulty.'

'But he must have had some secretary,' said Lord Colambre; 'who was his secretary? – we can apply to him.'

'His secretary is now *chargé d'affaires* in Vienna – we cannot get at him.'

'Into whose hands have that ambassador's papers fallen – who is his executor?' said Lord Colambre.

'His executor! – now you have it,' cried the count. 'His executor is the very man who will do your business – your friend Sir James Brooke is the executor. All papers, of course, are in his hands; or he can have access to any that are in the hands of the family. The family seat is within a few miles of Sir James Brooke's, in Huntingdonshire, where, as I told you before, he now is.'

'I'll go to him immediately – set out in the mail this night. Just in time!' cried Lord Colambre, pulling out his watch with one hand, and ringing the bell with the other.

'Run and take a place for me in the mail for Huntingdon. Go directly,' said Lord Colambre to the servant.

'And take two places, if you please, sir,' said the count. 'My lord, I will accompany you.'

But this Lord Colambre would not permit, as it would be unnecessary to fatigue the good old general; and a letter from him to Sir James Brooke would do all that the count could effect by his presence; the search for the papers would be made by Sir James, and if the packet could be recovered, or if any memorandum or mode of ascertaining that it had actually been delivered to old Reynolds could be discovered, Lord Colambre said he would then call upon the count for his assistance, and trouble him to identify the packet; or to go with him to Mr Reynolds to make farther inquiries; and to certify, at all events, the young man's dying acknowledgment of his marriage and of his child.

The place in the mail, just in time, was taken. Lord Colambre sent a servant in search of his father, with a note explaining the necessity of his sudden departure. All the business which remained to be done in town he knew Lord Clonbrony could accomplish without his assistance. Then he wrote a few lines to his mother, on the very sheet of paper on which, a few hours before, he had sorrowfully and slowly begun –

My dear Mother – Miss Nugent.

He now joyfully and rapidly went on –

My dear Mother and Miss Nugent,

I hope to be with you on Wednesday se'nnight; but if unforeseen circumstances should delay me, I will certainly write to you again. – Dear mother, believe me, your obliged and grateful son,

COLAMBRE.

The count, in the meantime, wrote a letter for him to Sir James Brooke, describing the packet which he had given to the ambassador, and relating all the circumstances that could lead to its recovery. Lord Colambre, almost before the wax was hard, seized possession of the letter; the count seeming almost as eager to hurry him off as he was to set out. He thanked the count with few words, but with strong feeling. Joy and love returned in full tide upon our hero's soul; all the military ideas, which but an hour before filled his imagination, were put to flight: Spain vanished, and green Ireland reappeared.

Just as they shook hands at parting, the good old general, with a smile, said to him, 'I believe I had better not stir in the matter of Benson's commission till I hear more from you. My harangue, in favour of the military profession, will, I fancy, prove like most other harangues, *en pure perte*.'

Chapter 16

IN WHAT WORDS of polite circumlocution, or of cautious diplomacy, shall we say, or hint, that the deceased ambassador's papers were found in shameful disorder. His excellency's executor, Sir James Brooke, however, was indefatigable in his researches. He and Lord Colambre spent two whole days in looking over portfolios of letters and memorials, and manifestoes, and bundles of paper of the most heterogeneous sorts; some of them without any docket or direction to lead to a knowledge of their contents; others written upon in such a manner as to give an erroneous notion of their nature; so that it was necessary to untie every paper separately. At last, when they had opened, as they thought, every paper, and, wearied and in despair, were just on the point of giving up the search, Lord Colambre spied a bundle of old newspapers at the bottom of a trunk.

'They are only old Vienna Gazettes; I looked at them,' said Sir James.

Lord Colambre, upon this assurance, was going to throw them into the trunk again; but observing that the bundle had not been untied, he opened it, and within-side of the newspapers he found a rough copy of the ambassador's journal, and with it the packet, directed to Ralph Reynolds sen., Esq., Old Court, Suffolk, per favour of his excellency, Earl — , a note on the cover, signed O'Halloran, stating when received by him, and the date of the day when delivered to the ambassador – seals unbroken. Our hero was in such a transport of joy at the sight of this packet, and his friend Sir James Brooke so full of his congratulations, that they forgot to curse the ambassador's carelessness, which had been the cause of so much evil.

The next thing to be done was to deliver the packet to Ralph Reynolds, Old Court, Suffolk. But when Lord Colambre arrived at Old Court, Suffolk, he found all the gates locked, and no admittance to be had. At last an old woman came out of the porter's lodge, who said Mr Reynolds was not there, and she could not say where he was. After our hero had opened her heart by the present of half a guinea, she explained, that she 'could not *justly* say where he was, because that he never let anybody of his own people know where he was any day; he had several different houses and places in different parts, and far-off counties, and other shires, as she heard, and by times he was at one, and by times at another.' The names of two of the places, Toddrington and Little Wrestham, she knew; but there were others to which she could give no direction. He had houses in odd parts of London, too, that he let; and sometimes, when the lodgers' time was out, he would go, and be never heard of for a month, maybe, in one of them. In short, there was no telling or saying where he was or would be one day of the week, by where he had been the last.'

When Lord Colambre expressed some surprise that an old gentleman, as he conceived Mr Ralph Reynolds to be, should change places so frequently, the old woman answered, 'That though her master was a deal on the wrong side of seventy, and though, to look at him, you'd think he was glued to his chair, and would fall to pieces if he should stir out of it, yet was as alert, and thought no more of going about, than if he was as young as the gentleman who was now speaking to her. It was old Mr Reynolds' delight to come down and surprise his people at his different places, and see that they were keeping all tight.'

'What sort of a man is he? – Is he a miser?' said Lord Colambre.

'He is a miser, and he is not a miser,' said the woman. 'Now he'd think as much of the waste of a penny as another man would of a hundred pounds, and yet he would give a hundred pounds easier than another would give a penny, when he's in the humour. But his humour is very odd, and there's no knowing where to have him; he's grossgrained, and more *positiver*-like than a mule; and his deafness made him worse in this, because he never heard what nobody said, but would say on his own way – he was very *odd*, but not *cracked* – no, he was as clear-headed, when he took a thing the right way, as any man could be, and as clever, and could talk as well as any member of Parliament, – and good-natured, and kind-hearted, where he would take a fancy – but then, maybe, it would be to a dog (he was remarkable fond of dogs), or a cat, or a rat even, that he would take a fancy, and think more of 'em than he would of a Christian. But, poor gentleman, there's great allowance,' said she, 'to be made for him, that lost his son and heir – that would have been heir to all, and a fine youth that he doted upon. But,' continued the old woman, in whose mind the transitions from *great* to little, from serious to trivial, were ludicrously abrupt, 'that was no reason why the old gentleman should scold me last time he was here, as he did, for as long as ever he could stand over me, only because I killed a mouse who was eating my cheese; and, before night, he beat a boy for stealing a piece of that same cheese; and he would never, when down here, let me set a mouse-trap.'

'Well, my good woman,' interrupted Lord Colambre, who was little interested in this affair of the mouse-trap, and nowise curious to learn more of Mr Reynolds' domestic economy, 'I'll not trouble you any farther, if you can be so good as to tell me the road to Toddrington, or to Little Wickham, I think you call it.'

'Little Wickham!' repeated the woman, laughing – 'Bless you, sir, where do you come from? – It's Little Wrestham; surely everybody knows, near Lantry; and keep the *pike* till you come to the turn at Rotherford, and then you strike off into the by-road to the left, and then again turn at the ford to the right. But, if you are going to Toddrington, you don't go the road to market, which is at the first turn to the left, and the cross-country road, where there's no quarter, and Toddrington lies – but for Wrestham, you take the road to market.'

It was some time before our hero could persuade the old woman to stick to Little Wrestham, or to Toddrington, and not to mix the directions for the different roads together – he took patience, for his impatience only confused his director the more. In process of time, he made out, and wrote down, the various turns that he was to follow, to reach Little Wrestham; but no human power could get her from Little Wrestham to Toddrington, though she knew the road perfectly well; but she had, for the seventeen last years, been used to go 'the other road,' and all the carriers went that way, and passed the door, and that was all she could certify.

Little Wrestham, after turning to the left and right as often as his directory required, our hero happily reached; but, unhappily, he found no Mr Reynolds there; only a steward, who gave nearly the same account of his master as had been given by the old woman, and could not guess even where the gentleman might now be. Toddrington was as likely as any place – but he could not say.

'Perseverance against fortune.' To Toddrington our hero proceeded, through cross-country roads – such roads! – very different from the Irish roads. Waggon ruts, into which the carriage wheels sunk nearly to the nave – and, from time to time, 'sloughs of despond,' through which it seemed impossible to drag, walk, wade, or swim, and all the time with a sulky postillion. 'Oh, how unlike my Larry!' thought Lord Colambre.

At length, in a very narrow lane, going up a hill, said to be two miles of ascent, they overtook a heavy laden waggon, and they were obliged to go step by step behind it, whilst, enjoying the gentleman's impatience much, and the postillion's sulkiness more, the waggoner, in his embroidered frock, walked in state, with his long sceptre in his hand.

The postillion muttered 'curses not loud, but deep.' Deep or loud, no purpose would they have answered; the waggoner's temper was proof against curse in or out of the English language; and from their snail's pace neither *Dickens* nor devil, nor any postillion in England, could make him put his horses. Lord Colambre jumped out of the chaise, and, walking beside him, began to talk to him; and spoke of his horses, their bells, their trappings; the beauty and strength of the thill-horse – the value of the whole team, which his lordship happening to guess right within ten pounds, and showing, moreover, some skill about road-making and waggon-wheels, and being fortunately of the waggoner's own opinion in the great question about conical and cylindrical rims, he was pleased with the young chap of a gentleman; and, in spite of the chuffiness of his appearance and churlishness of his speech, this waggoner's bosom 'being made of penetrating stuff,' he determined to let the gentleman pass. Accordingly, when half-way up the hill, and the head of the fore-horse came near an open gate, the waggoner, without saying one word or turning his head, touched the horse with his long whip – and the horse turned in at the gate, and then came –

'Dobbin! – Jeho!' and strange calls and sounds, which all the other horses of the team obeyed; and the waggon turned into the farmyard.

'Now, master! while I turn, you may pass.'

The covering of the waggon caught in the hedge as the waggon turned in; and as the sacking was drawn back, some of the packages were disturbed – a cheese was just rolling off on the side next Lord Colambre; he stopped it from falling; the direction caught his quick eye – 'To Ralph Reynolds, Esq.' – '*Toddrington*' scratched out; 'Red Lion Square,

London,' written in another hand below.

'Now I have found him! And surely I know that hand!' said Lord Colambre to himself, looking more closely at the direction.

The original direction was certainly in a handwriting well known to him – it was Lady Dashfort's.

'That there cheese, that you're looking at so cur'ously,' said the waggoner, 'has been a great traveller; for it came all the way down from Lon'on, and now it's going all the way up again back, on account of not finding the gentleman at home; and the man that booked it told me as how it came from foreign parts.'

Lord Colambre took down the direction, tossed the honest waggoner a guinea, wished him good-night, passed, and went on. As soon as he could, he turned into the London road – at the first town, got a place in the mail – reached London – saw his father – went directly to his friend, Count O'Halloran, who was delighted when he beheld the packet. Lord Colambre was extremely eager to go immediately to old Reynolds, fatigued as he was; for he had travelled night and day, and had scarcely allowed himself, mind or body, one moment's repose.

'Heroes must sleep, and lovers too; or they soon will cease to be heroes or lovers!' said the count. 'Rest, rest, perturbed spirit! this night; and tomorrow morning we'll finish the adventure in Red Lion Square, or I will accompany you when and where you will; if necessary, to earth's remotest bounds.'

The next morning Lord Colambre went to breakfast with the count. The count, who was not in love, was not up, for our hero was half an hour earlier than the time appointed. The old servant Ulick, who had attended his master to England, was very glad to see Lord Colambre again, and, showing him into the breakfast parlour, could not help saying, in defence of his master's punctuality –

'Your clocks, I suppose, my lord, are half an hour faster than ours; my master will be ready to the moment.'

The count soon appeared – breakfast was soon over, and the carriage at the door; for the count sympathised in his young friend's impatience. As they were setting out, the count's large Irish dog pushed out of the house door to follow them; and his master would have forbidden him, but Lord Colambre begged that he might be permitted to accompany them; for his lordship recollected the old woman's having mentioned that Mr Reynolds was fond of dogs.

They arrived in Red Lion Square, found the house of Mr Reynolds, and, contrary to the count's prognostics, found the old gentleman up, and they saw him in his red night-cap at his parlour window. After some minutes' running backwards and forwards of a boy in the passage, and two or three peeps taken over the blinds by the old gentleman, they were admitted.

The boy could not master their names; so they were obliged reciprocally to announce themselves – 'Count O'Halloran and Lord Colambre.' The names seemed to make no impression on the old gentleman; but he deliberately looked at the count and his lordship, as if studying *what* rather than *who* they were. In spite of the red night-cap, and a flowered dressing-gown, Mr Reynolds looked like a gentleman, an odd gentleman – but still a gentleman.

As Count O'Halloran came into the room, and as his large dog attempted to follow, the count's voice expressed: 'Say, shall I let him in, or shut the door?'

'Oh, let him in, by all means, sir, if you please! I am fond of dogs; and a finer one I never saw; pray, gentlemen, be seated,' said he – a portion of the complacency inspired by the sight of the dog, diffusing itself over his manner towards the master of so fine an animal, and even extending to the master's companion, though in an inferior degree. Whilst Mr Reynolds stroked the dog, the count told him that 'the dog was of a curious breed, now almost extinct – the Irish greyhound, of which only one nobleman in Ireland, it is said, has now a few of the species remaining in his possession Now, lie down, Hannibal,' said the count. 'Mr Reynolds, we have taken the liberty, though strangers, of waiting upon you – '

'I beg your pardon, sir,' interrupted Mr Reynolds; 'but did I understand you rightly, that a few of the same species are still to be had from one nobleman in Ireland? Pray, what is his name?' said he, taking out his pencil.

The count wrote the name for him, but observed, that 'he had asserted only that a few of these dogs remained in the possession of that nobleman; he could not answer for it that they were *to be had.*'

'Oh, I have ways and means,' said old Reynolds; and, rapping his snuff-box, and talking, as it was his custom, loud to himself, 'Lady Dashfort knows all those Irish lords; she shall get one for me – ay! ay!'

Count O'Halloran replied, as if the words had been addressed to him –

'Lady Dashfort is in England.'

'I know it, sir; she is in London,' said Mr Reynolds, hastily. 'What do you know of her?'

'I know, sir, that she is not likely to return to Ireland, and that I am; and so is my young friend here; and if the thing can be accomplished, we will get it done for you.'

Lord Colambre joined in this promise, and added that, 'if the dog could be obtained, he would undertake to have him safely sent over to England.'

'Sir – gentlemen! I'm much obliged; that is, when you have done the thing I shall be much obliged. But, maybe, you are only making me civil speeches!'

'Of that, sir,' said the count, smiling with much temper, 'your own sagacity and knowledge of the world must enable you to judge.'

'For my own part, I can only say,' cried Lord Colambre, 'that I am not in the habit of being reproached with saying one thing and meaning another.'

'Hot! I see,' said old Reynolds, nodding, as he looked at Lord Colambre. 'Cool!' added he, nodding at the count. 'But a time for everything; I was hot once – both answers good, for their ages.'

This speech Lord Colambre and the count tacitly agreed to consider as another *apart*, which they were not to hear, or seem to hear. The count began again on the business of their visit, as he saw that Lord Colambre was boiling with impatience, and feared that he should *boil over*, and spoil all. The count commenced with –

'Mr Reynolds, your name sounds to me like the name of a friend; for I had once a friend of that name; I had once the pleasure (and a very great pleasure it was to me) to be intimately acquainted abroad, on the Continent, with a very amiable and gallant youth – your son!'

'Take care, sir,' said the old man, starting up from his chair, and instantly sinking down again, – 'take care! Don't mention him to me – unless you would strike me dead on the spot!'

The convulsed motions of his fingers and face worked for some moments; whilst the count and Lord Colambre, much shocked and alarmed, stood in silence.

The convulsed motions ceased; and the old mall unbuttoned his waistcoat, as if to relieve some sense of expression; uncovered his gray hairs; and, after leaning back to rest himself, with his eyes fixed, and in reverie for a few moments, he sat upright again in his chair, and exclaimed, as he looked round –

'Son! – Did not somebody say that word? Who is so cruel to say that word before me? Nobody has ever spoken of him to me – but once, since his death! Do you know, sir,' said he, fixing his eyes on Count O'Halloran, and laying his cold hand on him, 'do you know where he was buried, I ask you, sir? do you remember how he died?'

'Too well! too well!' cried the count, so much affected as to be scarcely able to pronounce the words; 'he died in my arms; I buried him myself!'

'Impossible!' cried Mr Reynolds. 'Why do you say so, sir?' said he, studying the count's face with a sort of bewildered earnestness. 'Impossible! His body was sent over to me in a lead coffin; and I saw it – and I was asked – and I answered, "in the family vault." But the shock visit relates to that subject, I trust I am now sufficiently composed to attend to you. Indeed, I ought to be prepared; for I had reason, for years, to expect the stroke; and yet, when it came, it seemed sudden! – it stunned me put an end to all my worldly prospects – left me childless, without a single descendant or relation near enough to be dear to me! I am an insulated being!'

'No, sir, you are not an insulated being,' said Lord Colambre; 'you have a near relation, who will, who must be dear to you; who will make you amends for all you have lost, all you have suffered – who will bring peace and joy to your heart. You have a grand-daughter.'

'No, sir; I have no grand-daughter,' said old Reynolds, his face and whole form becoming rigid with the expression of obstinacy. 'Rather have no descendant than be forced to acknowledge an illegitimate child.'

'My lord, I entreat as a friend – I command you to be patient,' said the count, who saw Lord Colambre's indignation suddenly rise.

'So, then, this is the purpose of your visit,' continued old Reynolds; 'and you come from my enemies, from the St Omars, and you are in a league with them,' continued old Reynolds; 'and all this time it is of my eldest son you have been talking.'

'Yes, sir,' replied the count; 'of Captain Reynolds, who fell in battle, in the Austrian service, about nineteen years ago – a more gallant and amiable youth never lived.'

Pleasure revived through the dull look of obstinacy in the father's, eyes.

'He was, as you say, sir, a gallant, an amiable youth, once – and he was my pride, and I loved him, too, once – but did not you know I had another?'

'No, sir; we did not – we are, you may perceive, totally ignorant of your family and of your affairs – we have no connection whatever or knowledge of any of the St Omars.'

'I detest the sound of the name,' cried Lord Colambre.

'Oh, good! good! – Well! well! I beg your pardon, gentlemen, a thousand times – I am a hasty, very hasty old man; but I have been harassed, persecuted, hunted by wretches, who got a scent of my gold; often in my rage I longed to throw my treasure-bags to my pursuers, and bid them leave me to die in peace. You have feelings, I see, both of you, gentlemen; excuse me, and bear with my temper.'

'Bear with you! Much enforced, the best tempers will emit a hasty spark,' said the count, looking at Lord Colambre, who was now cool again; and who, with a countenance full of compassion, sat with his eyes fixed upon the poor – no, not the poor, but the unhappy old man.

'Yes, I had another son,' continued Mr Reynolds, 'and on him all my affections concentrated when I lost my eldest, and for him I desired to preserve the estate which his mother brought into my family. Since you know nothing of my affairs, let me explain to you; that estate was so settled, that it would have gone to the child, even the daughter of my eldest son, if ere had been a legitimate child. But I knew there was no marriage, and I held out firm to my opinion. "If there was marriage," said I, "show me the marriage certificate, and I will acknowledge the marriage, and acknowledge the child;" but they could not, and I knew they could not; and I kept he estate for my darling boy,' cried the old gentleman, with he exultation of successful positiveness again appearing strong n his physiognomy; but suddenly changing and relaxing, his countenance fell, and he added, 'But now I have no darling boy. What use all! – all must go to the heir-at-law, or I must will it to a stranger – a lady of quality, who has just found out she is my relation – God knows how – I'm no genealogist – and sends me Irish cheese and Iceland moss, for my breakfast, and her waiting-gentlewoman to namby-pamby me. Oh, I'm sick of it all see through it – wish I was blind – wish I had a hiding-place, where flatterers could not find me – pursued, chased – must change my lodgings again tomorrow – will, will – I beg your pardon, gentlemen, again; you were going to tell me, sir, something more of my eldest son; and how I was led away from the subject, I don't know; but I meant only to have assured you that his memory was dear to me, till I was so tormented about that unfortunate affair of his pretended marriage, that at length I hated to hear him named; but the heir-at-law, at last, will triumph over me.'

'No, my good sir, not if you triumph over yourself, and do justice,' cried Lord Colambre; 'if you listen to the truth, which my friend will tell you, and if you will read and believe the confirmation of it, under your son's own hand, in this packet.'

'His own hand indeed! His seal – unbroken. But how – when – where – why was it kept so long, and how came it into your hands?'

Count O'Halloran told Mr Reynolds that the packet had been given to him by Captain Reynolds on his deathbed; related the dying acknowledgment which Captain Reynolds had made of his marriage; and gave an account of the delivery of the packet to the ambassador, who had promised to transmit it faithfully. Lord Colambre told the manner in which it had been mislaid, and at last recovered from among the deceased ambassador's papers. The father still gazed at the direction, and re-examined the seals.

'My son's handwriting – my son's seals! But where is the certificate of the marriage?' repeated he; 'if it is withinside of this packet, I have done great *in* – but I am convinced it never was a marriage. Yet I wish now it could be proved – only, in that case, I have for years done great – '

'Won't you open the packet, sir?' said Lord Colambre. Mr Reynolds looked up at him with a look that said, 'I don't clearly know what interest you have in all this.' But, unable to speak, and his hands trembling so that he could scarcely break the seals, he tore off the cover, laid the papers before him, sat down, and took breath. Lord Colambre, however impatient, had now too much humanity to hurry the old gentleman; he only ran for the spectacles, which he espied on the chimney-piece, rubbed them bright, and held them ready. Mr Reynolds stretched his hand out for them, put them on, and the first paper he opened was the certificate of the marriage; he read it aloud, and, putting it down, said –

'Now I acknowledge the marriage. I always said, if there is a marriage there must be a certificate. And you see now there is a certificate – I acknowledge the marriage.'

'And now,' cried Lord Colambre, 'I am happy, positively happy. Acknowledge your grand-daughter, sir – acknowledge Miss Nugent.'

'Acknowledge who, sir?'

'Acknowledge Miss Reynolds – your grand-daughter; I ask no more – do what you will with your fortune.'

'Oh, now I understand – I begin to understand this young gentleman is in love – but where is my grand-daughter? – how shall I know she is my grand-daughter? I have not heard of her since she was an infant – I forgot her existence – I have done her great injustice.'

'She knows nothing of it, sir,' said Lord Colambre, who now entered into a full explanation of Miss Nugent's history, and of her connection with his family, and of his own attachment to her; concluding the whole by assuring Mr Reynolds that his grand-daughter had every virtue under heaven. 'And as to your fortune, sir, I know that she will, as I do, say – '

'No matter what she will say,' interrupted old Reynolds; 'where is she? When I see her, I shall hear what she says. Tell me where she is – let me see her. I long to see whether there is any likeness to her poor father. Where is she? Let me see her immediately.'

'She is one hundred and sixty miles off, sir, at Buxton.'

'Well, my lord, and what is a hundred and sixty miles? I suppose you think I can't stir from my chair, but you are mistaken. I think nothing of a journey of a hundred and sixty miles – I'm ready to set off tomorrow – this instant.'

Lord Colambre said, that he was sure Miss Reynolds would obey her grandfather's slightest summons, as it was her duty to do, and would be with him as soon as possible, if this would be more agreeable to him. 'I will write to her instantly,' said his lordship, 'if you will commission me.'

'No, my lord, I do not commission – I will go – I think nothing, I say, of a journey of a hundred and sixty miles – I'll go – and set out tomorrow morning.'

Lord Colambre and the count, perfectly satisfied with the result of their visit, now thought it best to leave old Reynolds at liberty to rest himself, after so many strong and varied feelings. They paid their parting compliments, settled the time for the next day's journey, and were just going to quit the room when Lord Colambre heard in the passage a well-known voice – the voice of Mrs Petito.

'Oh no, my compliments, and my Lady Dashfort's best compliments, and I will call again.'

'No, no,' cried old Reynolds, pulling his bell; 'I'll have no calling again – I'll be hanged if I do! Let her in now, and I'll see her – Jack! let in that woman now or never.'

'The lady's gone, sir, out of the street door.'

'After her, then – now or never, tell her.'

'Sir, she was in a hackney coach.'

Old Reynolds jumped up, and went to the window himself, and, seeing the hackney coachman just turning, beckoned at the window, and Mrs Petito was set down again, and ushered in by Jack, who announced her as –

'The lady, sir.' The only lady he had seen in that house.

'My dear Mr Reynolds, I'm so obliged to you for letting me in,' cried Mrs Petito, adjusting her shawl in the passage, and speaking in a voice and manner well mimicked after her betters. 'You are so very good and kind, and I am so much obliged to you.'

'You are not obliged to me, and I am neither good nor kind,' said old Reynolds.

'You strange man,' said Mrs Petito, advancing graceful in shawl drapery; but she stopped short. 'My Lord Colambre and Count O'Halloran, as I hope to be saved!'

'I did not know Mrs Petito was an acquaintance of yours, gentlemen,' said Mr Reynolds, smiling shrewdly.

Count O'Halloran was too polite to deny his acquaintance with a lady who challenged it by thus naming him; but he had not the slightest recollection of her, though it seems he had met her on the stairs when he visited Lady Dashfort at Killpatrickstown. Lord Colambre was 'indeed *undeniably an old acquaintance*:' and as soon as she had recovered from her first natural start and vulgar exclamation, she with very easy familiarity hoped 'My Lady Clonbrony, and my lord, and Miss Nugent, and all her friends in the family, were well;' and said, 'she did not know whether she was to congratulate his lordship or not upon Miss Broadhurst, my Lady Berryl's marriage, but she should soon have to hope for his lordship's congratulations for another marriage in *her* present family – Lady Isabel to Colonel Heathcock, who has come in for a large *portion*, and they are buying the wedding clothes – sights of clothes – and the di'monds, this day; and Lady Dashfort and my Lady Isabel sent me especially, sir, to you, Mr Reynolds, and to tell you, sir, before anybody else; and to hope the cheese *come* safe up-again at last; and to ask whether the Iceland moss agrees with your chocolate, and is palatable; it's the most *diluent* thing upon the universal earth, and the most *tonic* and fashionable – the *Dutches* of Torcaster takes it always for breakfast, and Lady St James' too is quite a convert, and I hear the Duke of V— takes it too.'

'And the devil may take it too, for anything that I care,' said old Reynolds.

'Oh, my dear, dear sir! you are so refractory a patient.'

'I am no patient at all, ma'am, and have no patience either; I am as well as you are, or my Lady Dashfort either, and hope, God willing, long to continue so.'

Mrs Petito smiled aside at Lord Colambre, to mark her perception of the man's strangeness. Then, in a cajoling voice, addressing herself to the old gentleman –

'Long, long, I hope, to continue so, if Heaven grants my daily and nightly prayers, and my Lady Dashfort's also. So, Mr Reynolds, if the ladies' prayers are of any avail, you ought to be purely, and I suppose ladies' prayers have the precedency in efficacy. But it was not of prayers and deathbed affairs I came commissioned to treat – not of burials, which Heaven above forbid, but of weddings my diplomacy was to speak; and to premise my Lady Dashfort would have come herself in her carriage, but is hurried out of her senses, and my Lady Isabel could not in proper modesty; so they sent me as their *double*, to hope you, my dear Mr Reynolds, who is one of the family relations, will honour the wedding with your presence.'

'It would be no honour, and they know that as well as I do,' said the intractable Mr Reynolds. 'It will be no advantage, either; but that they do not know as well as I do. Mrs Petito, to save you and your lady all trouble about me in future, please to let my Lady Dashfort know that I have just received and read the certificate of my son Captain Reynolds' marriage with Miss St Omar. I have acknowledged the marriage. Better

late than never; and tomorrow morning, God willing, shall set out with
this young nobleman for Buxton, where I hope to see, and intend
publicly to acknowledge, my grand-daughter – provided she will
acknowledge me.'

'*Crimini*!' exclaimed Mrs Petito, 'what new turns are here! Well, sir,
I shall tell my lady of the *metamorphoses* that have taken place, though
by what magic (as I have not the honour to deal in the black art) I can't
guess: But, since it seems annoying and inopportune, I shall take my
finale, and shall thus have a verbal *P.P.C.* – as you are leaving town, it
seems, for Buxton so early in the morning. My Lord Colambre, if I see
rightly into a millstone, as I hope and believe I do on the present
occasion, I have to congratulate your lordship (haven't I?) upon
something like a succession, or a windfall, in this *denewment*. And I beg
you'll make my humble respects acceptable to the ci-devant Miss
Grace Nugent that was; and I won't *derrogate* her by any other name in
the interregnum, as I am persuaded it will only be a temporary name,
scarce worth assuming, except for the honour of the public adoption;
and that will, I'm confident, be soon exchanged for a viscount's title, or
I have no sagacity nor sympathy. I hope I don't (pray don't let me) put
you to the blush, my lord.'

Lord Colambre would not have let her, if he could have helped it.

'Count O'Halloran, your most obedient! I had the honour of
meeting you at Killpatrickstown,' said Mrs Petito, backing to the door,
and twitching her shawl. She stumbled, nearly fell down, over the large
dog – caught by the door, and recovered herself. Hannibal rose and
shook his ears. 'Poor fellow! you are of my acquaintance too.' She
would have stroked his head; but Hannibal walked off indignant, and so
did she.

Thus ended certain hopes; for Mrs Petito had conceived that her
diplomacy might be turned to account; that in her character of an
ambassadress, as Lady Dashfort's double, by the aid of Iceland moss in
chocolate, flattery properly administered; that, by bearing with all her
dear Mr Reynolds' *oddnesses* and *roughessess* she might in time – that is to
say, before he made a new will – become his dear Mrs Petito; or (for
stranger things have happened and do happen every day) his dear Mrs
Reynolds! Mrs Petito, however, was good at a retreat; and she flattered
herself that at least nothing of this underplot had appeared; and at
all events she secured by her services in this embassy, the long-looked-
for object of her ambition, Lady Dashfort's scarlet velvet gown – 'not
yet a thread the worse for the wear!' One cordial look at this comforted
her for the loss of her expected *octogenaire*; and she proceeded to
discomfit her lady, by repeating the message with which strange old

Mr Reynolds had charged her. – So ended all lady Dashfort's hopes of his fortune.

Since the death of his youngest son, she had been indefatigable in her attentions, and sanguine in her hopes; the disappointment affected both her interest and her pride as an *intrigante*. It was necessary, however, to keep her feelings to herself; for if Heathcock should hear anything of the matter before the articles were signed, he might 'be off!' – so she put him and Lady Isabel into her coach directly – drove to Gray's, to make sure at all events of the jewels.

In the meantime Count O'Halloran and Lord Colambre, delighted with the result of their visit, took leave of Mr Reynolds, after having arranged the journey, and appointed the hour for setting off the next day. Lord Colambre proposed to call upon Mr Reynolds in the evening, and introduce his father, Lord Clonbrony; but Mr Reynolds said –

'No, no! I'm not ceremonious. I have given you proofs enough of that, I think, in the short time we've been already acquainted. Time enough to introduce your father to me when we are in a carriage, going our journey; then we can talk, and get acquainted; but merely to come this evening in a hurry, and say, "Lord Clonbrony, Mr Reynolds; – Mr Reynolds, Lord Clonbrony," and then bob our two heads at one another, and scrape one foot back, and away! – where's the use of that nonsense at my time of life, or at any time of life? No, no! we have enough to do without that, I daresay. – Good-morning to you, Count O'Halloran! I thank you heartily. From the first moment I saw you, I liked you; lucky too that you brought your dog with you! 'Twas Hannibal made me first let you in; I saw him over the top of the blind. – Hannibal, my good fellow! I'm more obliged to you than you can guess.'

'So are we all,' said Lord Colambre.

Hannibal was well patted, and then they parted. In returning home they met Sir James Brooke.

'I told you,' said Sir James, 'I should be in London almost as soon as you. Have you found old Reynolds?'

'Just come from him.'

'How does your business prosper? I hope as well as mine.'

A history of all that had passed up to the present moment was given, and hearty congratulations received.

'Where are you going now, Sir James? – cannot you come with us?' said Lord Colambre and the count.

'Impossible,' replied Sir James; – 'but, perhaps, you can come with me – I'm going to Gray's, to give some old family diamonds, either to be new set or exchanged. Count O'Halloran, I know you are a judge of these things; pray, come and give me your opinion.'

'Better consult your bride elect!' said the count.

'No; she knows little of the matter – and cares less,' replied Sir James.

'Not so this bride elect, or I mistake her much,' said the count, as they passed by the window and saw Lady Isabel, who, with Lady Dashfort, had been holding consultation deep with the jeweller; and Heathcock, playing *personnage muet*.

Lady Dashfort, who had always, as old Reynolds expressed it, 'her head upon her shoulders' – presence of mind where her interests were concerned – ran to the door before the count and Lord Colambre could enter, giving a hand to each – as if they had all parted the best friends in the world.

'How do? how do? – Give you joy! give me joy! and all that. But mind! not a word,' said she, laying her finger upon her lips – 'not a word before Heathcock of old Reynolds, or of the best part of the old fool, – his fortune!'

The gentlemen bowed, in sign of submission to her ladyship's commands; and comprehended that she feared Heathcock might *be off*; if the best part of his bride (her fortune, or her *expectations*) were lowered in value or in prospect.

'How low is she reduced,' whispered Lord Colambre, 'when such a husband is thought a prize – and to be secured by a manœuvre!' He sighed.

'Spare that generous sigh!' said Sir James Brooke; 'it is wasted.'

Lady Isabel, as they approached, turned from a mirror, at which she was trying on a diamond crescent. Her face clouded at sight of Count O'Halloran and Lord Colambre, and grew dark as hatred when she saw Sir James Brooke. She walked away to the farther end of the shop, and asked one of the shopmen the price of a diamond necklace which lay upon the counter.

The man said, 'He really did not know; it belonged to Lady Oranmore; it had just been new set for one of her ladyship's daughters, who is going to be married to Sir James Brooke – one of the gentlemen, my lady, who are just come in.'

Then, calling to his master, he asked him the price of the necklace; he named the value, which was considerable.

'I really thought Lady Oranmore and her daughters were vastly too philosophical to think of diamonds,' said Lady Isabel to her mother, with a sort of sentimental sneer in her voice and countenance. 'But it is some comfort to me to find, in these pattern-women, philosophy and love do not so wholly engross the heart, that they "feel every vanity in fondness lost." '

' 'Twould be difficult, in some cases,' thought many present.

' 'Pon honour, di'monds are cursed expensive things, I know!' said Heathcock. 'But, be that as it may,' whispered he to the lady, though loud enough to be heard by others, 'I've laid a damned round wager, that no woman's diamonds married this winter, under a countess, in Lon'on, shall eclipse Lady Isabel Heathcock's! – and Mr Gray here's to be judge.'

Lady Isabel paid for this promise one of her sweetest smiles; with one of those smiles which she had formerly bestowed upon Lord Colambre, and which he had once fancied expressed so much sensibility – such discriminative and delicate application.

Our hero felt so much contempt, that he never wasted another sigh of pity for her degradation. Lady Dashfort came up to him as he was standing alone; and, whilst the count and Sir James were settling about the diamonds –

'My Lord Colambre,' said she, in a low voice, 'I know your thoughts, and I could moralise as well as you, if I did not prefer laughing – you are right enough; and so am I, and so is Isabel; we are all right. For look here: women have not always the liberty of choice, and therefore they can't be expected to have always the power of refusal.'

The mother, satisfied with her convenient optimism, got into her carriage with her daughter, her daughter's diamonds, and her precious son-in-law, her daughter's companion for life.

'The more I see,' said Count O'Halloran to Lord Colambre, as they left the shop, 'the more I find reason to congratulate you upon your escape, my dear lord.'

'I owe it not to my own wit or wisdom,' said Lord Colambre; 'but much to love, and much to friendship,' added he, turning to Sir James Brooke; 'here was the friend who early warned me against the siren's voice; who, before I knew the Lady Isabel, told me what I have since found to be true, that

> Two passions alternately govern her fate –
> Her business is love, but her pleasure is hate.'

'That is dreadfully severe, Sir James,' said Count O'Halloran; 'but I am afraid it is just.'

'I am sure it is just, or I would not have said it,' replied Sir James Brooke. 'For the foibles of the sex, I hope, I have as much indulgence as any man, and for the errors of passion as much pity; but I cannot repress the indignation, the abhorrence I feel against women, cold and vain, who use their wit and their charms only to make others miserable.'

Lord Colambre recollected at this moment Lady Isabel's look and voice, when she declared that 'she would let her little finger be cut off to purchase the pleasure of inflicting on Lady de Cresey, for one hour, the torture of jealousy.'

'Perhaps,' continued Sir James Brooke, 'now that I am going to marry into an Irish family, I may feel, with peculiar energy, disapprobation of this mother and daughter on another account; but you, Lord Colambre, will do me the justice to recollect that, before I had any personal interest in the country, I expressed, as a general friend to Ireland, antipathy to those who return the hospitality they received from a warm-hearted people, by publicly setting the example of elegant sentimental hypocrisy, or daring disregard of decorum, by privately endeavouring to destroy the domestic peace of families, on which, at last, public as well as private virtue and happiness depend. I do rejoice, my dear Lord Colambre, to hear you say that I had any share in saving you from the siren; and now, I will never speak of these ladies more. I am sorry you cannot stay in town to see – but why should I be sorry – we shall meet again, I trust, and I shall introduce you; and you, I hope, will introduce me to a very different charmer. Farewell! – you have my warm good wishes wherever you go.'

Sir James turned off quickly to the street in which Lady Oranmore lived, and Lord Colambre had not time to tell him that he knew and admired his intended bride. Count O'Halloran promised to do this for him. 'And now,' said the good count, 'I am to take leave of you; and I assure you I do it with so much reluctance that nothing less than positive engagements to stay in town would prevent me from setting off with you tomorrow; but I shall be soon, very soon, at liberty to return to Ireland; and Clonbrony Castle, if you will give me leave, I will see before I see Halloran Castle.'

Lord Colambre joyfully thanked his friend for this promise.

'Nay, it is to indulge myself. I long to see you happy – long to behold the choice of such a heart as yours. Pray do not steal a march upon me – let me know in time. I will leave everything – even the siege of — for your wedding. But I trust I shall be in time.'

'Assuredly you will, my dear count; if ever that wedding – '

'If,' repeated the count.

'If,' repeated Lord Colambre. 'Obstacles which, when we last parted, appeared to me invincible, prevented my having ever even attempted to make an impression on the heart of the woman I love; and if you knew her, count, as well as I do, you would know that her love could "not unsought be won." '

'Of that I cannot doubt, or she would not be your choice; but when her love is sought, we have every reason to hope,' said the count, smiling, 'that it may, because it ought to be won by tried honour and affection. I only require to be left in hope.'

'Well, I leave you hope,' said Lord Colambre; 'Miss Nugent – Miss Reynolds, I should say, has been in the habit of considering a union with me as impossible; my mother early instilled this idea into her mind. Miss Nugent thought that duty forbad her to think of me; she told me so: I have seen it in all her conduct and manners. The barriers of habit, the ideas of duty, cannot, ought not, to be thrown down or suddenly changed in a well-regulated female mind. And you, I am sure, know enough of the best female hearts, to be aware that time '

'Well, well, let this clear good charmer take her own time, provided there's none given to affectation, or prudery, or coquetry; and from all these, of course, she must be free; and of course I must be content. *Adieu, au revoir.*'

Chapter 17

As Lord Colambre was returning home, he was overtaken by Sir Terence O'Fay.

'Well, my lord,' cried Sir Terence, out of breath, 'you have led me a pretty dance all over the town; here's a letter somewhere down in my safe pocket for you, which has cost me trouble enough. Phoo! where is it now? – it's from Miss Nugent,' said he, holding up the letter. The direction to Grosvenor Square, London, had been scratched out; and it had been re-directed by Sir Terence to the Lord Viscount Colambre, at Sir James Brooke's, Bart., Brookwood, Huntingdonshire, or elsewhere, with speed. 'But the more haste the worse speed; for away it went to Brookwood, Huntingdonshire, where I knew, if anywhere, you was to be found; but, as fate and the post would have it, there the letter went coursing after you, while you were running round, and *back* and forwards, and everywhere, I understand, to Toddrington and Wrestham, and where not, through all them English places, where there's no cross-post; so I took it for granted that it found its way to the dead-letter office, or was sticking up across a pane in the d—d postmaster's window at Huntingdon, for the whole town to see, and it a love-letter, and some puppy to claim it, under false pretence; and you all the time without it, and it might breed a coolness betwixt you and Miss Nugent.'

'But, my dear Sir Terence, give me the letter now you have me.'

'Oh, my dear lord, if you knew what a race I have had, missing you here by five minutes, and there by five seconds – but I have you at last, and you have it – and I'm paid this minute for all I liquidated of my substance, by the pleasure I have in seeing you crack the seal and read it. But take care you don't tumble over the orange woman – orange barrows are a great nuisance, when one's studying a letter in the streets of London, or the metropolis. But never heed; stick to my arm, and I'll guide you, like a blind man, safe through the thick of them.'

Miss Nugent's letter, which Lord Colambre read in spite of the jostling of passengers, and the incessant talking of Sir Terence, was as follows: –

Let me not be the cause of banishing you from your home and your country, where you would do so much good, and make so many happy. Let me not be the cause of your breaking your promise to your mother; of your disappointing my dear aunt, so cruelly, who has complied with all our wishes, and who sacrifices, to oblige us, her favourite tastes. How could she ever be happy in Ireland – how could Clonbrony Castle be a home to her, without her son? If you take away all she had of amusement and *pleasure*, as it is called, are not you bound to give her, in their stead, that domestic happiness, which she can enjoy only with you, and by your means? If, instead of living with her, you go into the army, she will be in daily, nightly anxiety and alarm about you; and her son will, instead of being a comfort, be a source of torment to her.

I will hope that you will do now, as you have always hitherto done, on every occasion where I have seen you act, what is right, and just, and kind. Come here on the day you promised my aunt you would; before that time I shall be in Cambridgeshire, with my friend Lady Berryl; she is so good as to come to Buxton for me – I shall remain with her, instead of returning to Ireland. I have explained my reasons to my dear aunt – Could I have any concealment from her, to whom, from my earliest childhood, I owe everything that kindness and affection could give? She is satisfied – she consents to my living henceforward with Lady Berryl. Let me have the pleasure of seeing, by your conduct, that you approve of mine. – Your affectionate cousin and friend,

GRACE NUGENT.

This letter, as may be imagined by those who, like him, are capable of feeling honourable and generous conduct, gave our hero exquisite pleasure. Poor, good-natured Sir Terence O'Fay enjoyed his lordship's delight; and forgot himself so completely, that he never even inquired whether Lord Colambre had thought of an affair on which he had spoken to him some time before, and which materially concerned Sir Terence's interest. The next morning, when the carriage was at the door, and Sir Terence was just taking leave of his friend Lord Clonbrony, and actually in tears, wishing them all manner of happiness, though he said there was none left now in London, or the wide world, even, for him – Lord Colambre went up to him, and said, 'Sir Terence, you have never inquired whether I have done your business?'

'Oh, my dear, I'm not thinking of that now – time enough by the post – I can write after you; but my thoughts won't turn for me to business now – no matter.'

'Your business is done,' replied Lord Colambre.

'Then I wonder how you could think of it, with all you had upon your mind and heart. When anything's upon my heart, good-morning to my head, it's not worth a lemon. Good-bye to you, and thank you kindly, and all happiness attend you.'

'Good-bye to you, Sir Terence O'Fay,' said Lord Clonbrony; 'and, since it's so ordered, I must live without you.'

'Oh! you'll live better without me, my lord; I am not a good liver, I know, nor the best of all companions for a nobleman, young or old; and now you'll be rich, and not put to your shifts and your wits, what would I have to do for you? – Sir Terence O'Fay, you know, was only *the poor nobleman's friend*, and you'll never want to call upon him again, thanks to your jewel, your Pitt's-di'mond of a son there. So we part here, and depend upon it you're better without me – that's all my comfort, or my heart would break. The carriage is waiting this long time, and this young lover's itching to be off. God bless you both! – that's my last word.'

They called in Red Lion Square, punctual to the moment, on old Mr Reynolds, but his window-shutters were shut; he had been seized in the night with a violent fit of the gout, which, as he said, held him fast by the leg. 'But here,' said he, giving Lord Colambre a letter, 'here's what will do your business without me. Take this written acknowledgment I have penned for you, and give my grand-daughter her father's letter to read – it would touch a heart of stone – touched mine – wish I could drag the mother back out of her grave, to do her justice – all one now. You see at last I'm not a suspicious rascal, however, for I don't suspect you of palming a false grand-daughter upon me.'

'Will you,' said Lord Colambre, 'give your grand-daughter leave to come up to town to you, sir? You would satisfy yourself, at least, as to what resemblance she may bear to her father; Miss Reynolds will come instantly, and she will nurse you.'

'No, no; I won't have her come. If she comes, I won't see her – shan't begin by nursing me – not selfish. As soon as I get rid of this gout, I shall be my own man, and young again, and I'll soon be after you across the sea, that shan't stop me; I'll come to – what's the name of your place in Ireland? – and see what likeness I can find to her poor father in this grand-daughter of mine, that you puffed so finely yesterday. And let me see whether she will wheedle me as finely as Mrs Petito would. Don't get ready your marriage settlements, do you hear, till you have seen my will, which I shall sign at – what's the name of your place? Write it down there; there's pen and ink; and leave me, for the twinge is coming, and I shall roar.'

'Will you permit me, sir, to leave my own servant with you to take care of you? I can answer for his attention and fidelity.'

'Let me see his face, and I'll tell you.' Lord Colambre's servant was summoned.

'Yes, I like his face. God bless you! – Leave me.'

Lord Colambre gave his servant a charge to bear with Mr Reynolds' rough manner and temper, and to pay the poor old gentleman every possible attention. Then our hero proceeded with his father on his journey, and on this journey nothing happened worthy of note. On his first perusal of the letter from Grace, Lord Colambre had feared that she would have left Buxton with Lady Berryl before he could reach it; but, upon recollection, he hoped that the few lines he had written, addressed to his mother *and* Miss Nugent, with the assurance that he should be with them on Wednesday, would be sufficient to show her that some great change had happened, and consequently sufficient to prevent her from quitting her aunt, till she could know whether such a separation would be necessary. He argued wisely, more wisely than Grace had reasoned; for, notwithstanding this note, she would have left Buxton before his arrival, but for Lady Berryl's strength of mind, and positive determination not to set out with her till Lord Colambre should arrive to explain. In the interval, poor Grace was, indeed, in an anxious state of suspense; and her uncertainty, whether she was doing right or wrong, by staying to see Lord Colambre, tormented her most.

'My dear, you cannot help yourself; be quiet,' said Lady Berryl; 'I will take the whole upon my conscience; and I hope my conscience may never have anything worse to answer for.'

Grace was the first person who, from her window, saw Lord Colambre, the instant the carriage drove to the door. She ran to her friend Lady Berryl's apartment –

'He is come! – Now, take me away!'

'Not yet, my sweet friend! Lie down upon this sofa, if you please; and keep yourself tranquil, whilst I go and see what you ought to do; and depend upon me for a true friend, in whose mind, as in your own, duty is the first object.'

'I depend on you entirely,' said Grace, sinking down on the sofa; 'and you see I obey you!'

'Many thanks to you for lying down, when you can't stand.'

Lady Berryl went to Lady Clonbrony's apartment; she was met by Sir Arthur.

'Come, my love! come quick! – Lord Colambre is arrived.'

'I know it; and does he go to Ireland? Speak instantly, that I may tell Grace Nugent.'

'You can tell her nothing yet, my love; for we know nothing. Lord Colambre will not say a word till you come; but I know, by his countenance, that he has good and extraordinary news.'

They passed rapidly along the passage to Lady Clonbrony's room.

'Oh, my dear, dear Lady Berryl, come! or I shall die with impatience,' cried Lady Clonbrony, in a voice and manner between laughing and crying. 'There, now you have congratulated, are very happy, and very glad, and all that – now, for mercy's sake, sit down, Lord Clonbrony! for Heaven's sake, sit down – beside me here – or anywhere! Now, Colambre, begin; and tell us all at once!'

But as nothing is so tedious as a twice-told tale, Lord Colambre's narrative need not here be repeated. He began with Count O'Halloran's visit, immediately after Lady Clonbrony had left London; and went through the history of the discovery that Captain Reynolds was the husband of Miss St Omar, and the father of Grace; the dying acknowledgment of his marriage; the packet delivered by Count O'Halloran to the careless ambassador – how recovered, by the assistance of his executor, Sir James Brooke; the travels from Wrestham to Toddrington, and thence to Red Lion Square; the interview with old Reynolds, and its final result; all was related as succinctly as the impatient curiosity of Lord Colambre's auditors could desire.

'Oh, wonder upon wonder! and joy upon joy!' cried Lady Clonbrony. 'So my darling Grace is as legitimate as I am, and an heiress after all. Where is she? where is she? In your room, Lady Berryl? – Oh, Colambre! why wouldn't you let her be by? Lady Berryl, do you know, he would not let me send for her, though she was the person of all others most concerned!'

'For that very reason, ma'am; and that Lord Colambre was quite right, I am sure you must be sensible, when you recollect, that Grace has no idea that she is not the daughter of Mr Nugent; she has no suspicion that the breath of blame ever lighted upon her mother. This part of the story cannot be announced to her with too much caution; and, indeed, her mind has been so much harassed and agitated, and she is at present so far from strong, that great delicacy – '

'True! very true, Lady Berryl,' interrupted Lady Clonbrony; 'and I'll be as delicate as you please about it afterwards; but, in the first and foremost place, I must tell her the best part of the story – that she's an heiress, madam, never killed anybody!' So, darting through all opposition, Lady Clonbrony made her way into the room where Grace was lying – 'Yes, get up! get up! my own Grace, and be surprised – well you may! – you are an heiress, after all.'

'Am I, my dear aunt?' said Grace.

'True, as I'm Lady Clonbrony – and a very great heiress – and no more Colambre's cousin than Lady Berryl here. So now begin and love him as fast as you please – I give my consent – and here he is.'

Lady Clonbrony turned to her son, who just appeared at the door.

'Oh, mother! what have you done?'

'What have I done?' cried Lady Clonbrony, following her son's eyes: – 'Lord bless me! – Grace fainted dead – Lady Berryl? Oh, what have I done? My dear Lady Berryl, what shall we do?'

'There! her colour's coming again,' said Lord Clonbrony; 'come away, my dear Lady Clonbrony, for the present, and so will I – though I long to talk to the darling girl myself; but she is not equal to it yet.'

When Grace came to herself, she first saw Lady Berryl leaning over her, and, raising herself a little, she said –

'What has happened? – I don't know yet – I don't know whether I am happy or not.'

Then seeing Lord Colambre, she sat quite upright. 'You received my letter, cousin, I hope? – Do you go to Ireland with my aunt?'

'Yes; and with you, I hope, my beloved friend,' said Colambre; 'you once assured me that I had such a share of your esteem and affection, that the idea of my accompanying you to Ireland was not disagreeable to you; you flattered me that I formed part of your agreeable associations with home.'

'Yes – sit down by me, won't you, my dear Lady Berryl – but then I considered you as my cousin, Lord Colambre, and I thought you felt the same towards me; but now – '

'But now, my charming Grace,' said Lord Colambre, kneeling beside her, and taking her hand, 'no invincible obstacle opposes my passion – no *invicible* obstacle, did I say? let me hope that I may say no obstacle, but what depends on the change in the nature of your sentiments. You heard my mother's consent; you saw her joy.'

'I scarcely knew what I heard or saw,' said Grace, blushing deeply, 'or what I now see and hear; but of this I feel secure, before I comprehend the mystery, before you explain to me the causes of your – change of conduct, that you have never been actuated by caprice, but governed by wise and honourable motives. As to my going to Ireland, or remaining with Lady Berryl, she has heard all the circumstances – she is my friend and yours – a better friend cannot be; to her I appeal – she will decide for me what I ought to do; she promised to take me from hence instantly, if I *ought* to go.'

'I did; and I would do so without hesitation, if any duty or any prudence required it. But, after having heard all the circumstances, I can only tell you that I willingly resign the pleasure of your company.'

'But tell her, my dear Lady Berryl,' said Lord Colambre, 'excellent friend as you are – explain to her you can, better than any of us, all that is to be known; let her know my whole conduct, and then let her decide for herself, and I shall submit to her decision. It is difficult, my dear Grace, to restrain the expression of love, of passion, such as I feel; but I have some power over myself – you know it – and this I can promise you, that your affections shall be free as air – that no wishes of friends, no interference, nothing but your own unbiased choice will I allow, if my life depended upon it, to operate in my favour. Be assured, my dearest Grace,' added he, smiling as he retired, 'you shall have time to know whether you are happy or not.'

The moment he had left the room, she threw herself into the arms of her friend, and her heart, oppressed with various feelings, was relieved by tears – a species of relief to which she was not habituated.

'I am happy,' said she; 'but what was the *invincible obstacle*? – what was the meaning of my aunt's words? – and what was the cause of her joy? Explain all this to me, my dear friend; for I am still as if I were in a dream.'

With all the delicacy which Lady Clonbrony deemed superfluous Lady Berryl explained. Nothing could surpass the astonishment of Grace, on first learning that Mr Nugent was not her father. When she was told of the stigma that had been cast on her birth; the suspicions, the disgrace, to which her mother had been subjected for so many years – that mother, whom she had so loved and respected; who had, with such care, instilled into the mind of her daughter the principles of virtue and religion; that mother whom Grace had always seen the example of every virtue she taught; on whom her daughter never suspected that the touch of blame, the breath of scandal, could rest – Grace could express her sensations only by repeating, in tones of astonishment, pathos, indignation – 'My mother! – my mother! – my mother!'

For some time she was incapable of attending to any other idea, or of feeling any other sensations. When her mind was able to admit the thought, her friend soothed her, by recalling the expressions of Lord Colambre's love – the struggle by which he had been agitated, when he fancied a union with her opposed by an invincible obstacle.

Grace sighed, and acknowledged that, in prudence, it ought to have been an *invincible* obstacle – she admired the firmness of his decision, the honour with which he had acted towards her. One moment she exclaimed, 'Then, if I had been the daughter of a mother who had conducted herself ill, he never would have trusted me!'

The next moment she recollected, with pleasure, the joy she had just seen in his eyes – the affection, the passion, that spoke in every word and look; then dwelt upon the sober certainty, that all obstacles were removed.

'And no duty opposes my loving him! And my aunt wishes it! my kind aunt! And I may think of him. – You, my best friend, would not assure me of this if you were not certain of the truth. – Oh, how can I thank you for all your kindness, and for that best of all kindness, sympathy. You see, your calmness, your strength of mind supports and tranquillises me. I would rather have heard all I have just learnt from you than from any other person living. I could not have borne it from any one else. No one else knows my mind so perfectly – yet my aunt is very good, – and my dear uncle! should not I go to him? – But he is not my uncle, she is not my aunt. I cannot bring myself to think that they are not my relations, and that I am nothing to them.'

'You may be everything to them, my dear Grace,' said Lady Berryl; 'whenever you please, you may be their daughter.'

Grace blushed, and smiled, and sighed, and was consoled. But then she recollected her new relation Mr Reynolds, her grandfather, whom she had never seen, who had for years disowned her – treated her mother with injustice. She could scarcely think of him with complaisancy; yet, when his age, his sufferings, his desolate state, were represented, she pitied him; and, faithful to her strong sense of duty, would have gone instantly to offer him every assistance and attention in her power. Lady Berryl assured her that Mr Reynolds had positively forbidden her going to him; and that he had assured Lord Colambre he would not see her if she went to him. After such rapid and varied emotions, poor Grace desired repose, and her friend took care that it should be secured to her for the remainder of the day.

In the meantime, Lord Clonbrony had kindly and judiciously

employed his lady in a discussion about certain velvet furniture, which Grace had painted for the drawing-room at Clonbrony Castle.

In Lady Clonbrony's mind, as in some bad paintings, there was no *keeping*; all objects, great and small, were upon the same level.

The moment her son entered the room, her ladyship exclaimed –

'Everything pleasant at once! Here's your father tells me, Grace's velvet furniture's all packed; really, Soho's the best man in the world of his kind, and the cleverest – and so, after all, my dear Colambre, as I always hoped and prophesied, at last you will marry an heiress.'

'And Terry,' said Lord Clonbrony, 'will win his wager from Mordicai.'

'Terry!' repeated Lady Clonbrony, 'that odious Terry! – I hope, my lord, that he is not to be one of my comforts in Ireland.'

'No, my dear mother; he is much better provided for than we could have expected. One of my father's first objects was to prevent him from being any encumbrance to you. We consulted him as to the means of making him happy; and the knight acknowledged that he had long been casting a sheep's eye at a little snug place, that will soon be open, in his native country – the chair of assistant barrister at the sessions. "Assistant barrister!" said my father; "but, my dear Terry, you have all your life been evading the laws, and very frequently breaking the peace; do you think this has qualified you peculiarly for being a guardian of the laws?" Sir Terence replied, "Yes, sure; set a thief to catch a thief is no bad maxim. And did not Mr Colquhoun, the Scotchman, get himself made a great justice, by his making all the world as wise as himself, about thieves of all sorts, by land and by water, and in the air too, where he detected the mud-larks? – And is not Barrington chief-justice of Botany Bay?"

'My father now began to be seriously alarmed, lest Sir Terence should insist upon his using his interest to make him an assistant barrister. He was not aware that five years' practice at the bar was a necessary accomplishment for this office; when, fortunately for all parties, my good friend, Count O'Halloran, helped us out of the difficulty, by starting an idea full of practical justice. A literary friend of the count's had been for some time promised a lucrative situation under Government; but, unfortunately, he was a man of so much merit and ability, that they could not find employment for him at home, and they gave him a commission, I should rather say a contract, abroad, for supplying the army with Hungarian horses. Now the gentleman had not the slightest skill in horseflesh; and, as Sir Terence is a complete *jockey*, the count observed that he would be the best possible deputy for his literary friend. We warranted him to be a thoroughgoing friend; and I do think the coalition will be well for both parties. The count has settled it all, and I left Sir Terence comfortably provided for, out of your way, my dear mother, and as happy as he could be, when parting from my father.'

Lord Colambre was assiduous in engaging his mother's attention upon any subject which could for the present draw her thoughts away from her young friend; but, at every pause in the conversation, her ladyship repeated, 'So Grace is an heiress, after all – so, after all, they know they are not cousins! Well! I prefer Grace, a thousand times over, to any other heiress in England. No obstacle, no objection. They have my consent. I always prophesied Colambre would marry an heiress; but why not marry directly?'

Her ardour and impatience to hurry things forward seemed now likely to retard the accomplishment of her own wishes; and Lord Clonbrony, who understood rather more of the passion of love than his lady ever had felt or understood, saw the agony into which she threw her son, and felt for his darling Grace. With a degree of delicacy and address of which few would have supposed Lord Clonbrony capable, his lordship co-operated with his son in endeavours to keep Lady Clonbrony quiet, and to suppress the hourly thanksgivings of Grace's *turning out an heiress*. On one point, however, she vowed she would not be overruled – she would have a splendid wedding at Clonbrony Castle, such as should become an heir and heiress; and the wedding, she hoped, would be immediately on their return to Ireland; she should announce the thing to her friends directly on her arrival at Clonbrony Castle.

'My dear,' said Lord Clonbrony, 'we must wait, in the first place, the pleasure of old Mr Reynolds' fit of the gout.'

'Why, that's true, because of his will,' said her ladyship; 'but a will's soon made, is not it? That can't be much delay.'

'And then there must be settlements,' said Lord Clonbrony; 'they take time. Lovers, like all the rest of mankind, must submit to the law's delay. In the meantime, my dear, as these Buxton baths agree with you so well, and as Grace does not seem to be over and above strong for travelling a long journey, and as there are many curious and beautiful scenes of nature here in Derbyshire – Matlock, and the wonders of the Peak, and so on – which the young people would be glad to see together, and may not have another opportunity soon – why not rest ourselves a little? For another reason, too,' continued his lordship, bringing together as many arguments as he could – for he had often found, that though Lady Clonbrony was a match for any single argument, her understanding could be easily overpowered by a number, of whatever sort – 'besides, my dear, here's Sir Arthur and Lady Berryl come to Buxton on purpose to meet us; and we owe them some come to Buxton on purpose to meet us; and we owe them some compliment, and something more than compliment, I think; so I don't see why we should be in a hurry to leave them, or quit Buxton – a few weeks sooner or later can't signify – and Clonbrony Castle will be getting all the while into better order for us. Burke is gone down there; and if we stay here quietly, there will be time for the velvet furniture to get there before us, and to be unpacked, and up in the drawing-room.'

'That's true, my lord,' said Lady Clonbrony; 'and there is a great deal of reason in all you say – so I second that motion, as Colambre, I see, subscribes to it.'

They stayed some time in Derbyshire, and every day Lord Clonbrony proposed some pleasant excursion, and contrived that the young people should be left to themselves, as Mrs Broadhurst used so strenuously to advise; the recollection of whose authoritative maxims fortunately still operated upon Lady Clonbrony, to the great ease and advantage of the lovers.

Happy as a lover, a friend, a son; happy in the consciousness of having restored a father to respectability, and persuaded a mother to quit the feverish joys of fashion for the pleasures of domestic life; happy in the hope of winning the whole heart of the woman he loved, and whose esteem, he knew, he possessed and deserved; happy in developing every day, every hour, fresh charm in his destined bride – we leave our hero, returning to his native country.

And we leave him with the reasonable expectation that he will support through life the promise of his early character; that his patriotic views will extend with his power to carry wishes into action; that his attachment to his warm-hearted countrymen will still increase upon further acquaintance; and that he will long diffuse happiness through the wide circle, which is peculiarly subject to the influence and example of a great resident Irish proprietor.

LETTER FROM LARRY TO HIS BROTHER, PAT BRADY, AT MR MORDICAI'S, COACHMAKER, LONDON.

MY DEAR BROTHER,

Yours of the 16th, enclosing the five pound note for my father, came safe to hand Monday last; and with his thanks and blessing to you, he commends it to you herewith enclosed back again, on account of his being in no immediate necessity, nor likelihood to want in future, as you shall hear forthwith; but wants you over with all speed, and the note will answer for travelling charges; for we can't enjoy the luck it has pleased God to give us without *yees:* put

Old Nick's gone, and St Dennis along with him, to the place he come from – praise be to God! The *ould* lord has found him out in his tricks; and I helped him to that, through the young lord that I driv, as I informed you in my last, when he was a Welchman, which was the best turn ever I did, though I did not know it no more than Adam that time. So *ould* Nick's turned out of the agency clean and clear; and the clay after it was known, there was surprising great joy through the whole country; not surprising either, but just what you might, knowing him, r*a*sonably expect. He (that is, old Nick and St Dennis) would have been burnt that night – I *mane*, in *effigy*, through the town of Clonbrony, but that the new man, Mr Burke, come down that day too soon to stop it, and said, 'it was not becoming to trample on the fallen,' or something that way, that put an end to it; and though it was a great disappointment to many, and to me in particular, I could not but like the jantleman the better for it anyhow. They say, he is a very good jantleman, and as unlike old Nick or the saint as can be; and takes no duty fowl, nor glove, nor sealing-money; nor asks duty work nor duty turf. Well, when I was disappointed of the *effigy*, I comforted myself by making a bonfire of old Nick's big rick of duty turf, which, by great luck, was out in the road, away from all dwelling-house, or thatch, or yards, to take fire; so no danger in life or objection. And such another blaze! I wished you'd seed it – and all the men, women, and children in the town and country, far and near, gathered round it, shouting and dancing like mad! – and it was light as day quite across the bog, as far as Bartley Finnigan's house. And I heard after, they seen it from all parts of the three counties, and they thought it was St John's Eve in a mistake – or couldn't make out what it was; but all took it in good part, for a good sign, and were in great joy. As for St Dennis and *ould* Nick, an attorney had his foot upon 'em, with an habere a latitat, and three executions hanging over 'em; and there's the end of rogues! and a great example in the country. And – no more about it; for I can't be wasting more ink upon them that don't desarve it at my hands, when I want it for them that do, you shall see. So some weeks past, and there was great cleaning at Clonbrony Castle, and in the town of Clonbrony; and the new agent's smart and clever; and he had the glaziers, and the painters, and the slaters up and down in the town wherever wanted; and you wouldn't know it again. Thinks I, this is no bad sign! Now, cock up your ears, Pat! for the great news is coming, and the good. The master's come home – long life to him! – and family come home yesterday, all entirely! The *ould* lord and the young lord (ay, there's the man,

Paddy!), and my lady, and Miss Nugent. And I driv Miss Nugent's maid, that maid that was, and another; so I had the luck to be in it along *wid* 'em, and see all, from first to last. And first, I must tell you, my young Lord Colambre remembered and noticed me the minute he lit at our inn, and condescended to beckon at me out of the yard to him, and axed me – 'Friend Larry,' says he, 'did you keep your promise?' – 'My oath again' the whiskey, is it?' says I. 'My lord, I surely did,' said I; which was true, as all the country knows I never tasted a drop since. 'And I'm proud to see your honour, my lord, as good as your word too, and back again among us.' So then there was a call for the horses; and no more at that time passed betwix' my young lord and me, but that he pointed me out to the *ould* one, as I went off. I noticed and thanked him for it in my heart, though I did not know all the good was to come of it. Well, no more of myself, for the present.

Ogh, it's I driv 'em well; and we all got to the great gate of the park before sunset, and as fine an evening as ever you see; with the sun shining on the tops of the trees, as the ladies noticed; the leaves changed, but not dropped, though so late in the season. I believe the leaves knew what they were about, and kept on, on purpose to welcome them; and the birds were singing, and I stopped whistling, that they might hear them; but sorrow bit could they hear when they got to the park gate, for there was such a crowd, and such a shout, as you never see – and they had the horses off every carriage entirely, and drew 'em home, with blessings, through the park. And, God bless 'em! when they got out, they didn't go shut themselves up in the great drawing-room, but went straight out to the *tir*rass, to satisfy the eyes and hearts that followed them. My lady *laning* on my young lord, and Miss Grace Nugent that was, the beautifullest angel that ever you set eyes on, with the finest complexion and sweetest of smiles, *laning* upon the ould lord's arm, who had his hat off, bowing to all, and noticing the old tenants as he passed by name. Oh, there was great gladness and tears in the midst; for joy I could scarce keep from myself.

After a turn or two upon the *tir*rass, my Lord Colambre *quit* his mother's arm for a minute, and he come to the edge of the slope, and looked down and through all the crowd for some one.

'Is it the widow O'Neill, my lord?' says I; 'she's yonder, with the spectacles on her nose, betwixt her son and daughter, as usual.'

Then my lord beckoned, and they did not know which of the *tree* would stir; and then he gave *tree* beckons with his own finger, and they all *tree* came fast enough to the bottom of the slope forenent my lord; and he went down and helped the widow up (Oh, he's the true jantleman), and brought 'em all *tree* up on the *tir*rass, to my lady and Miss Nugent; and I was up close after, that I might hear, which wasn't manners, but I couldn't help it. So what he said I don't well know, for I could not get near enough, after all. But I saw my lady smile very kind, and take the widow O'Neill by the hand, and then my Lord Colambre '*troduced* Grace to Miss Nugent, and there was the word *namesake*, and something about a check curtains; but, whatever it was, they was all greatly pleased; then my Lord Colambre turned and looked for Brian, who had fell back, and took him with some commendation to my lord his father. And my lord the master said, which I didn't know till after, that they should have their house and farm at the *ould* rent; and at the surprise, the widow dropped down dead; and there was a cry as for ten *berrings*. 'Be qui'te,' says I, 'she's only kilt for joy;' and I went and lift her up, for her son had no more strength that minute than the child new born; and Grace trembled like a leaf, as white as the sheet, but not long, for the mother came to, and was as well as ever when I brought some water, which Miss Nugent handed to her with her own hand.

'That was always pretty and good,' said the widow, laying her hand upon Miss Nugent, 'and kind and good to me and mine.'

That minute there was music from below. The blind harper, O'Neill, with his harp, that struck up 'Gracey Nugent.'

And that finished, and my Lord Colambre smiling, with the tears standing in his eyes too, and the *ould* lord quite wiping his, I ran to the *tir*rass brink to bid O'Neill play it again; but as I run, I thought I heard a voice call Larry.

'Who calls Larry?' says I.

'My Lord Colambre calls you, Larry,' says all at once; and four takes me by the shoulders and spins me round. 'There's my young lord calling you, Larry – run for your life.'

So I run back for my life, in my hand, when I got near.

'Put on your hat, my father desires it,' says my Lord Colambre. The ould lord made a sign to that purpose, but was too full to speak. 'Where's your father?' continues my young lord. – 'He's very ould, my lord,' says I. 'I didn't *ax* you how ould he was,' says he; 'but where is he?' – 'He's behind the crowd below, on account of his infirmities; he couldn't walk so fast as the rest, my lord,' says I; 'but his heart is with you, if not his body.' 'I must have his body too, so bring him bodily before us; and this shall be your warrant for so doing,' said my lord, joking; for he knows the *natur* of us,

Paddy, and how we love a joke in our hearts, as well as if he had lived all his life in Ireland; and by the same token will, for that *rason*, do what he pleases with us, and more maybe than a man twice as good, that never would smile on us.

But I'm telling you of my father. 'I've a warrant for you, father,' says I; 'and must have you bodily before the justice, and my lord chief-justice.' So he changed colour a bit at first; but he saw me smile. 'And I've done no sin,' said he; 'and, Larry, you may lead me now, as you led me all my life.'

And up the slope he went with me as light as fifteen; and, when we got up, my Lord Clonbrony said, 'I am sorry an old tenant, and a good old tenant, as I hear you were, should have been turned out of your farm.'

'Don't fret, it's no great matter, my lord,' said my father. 'I shall be soon out of the way; but if you would be so kind to speak a word for my boy here, and that I could afford, while the life is in me, bring my other boy back out of banishment – '

'Then,' says my Lord Clonbrony, 'I'll give you and your sons three lives, or thirty-one years, from this day, of your former farm. Return to it when you please.' 'And,' added my Lord Colambre, 'the flaggers, I hope, will be soon banished.' Oh, how could I thank him – not a word could I proffer – but I know I clasped my two hands, and prayed for him inwardly. And my father was dropping down on his knees, but the master would not let him; and *obsarved*, that posture should only be for his God. And, sure enough, in that posture, when he was out of sight, we did pray for him that night, and will all our days.

But, before we quit his presence, he called me back, and bid me write to my brother, and bring you back, if you've no objections, to your own country.

So come, my dear Pat, and make no delay, for joy's not joy *complate* till you're in it – my father sends his blessing, and Peggy her love. The family entirely is to settle for good in Ireland, and there was in the castle yard last night a bonfire made by my lord's orders of the ould yellow damask furniture, to plase my lady, my lord says. And the drawing-room, the butler was telling me, is new hung; and the chairs with velvet as white as snow, and shaded over with natural flowers, by Miss Nugent. Oh! how I hope what I guess will come true, and I've *rason* to believe it will, for I dreamt in my bed last night it did. But keep yourself to yourself – that Miss Nugent (who is no more Miss Nugent, they say, but Miss Reynolds, and has a new-found grandfather, and is a big heiress, which she did not want in my eyes, nor in my young lord's), I've a notion will be sometime, and maybe sooner than is expected, my Lady Viscountess Colambre – so haste to the wedding. And there's another thing: they say the rich ould grandfather's coming over; – and another thing, Pat, you would not be out of the fashion – and you see it's growing the fashion not to be an Absentee. – Your loving brother,

LARRY BRADY.

WORDSWORTH CLASSICS

General Editors: Marcus Clapham and Clive Reynard
Titles in this series

Distribution

AUSTRALIA, BRUNEI
& MALAYSIA
Reed Editions
22 Salmon Street, Port Melbourne
Vic 3207, Australia
Tel: (03) 245 7111
Fax (03) 245 7333

DENMARK
BOG-FAN
St. Kongensgade 61A
1264 København K

BOGPA SIKA
Industrivej 1, 7120 Vejle Ø

FRANCE
Bookking International
16 Rue des Grands Augustins
75006 Paris

GERMANY, AUSTRIA
& SWITZERLAND
Swan Buch-Marketing GmbH
Goldscheuerstrabe 16
D-7640 Kehl Am Rhein, Germany

GREAT BRITAIN & IRELAND
Wordsworth Editions Ltd
Cumberland House, Crib Street,
Ware, Hertfordshire SG12 9ET

Selecta Books
The Selectabook
Distribution Centre
Folly Road, Roundway, Devizes
Wiltshire SN10 2HR

HOLLAND & BELGIUM
Uitgeverlj en Boekhandel
Van Gennep BV, Spuistraat 283
1012 VR Amsterdam, Holland

INDIA
OM Book Service
1690 First Floor
Nai Sarak, Delhi – 110006
Tel: 3279823-3265303 Fax: 3278091

ITALY
Magis Books
Piazza Della Vittoria I/C
42100 Reggio Emilia
Tel: 0522-452303 Fax: 0522-452845

NEW ZEALAND
Whitcoulls Limited
Private Bag 92098, Auckland

NORWAY
Norsk Bokimport AS
Bertrand Narvesensvei 2
Postboks 6219, Etterstad, 0602 Oslo

PORTUGAL
Cashkeen Limited
(Isabel Leao) 25 Elmhurst Avenue
London N2 0LT
Tel: 081-444 3781 Fax: 081-444 3171

SINGAPORE
Book Station
18 Leo Drive, Singapore
Tel: 4511998 Fax: 4529188

SOUTH EAST CYPRUS
Tinkerbell Books
19 Dimitri Hamatsou Street, Paralimni
Famagusta, Cyprus
Tel: 03-8200 75

SOUTH WEST CYPRUS & GREECE
Huckleberry Trading
4 Isabella, Anavargos, Pafos, Cyprus
Tel: 06-231313

SOUTH AFRICA, ZIMBABWE
CENTRAL & E. AFRICA
Trade Winds Press (Pty) Ltd
P O Box 20194, Durban North 4016

SPAIN
Ribera Libros
Dr. Areilza No.19, 48011 Bilbao
Tel: 441-87-87 Fax: 441-80-29

USA, CANADA & MEXICO
Universal Sales & Marketing
230 Fifth Avenue, Suite 1212
New York, N Y 10001 USA
Tel: 212-481-3500 Fax: 212-481-3534

DIRECT MAIL
Redvers
Redvers House, 13 Fairmile,
Henley-on-Thames, Oxfordshire RG9 2JR
Tel: 0491 572656 Fax: 0491 573590